BRODERICK

BRODERICK

a novel by
WILLIAM HEFFERNAN

CROWN PUBLISHERS, INC. NEW YORK

Inquiries should be addressed to Crown Publishers, Inc., One Park
Avenue, New York, New York 10016

Printed in the United States of America

Published simultaneously in Canada by General Publishing Company Limited

Library of Congress Cataloging in Publication Data
Heffernan, William, 1940–
  Broderick.

  1. Broderick, John J., 1892–1966—Fiction.
PZ4.H45854Br 1980   [PS3558.E4143]   813'.5'4   79-24855

ISBN: 0-517-53732X

10   9   8   7   6   5   4   3   2   1

First edition

This book is for my father,
William H. Heffernan, who spent his life
making sure his sons had opportunities
denied to him.

Acknowledgments

A very special one to Philip Leshin, whose original idea was the basis of this book and whose help in the months of research that followed was invaluable.

Also to the New York City Police Department and the many officers who helped research its proud past; to the Retired Detective Association of the New York City Police Department and its members who worked during and were willing to speak about the days in question; the New York City Department of Correction, especially John Walsh; the Brooklyn Public Library and its staff for exceptional assistance; and especially to Larry Freundlich and Gloria Loomis, whose faith, help, and encouragement can never be repaid.

And also for my family, who graciously put up with the lunacy of a man writing his first novel.

Under blank eyes and fingers never still
The particular is pounded till it is man.
When had I my own will?
O not since life began.

Constrained, arraigned, baffled, bent and unbent
By these wire-jointed jaws and limbs of wood,
Themselves obedient,
Knowing not evil and good. . . .

WILLIAM BUTLER YEATS

Preface

The prospect of writing a historically accurate novel set in 1926 was at first a staggering thought. Despite the popularity of the era, the events to be fictionalized took place nearly twenty years before my birth. But there were advantages as well. Working for a major New York City newspaper provided access to the recorded history of daily events set down in the more than twenty newspapers that then existed in the city—reports that were meticulously preserved in the paper's library. There were also the magnificent old gentlemen—retired detectives all—who lived and worked in that era and who—"since the statute has passed" as one aptly put it—spoke freely about the crime, the corruption, and the magnificent mayhem that existed in those days. There was also the elderly gentleman now living in Las Vegas (who asked that his name never be credited), who once served as Arnold Rothstein's accountant, a man who provided insights that only one who lived on the other side of the law could have offered. What was first a threat, therefore, became an adventure in research and an education that even fifteen years of journalism could not match.

In the writing, of course, certain liberties have been taken: fictional characters added, some dates of events changed, some names altered, and some conclusions drawn in the interest of smooth, readable fiction. Some may consider this an outrageous impertinence, which is perhaps the most accurate definition of what a novel is. And *Broderick* is fiction, even though it includes many events that actually occurred.

Broderick also is a story of 1926, but in many ways it could as easily take place today. There are great similarities between the twenties and the days we now pass through. Much like today, there were those in the twenties who believed in the ability to legislate morality and, like today, each attempt to do so produced an inevitable degree of corruption. An old political science professor once told me that morality could never be legislated, whether it be the attempt to abolish alcohol during the twenties or soft drugs today, or the insistence that gambling, prostitution, or homosexuality could be brought to an abrupt halt, like automobiles at traffic lights, merely because laws and accompanying punishments had been agreed upon.

Ironically, in the twenties, like today, it was the police, along with those who made and administered the laws who first recognized the futility of the attempt and who capitalized on the corruption that naturally followed. It was true in the twenties; it is true today and it undoubtedly will be true tomorrow. One need only point to the Knapp Commission and remember Judge Seabury; to Watergate and recall Teapot Dome, along with a myriad of others, to recognize the validity of that old professor's premise. What we are speaking of is an aura of corruption produced by men who suffer from spiritual, not material, poverty.

There was, however, one striking difference discovered during the research that went into this book. The corruption of 1926 was far more open, far more accepted, the sense of amorality, whether official or personal, more honestly acknowledged. Perhaps that, along with the blatant violence of the day, is why that era became known as the Roaring Twenties, that romantic period of our history that still leaves its mark on us all.

New York City   WILLIAM HEFFERNAN

BRODERICK

CHAPTER ONE

Ossining, New York, 1926

EARLY IN AUGUST, ONLY ONE MONTH BEFORE THE
planned execution would take place, Hyman Amberg stood at the south gate
of Sing Sing Prison waiting for the heavy steel doors to swing open. It was
hot, and like the men inside, the heat seemed trapped behind the thirty-foot
walls and the guard operating the gate was in no hurry to exert himself.
When the doors finally swung away Amberg stepped through almost as
though leaving did not matter. His small, wiry body seemed listless, his mind
unmoved, riveted on something beyond the moment. Outside, the rural air
filled his lungs and he breathed in deeply, feeling his chest expand against the
cheap blue suit they had given him. The prison doors closed behind him and
the sound of the steel ringing shut brought him back and sent a sudden
tremor through his body. It was in that first minute he sensed something was
wrong; his strength seemed to leave him and for a moment he felt unable to
move. To his left, down the long cobblestone path that led to the parking
area, a heavy, round-faced man stood waiting beside a black Packard sedan.
The feeling passed and he started down the path pulling at his right leg in the
slightly altered gait he had carried with him for twenty years now. He felt
sure of himself again, sure it would all go as he had planned during the long
three years that had just ended.

When he reached the car Moe Berg grabbed his shoulders and squeezed

1

them between his hands. "You look great, Hy. A helluva lot better than most guys who come out of there."

"I look like a washed-out piece of shit," Amberg said. "Did you take care of things?"

"Everything's all set. I got two new guys. We're just waiting for your say-so and we're back in business."

Amberg smiled for the first time, his thin lips curling up at the corners of his mouth. It would go well; everything would be all right, he was sure of it now.

The car headed south on Route 9. To the right the Hudson River slid past and the white sails of small boats could be seen near the opposite shore struggling against the outgoing tide. He had been able to see the river from the upper levels of the prison and he had hated the sight of the boats then. They had planned the prison that way, he had thought. Giving you a glimpse of what you couldn't have. Not for years. Now he was seeing the boats again, this time outside the walls. He still hated the sight of them. He hated the people sitting behind the sails, people who would soon slide past the prison thinking about the men locked up there. Glad they were there, just as he knew they had been glad three years ago when the newspapers told about his conviction for armed robbery.

"I got us a couple of rooms in the Manhattan Hotel," Moe said. "It's not the Waldorf, but the rooms are big enough for the three of us."

"The three of us?" Amberg said. He looked across at Moe. He was staring ahead at the road, his face as expressionless as it had been as long as Amberg had known him.

"Yeah, Gillie's there. She moved in right away. She would have been here with me but she wanted to stay behind to get a little party together." He glanced across at Amberg. "We're gonna celebrate this, Hy. You, me, Gillie, and the two new guys."

"Who are they, these new guys?" Amberg asked, not really caring at the moment.

"They're young kids, but they're good. Both of them have plenty of nerve and as soon as I mentioned your name they wanted in. One kid's name is Dunniger, Rudy Dunniger. The other guy is Jimmy Crowley. He got a name for himself when the newspapers called him Two Gun Crowley after he got caught heisting a store in Harlem." Moe chuckled over the nickname. "Maybe you read about it. The cops found two guns on him and the newspapers heard about it and made up the name. They're both a little wild, but they'll do what they're told." He shrugged his thick shoulders, still looking at the road. "You know the other boys are all still locked up, so there wasn't a lot to pick from."

"They'll do," Amberg said. "I need bodies, not brains." He looked back at the river. Somehow it now made him feel more relaxed, more certain of

2

himself. Even the cold gray of his eyes seemed to soften. But the hatred was still there, the hatred for *the* man and that would not change. Three years could be a lifetime, he had learned, and certainly worth a life in return. *He* had put him there, stolen the three years, and whether he had belonged behind the walls of Sing Sing or not really did not matter. He had been put there by one person who had used treachery and lies to do it and now he was going to pay in kind.

Amberg drew a long breath, keeping his eyes on the river. He had given three years of thought to what he would do, but still only the end result was a certainty in his mind. But the rest would come to him, he had decided. He had prepared a story for Moe and the others, one he felt they would believe and one he believed himself might eventually become a reality. But only one thing was important to him now and that was the end result. The means to the end would present itself and when it did he would recognize it instantly.

"We lined up some jobs," Moe said. "I've got a couple of places spotted that are pushovers. All we have to do is walk in and pick up the money."

"I'm not doing stickups," Amberg said. "I'm through with that. It's over." He snapped his fingers to emphasize his pronouncement. "I've still got some money stashed away from the last job and that will hold us for a while. We're going to do something different, something that will cut us in on the real money." He paused a moment, smiling to himself. "What would you think about going into the liquor business, Moe? Then the only jobs you and the new guys would have to pull would be to finance that. And while you were doing it I could take care of one special job that I've been planning for a long time."

Moe forced his eyes away from the road and looked briefly at Amberg. "That liquor business is heavy stuff, Hy. Everything is pretty tied up."

"So we'll untie it." He grinned at the bigger man. It was a strange, almost cruel half smile. "But that'll all come as soon as I take care of my special business."

He was off and running again, Moe thought. For as long as he had known him, for more than ten years now, there had always been some big scheme that never came off. He had usually been able to talk him out of them, but it always took time. When things were clean and simple and violent nobody could do them better than Hy, but he wasn't somebody who could plan things that weren't straightforward—and he had been away three years now and didn't have any idea how completely wrapped up all the big action had become. Moe watched the road ahead almost absentmindedly. Now there was some special job too. He found he was almost afraid to ask about it. He had thought about getting away from Hy while he was away but had done nothing about it. All those years; it was just a hard habit to break.

"What's this special business?" Moe finally asked. He was trying to watch Amberg out of the corner of his eye, trying to gauge his mood.

3

Amberg rested his head against the seat and slid his hat down over his eyes until the brim followed the hook shape of his nose. "I'm gonna kill Johnny Broderick. I'm gonna kill him right out in the open so people can watch him die."

Moe kept his eyes on the road but his hands tightened on the steering wheel. His neck jerked nervously as it always did when something disturbed him. "Killing a cop, Hy, that's a little rough. I know he sent you up but an awful lot of heat would come down if you did that."

"There won't be any heat. The only heat is gonna be on Broderick." He raised his head from the seat and straightened his hat. His voice was calm but his eyes seemed to burn out of his thin, sunken face. "I'm not just going to kill him, I'm going to execute him." He took a deep breath as though struggling to keep his voice calm. "When I was inside I worked a month in the death house and I saw how they kept those guys there, how they let them count off the days they had left. Broderick's gonna have the same thing. I won't tell him right out but he'll know it's coming just the same. And every time he sees me he'll know it's getting closer." He was staring straight ahead and his voice was almost mechanical. "I want him to remember how he set me up and how his pals held my arms while he beat the shit out of me. I want him to think about every fucking punch and every time he does I want him to sweat." He let out a small laugh and looked across at Moe. "And the funny thing, Moe, is that I'm not going to do a thing he can get me for. I'll sit and wait and I'll be good as gold. I'll go to all the places he goes to and every time he sees me he'll know it's coming and he'll know there's not a thing he can do about it."

Amberg's mind drifted away with the sound of his own words. He was unaware of Moe's sudden silence and he stared back at the river. He was smiling to himself again and far down in the distance he could see the Palisades rising up, secure and immovable. Across the river from those cliffs millions of people were going about their business on crowded Manhattan streets. And soon some of those same people would become part of his plan. They would be witnesses to an execution.

4

CHAPTER TWO

THE INDUSTRIAL SQUAD OFFICE WAS CRAMPED AND dark, the only light coming from a single ceiling fixture that was coated with years of dust. The office was in a converted storeroom on the second floor of Police Headquarters. It was a small, squalid room and the once bright walls had never been repainted and were now a dingy brown. They had squeezed four battered desks into the twelve-by-twelve-foot work area and the panes of glass in the lone window were covered with grime, making the room seem even smaller and darker than it was. Johnny Broderick's desk was next to the window. He had claimed that place for himself when the squad had moved to the office one and a half years ago, thinking ahead to the humid summers and the hours he would have to spend in the small cramped room. The window was open now but the amount of air that entered gave little relief. The only breeze, he had found, came in the winter, when the air pushed through the rotting window frame and forced him to sit working in a topcoat.

He sat there now with his feet propped up on the desk, his thick shoulders and chest obscuring the back of his wooden swivel chair. Behind him the jacket of his blue, double-breasted suit hung neatly from a clothes tree and above it a pale, straw skimmer dangled from a hook. There was a clutter of papers spread out on the desk and in one corner there was an upright tele-phone. Throughout the morning he had found himself staring at the telephone, hoping it would ring, giving him some excuse to get out of there.

To the right of the desk a photograph was tacked on the wall. It showed a dapper man dressed in a top hat, morning coat, and spats. There was a smooth, self-assured smile on his face and he was holding a cane cavalierly tucked under one arm. At the bottom right-hand corner there was a hand-written inscription that read: "To Johnny Broderick, the toughest cop in New York, from his strongest admirer." It was signed, "Jimmy."

Broderick looked at the photograph of Jimmy Walker, studying, as he had many times before, the perfect cut of the clothes, the confident tilt of the top hat. He smiled to himself, then looked down again at the papers on his desk. Reports that had to be filled out. It was the part of being a detective that made little sense to him. Everything had to be reduced to writing—the one thing that made every detective look foolish, trying to explain what he had done in words. Fuckers, he thought to himself. They hired you to be a cop and then they turned you into a pencil pusher, just so the bosses had some papers to shuffle around their desks. But it was more than that. He knew how those same bosses could use reports to trap a cop. If you left something out, or didn't explain exactly what you had done and why and under what au-thority, they could use it against you. He stared at the papers and shook his head. Someday you'll have to fill out a report every time you go to the crapper. He smiled to himself again. He could almost see the questions. Time of arrival. Time of departure. How many sheets of paper used. Authorized by what command. And God help you if you got there and couldn't go. They'd bring you up on charges. Failure to complete assignment. He almost laughed out loud. No, not that. Failure to do your duty. He pushed the papers off to one side. The hell with them, he thought. They could be done later.

He looked at the telephone again and then let his eyes wander to his black shoes. The high level of the shine pleased him. His appearance had always been important, he told himself. Even when he was in uniform. Most cops were slobs and that was why so few ever got out of the uniformed division. A slob doesn't become a detective. A detective had to show a little class. If he was sloppy about himself, he'd be sloppy about his work. He had guarded against that from the beginning and he had remained in uniform for only three years. Now, after almost six years in the department, he was a first-grade detective, something few had managed that quickly. He smiled, think-ing about his success. Even fewer had received the kind of newspaper coverage he had with every good arrest. He glanced at the photograph again. And now he had Jimmy Walker in his corner and he could even escape some of the pressures the senior commanders handed down to prove how impor-tant they were. That's what you need to get along in this department, Brod-erick mused. A good image, some good arrests with good publicity and a strong goddamned rabbi.

He glanced down at his shoes again, reassuring himself of the shine, then glanced across the room where Johnny Cordes and Barney Ruditsky sat filling out reports.

"Hey, what do you think the department would do if I started wearing spats and carried a cane?" he asked.

Cordes looked up from his paper work, his handsome, dark Spanish features unmoved by the question. "I think they'd tell you to eat the spats and stick the cane up your ass," he said.

Broderick lowered his eyes to his shoes again. "That's the trouble with this place," he said. "Nobody's got any style."

Barney Ruditsky leaned back in his chair, then looked over at Cordes and winked. "Look, don't pay any attention to Cordes," he said. "There's nothin' wrong with spats and a cane. I've thought about it myself. You could probably even get somebody to make a cane with a gun in it."

Broderick looked at him thoughtfully. Ruditsky's puffy red face was serious and his attitude seemed reassuring. He had a broad red nose lined with veins that made him look more like somebody's drunken uncle than a cop and somehow it seemed to give him a note of stability. He was more like a bank teller or clerk than a first-grade detective.

Ruditsky got slowly out of his chair and swaggered across the room to Broderick's desk. His vest was unbuttoned and flapped about his long, slender frame. His face broke into a grin as he leaned across the desk and stared at the picture of Jimmy Walker.

"Yeah, after all, who's gonna tell the toughest cop in New York to stick a cane up his ass?" he said.

Broderick swung his feet off the desk and started to rise from his chair, annoyed he had been taken in so easily. "You touch that picture and I'll break your fucking arm," he said.

Ruditsky threw his hands up in front of his face and backed away from the desk. He eased back toward the door and picked his jacket up from the chair. He slipped the jacket on and ran his hands through his curly brown hair, still looking across at Broderick.

"Hey, Johnny," he said. "Stick the cane up your ass."

Broderick stepped from behind the desk and Ruditsky quickly opened the door and stepped outside. Turning, he bowed toward Broderick and giggled, then slammed the door shut as Broderick grabbed a paperweight from the desk and threw it across the room. The paperweight banged against the door, then bounced harmlessly to the floor and rolled under a desk.

"You better run you goddamned Jew bastard," he shouted.

The telephone rang and Cordes grabbed it with both hands and placed the tubelike receiver to his ear.

"Yeah, I understand, Cap," he said. "We'll meet the uniformed guys downstairs." He banged his finger on the receiver cradle and asked for the desk sergeant, then continued. "Sarge, Barney Ruditsky is leaving the building.

7

Stop him, will you. We got a job to go out on." He placed the telephone on the desk and reached for his coat.

Broderick was already buttoning his suit coat and adjusting the white handkerchief in its breast pocket.

"That was the captain," Cordes said. "City Hall called. They got some pickets outside the Goldspan Building in the fur district and they want we should explain how picketing isn't allowed."

Broderick opened the top drawer of his desk and took out a pair of brass knuckles and slid them into the right-hand pocket of his suit coat. He grimaced slightly thinking how they would ruin the line of the suit.

The car moved slowly along Sixth Avenue. Broderick sat in the front seat on the passenger side. Cordes was behind the wheel, whistling between his teeth, and in back Ruditsky sat resting his head back, his hat pulled low over his eyes. Behind them two cars of uniformed men and a paddy wagon followed.

The car moved through the twenties and Broderick glanced to the right watching the side streets slip by. He had grown up on the east side of those streets, a skinny Irish kid who had thought the whole world was a collection of tenements. His mother had been dead by the time he had claimed the streets as his own, learning how to use his hands effectively, picking up the little tricks a smart kid learns, like putting a well-shaped rock in your hand so you could hit with power even though you only weighed a hundred and ten pounds.

The car passed Twenty-eighth Street. Far down, near the East River, his father had once beaten him in the street. He had caught him fighting and had beaten his face bloody. He had never told his father that the kid he was fighting with had called the old man a drunk. He was drunk when he beat him that day. The smell of booze had surrounded him like a mist as it did most of the time, and on hot days, when he sat drinking ale in their cold-water flat, the sweat from his body had seemed to radiate the smell, spreading it throughout the two rooms they lived in. When he left to join the navy at seventeen he never came home to the old man again. He had seen him on the street several times before he died and once when he had been called down to the Tenth Precinct. He was in uniform then and the old man had been arrested for drunkenness and had told the sergeant that his son was a cop. When he arrived at the precinct the sergeant had taken him aside, telling him to take the old man home and to keep him out of trouble. It was a courtesy from one member of the force to another, the sergeant had said. He remembered how embarrassed he had been and how he had taken the old man out of the precinct that night and around the corner to an alley. There, he had grabbed the old man by the shirt, telling him that if he ever told anyone again that he was his son he would beat his goddamned brains out. For a moment the old man's image flashed back to him, the tears that had suddenly filled his eyes, the way he had raised his hand to slap him, but the hand falling helplessly at his side before he walked away talking to himself. The next time he saw him the old man was in his coffin. It was the first time he could remember his father not smelling of liquor.

The car pulled around the corner and in the distance they could see more than twenty pickets walking in a line in front of the Goldspan Building. There were a few women among them and, like many of the others, they carried placards demanding the right to unionize. The police cars pulled to the curb as the paddy wagon came up alongside. The three detectives climbed out of the car and walked toward the pickets, who had stopped moving and were now gathered close together.

"You've got two seconds to fold up your signs and get your asses out of here," Broderick shouted.

Angry voices shot back. Several screamed for the police to get out, to leave them alone.

Broderick fixed his eyes on a large, hulking man in the center of the crowd. Always get the biggest guy first, he thought, as he slid his right hand into his suit-coat pocket and slipped his fingers into the brass knuckles. His first punch caught the man squarely between the eyes and he could feel the flesh go soft under the weight of the punch and blood splattered on the sleeve of his coat as the man crumpled to the ground. Ruditsky and Cordes moved in behind him striking out with blackjacks, and the uniformed men rushed forward swinging their nightsticks.

It was over within seconds. Those who were able to run raced down the street with uniformed men in pursuit. Other cops, trying to keep blood off their uniforms, dragged the injured toward the paddy wagon. One brawny cop held a small, bespectacled man by the scruff of the neck.

"This guy's the ringleader," he called out. He shook the man roughly. "Aren't you, you little creep?"

The small man stood limply in the big cop's grasp. His eyes were wide and the thick lenses of the spectacles he wore made them seem even larger. Broderick walked toward him, flexing his heavy shoulder muscles beneath his suit coat. He took off his skimmer and ran a hand through his straight black hair and began fanning himself with his hat. He was a ruggedly handsome man and when his square jaw was set he seemed awesome. His eyes remained fixed on the little man.

"Hot day, isn't it?" he said, placing the hat back on his head.

The man stared up at him but did not answer.

"It must be hot," Broderick said. "You're sweating your balls off."

"Yes, it's very hot," the man said.

"What's your name?" Broderick asked.

"Johannes. Lester Johannes," he said.

Broderick looked at the cop. "Well, you bring Mr. Lester Johannes to our

9

office," he said. "We have a few questions we want to ask him. You book him first, then you bring him up for a visit."

He looked down at the little man again and noticed his lips were trembling. He smiled, then looked at the brass knuckles that were still on his hand. There was blood on them. He slipped them off, turning them over in his hand. With his other hand he reached out and took hold of Johannes's necktie and slowly he began to wipe the brass knuckles clean.

"We'll be waiting for you, Mr. Johannes," he said.

Back in the squad room Johannes sat in a chair in the center of the room. His arms were behind his back, held there by handcuffs, and he stared at the floor, where Broderick's shiny black shoes glistened back at him. Dried blood crusted around his mouth and his lips were badly swollen. Broderick's voice boomed down at him.

"We'd like to know who put you up to picketing Mr. Goldspan's building," he said.

"The union," Johannes said, his voice weak.

"That doesn't tell me anything," Broderick growled. "Who in the union?"

"The action committee took a vote. It was decided that way," Johannes said.

"Who runs the action committee?" Broderick said.

"No one person runs it. It's a committee. Everybody on it has a voice. Every worker is equal," he said.

"Every worker," Broderick shouted. "Every worker. You fucking Bolshevik." He reached down and grabbed Johannes by the shirt and pulled him to his feet. "Are you a fucking Bolshevik?" he shouted.

Johannes stared into Broderick's chest and shook his head.

"Don't tell me you're not a fucking Bolshevik. I know a fucking Bolshevik when I see one."

Ruditsky and Cordes sat behind their desks suppressing laughter.

"He looks like a fucking Bolshevik if I ever saw one," Ruditsky said. "I'll bet you he's got a picture of Lenin tattooed on his ass."

"You see," Broderick said. "These two detectives think you're a fucking Bolshevik. And they're not stupid, are they?"

Johannes shook his head again.

"Then you must be a Bolshevik, right?"

Broderick placed his hand under Johannes's chin and lifted his face. "Right?" he said.

Squeezing his fingers into his jaw Broderick moved Johannes's head up and down. The little man stared into his face, his lips trembling.

"Now doesn't it feel better to tell the truth?" Broderick asked.

He forced his head up and down again, then let go of his face and smiled down at him. Johannes was trying to smile in return when Broderick's knee came up into his groin. The small man's mouth dropped and his eyes bulged in his head. He groaned, high and shrill, as his body collapsed to the floor.

Broderick looked down at him. His voice was now calm and even. "How many times do I have to tell you Bolshevik bastards that we don't allow no pickets in New York?" He kicked Johannes in the stomach. "The mayor doesn't want any pickets making trouble and it's our job to make sure there isn't any trouble." He kicked him hard again.

The door to the squad room swung open and a well-dressed man stepped inside. He was carrying a briefcase and he stopped just inside the door and looked down at Johannes twisting on the floor in pain. Then he looked up at Broderick and smiled.

"Excuse me. They told me downstairs I could find Detective Broderick here," he said.

"I'm Broderick."

"Good," he said, walking forward. "My name is Arthur Greenberg, and I represent Mr. Arnold Rothstein, who has asked me to speak with you about a matter that concerns him."

Broderick watched the lawyer closely. He was a weasel of a man, with closely set eyes that appeared to suggest more than was said. There was a large diamond stickpin in his necktie and his clothing looked expensive and tailor-made. A high-priced character, Broderick thought.

"Is there someplace we might talk in private?" the lawyer said.

"There might be," Broderick answered.

Broderick knew Rothstein was behind the labor problems in the fur district. He had expanded his horizons. He was no longer content being the city's most powerful gambler, the grand fixer of sporting events, the money man behind the illegal liquor racket. There was money in the labor movement and he wanted his share of it. Now his lawyer walks in and sees one of his *workers* bleeding on the floor and he doesn't think twice about it. The idea brought a smile to Broderick's lips.

"I think you'll find our conversation rather interesting," Greenberg said. "Perhaps a restaurant nearby?"

Broderick looked at Cordes and Ruditsky. "I'll be at the Villa Penza," he said. "Have the sergeant lock this creep up. He's not going anywhere for a while." He looked at Greenberg and smiled. "After you, Mr. Greenberg," he said.

An hour later Broderick sat outside Chris Nolan's office in City Hall, his skimmer resting on his lap. He had always been impressed by the lavishness of the mayor's offices. The thick red carpeting and the white paneled walls gave off a sense of wealth and authority. There was little furniture in the office of the mayor and his staff, only what was needed plus the occasional odd table or chair, each ornate and impressive. It gave the office a feeling of openness, a place that housed men who wielded power but one where there was also nothing to hide.

11

A secretary sat across from him sifting through the stacks of papers spread out on her desk and sporadically answering the telephone. She was a prim-looking woman, about forty years of age. Her hair was drawn back tightly against her head and he thought she must have been attractive once, years ago. Now her looks had left her and like most once attractive women, only the shell of what had been remained. His wife was like that, he thought. Once people had stopped to look at her as she walked along the street, a slender almost delicate woman moving quietly through the squalor that had sur- rounded them. They had grown up together in the same filth-ridden tene- ments and he had been overwhelmed by the contrast she had set against the poverty and the grime. Then he had left for the navy and she had waited for him until he had returned and they had married when he had joined the Fire Department. He smiled to himself. Later she had urged him to leave that job and transfer to the Police Department. She had been afraid of the danger that surrounded men who ran into burning buildings. He shook his head thinking about those years. There was little left of what he remembered. She was twenty-eight now, two years younger than he, and the birth of their daughter seven years ago had left behind a dull, frumpy woman who shuffled about the house with spreading hips. Soon after, religion had filled her life and she would go off to mass every morning and to a novena each Friday and their love-making had become a brief, dissatisfying thing, something performed in the dark dressed in bed clothes. Now two years had passed since he had left their house to take the hotel room he still occupied. At first he had visited her each week but gradually the visits to the house in Queens had become less frequent, due to the pressures of the job he had told her. But they both knew the marriage was over. Only she continued the pretense.

But soon he knew he would have to go out there again. It had been weeks now and she would need money and a call to her parish priest would bring another call to the department. Those calls always had to be avoided.

The door to Chris Nolan's office swung open and his bulky form filled the entrance as he beckoned Broderick forward. There was a sizable gap between Nolan's vest and his trousers and the smooth white of his shirt that showed through pressed against a protruding paunch.

Broderick closed the door behind him as Nolan slipped into the chair behind his desk. He ran a hand across his thinning hair and peered at Brod- erick over the rims of his steel-framed glasses.

"You said it was important when you called, John. What is it?" Nolan bit off the tip of a cigar and spit it off to his left. He was a crude, cold man and Broderick could not remember ever seeing him without a cigar stuffed into his mouth.

"I was contacted by this lawyer who wants to make a contribution for a certain favor," Broderick said, forcing himself into an almost boyish smile.

Nolan raised his eyebrows, then struck a match and puffed on his cigar until it was drawing properly.

"What favor, John?" he said.

"Well, this guy works for Arnold Rothstein. He showed up at the squad just after we rousted some pickets in the fur district. There was a demonstration there this morning," Broderick said.

"Yes, I know. I sent out the order to have it broken up," Nolan said.

Broderick twisted in his chair. "I figured it came from the Hall," he said. "Well, anyway, this guy, Greenberg is his name, he asked me to meet with him and he suggested that the pickets could be left alone. He said Rothstein, and you know he's behind all the stuff there, was very interested in getting a union in the fur district. Then he said Rothstein would like to make a contribution to the favorite charity of anybody who could help him. He says they've invested a lot of money in the union and that he felt a sizable contribution, say a hundred grand, was something he'd like to do."

"And what did you say, John?" Nolan had turned his chair to the side and was staring out a window, puffing away on his cigar.

Broderick could feel the sweat forming on his forehead. "Well, Chris, I laughed at him and said why not a hundred and ten grand. And this little Jew just looked at me and smiled and said, make it a hundred and ten. So I told him it would all have to be in cash and I would have to talk to some people first."

Nolan spun around in his chair and looked across his desk at Broderick. "Did you report this attempted bribe to your superiors, John?" he asked.

Broderick could feel his face turning red and sweat poured into the palms of his hands as he twisted his skimmer between them.

"No, Chris. I came here first. I always talk to you first," he said.

Nolan stood up and walked around the desk. "Good boy, Johnny," he said. He was smiling with the cigar still clenched between his teeth. "You wait here. I have to see someone but I'll be right back. Don't worry. You did the right thing, just like always."

Nolan strode out of the office leaving Broderick alone. He took a deep breath. Why the hell do we always have to play games, he thought. If I didn't come here they'd think I was trying to keep the score for myself. He had been told by Nolan that labor matters had to be reported to the Hall. No petty stuff, just good labor matters, and he had known that had meant money matters. It was like the rule in the Police Department. The men who made the score kept half and shared it among themselves. The immediate superior then got half and he split it with the boss above him who, in turn, split it with the boss above him. It went on like that all the way to the commissioner, who everyone knew split with the Hall. God, he thought, as he had many times before, those at the top had envelopes coming in from everywhere. Even the

13

secondary bosses had money coming in from dozens of squads. For borough commanders, hundreds of squads were involved, and when it reached the commissioner and the Hall, the amounts had to be unbelievable.

Broderick thought about this score. A hundred and ten grand, the largest he had ever heard of. The guys who made the score, the guys in the squad, should keep half, that was the rule. But Nolan was no fool. He might say that the share for the bosses would have to come out of that half. That wouldn't be fair, he thought. But who's going to argue. You take it and keep your mouth shut.

The door to the office swung open again and Nolan moved heavily back into the room. He walked over to Broderick and put his hand on his shoulder. "Johnny boy," he said. "You make the contact and pick up that contribution. How many of the boys in the squad know about this?"

"Well, you got Ruditsky and Johnny Cordes," Broderick said. "Then you got the lieutenant, but he doesn't know about it yet."

"Forget the lieutenant," Nolan said, walking around his desk and picking up another cigar. "You hold out twenty grand and tell the boys it's a bonus from the Hall. They don't have to know any more than they do already. In fact don't even mention the Hall, just tell them they shouldn't discuss it with anyone. Any problem from the squad commander or anyone else, including the other guys in the squad, you tell them to call me here. That should put a stop to it. But if you handle it right there shouldn't be any problems. You understand me, John?"

"No problem at all, Chris," he said. "I'll take care of things and I'll stop by here tomorrow."

He turned to go but Nolan's voice stopped him.

"No, you call me and I'll have someone meet you. One other thing, John. You tell Mr. Greenberg that his client has a six-month grace period to get his union going. After that he'll have to talk to us again. And if there are any complaints from the fur people, you just refer them to the Hall."

Broderick stood smiling across at Nolan. Twenty grand, he thought, and maybe more six months from now.

Outside Nolan's office the double doors leading into the mayor's office were open. Jimmy Walker was standing behind his desk. The secretary was standing next to him and Walker was pointing to something on his desk. "Just change that one point and it will be fine," he said.

Walker looked up and saw Broderick standing in the outer office. A smile flashed across his face. "Johnny boy," he called, waving him into the office.

Broderick strode through the double doors as the prim-looking secretary moved out past him, closing the doors behind her. Walker remained standing behind his desk, appearing almost regal amid the well-appointed surroundings of his office. It was a large room, slightly longer than it was wide. The large doors and the paneled wainscoting were painted white and contrasted perfectly against the field of blue wallpaper and the blue carpeting. In the center of the room a large crystal chandelier hung from the ceiling, adding a touch of magnificence much like some fine jewelry hanging about the neck of a beautiful woman. It all seemed to befit the mayor as he stood there impeccably dressed in a light gray suit, a red and gray striped tie protruding at a precise angle from his vest.

The mayor extended his hand, still smiling. His handsome slender face seemed soft and in perfect harmony with his surroundings. Not a hair on his head was out of place.

"Sit down, John, and tell me what you've been doing. It's been weeks since I've had a chance to talk to you."

Walker waited for Broderick to seat himself in a leather chair across from him, then slid gracefully into his own high-backed chair. He removed a handkerchief from his breast pocket with his left hand and dabbed his forehead, then returned it, still using the left hand as he rearranged it in its proper position. Broderick had once asked him why he used his left hand that way and Walker had told him it was an old show business trick. If you use your right hand you must bring it across your body, he had said. That separates you from your audience and you must never allow yourself to be separated from your audience.

They were talking now about the Police Department and about the bootleggers who were vying with each other for control of the illegal liquor market and the violence that regularly erupted when individual territories were violated. Walker laughed raucously as Broderick told him about a gangster Walker knew who had been shot in the buttocks during one of the recent battles. He was a great fan of the Police Department, a devoted buff to the individual actions of cops, almost as though they were men apart from him, not actually under his direct command, as of course they were. He seemed to revel in stories about the police and the criminals who permeated the city and were regarded almost as a special breed of celebrity. It was all part of the New York that he loved, Broderick had often thought, the romance that always seemed more exciting when it was surrounded by something tainted.

"These are great days, John," Walker said. "And we're all lucky to be part of them. We have an opportunity to see that people have what they want. It may not always be what the existing laws say they should have. But that's part of the job too, deciding how the law should be applied and to what degree. And it does have its rewards."

He placed his palms down on the desk and rose from his chair. Broderick got to his feet as Walker moved around the desk and stood next to him. He placed an arm around Broderick's shoulder and began walking across the office, stopping for a moment under the chandelier.

"You've been doing a fine job for us, John," he said. "I want you to know that I'm aware of what you're doing and I appreciate it. Your loyalty is

15

important to me. It's not something we seem to have a great deal of today and it's something that should be rewarded."

"You know you'll always have that from me, Jim," Broderick said. He had called Walker by his first name almost from the beginning. It was something he knew the mayor favored. In the beginning it had been Mr. Mayor, but Walker had quickly put an end to that, explaining that formalities were not needed among friends. He had become Walker's friend when some newspapermen had introduced them during the campaign, almost two years ago now. There had been a story in the papers that day about an arrest he had made and Walker had been delighted with the first-hand account Broderick had given him. There had been some jobs that had followed, jobs that he had done surreptitiously at first until it had become obvious that Walker would be elected. The work had been a wise step, he learned later. Three weeks after Walker took office Broderick was promoted from third- to first-grade detective and assigned to the newly formed Industrial Squad, the small elite force established to handle labor problems and major crimes.

They walked on toward the door, Walker's arm still draped around Broderick's shoulder. Walker was a full four inches shorter than the heavyset detective. From a distance he appeared taller, probably because of his slender build, Broderick thought. But he was no more than five foot eight, an average-sized man at best.

"Chris Nolan has been speaking highly of you, John," Walker continued. "He feels you're a valuable asset to us and I personally want you to continue to work closely with him. The mayor has to keep his pulse on the Police Department and its problems. But with everything that goes on in this office, that's becoming very hard to do. So you keep Chris apprised on any new problems that develop so we can be on top of them."

On the way back to the office, amid the clatter of passing trolley cars, he tried to review the conversation in his mind. Except for his story about the bootleggers he had said little, no more than a few dozen words. Walker had dominated as usual. It was always that way, it seemed. He always became tongue-tied in the mayor's presence, and when he did talk his voice sounded awkward to him and his mind immediately reviewed each statement as though trying to be certain he had not said something foolish, something that might jeopardize the relationship. But it didn't matter. Walker had not said much himself, nothing at all about the earlier meeting with Chris Nolan. There had been hints but nothing certain, nothing solid to indicate the mayor even knew about the "contribution" he would deliver tomorrow. It was simply a meeting between friends and even if Walker wasn't his friend he was something far more important. He was his rabbi. And he was the only rabbi any New York cop needed.

Johnny Cordes and Barney Ruditsky had the look of two vultures anticipating carrion when he returned. Cordes was a solidly built man, smaller than

16

Broderick but with a sleek, almost feline look about him and Broderick had never seen him lose his composure, even in the worst of situations. Just a cold-blooded Spaniard, he had often thought. Now he sat behind his desk watching Broderick with an amused smirk on his face.

Broderick just grinned at him.

"So what happened?" Cordes said.

"Nothin' much. We got a little contribution coming our way and we don't have to worry about the fur district anymore, not for six months anyway."

Both detectives had their eyes fixed on him waiting for more.

"You gonna tell us how much, or is it a secret?" Cordes said.

Broderick glanced at the door that led to the lieutenant's office. "Where is he?" he asked.

"Gone for the day, like always," Ruditsky said, alluding to the near constant absenteeism of their boss.

"Well, we don't have to tell him about this, nothing except that City Hall called and all fur district problems are to be referred there from now on."

"So what about the contribution?" Cordes said.

"What's the matter, you lose a bundle at the track, Cordes?" Broderick was smirking himself now, playing the string completely out.

"Don't fuck around, John," Cordes said.

"We have some money to divide up between the three of us tomorrow," Broderick said. "What would you say to fifteen grand split three ways?"

There was silence, then Ruditsky jumped to his feet.

"Fifteen big ones, I love it. I'll take my five in hundreds and God help those suckers at the track," he said.

Broderick looked at him and smiled. "Like the man said, there's a sucker to be had every minute of the day. I'll tell you what. I'll even buy the drinks to celebrate."

CHAPTER THREE

MOE BERG OPENED THE DOOR TO THE HOTEL ROOM, then stepped aside to let Hy Amberg enter first. Inside, a mixture of odors filled his nostrils. The furniture was old and heavy with years of dust, and its musty smell mingled with the aromas of the food and liquor that covered a large table to his left, and underlying it all was the strong scent of a cheap perfume.

Across the room a well-proportioned blonde jumped to her feet and rushed toward him, her full breasts bouncing heavily under a loose-fitting dress.

"Hy, honey," she squealed, then threw her arms around his neck and kissed his face repeatedly. "Oh, it's so good to see you, honey."

Amberg pushed her away to arm's length and stared at her, studying the tightly curled hair that puffed out over her ears. "A new hair style," he said. "What other new things have you been doing while I've been gone?" A slight smile crossed his lips and he reached out and pinched her cheek, a little harder than necessary.

Gillie winced. Not unlike Moe, Gillie too had thought of deserting Amberg before he returned but she had been afraid. The brutality of the man and his insane anger had held her, kept her waiting as sure as if he had locked her in a room. There had been tenderness between them and passion and she enjoyed his body like she enjoyed the bodies of most men. But there was also the fear. "Nothing, Hy. Ask Moe if you don't believe me. It's been awful without you." She began to pout.

Amberg patted her cheek, then looked past her, across the room to where two young men stood watching. They were both about the same size; both were thin with hard young bodies. They were approximately twenty, no more than twenty-two, Amberg guessed. The one with blond, curly hair and the handsome boyish face was wearing two .38 caliber revolvers in shoulder holsters. Crowley, Amberg said to himself. The other would be Dunniger, standing there with his mouth open in a half smile, his hair hanging across his forehead like brown straw. He was absentmindedly kneading his crotch with his left hand and there was a large .38 stuck in his belt. A fucking farmboy, Amberg thought.

Amberg spoke over his shoulder to Moe.

"Are these the two guys you told me about?" he said.

"Yeah. This is them." Moe moved across the room and stopped in front of the two men and then turned to face Amberg. "This is Jimmy Crowley, Hy," he said, placing a hand on Crowley's shoulder.

Crowley nodded. "It's good to meet you, Hy. I heard a lot about you."

Amberg's eyes bore into Crowley's face, then switched to Dunniger.

"And this is Rudy Dunniger, Hy. They're both good boys," Moe said.

The smile on Dunniger's face widened, then faded slightly under Amberg's stare. His hand drifted back to his crotch and he began pulling at his genitals again. "Hey, I'm really lookin' forward to workin' with you, Hy," he said.

Amberg moved slowly across the room. His limp was more noticeable now and he caught Dunniger's eyes shift to his right leg.

"You see something you don't like," he said.

"No, Hy. I like everything I see."

Amberg stood before him, watching with pleasure as the young man's cheeks turned red. He was trying to smile again and his hand began to move more feverishly and for a moment Amberg wondered if he was actually jerking off.

Amberg motioned to the revolver in his belt.

"You always carry it that way?" he asked.

"Yeah, I like it that way."

"Well, I don't," Amberg snapped. "You're gonna blow your balls off that way." He smiled at Dunniger. "Tomorrow, first thing, you get yourself a holster. I like people who have balls. And you seem to like yours."

"Yeah. Sure thing," Dunniger said. The foolish half smile had returned to his face and he began to laugh. Crowley and Moe laughed with him.

"And you like two guns, I see," Amberg said, turning toward Crowley.

"Yeah, uh, I . . . I guess I do," Crowley stammered.

19

"I guess you're ambidextrous, eh, kid?" Amberg said.

Confusion spread across Crowley's face and his mouth began to move in an attempted answer that did not come.

"That means you can use both hands as good as most guys use one," Amberg said, his lips curving up in a self-satisfied grin.

"Yeah, that's it. That's what I can do," Crowley said.

Amberg turned away and walked over to the table that held an array of delicatessen food and opened bottles of liquor. There was a large single layer cake covered with white frosting and bearing the inscription, "Welcome Home Hy," in large red letters. He dipped a finger into the frosting and tasted it. "Some spread," he said.

"It's all for you, Hy," Gillie said, moving up beside him. "You want me to make you a sandwich or something?"

Amberg ignored her, turned and walked slowly across the length of the room, surveying the heavy worn furniture and the faded yellow wallpaper. As he reached the end of the room he stopped in front of a second door.

"What's in here?" he said.

"It's the bedroom," Moe said as Amberg opened the door and looked inside. "It's a good bed. I figured you and Gillie could stay in there. I got a roll-away bed in the closet so I can sleep out here. I thought Rudy and Jimmy could stay at their own places for now, since they only live a few blocks away. But if you want them here we can get a couple more roll-aways."

Amberg stood in the doorway, his back still turned to the others. It was a sparsely decorated room. The large four-poster bed, dresser, and armoire were an aging matched set and each carried the scratches and wood stains that came with that age. There was a small upholstered chair in one corner and beneath it he could see a large stain on the flowered carpet. He turned to face Moe.

"It's a dump," he said. "But it'll do for what I have in mind, for the time being anyway. For now Rudy and Jimmy can stay at their places. If that changes later we'll move them in here. How far in advance did you pay for this place?"

"Just a week," Moe said.

"Pay it up for a month and slip each of the desk clerks something so we're sure we know ahead of time about anybody coming to pay us a visit."

"Sure, I'll do it first thing in the morning," Moe said.

Amberg took off his wide-brimmed hat and dropped it on a small table next to an overstuffed sofa. He ran his hands through his thin, sandy-colored hair, then rubbed his chin, feeling the roughness of the five o'clock stubble. He looked at Gillie.

"Did you bring my clothes?" he asked.

"Sure, honey. They're in the bedroom," she said, coming quickly to his side.

20

Amberg glanced about the room again, then addressed the three men. "Look. You boys have a drink, relax and give me a few minutes. I want to clean up and get rid of this crap they gave me to wear."

He motioned Gillie toward the bedroom with his head, then allowed his eyes to shift back to Moe, Dunniger, and Crowley. He winked at them. All three were grinning.

Inside the bedroom Amberg stripped off the cheap blue suit and thin cotton shirt he had been given at Sing Sing earlier that day. He stood in his shorts and T-shirt a few feet from Gillie. She sat on the edge of the bed, her legs crossed, the knee-length hemline of her dress pulled up, exposing her smooth, slender legs to mid-thigh. She looked at him and smiled. There was a knowing look in her eyes and as he stood there Amberg could feel the excitement building within him.

"It's been a long time," Gillie said.

"Too long," Amberg said. "You show me how long it's been for you."

Her smile widened and she rose slowly from the bed and reached behind her back with her right hand and unfastened her dress, allowing it to slip gradually along her body to the floor. She stood before him now wearing only panties, a garter belt and silk stockings, her full, ample breasts rising with each breath, the nipples taut and erect. Slowly she lowered her eyes to the bulge inside his shorts, then moistened her lips with her tongue and reached out with her hand, sliding it softly into the opening of his shorts and gently drawing him to her.

He wanted her desperately now. Not so much because he cared but because it had been three years and like most men who spent long years behind bars he had turned to young boys for satisfaction—and the fact frightened him.

A sudden warmth filled Amberg's cheeks as he moved to her now and he could feel his hands tremble as he placed them on her shoulders and slowly eased her back to the bed, moving one hand to the back of her head in the same motion and pressing it down until her mouth met his protruding erection. A soft, low moan rose from deep within Gillie's throat and Amberg could feel a shudder course through his body as her head slid back and forth, her tongue moving violently against him. Gradually his head dropped forward and both hands pressed her head against him.

"Oh, baby," he said, his voice little more than a whisper, "just do it, baby. Do it." He closed his eyes and he could feel his muscles tighten and then go limp.

In the other room the three men sat at the table eating and drinking. Dunniger, his cheek stuffed with a large piece of sandwich, glanced toward the bedroom door. A smirk appeared on his face.

"He's been in there a long time," he said, looking at the others for some sign his humor had been appreciated.

21

"Three years is a long time," Moe said. "You can work up a pretty stiff prick in three years."

They all laughed. Crowley took a long sip of bourbon, watching his reflection in a mirror on the wall across from him.

"What do you think he has planned for us, Moe?" he said, still watching himself.

"He'll tell both of you when he's through," Moe said. "One thing you two have to learn about him is that he don't like questions. Hy likes to do things his own way and he don't like anybody to object to his ideas. I don't mean that you can't change his mind, but you have to know how to do it. The best thing is for you guys to just say yes to whatever he wants and if you have a problem with it you come to me and let me work it out."

Crowley and Dunniger nodded their approval.

"That's fine with me," Crowley said. "You been with him a long time?"

"About eight years. We were just a little older than you guys when we started out together. We were crazy then. Shit, we never planned anything. We'd just bust into a joint and stick it up and then get away any way we could. But now things are different, now you have to plan everything right down to the last detail."

"If you guys are so careful how'd he get caught this last time," Dunniger asked.

"He *didn't* get 'caught,' " Moe said. "He got set up by a lousy cop named Broderick."

"I heard about him. They say he's a mean bastard," Crowley said.

"Yeah, that's what they say. But don't even mention his name around here. Hy goes fucking crazy when he even thinks about him."

A chill passed through Moe and the nervous twitch returned to his neck as he thought about Broderick and the look on Amberg's face as they talked about his plans driving back from Sing Sing. He would not tell the others about those plans, he thought. He would leave that for Amberg. There was still a chance he could change things, convince Hy it was too dangerous, and he only hoped there would be enough time to do it.

Moe's thoughts were interrupted by Dunniger's voice.

"What'd you say, kid?" he asked.

"I said how'd he get the bum leg?" Dunniger whispered the question.

"That's another thing I wouldn't talk about. He's touchy about that leg. He told me once that he got kicked by a horse when he was a kid. He really hates horses. One time, years ago, we pulled this job up in the Bronx and as we're coming out of this place there's this nag hitched up to an ice wagon in front of the place. Hy takes one look at that horse and he stops and shoots it right between the eyes. The sound of that cannon going off without warning scared the shit out of me. But you should of seen that nag hit the ground. It went down like a bag of bricks and Hy was laughing so hard he almost couldn't move. Hell, he sat in the car and laughed for six blocks and I was so scared I almost drove the fuckin' car up on the sidewalk."

All three men were laughing as the bedroom door opened. Amberg stood there watching them, dressed now in tan, pleated slacks and a white silk shirt open at the collar.

"You guys sound like you're having a good time," he said.

"Yeah. I was just telling them about some of the old jobs we pulled together, like the time you blew that horse away and scared the hell out of me. Remember how I almost drove the car up on the sidewalk?" Moe was smiling, but he was watching Amberg closely, trying to gauge his reaction.

Amberg nodded. "I hate fucking horses," he said.

He walked to the window and drew back the thin, white curtains. Below, four stories down on Eighth Avenue, a trolley car moved by, its bell clanging at the slow-moving traffic. It was seven o'clock now and the darkened streets were filled with well-dressed couples probably heading for restaurants for a quick meal and a few drinks from a secreted hip flask before going on to the theater. It had been three years now since he had been a part of the night life of the city, he thought. Three years and all because of one man. But those three years would be paid for, he knew. Paid in full. His way.

Amberg turned away from the window and walked to the table.

"You want a drink?" Moe asked.

"Yeah. A little Scotch in a tall glass."

Moe poured the drink. "This is the good stuff, imported. Not the crap they're peddling in the speaks these days."

Amberg held the glass up, allowing the amber color to catch the light. He took a long drink. "Don't knock that stuff. We're gonna be selling that crap soon *ourselves*," he said, watching for reactions from the new men.

"The liquor racket, hey, that's great," Dunniger said. "But I thought that was all tied up."

"We're gonna untie it, right, Moe?"

Moe nodded. "You heard the man."

"First thing tomorrow I want both of you guys to start moving around. You find out who's selling, and where they're buying their stuff. I want to know how they ship it in, the routes the trucks use, who peddles it to the speaks, everything. I know it's gonna take some time, but we got time. I got some personal business to take care of first and that's gonna take some time too. You guys understand what I want?"

Crowley and Dunniger assured him they did, then looked at each other and grinned.

"Man, there's big dough in that," Crowley said.

"What you think you were joining up with, some two-bit stickup team?" Amberg said. "The only jobs we do from now on is to finance this. And those have to be safe jobs. Otherwise you two keep your noses clean, understand?"

23

Dunniger was still grinning. "I think it's great, but how do we cut ourselves in?" he asked.

"The same way the guineas did. We'll ask for a piece of the action and if they don't give it to us we'll take it. If the people they buy from won't sell to us, we'll take the booze away from the people they do sell it to. We'll need some more men, but we'll get them as we need them. That'll be your job, Moe. You start lining up the right people. Some of the old gang will be getting out of stir in a few months, but in the meantime you scout up some others. We're gonna need some good drivers and some good muscle. You know the kind of people I want." He turned to Dunniger and Crowley. "Now you boys take off. Have a good time. Me and Moe, we've got some other business to talk over. You check with me here tomorrow night, about this time."

When Dunniger and Crowley had left, Amberg poured himself another drink and leaned back in his chair.

"Now tell me everything you know about Broderick," he said. He was in command again. He had intimidated everyone as he intended and he could feel his confidence surging.

"I don't know too much," Moe said. "I've been layin' kind of low, keepin' pretty much out of sight up in the Bronx."

"Does he still hang out on Broadway, like he used to?"

"Yeah, pretty much so. Most of what I get on him I get from the newspapers," Moe said. "I've seen him a couple of times going into Lindy's at lunch time. A lot of the newspaper guys hang out there and he likes to be around them. You know they've been making a big thing about him the last couple of years, Winchell, Considine, Gene Fowler, all of them. They call him the toughest cop in New York, Johnny 'the beater' Broderick, they call him. They write all kinds of bullshit about him, like how he's not supposed to carry a gun because he's so good with his hands. Stuff like that. Pure bullshit."

Amberg was staring straight into Moe's face. His eyes were almost gleaming now and his teeth were clenched, causing the muscles in his jaw to dance nervously along his thin, angular face. "How about the Garden? Does he still moonlight for Tex Rickard when there's something big going on?"

"I saw him there a couple of times at big fights," Moe said. "But he's usually got somebody else with him. He'd be awful hard to reach there."

"We're not gonna reach him there. But maybe we'll see him there. We're going to see him in a lot of places. Every time he turns around he'll see me and before I get through with him he's going to be seeing me in his sleep. And that's when I kill him, not until then."

Moe watched Amberg closely. He had never seen his eyes as wild, not even in the early days when everything was played like the Wild West. His gun was a toy to him then and he played with it constantly, like Dunniger played with his prick, and a stickup without shots fired took the fun out of it. And in those days he had always made sure there was fun, even if it had meant only firing two shots into the ceiling. Moe's neck began to twitch again. There would be no talking to him now, he knew that. But still he had to try. But it would have to be done carefully.

"Look, Hy," Moe began, "you know this Broderick is about as dirty as a cop can get. I was thinking, maybe we could set him up for a fall. You know, have one of the new guys offer him some dough and then tip off some of the police brass. Can't you see him in the joint. They'd tear him up alive in there. Shit, he wouldn't last a week. Everybody would be waiting to stick a shiv in his back."

Amberg leaned forward, his eyes cutting into Moe's face. He was silent for a long time, then he spoke, his voice almost a whisper.

"I kill Johnny Broderick," he said. "Nobody else touches him. I do it and I do it my way. He's gonna die out on the street with people watching. He's gonna crawl in the gutter and he's gonna beg for his fucking life and then I'm gonna blow his brains out, right there in front of everybody. You understand me, Moe?" Amberg's face was glowing with controlled rage. He was on the edge now and seeing him that way sent a shiver through Moe's body.

"Sure, Hy. Sure," Moe said. "If you want it that way, it's fine with me. You just tell me what you want me to do."

A slight smile appeared on Amberg's lips and his breathing, which had been rapid moments ago, eased. He stood and walked back to the window and looked down into Eighth Avenue again.

The two detectives held him by the arms, supporting more than restraining him. Broderick's face hovered above, cold and expressionless. "You're a punk," the face said just before the heavy fist dug into the pit of the stomach, squeezing the air from the lungs so the cries and threats that came after were only meaningless gasps. "You'll talk now," the face said as the second punch came squarely into the mouth. Blood pouring into the throat, choking. The two detectives warning: "Not in the face, Johnny. We have to explain that. Don't be stupid. Use the body." Again the stomach and the ribs. "You're going away, creep. I got enough on you to make it stick. . . . Fuck You. . . . I'll kill you first"—Again the fist. Collapsing on the desk. Turning to speak and again the fist crashing down, this time into the kidneys—pissing blood for months.

Amberg's hands trembled as he pulled back the curtains. The foot traffic had lessened now. It was after eight o'clock and the people were in the theaters. Most of the restaurants would be nearly deserted, waiting to come to life again at ten-thirty when the theaters would empty and Broadway would again carry the laughter of beautiful women walking on the arms of well-dressed men.

"Tell Gillie to get her ass dressed," Amberg said, still looking out the window. "We're going to get something to eat in a good joint and then we're going to hit some nightspots . . . the ones my pal Johnny Broderick likes to go to."

Moe took a deep breath, then walked across the room and knocked on the bedroom door.

"Gillie," he said. "Get dressed. Hy says we're going out."

A few blocks away in a small speakeasy on Ninth Avenue, Crowley and Dunniger sat at the bar, talking. There was a mirror behind the bar and Crowley studied himself, then rearranged a blond curl that had tumbled onto his forehead.

"We are *really* gonna score this time," Dunniger said. "No more petty shit. The liquor business. That is big time, really big time. What'd you think of the boss, Jimmy? Real tough, ain't he?"

"You think everybody's tough," Crowley said. "But he does have good taste in broads. I'd really like to get my prick into that Gillie bitch. Did you see the tits on her?"

Dunniger began rubbing himself again. "Yeah, and Amberg'll blow your prick right off if you even look at that skirt. You better forget about that. There's plenty of other stuff around."

"But not with tits like that," Crowley grinned at himself in the mirror, then took a heavy drink of bourbon. "But I can wait," he added. "But damn if it didn't drive me crazy sitting out there while he was in the bedroom screwing the ass off her. Shit."

"Like Moe said, you can work up some kind of hard-on in three years," Dunniger slapped his hand on the bar and began to laugh. He held up both hands extending them nearly two feet apart. "About this fucking big," he said.

They laughed again and Crowley waved to the bartender for another round of drinks.

"Speaking of hard-ons, I guess Amberg's got a big one for that Broderick," Dunniger said.

"Yeah, I guess so," Crowley said. "I wouldn't be surprised if that was the personal business he was talking about."

"You mean take him out?" Dunniger whispered.

"I don't think he's planning to send him a Christmas card," Crowley said.

"Holy shit. I never thought of that. Man, that would be something. Kill fucking Johnny Broderick. The whole fucking town would sit up and take notice if he did that. Man, I'm glad I ain't him," Dunniger said.

"You ought to be glad you're not a fucking horse either," Crowley said.

"Yeah, you bet your sweet ass on that. Imagine, blasting a fucking horse. That's the craziest thing I ever heard of."

"I know. That's one of the things that bothers me," Crowley said.

26

CHAPTER FOUR

WORTH & WORTH CLOTHIERS STOOD IN UNOBTRU-
ive elegance on West Fifty-third Street, only a few doors from the bawdiness
of Broadway. The exterior of the shop was lined with heavy wood framing
along the doors and windows and set off by a highly polished brass doorplate
and ornate gold lettering on the display window that intoned: "Catering to
New York's Gentry Since 1850." All of it exuded a quiet sense of dignity that
even the clanging of streetcars a few steps away seemed unable to disturb.

Inside, the effect, like the paneling, continued throughout the long, narrow
room, adding a certain distinction to the racks of ready-made suits that lined
three walls. A large Oriental rug occupied most of the room and, in the
center of the rug there was a full-length mirror with potted palms on each
side, the branches rustling faintly under the breeze of two overhead fans. It
was a place designed exclusively for men, a sanctum safe from the intrusion
of women, and Johnny Broderick seemed perfectly at home as he stood before the mirror, turning slowly to each side, his eyes fixed on the reflection of
a blue serge suit coat.

A short, slender man of about fifty stood beside Broderick, his own tailor-
ing impeccable, his eyes also fixed approvingly on the mirror. Behind him a
young clerk stood in shirt sleeves awaiting any command. There was a
slightly bored look on his face.

Broderick turned to one side again, then faced the mirror squarely and flexed his shoulders as though he expected the muscles to come bursting through the fabric. He nodded his approval.

"Looks good. I like it," he said, turning toward the slender man. "Let me try the brown one again."

The man snapped his fingers and the clerk hurried forward and helped Broderick remove the jacket, then moved away to a nearby chair where a brown suit coat lay neatly folded.

"In all my years in this business I haven't seen a more perfect fit, Detective Broderick," the man said. He spoke with a slight English accent that was obviously contrived.

"Adolf, every time I come in here you tell me that. But this time I think you're right," Broderick said.

He was standing in his shirt sleeves now and the gun and holster attached to the right side of his belt seemed to jar the quiet dignity of the room. The clerk returned and helped him with the brown suit coat and Broderick buttoned it and turned to his left, observing the slight bulge made by the weapon. He frowned.

"This one seems a little tight," he said. "You'll have to make some adjustments so the gun doesn't show. I think the blue one was okay the way it was."

"It was perfect," Adolf said affectedly. "A beautiful fit. It's a shame you have to wear a weapon. You have a perfect physique for clothing. Broad shoulders, narrow waist, it's a shame to alter them."

Broderick turned back to the mirror and frowned again at the bulge along his right side. "Yeah, I know, Adolf. But if I didn't wear it somebody would be putting little round holes in your suits."

Adolf nodded in mock sadness, then took a clothes brush from the clerk and began to move about Broderick brushing furiously. He helped remove the suit coat, then motioned to the clerk, who hurried off and returned with the jacket to Broderick's own suit.

Slipping it on, Broderick stood before the mirror and adjusted the lapels, then flexed his shoulders again.

"You know, you should really tell the mayor about our shop," Adolf said. "He couldn't find better fabric and I'm sure he'd be very happy with our selection." Adolf again began moving about Broderick brushing his suit coat.

Broderick smiled at the smaller man, then took his skimmer from the clerk and adjusted it on his head. "You'd never get the mayor to buy off-the-rack suits, Adolf, even if they do cost two hundred bucks. All his suits are custom made. Besides, he already has a dozen suits like those two."

"Will you be taking both the suits then?" Adolf asked. He had raised his chin slightly, adding to the affectation.

"Yeah, I think I will. You fix the coat on the brown one. The trousers were fine on both. Just keep the drape over the shoe tops the way we had it."

Broderick started toward the door, his shoulders swaying slightly from side to side. At the door he turned. "Oh, Adolf. These get delivered to my hotel, not my house. And put both of them on my tab."

"Certainly." Adolf offered a small bow. "They'll be there by the first of the week, if that's agreeable?"

Broderick nodded and opened the door, allowing the blare of the traffic to intrude for a moment into the quiet dignity of the shop.

When the door closed behind him the clerk shot a glance at Adolf. "Put it on his tab," he said. "Everything seems to go on his tab. But he never pays it."

Adolf stiffened and fixed the clerk with his most imperious stare. "Did I ask for your financial advice?" he snapped. "You really have a great deal to learn about commerce, young man. If Detective Broderick did pay, a dozen hoodlums would come in here and put clothing on *their* tabs. And I assure you they would not pay their bills." Adolf paused and drew himself up to full dignity. "Detective Broderick has one beneficial characteristic. He never allows anyone to play where he plays. So I keep him furnished with suits and shirts and neckwear and even monogrammed undergarments if he wants them and he makes sure no one bothers me. It's an investment. If you expect to prosper in this business you should learn about these things."

Outside, Broderick stood at the corner of Broadway and Fifty-third Street surveying the lunch hour chaos of Broadway. Young women in loose-fitting, knee-length dresses paraded by, their casual hats pulled down along their ears, the delicate puffs of tightly curled hair protruding fashionably from the sides and back. Across the street a uniformed cop stood next to a black Duesenberg, his foot on the running board, his summons book propped on his knee. He appeared to be lecturing the driver, who probably went over the twenty-mile speed limit, Broderick thought.

Broderick smiled, quietly pleased he was no longer in uniform himself. He started south on Broadway, his shoulders swaying as he moved through the noontime crowds. All about him the buildings rose with a power and brashness that seemed unassailable. The sun was bright and directly overhead and it caught the asphalt paving bricks in the street and the steel of the trolley tracks, causing them to give off flashes of light as the traffic moved past. There was no place in the world like this street, he thought.

Three blocks south at Fiftieth Street and Broadway Lindy's Restaurant was conducting the noontime war that was the daily lunch hour. Waiters moved through the long, narrow room at breakneck speed, dropping plates of food unceremoniously in front of customers, then dashing back to the kitchen, shouting orders at the chef and each other. Amid the clatter of dishes, shouting waiters, and the constant buzz of conversation, Leo Lindy moved graciously among the tables like a grand conductor directing some mad Chinese symphony. Occasionally he would stop to inquire about a customer's satisfac-

29

tion or to pass on some bit of Broadway gossip, then return to his customary station near the door ready to greet new arrivals, looking very much the proprietor in his neatly tailored dark suit. It was a good luncheon crowd, the only open tables were those reserved for regular customers. But then it was always good at lunch, even though it was something Leo worried about daily.

He looked about the room with satisfaction, his eyes coming to rest on a small bar in the center of the north wall. The bar annoyed him. It was a useless fixture now with the madness of prohibition besetting everyone. He had thought about removing the bar but had decided against it. There would be room for only three more tables with the bar gone and he considered the cost of removing it excessive compared to the benefits it would produce. Besides there was always hope that President Coolidge would come to his senses.

There were tables on each side of the bar and others extended out into the center of the room. The south wall was lined with booths that were occupied by newspapermen and other regular customers who preferred the false privacy that the high-backed seats pretended to give. They were all filled now and Leo looked down the long line of booths with pleasure, his eyes passing over the framed line drawings of Broadway scenes and the photographs of celebrities that covered the wall above them.

Lindy walked to the second booth where two young reporters sat with oversized sandwiches in front of them. The smaller of the two was thin and intense with eyes that constantly darted about as though afraid their owner might be missing some important subtlety. His dress was poor. The suit appeared rumpled and the hat needed blocking and was pushed to the back of his head. But Leo liked the young man. Everywhere he went he seemed to meet Walter Winchell and he had become convinced he would soon make his mark on the city. The other young man he knew only as Murphy, James, he thought, and although he also worked for the *Graphic,* he was a bit too foppish for Leo's taste.

"How is everything, Walter, Mr. Murphy?" Leo said, stopping beside the slightly elevated booth.

"Perfect, Leo," Winchell said. "I'm just taking my time and waiting for our friend Broderick to come in. We could have some excitement here today."

Leo stared at Winchell. "Excitement?" he said, his voice carrying a trace of concern.

Winchell motioned behind him with his head. "Back there," he said. "At the table in the opposite corner. You see the two guys back there, the ones with the good-looking blonde?"

Lindy looked back, allowing his eyes to pass discreetly over the three customers and sized them up in his mind. One of the men was hard and wiry with ferretlike eyes that seemed exceptionally cruel. The other was a large hulk of a man who appeared to have no neck at all. The blonde was indeed attractive but her clothes were garish and it gave her an air of cheapness. He turned back to Winchell. "So?" he said.

"That's Hy Amberg and company," Winchell said. "Johnny put him away three years ago and he did a lot of screaming and yelling at the time about how he was going to pay Johnny back."

"Three years is a long time," Leo said, without conviction. "A person can forget a lot of things in three years."

"Not if you're Hy Amberg, you don't," Winchell said. "He's a little crazy upstairs and he hates Johnny's guts. It's a mutual feeling, of course. In fact I think he may be the one guy in this town who scares Johnny just a little."

"According to your articles Johnny Broderick isn't afraid of man or beast, Walter." Murphy was grinning as he spoke. "Besides, from what I know about Amberg, he'd starve to death if he didn't have small storekeepers to stick up. He's not exactly Legs Diamond, you know."

"I'm not saying he's not a punk," Winchell said, his voice high and raspy. "But he's a crazy punk. You could just say hello to that character and he might decide to shoot you for doing it. His last babe, well, let's say he took a broken bottle to her face because she didn't do something he wanted. At least that's the book on him."

Murphy laughed. "Or perhaps she did, but not sufficiently well enough."

Lindy shook his head. "This conversation is getting too morbid for me, gentlemen. You don't really think there could be trouble, do you?" he said.

"You never know, Lindy," Winchell said. "You never know." He and Murphy laughed.

Lindy shook his head again and walked back toward the kitchen, taking care to again inspect the three people sitting at the rear table. Trouble was something he didn't need, he told himself.

Amberg sat at the small round table facing the door, with Moe and Gillie on each side. There was a slight smile on his lips, more of anticipation than of pleasure. He inspected the room carefully, then nudged Gillie with his elbow. "You see those booths over there?" he said. "Most of them are reserved for the newspaper guys who come in here." He turned to Moe. "Those are my pal's friends, aren't they? The guys who tell everybody what a big man he is, what a tough cop he is." Amberg laughed. It was a low, broken laugh that held no pleasure in it.

Gillie looked up and down the booths. "Gee, that's interesting, Hy," she said. "Are they all from newspapers?"

Amberg's face registered disgust. "Who cares," he said. "Most of them are just flunkies. There are always flunkies hanging around big shots. That's why I keep you around."

Gillie began to pout, her lower lip protruding like a child denied an ice cream cone. "That's not nice, Hy. I'm no flunkie. Am I, Moe?"

31

Amberg reached out and took her wrist. He squeezed it. "Shut up," he said. "Just shut your goddamned mouth."

"You're hurting me," she said, trying to pull her hand away.

"Oh, baby. Did I hurt you?" Amberg held tightly to her wrist. The cold, pleasureless laugh returned, then stopped abruptly.

Moe tried to distract him. "Boss. What about this place on Forty-eighth Street. I tell you, the boys think it's an easy mark. Every morning there's just that old man in it and he's even got curtains behind the window display cases. You can't even see in from the street."

"I told you before, I've had enough of that crummy stuff." Amberg's voice was low and harsh and his attention was still fixed on Gillie as he spoke. He turned toward Moe, his voice softening. "That's small time and we've done too many of them. If places start getting knocked off this soon after I'm back on the street the cops are gonna know who's doing it. They know that's been our action and if we move too soon we're all gonna end up in the joint. And I'm never going back inside. You concentrate on what I told you. Find us some new boys. I don't want to have to depend on these kids, Crowley and Dunniger. They're too green. That Dunniger kid can't keep his hands off his prick and Crowley never stops looking at himself in the mirror." Amberg returned his attention to the crowded restaurant. "Some day those guys over there will start writing about Hy Amberg." He seemed transfixed by the booths along the far wall, as though expecting the scattering of newspapermen who sat there to turn and acknowledge his prediction.

"Of course they are, Hy," Gillie said, trying to regain his favor. "They ought to be writing about you right now."

Moe reached out and touched Amberg's arm and motioned toward the door. "Look who just showed up."

Across the room, just inside the etched glass double doors, Johnny Broderick stood with his heavy frame almost obscuring the entrance.

"Well, well. The big man, himself," Amberg said. "I hope you enjoy your lunch, tough guy."

"Who's that?" Gillie asked. She was studying Broderick and seemed pleased by what she saw.

Amberg ignored her, not noticing the attraction. His attention remained riveted on Broderick.

Standing next to Lindy's small reservations table, Broderick scanned the room. Cordes was not there yet, he probably . . . He stopped abruptly. At a small table at the rear of the room, Hy Amberg sat smiling at him. So they let that crazy bastard out, he thought. He hardened his stare, trying to conceal the surprising sense of discomfort that rose inside him. The feeling annoyed him, but still it was there and he tried to hide it by continuing his surveillance of the room. Winchell was in a booth to the left. The reporter was watching him.

32

Leo Lindy approached. "Hi, Johnny. Would you like to join Mr. Winchell's table? He's in the second booth with Mr. Murphy."

"No, I'm waiting for somebody, Leo, but I'll say hello." He walked to the second booth, removed his skimmer and smiled at Winchell. "Hello, Walter."

"Johnny. You know Jim Murphy, don't you?" Winchell said.

Broderick extended his hand. "Good to meet you, Jim."

"Will you join us?" Winchell said.

"No, but thanks. I'm waiting for Johnny Cordes. I just wanted to thank you for the plug you gave me in the paper this morning."

"Don't mention it. You deserved it. By the way, John, did you happen to notice who's sitting back there?" Winchell motioned to the rear of the room and began to smile.

"Yeah, I saw him," Broderick said. "But I smelled him first." The two reporters began to laugh. Leo Lindy started past them and Broderick reached out and stopped him. "What's that garbage doing in here, Leo?" He motioned toward the rear of the dining area with his eyes.

Lindy sighed and shrugged his shoulders apologetically. "It's a public place, John. As long as he doesn't cause any trouble, what can I do? There won't be any trouble, will there, John?" Lindy looked honestly concerned.

"Yes, John," Winchell offered. "Lindy wants to be sure that there isn't any shooting until everyone gets their dessert."

"Shooting. Oh, my God. Shooting they're talking about." Lindy shook his head and walked briskly away, leaving the three men laughing quietly.

Broderick looked up and saw Cordes coming through the swinging glass doors. "I'll have to see you guys later," he said. "Cordes just came in and we have some things to talk about." He placed his hand on Winchell's shoulder. "Thanks again, Walter."

Broderick met Cordes at the door and they moved without speaking to a small front table in the opposite corner of the room. Cordes slid into a chair, his back against the front wall, and Broderick bypassed the chair opposite him and sat to his right, his back against the north wall. Cordes spoke first.

"I see your buddy's here for lunch," he said, his eyes fixed on Amberg.

"Yeah, with his social secretary and his business manager. Maybe we should find them all a new place to eat, like Sing Sing," Broderick said.

"I didn't know he was out," Cordes said. "And he sure is paying a lot of attention to us. He just can't keep his eyes off us."

Broderick felt the emotion rise in his stomach again. He turned to his right. Amberg was still smiling. "Somebody ought to kill that creep," he said to Cordes.

"He's just a cheap hood," Cordes said. "Don't let him bother you."

Broderick turned to Cordes. His face was serious. "He's more than that," he said. "That clown is a maniac. I've had it up to here with creeps like that." He brought his hand up to his throat.

33

Cordes laughed. "You? Bothered by a punk like that. That's not the Johnny Broderick I keep reading about. You better watch out or I'll tell the newspaper boys and they'll destroy your image."

"Yeah, yeah," Broderick said. "But you mark my words. This garbage is different. You don't ever know what the scum is going to do. Even he doesn't know what he's gonna do. Rats like that should be put away."

"Screw him," Cordes said. "You worry about him too much. Let's talk business. I made the pickup at the Toledo." He took a gold toothpick from his vest—his trademark—and slipped it into his mouth.

"Did you check the amount?" Broderick asked.

"It's short, but I expected it. The guineas say business is off."

"Off, my ass," Broderick said. "Everybody's drinking, everybody's gambling. I dropped nearly a grand in the last two weeks, myself. They're bullshitting you. You're not being forceful enough."

"Then *you* make the pickup next time," Cordes said. "I don't want to shake those guys up. They spread a lot of grease around town. There's no way of telling who's on their pad and if we push them too hard it could mean trouble."

"Okay, forget it. But what the hell do you think the lieutenant is going to say when we come up short? You know damn good and well what he's going to say. He'll say straighten it out or it comes out of your end, that's what. I'll make a stop there and explain to those bastards."

They stopped talking abruptly as a slovenly waiter approached. He was a fat little man with an apron tied high around his chest. There was a towel over his arm and the stub of a pencil stuck behind his ear. He stopped in front of the table.

"Okay, gentlemen, what will it be today?"

"You know, Max," Broderick said. "The usual."

Max frowned. He was typical of Lindy's waiters. He yelled at his boss and talked back to customers. His main talent was cajoling his customers, convincing them he was privy to the daily secrets of the kitchen. It was a ploy, he believed, that produced larger tips.

"Look, Mr. Broderick," he began, "the bagels were delivered too early, the kitchen man forgot to cover them—a little stale. We're short of the good parts of the Nova Scotia. We had a run earlier. All we got left is a piece of lox and it's too salty. Listen to Max. Try the blintzes, cheese, with sour cream, a side of sturgeon, a nice Bermuda onion, and sliced tomato. This you'll enjoy."

Broderick grinned at the fat waiter. "You're a fucking phoney, Max, but we'll do it your way. Just bring it. The same for both of us." He turned to Cordes. "That okay with you?"

Cordes nodded, chewing on his toothpick and he began to laugh as he watched Max scribble down the order at inhuman speed, spin on his heels, and race off toward the kitchen. "He moves awful fast for a fat man," he said.

34

"Yeah, he sure does," Broderick said. "And listen. Don't worry about the guineas. I'll be gentle."

Cordes's eyes shot up. "Let's drop it, Johnny. Here comes your buddy and his friend. You know, she's not half bad at all."

Broderick watched Amberg approach. There was a smirk on his face and the woman with him was giggling. The muscles in Broderick's jaw tightened and he could feel the sensation in his stomach again. Cordes kept his eyes on Moe, who was moving along the opposite side of the restaurant heading for the door. Amberg and Gillie stopped in front of the table.

"Hey, Johnny Cordes and Johnny Broderick," he said. "The two Johnnies. The boys in blue who wear those beautiful two-hundred-dollar suits. How's tricks?" Amberg was smiling again but only with his mouth.

"Get lost, Amberg, and make it fast," Broderick said.

Amberg's smile broadened and he turned to Gillie. "Now see that. And here I am just wanting to introduce my lady to the toughest cop in New York."

"Hi," Gillie said. She smiled at Broderick.

"No, baby, not Johnny Broderick," Amberg said. "He's only tough in the newspapers. This guy, the man with the solid gold toothpick." He pointed to Cordes. "He's the tough guy."

Gillie looked confused, then turned to Cordes. "Hi," she said.

"Get out of here, Hy," Cordes said. "Lindy doesn't like trouble in his place."

"You better get out of here you little bastard," Broderick said. His eyes were dark and his jaw moved back and forth under his grinding teeth.

"Now, Detective Broderick. I don't want any trouble either. I'm just a citizen out having lunch, who wanted the lady here to meet you two prominent gentlemen." The smirk was back on Amberg's face.

"Hi," Gillie said again.

"That's not a lady. That's a broad out with a punk. Now get lost," Broderick said, looking away from Amberg for the first time.

"Hey, that's no way to talk to somebody. I didn't do anything to you," Gillie said. She turned to Amberg looking for some support.

Broderick turned his attention to Gillie. His eyes were hard. "You're not somebody, kid. And you're here with less than somebody."

Amberg was not smiling now and he placed both hands on the table and leaned down, directly across from Broderick. "You know, Johnny. Big, bad Johnny. I don't want any trouble here and neither do you. But some day, old pal, there just might be trouble. And it's going to be interesting to see what happens."

"You little bastard." Broderick began to rise from his seat but Cordes caught his arm.

"Easy, Johnny, easy," he said.

Amberg straightened up and took Gillie's arm. "That's right, Johnny boy. Take it easy. We'll be seeing each other. Old friends always run into each other now and then." Amberg let out a short, vicious laugh, then turned and moved slowly toward the door. He passed Leo Lindy who was standing by the reservations table. Lindy was wiping his forehead with a handkerchief. "Nice place you got here," Amberg said as he stepped through the frosted glass doors.

Outside, the smile faded from Amberg's face; his eyes became narrow and his body tensed.

"What's wrong, honey?" Gillie said.

"Some day I'm gonna kill that rotten bastard. I'm gonna spread his brains all over the street. He's nothing. Nothing."

"I know, baby. But it's all right. Don't let him bother you," Gillie said.

Amberg's eyes seemed to erupt with anger. "Shut up," he shouted, pushing her toward the black Packard that had just pulled to the curb with Moe behind the wheel. "Shut your goddamned mouth."

Inside, Broderick sat at the table in silence. He stared straight ahead. "That little bastard," he said.

"He really gets to you, doesn't he?" Cordes said.

"Did anybody see that? Any of the newspaper guys?"

"I don't know, Johnny. I suppose they saw him come over here. But nobody heard anything and even if they did, so what? He's nothing. He's a punk."

Broderick stared down into the table, fighting to control his appearance. Don't look like you're upset, he told himself. Look like nothing happened. He smiled falsely at Cordes. "Yeah, you're right," he said, still smiling. "But that little bastard isn't going to stop. I'm gonna have to stop that prick myself."

"Quiet, Johnny," Cordes said, indicating that someone was coming.

Max glided up to the table, his right hand and most of his forearm holding plates of food.

"And now gentlemen of the police, you are going to love this, I promise," he said, scattering the dishes about the table with deliberate abandon. "And what to drink?"

"A cold beer," Cordes said.

"A cold beer? You never heard about prohibition?" Max said.

"The kind you serve here in the frosted glasses, Max. A cold beer." Cordes laughed at the mock expression of surprise on Max's face. He had loose, sagging jowls and when he shook his head, which he did repeatedly, they quivered like jelly.

"A cold beer," Max said emphatically. "And for you, Mr. Broderick?"

"Just a glass of soda water, Max."

Max turned to Cordes and squinted at him out of the corner of one eye.

"See," he said. "Not only he obeys the law, but he doesn't drink either.

36

He's going to live forever. You and me, we'll probably wake up dead tomorrow."

"Just a cold beer, Max. And today, not tomorrow." Cordes was still laughing at the little waiter.

"Today not tomorrow. I'm going. I'm going. If the police don't obey the law why should Max worry." Max spun around and rushed off toward the kitchen again, his jowls quivering as he moved.

Cordes sat there chuckling. "They ought to have a cabaret license for that guy," he said. He looked at Broderick. His face was sour and the muscles along his jaw were still moving violently. "Johnny. Don't let that creep bother you," he said.

"He doesn't bother me."

"Yeah, I can tell," Cordes said.

Max returned with the drinks, dropped them on the table, then rushed off again. They sat there eating in silence. After a few minutes Broderick pushed his plate away, the food almost untouched.

"What's the matter," Cordes asked, "you're not hungry?"

"No. I don't like sturgeon that much," he said.

Cordes resumed his attack on the food in front of him. Across the room Walter Winchell stood at the reservations table paying his check. He studied Cordes and Broderick for a few moments, then walked toward them.

"Hello, Cordes," he said, patting him on the shoulder. "Good to see you." He shifted his stance to face Broderick. "What was that all about, Johnny? Between you and Amberg, I mean?"

Broderick flashed a smile, "Nothing, Walter. Nothing at all. The punk was trying to impress his girl friend. I'm afraid he didn't learn very much at Sing Sing and it looks like he's heading for another fall. Maybe one he won't get up from this time."

"That's very interesting," Winchell said. "I could always use something about you locking up Amberg again. You let me know when it's going down."

"You know I will, Walter. And it might be sooner than you think."

Winchell smiled at him. "That's the boy, Johnny," he said. "We'll see you soon, then." He turned and started to go, then stepped back to the table. "You know, John, you have a good reputation in this town and you can't let some cheap hood put a mark on it. You know I mean that as a friend."

"That creep isn't putting a mark on anything." Broderick could feel his face redden and he fought to control himself.

"That's good, John," Winchell said. "It's just that I worry about you. I'll be hearing from you soon, then. See you, Cordes." He turned and walked away before Cordes could respond.

Broderick and Cordes sat quietly. A few moments passed and then Cordes could stand the silence no longer.

"Look, Johnny, maybe it's none of my business, but what is this? You got to

37

perform on command for these newspaper clowns?"

"It's nothing like that," Broderick said. His voice was tight and defensive. "He's been good to me. I got some good press from him. He just wants to see me get more of the same. That's all there is to it."

"Yeah, okay," Cordes said. "But he talks like you should be busting a head whenever he wants to see one busted."

The remark cut into Broderick and he snapped back at Cordes. "Look, he's okay, I told you. That punk needs to get his head busted anyway. I should have busted it right here, today. Anyway, forget about it." Broderick pushed himself away from the table. "Let's get out of here," he said. "It's one-thirty."

Broderick and Cordes walked to the reservations table where Leo Lindy stood. "And how was lunch?" he inquired.

"Just great," Broderick said, reaching into his trouser pocket and withdrawing a roll of bills. He took two dollars off the top and handed it to Lindy. "Here, that ought to cover everything. Whatever's left over, give it to Max," he said.

Lindy looked at him openly surprised. "Johnny, you don't have to do that. Just leave something for Max, like always," he said.

"That's okay. I want to," he said.

Lindy took the money and then decided it deserved some gossip in return. "Say, have you boys caught the new show at the Palace? Jolson does this new song, 'Swanee,' and it's fantastic. It stops the show." His voice prattled on until he realized that Broderick and Cordes were only half listening. "Yeah, well, you fellas have a good day," he said. "I'll see you tomorrow." He turned, smiling at another customer arriving with a check in hand as Broderick and Cordes moved quickly out the door.

Broderick walked to the curb where an unmarked police Model A Ford stood waiting.

"This your car?" he said to Cordes.

"Yeah," Cordes said.

"You going back downtown?"

"No, I still have some stuff to do up here." Cordes reached in his pocket and took out the keys and tossed them to Broderick. "You take it," he said. "I won't be going back to Headquarters anyway."

Broderick climbed in the passenger side and slid across the seat. He looked back at Cordes. "Thanks," he said.

Cordes leaned inside the car. "Think nothing of it," he said. He was watching Broderick closely. "And take it easy."

"Sure." Broderick grinned at him, then started the engine.

Cordes slammed the passenger door and stood there as the car pulled out into traffic and headed south on Broadway. "Sure," he said aloud.

Two blocks south at Forty-eighth Street and Broadway, Broderick pulled the car to the curb and pressed the horn three times. He slid across the seat to the passenger side and leaned out the window as a small door in the side of a newsstand opened and a head popped out, the face like some craggy gnome. The head was followed by the body of a man no more than five feet tall. He rushed over to the car, smiling. His chin only came up to the bottom of the open window.

"Hi, Johnny. Hey, that was a great mention you got in the *Graphic* this morning. I saved a copy for you. You want it?"

"I got it at the office," Broderick said. "What do you have for me today, Danny?"

"Not too much," the little man said. "There's a new speakeasy that just opened up down in the Village. It's an independent operation, if you know what I mean, and so I don't think it's gonna last too long. I understand the boys are pretty upset about it."

"Who's running it?" Broderick asked.

"Some guys from New Jersey that I never heard of," Danny said. "My people tell me they're legit businessmen who opened it up as an investment. I think they're gonna be in for a big surprise." Danny's eye twitched as he spoke and he glanced around as if trying to be sure no one was watching him.

"Anything else?" Broderick asked.

"No, it's been kind of quiet today." Danny looked quickly around again as though he expected someone to come up behind him.

"Okay, Danny. Look, I want you to do something special for me."

Danny's eyes lit up. "Sure, Johnny. Anything you want."

"I want you to keep your eyes and ears open about anything—and I mean *anything*—that involves Hy Amberg in any way. The same thing for any of his goons. I want to know about anybody who's tied into him and what they're doing all the time. You understand me, Danny?"

"Sure, Johnny. I'll watch that whole crew like a hawk. I heard he came home yesterday and that two kids named Crowley and Dunniger may have hooked up with him. But they're just punks. But if you want I'll find out if they even spit on the sidewalk."

"That's my boy," Broderick said. He reached into his pocket and took out the roll of bills and peeled off a five and thrust it in Danny's hand. "Here, buy yourself a hat," he said.

"Johnny, you don't have to do that," Danny said, scratching his head through his workman's cap and glancing to each side again.

"I want to. You come up with something good for me on Amberg or any of his clowns and there'll be a lot more in it for you. Now you take care of yourself and I'll see you later tonight." Broderick slid back across the seat and gunned the engine.

As the car continued south Broderick looked in the rear-view mirror and watched the little man scurry back into the newsstand. It's time to start covering your ass, he thought. And that's only the beginning.

39

CHAPTER FIVE

HY AMBERG HAD SPENT THE AFTERNOON ALONE IN the bedroom, just lying on the bed, his eyes staring blindly at the ceiling. He had hardly moved. It was something he had learned in prison, an almost trancelike state that could be induced to escape the endless sounds of a hundred men fighting personal wars with their cages. It allowed him to think, to plan, to remember.

When he finally emerged from the bedroom at six o'clock he was still wearing the clothes he had worn at lunch, minus the suit coat and tie. There was one new addition now, a .45 caliber automatic held tightly under his left arm by a shoulder holster. The sight of the weapon, though not upsetting, surprised Moe. It was unlike Amberg to carry a gun unless he was going out with the intention of using it. Guns could be trouble; he had said so himself many times. A shakedown by an ambitious cop could put you back inside. It was a senseless risk and he had always avoided those risks, at least in the past.

Moe chose not to speak. He sat stoically at the table playing solitaire, keeping his attention indirectly on Amberg as he walked across the room and seated himself in an overstuffed chair near the window. Gillie was also silent, sitting on the sofa flipping the pages of a magazine. Moe hoped she would remain that way.

Amberg lit a cigarette, then pulled himself up from the chair and walked to the table. He poured himself an ample amount of Scotch and stood there drinking it. The rows of cards were spread out in front of Moe. He pointed to them. "Put the black seven on the red eight," he said.

"Thanks. I didn't even see that," Moe said. He placed the card into position and Amberg turned and walked back to the chair. He sat there only a few minutes, then was up again pacing about the room.

"What's wrong, honey," Gillie said, "you're moving around like a big old tomcat."

Amberg stopped moving. Gillie sat there examining the nails on one hand, fully occupied. He stared at her for a moment but did not speak. Slowly he walked to the window and pulled back the thin, white curtains. The sunlight was fading. Moe watched him for a long time, then looked across at Gillie. She looked up and smiled at him impishly.

"I think maybe that big good-looking cop in Lindy's got my honey all upset. What do you think, Moe?"

Moe shook his head violently and mouthed the word no, trying to get her off the subject.

"Sure that's it," Gillie said, returning to the magazine. "All those important people paid attention to that big cop and they ignored Hy. Is that what's got you so upset? Well, if you ask me it just shows how much they know."

Amberg's body became rigid and he turned slowly from the window. He moved to the sofa, stopping directly in front of her. She smiled at him. Behind Amberg, Moe dropped his face into his hands.

"You're a funny lady today," Amberg said. He reached out with his right hand and stroked her cheek affectionately. He too was smiling now.

"Oh, you know me, Hy. You know how I just love to kid around. You always liked it when . . ."

Gillie was still talking when Amberg's left fist came off his hip and crashed into the side of her head. There was a cry of shock and pain as she fell over on the sofa. He was on top of her immediately, both hands smashing down at her as she tried to cover her face with her arms, screaming at him to stop.

Moe jumped up from his chair. "Hy, stop. You'll kill her," he shouted.

"That's right. I'm gonna kill this bitch." His voice was breathless and he reached to his left and grabbed a lamp from the end table and raised it above his head.

Moe moved in quickly behind him, grabbing his arm. "No, Hy, don't do it. It'll mean bad trouble."

Amberg spun off the sofa like a cat, pulling the automatic from his shoulder holster and pushing it into Moe's throat. Moe lurched backward, the gun still pressed against his neck as Amberg moved with him. He fell into the chair near the window, pressing back into it until he could feel the springs pushing into his spine. Amberg cocked the hammer, the three separate clicks sounding progressively louder.

41

"No, Hy. No." Moe's voice was pleading, begging. His neck began to jerk in a nervous spasm.

"You stupid bastard. You touched me. You put your hands on me. I'll blow your fucking head off." Amberg's face was ashen. His eyes were glazed.

Moe continued to beg, pleading as loudly as he could with the barrel of the gun pressed into his windpipe. "Hy, listen to me. I just didn't want you to kill the bitch. We would of lost everything. It would of meant trouble. The liquor thing. Broderick. Everything would of been out the window. I mean here in the room. Somebody would of heard. I was just trying to protect you."

At the sound of Broderick's name the barrel of the automatic eased slightly off Moe's throat. Behind him Moe could hear the sound of someone running as Gillie rushed into the bedroom. Amberg's eyes cleared and he stared down at Moe. Slowly his thumb released the hammer and he stood up, his body swaying. Sweat covered Moe's face. He moved forward in the chair. His breath was coming in gasps and his arms and legs felt limp.

Amberg seemed dazed, far off in thought, and the gun now hung loosely at his side. He blinked his eyes, then put the gun back in his holster. "You know, Moe. You're a lot smarter than anybody gives you credit for. Anybody except me, that is." He walked to the table and poured himself another drink. He sat down and held the glass up to his face.

Moe sat motionless, then stood and walked unsteadily to the table. His legs were trembling and he sat quickly, uncertain of his ability to remain standing.

Amberg continued to look at the amber liquor. "But that bitch was right about one thing," he said. "I let him get to me today. I got to him, but I let him get to me too." He swirled the liquor in his glass. "I can't do that. I have to play this the right way." The distant look returned momentarily, then disappeared. "You gotta help me, Moe. You have to keep reminding me. You have to keep telling me how he's gonna crumble inside, how he's gonna sweat everytime he thinks about me." He was speaking quietly now, deliberately. There was no emotion in his voice.

Moe nodded. "You're right, Hy. That's what we have to do. We got to work on other things. The liquor thing. Getting the dough we need to set ourselves up proper." He was concentrating on Amberg, gauging his reaction.

"Yeah, that's what we have to do." Amberg was still toying with the glass in front of him. Then he smiled. "Yeah, we got other things to worry about. We gotta make some money, right, Moe?"

"That's right, Hy." Moe began to relax for the first time.

"And we need some more boys. Did you find anybody yet?"

"I made contact with two guys this afternoon. They just got out of stir and they're hungry. They're looking to hook up with something and they got no ties with anybody. But they're good."

"What are their names? No. Never mind. It doesn't matter what their names are as long as they're good. When can I see them?"

"I can have them here tomorrow, any time you want."

"Good." Excitement was returning to Amberg's eyes. "That's what we'll do. What else, Moe? What else?"

Moe spoke cautiously again and his neck gave a violent jerk. "Well, we still got that jewelry joint on Forty-eighth Street. Crowley and Dunniger are really hot for it and I think maybe they're right. I saw it. It's a pushover."

"That's *bad* for me," Amberg said, his voice still calm. "Right away the cops will try to place me there. I can't go near stuff like that. They'll show some lousy clerk a mug shot and I'll be right where they want me."

"But, Hy, you don't have to do nothin'. You don't have to go near the place. Look. We need the dough, right? And this is an easy mark. Me and the boys can do it without any problems. You can be here with Gillie and nobody can tie you into anything. Just give us the go-ahead. I think it's a sure thing for at least ten grand."

Amberg was quiet. Then he nodded. "You guys do it alone." He paused again. "That might work," he said. "That just might work. You sure the place is worth that much?"

"Easy, Hy. There's a lot of uncut stuff there. Stuff we could fence easy. We could take it right to the Bowery and have the cash before the cops even know the place was heisted."

"Okay. I like that. I want us to make our move with the booze fast, by the middle of next month maybe. The other thing will be finished by then and the heat will be off. We're gonna need some extra dough by then, anyway. When will you be ready to move on this Forty-eighth Street job?"

"Next week, Hy. Or the week after for sure. As soon as we're sure of a big score. I want to case it for a while first."

"I like that," Amberg said. "It's got to be planned right. Everything from now on has got to be planned right. We don't make any more mistakes. We do everything by the numbers, just like they do it on death row. We count the days. We let Broderick count the days." He began to laugh.

There was a tightening in Moe's stomach. "And we do that job, right, Hy?"

Amberg put the glass down and smiled. "Yeah, sure. Of course we do that job. We're gonna do everything just like I said."

The door to the bedroom opened and Gillie stood there, her eyes streaked with mascara. There was a swelling along the right side of her jaw and her lips were trembling.

"I'm sorry, Hy," she said. "Please don't be mad at me anymore. I didn't mean anything. Please let me make it up to you." Her voice was almost a whimper now.

Amberg stood and moved from behind the table. She took a frightened step backward. He held out his arms at his sides. "I'm not mad at you," he said, starting toward the bedroom.

She rushed to him and threw her arms around his neck. He rubbed his hand against the swelling on her jaw, then began walking her toward the bedroom, his arm around her waist.

Moe sat watching as the bedroom door closed behind them. Then he reached for the bottle of Scotch and poured himself a drink. He looked down at his hand. It was steady again.

CHAPTER SIX

IT WAS SIX-THIRTY WHEN JOHNNY BRODERICK ARRIVED at the records room at Police Headquarters. It was a dark, musty room and the lighting was poor. He went straight to a clerk seated at a large wooden desk, reading a magazine. The clerk seemed annoyed by the interruption.

"Yeah?" the clerk said. "What do you want?"

Broderick dropped his shield on the desk. "What I *want*," he said, "is everything you have on Hy Amberg, Rudy Dunniger, and James Crowley, including any reports on who they're tied in to and what they're involved in right now."

A pained expression moved across the clerk's face. "A lot of that'll be in surveillance reports and those are locked up now," he said.

"So you have a key, don't you?"

"Yeah, but I ain't supposed to—"

The clerk never finished. "Never mind what you ain't supposed to do," Broderick snapped. "Either you get it or I go to your boss and he gets it."

"All right. All right," the clerk said. "You don't have to get nasty. You know we both work for the same Police Department."

"That's what I'm trying to make you remember," Broderick said.

The clerk walked slowly to a row of filing cabinets that lined the rear wall. He was muttering to himself. He returned minutes later with three manila envelopes, each about a half-inch thick. Broderick took them and walked to a long table in the center of the room and began leafing through them.

The first was Amberg's and it contained various reports including his arrest record dating back to 1912, when he was sixteen, and numerous mug shots from that time up to three years ago when Broderick himself had been the arresting officer. In that latest photograph there was a swelling over Amberg's left eye and around his mouth. He looked as though he had been hit with a baseball bat, Broderick thought. A smile crossed his lips, then faded. At the back of the envelope there was an old wanted poster. "Should be considered armed and dangerous," it warned. It was something he didn't have to be reminded of. Amberg had always been dangerous: a maniac who enjoyed hurting people.

There were also prison reports, copies that had been sent to the department for use in court after subsequent arrests. They spoke about a "troublesome" prisoner, stretches in solitary confinement, insubordination—easy words used to describe a rotten little bastard, Broderick thought. In all, he had been arrested ten times in fifteen years, mostly petty juvenile arrests that sent him in and out of reformatories like a yo-yo. There had been several arrests for assault, but in each case the charges were dropped when the victims failed to appear in court. He had been held once in 1922 for suspicion of murder, but that too had failed to produce a conviction. The only major arrest was Broderick's: armed robbery—the one arrest that had put him away for three years.

There was another batch of papers, each with the same words, "past association," typed at the top of each page. There were six men listed. The only one currently on the street was Moe Berg. Four of the others were doing time and the fifth was dead, stabbed to death during an argument in a Harlem bar. Probably tried to pick up some nigger bitch, Broderick thought. There were photographs of all six. The dead man's had the word "deceased" written across his face.

The other two envelopes held similar information with photographs attached. James Crowley, age twenty-two. One arrest: armed robbery and assault. Possession of two weapons. One year, state reformatory, paroled to custody of parents at age twenty. Rudy Dunniger, twenty-one. Two arrests: assault with a deadly weapon and grand larceny. Two years, state reformatory. The files indicated that both were believed to be associating with known criminals. The brief descriptions were followed by the names of detectives assigned to uptown precincts. It was good work. Thorough police work, Broderick thought. Now he knew about the two men who were running with Amberg. It gave him a starting point, an edge. He wrote the information in his notebook. Crowley, Dunniger, Moe Berg. He would find out who the blonde had been as well. They could be watched now and he would know what they were doing, what Amberg had up his sleeve. And then he would come down on him, before he knew what hit him.

46

He picked up Amberg's mug shot again, the one from three years ago. There was a shifting again in his stomach. *He had screamed the whole time, screamed like a madman. I'll kill you. I'll kill you, you lousy bastard. You set me up.* His body was hard under the punches, he remembered that now. And the punches were heavy, with all his weight behind them. Set him up. The lousy creep. He deserved to be locked up. *He screamed as the others dragged him to the cell in Headquarters. A gasping sound, out of breath. A crazy man, screaming even though he couldn't breathe. And the eyes in court, eyes like a madman, staring and smiling. Then the judge said three years and he turns, his eyes looking like they're going to explode. Watching over his shoulder as they pulled him out the door.* Broderick shoved the photograph back into the envelope and walked back to the clerk and tossed the envelopes on his desk.

"You get what you want?" the clerk said.

"Yeah, I got it."

Broderick took the stairs two at a time down to the first floor and walked quickly to the duty sergeant's desk. "I want you to do something for me, Charlie," he said.

"Sure, Johnny, what's up?"

Broderick tore a page from his notebook. On it were the names of Berg, Dunniger, and Crowley with a bracket alongside and Amberg's name to the right of it. "I want dispatch to get a message out to all precincts in Manhattan, asking that all patrols keep an eye out for these guys and report to me in the Industrial Squad on any activity they observe. Have dispatch put down that we suspect them of planning a job. Okay, Charlie?"

"No sooner said than done," the sergeant said. "What do you think they're up to?"

"You name it, they're up to it," Broderick said.

The sergeant laughed. Broderick started to go. "Johnny. Wait a minute. There are two messages for you. One is from Mr. Nolan. He wants you to meet him and the mayor at the Owl Club at nine o'clock. I see you're still traveling in heavy company." The sergeant gave him a knowing smile.

Broderick smiled back, inwardly pleased with the recognition. "Who's the other one from?"

"That's the bad news," the sergeant said. "It's from Inspector Garfoli. He wants you to come up to his office before you leave the building. It's an order, not a request."

"What the fuck does he want?" Broderick said.

The sergeant shrugged his shoulders. "The word came down from his secretary, that fat little guinea sergeant who thinks he's so important. Anyway I don't question an inspector of patrol. I don't plan to end up counting sea gulls in Staten Island."

"Yeah, okay. Thanks." Broderick turned and headed back to the stairs. Garfoli's office was on the third floor. It was seven o'clock now and if he kept him waiting, as he was likely to, he'd be late for his meeting with the mayor and Nolan. What could he want anyway, he wondered. Maybe it was the Toledo. He had been there earlier and had come on strong with the guineas. Maybe Garfoli was in with them. It could be like Cordes said. Those grease-balls had connections and Garfoli was a wop too. But he was in patrol and he had no right to fuck around with a detective. He should go through the chain of command. But if he wasn't doing that it could mean something too.

Broderick reached the third floor and went straight to Garfoli's office. Inside, the main office was empty, except for the sergeant sitting at a desk in front of the inspector's glass-enclosed private office. There was a light on in his office, but the glass had been painted for privacy and he couldn't tell if Garfoli was inside. He approached the overweight sergeant. "I understand the inspector wanted to see me," he said.

"That's right," the sergeant said, his voice rising slightly on the last word.

Little greaseball, Broderick thought. Go fuck yourself.

"Would you like to tell him I'm here?" Broderick said.

The sergeant smiled, raising his overweight body from his chair. "Sure, Detective," he said. He took the few steps to the door, knocked twice, then opened it. "Detective Broderick is here, Inspector," he said.

"Tell him to have a seat," a voice inside the office said.

The sergeant turned, smiled again, and started to speak.

"I heard," Broderick said, cutting him off. He walked to a row of wooden chairs outside the inspector's office and sat down. He kept his hat on. There was no reason to take his hat off for some guinea, inspector or not, he thought. The minutes passed. Broderick took his watch from his vest pocket and studied it. Seven-thirty. He would barely have time to shave, change his clothes, and get to the Owl Club on time. If this kept up he would have to shave in his office and go the way he was. Goddamned guinea, he thought.

The door to the office opened and Garfoli stood there in full uniform. He was tall and stocky, but still in good condition for a man of fifty, even though his black, curly hair was streaked with gray. "In here, Broderick," he commanded.

Broderick walked into the office and stood there before Garfoli's desk as the inspector settled back into his leather chair. He looked over some papers on his desk, then turned his eyes to the man before him.

"It's customary, Detective, for people coming into this office to take off their hats," he said. He stared directly into Broderick's face, watching as he removed the hat, his face reddening.

"You asked to see me, Inspector?" Broderick said. His voice sounded even to him. Unconcerned. That was the way it should be, he thought.

"That's right, Detective." Garfoli looked back down at the papers, then back at Broderick. "I've heard some very disturbing reports about you," he said.

"From who, sir?" Broderick said.

"That doesn't matter," Garfoli snapped. "All that matters is that I'm disturbed. As a senior officer in this department I don't like to hear reports about excessive force being used and constant hints about payoffs and looking the other way when the *right people* are involved in something. Do you get my drift, Detective?"

Broderick stared at Garfoli. "Not at all, Inspector," he said. If Garfoli had anything on him he'd be locking him up, not talking to him. He knew that. Let him play his game.

"You don't, eh?" Garfoli leaned back in his chair. "Well, I think *I* do. I think you and your buddies in the squad are the most corrupt bunch of cops there are in this city and I'm not talking about lifting apples from fruit stands."

Broderick averted his eyes and concentrated on the wall behind the senior officer. He knew now that he was safe.

"If you have any evidence to *prove* that, sir, I'd like to know what it is," he said.

"I bet you would, Broderick." The inspector stood behind his desk, forcing Broderick's eyes to meet his. "I bet you'd love to know what it is. Then you could go running to those political cronies of yours and see what they could do to cover up for you. But you're not going to play this your way. You're going to play it *my* way."

"If you have any proof of corruption, sir, I believe you should be reporting it to my superior in the *Detective Bureau*. Inspector—"

The inspector's voice rose to a near roar, cutting Broderick off mid-sentence. "Don't you *ever* presume to tell me procedure. Don't you ever presume to tell me anything, *Detective*," he shouted. "I came up through the ranks on merit, not by kissing every politician's ass in sight."

"I think my record speaks for itself, Inspector," Broderick snapped.

"Your record stinks like shit." Garfoli slammed his fist on the desk. "If you were in uniform I would have busted your ass out of this department. And I still intend to do it."

"Is that all, *sir?*" Broderick said.

Garfoli slid back into his chair. "What I have in front of me are allegations. But they're enough for me to have a reason to keep an eye on you. And that's just what I'm going to do. I'm going to watch you all the time. If you so much as spit, Broderick, I'm going to know about it. You take one dime, one free ticket to the ball park and I'm going to come down on you with both feet. And you tell those bums you work with the same thing. Do you understand me?"

"I heard you, sir," Broderick said. His voice was cold and flat.

"I didn't ask if you heard me. I asked if you understood me?"

Broderick looked down at the inspector. William Garfoli, guinea inspector, he thought. He kept his face calm, almost smiling. "I understood you, Inspector. I'll let *all* the people concerned know exactly what you said."

Garfoli's face reddened and he stood up abruptly. "If that's supposed to be some kind of threat you can stick it right up your ass, mister," he snapped. "Now you get out of this office and you remember what I said. From now on you belong to me."

Broderick turned and walked briskly out the door. Outside, the sergeant sat smirking. Broderick gave him a kiss-my-ass look and walked straight out of the office. Outside, as the outer door closed behind him, he took a deep breath. Just what I needed, he thought. More fucking trouble. He'd have to be careful now. Very careful—at least until the next good arrest. After that even Garfoli would have to lay off for a while. Maybe he should talk to Nolan, he thought. No, he would wait for that. There was no point in asking for favors until they were needed. Right now he was still safe. He was sure of that.

Garfoli's voice boomed out of his office, causing the fat sergeant to bolt out of his chair and rush to the door.

"Yes, Inspector?" he said.

"Come in here and close the door behind you," Garfoli said.

The sergeant obeyed the order and placed himself in front of the desk. "First thing tomorrow morning, I want you to pass the word to my commanders that I personally want to know whenever Broderick does anything in their precincts. I want to know what he's doing, no matter what it is. Is that understood?"

"Yes, sir," the sergeant said. "Sir?"

"What?"

"I happen to know some of the places he hangs out. You know, I've seen him around. Well, what I mean, sir, is that it wouldn't be too hard for me to keep an eye out for him in my spare time."

"That's very good, Sergeant," Garfoli said. "You do that. Strictly unofficial, of course. But you do that and report directly to me."

"Yes, sir," the sergeant said.

Garfoli watched him as he moved out the door. Maybe his fat-assed sergeant was good for something after all, he thought. Ambition was a wonderful thing, he mused. Especially in the Police Department. He leaned back in his chair and began strumming his fingers on the desk, then looked down at the brass buttons on his tunic and frowned. With the sleeve of one arm he rubbed one of the buttons vigorously. It was an idiosyncrasy he had never been able to escape. He hated dirty brass.

CHAPTER SEVEN

JOHNNY BRODERICK WALKED THROUGH THE DOOR OF the Owl Club at eight fifty-five that evening. Nolan had asked him to be there at nine and he had rushed to be early. Inside, in the red decorated lobby, an attractive blonde with large breasts stood behind a waist-high door. She smiled coyly as Broderick handed her his straw skimmer.

Very nice, he thought, as he crossed the thick red carpet and approached a formally dressed captain stationed beside a large potted palm. Too bad to-night is business, he thought, looking back at her. She was still smiling.

"I'm supposed to meet the mayor here," he said coldly.

"The mayor hasn't arrived yet, sir." The captain's voice was equally cool and he looked Broderick over with suspicion. Broderick's eyes hardened and he stared straight into the captain's face. The thin little man softened immediately.

"Mr. Nolan is inside, sir. He's also waiting for the mayor. May I have your name?" His voice was nervous now, but still efficient. He was fondling his bow tie with his fingertips.

Little fag, Broderick thought. "The name's Broderick." His voice was low and harsh. Let the little bastard squirm a bit. A slight smile crossed his lips.

The captain picked up a book from a table behind him and glanced quickly through a list of names. "Yes, sir. The mayor's expecting you. Would you care to join Mr. Nolan?" He raised his fingers to his tie again.

51

Broderick nodded. "Where is he?"

"In the main room, at ringside, sir. May I show you the way?"

Broderick fell in behind the captain as he moved ahead into the main room. He looked back at the blonde. She was still watching him.

Stepping from the lobby to the main room the color scheme changed abruptly from red to gold and Broderick could see the room was already crowded and only a few tables far from the bandstand were still empty. There were large fans suspended from the ceiling that circulated air through the room, creating a slight breeze. But it seemed to do little good, and as he moved through the narrow spaces between the tables he could see Chris Nolan seated just to the left of the band mopping his face with a large white handkerchief. He had the usual large cigar stuffed into his mouth and when he saw Broderick coming toward him his mouth turned upward, exposing teeth that clamped down on the cigar like a great, glistening vise.

They reached the table and the captain drew back a chair directly opposite Nolan. Broderick ignored him and seated himself next to Chris. Kiss my ass, you little faggot, he thought, as the captain withdrew in a flurry of annoyance.

"You got the captain all upset," Chris said.

"Fuck the little fag."

Chris chuckled and his large belly shook lightly under his vest. "That's what I like about you, Johnny boy, you never mince your words."

Broderick eased back in his chair, his large hands falling loosely into his lap. "You said to be here at nine, is there some kind of problem, Chris?"

"Yes, but I'll let Jimmy tell you about it. It's nothing serious. Just a little job. Why don't you have a drink?"

"Just some coffee."

Nolan smiled again and took the cigar from his mouth. "Someday I'm going to get you off the wagon, Johnny boy, and introduce you to some good Scotch whisky." He motioned to a passing waiter, using the cigar like a wand. "One large Scotch and a cup of coffee," he said.

He turned back to Broderick as an attractive brunette began to sing in a low, sultry voice. "Look at the legs on that babe. When Jimmy gets here he'll have her at the table in ten minutes, unless he brings Betty with him, of course." Nolan laughed again, his belly shaking more violently.

Broderick took a pocketwatch from his vest and looked at it. "He's late," he said, looking up at Nolan.

"It's only ten after, John. Hell, that's not very late for Jimmy. Three hours isn't very late for Jimmy. You should know that. What's the matter? You have someplace to go?" Nolan's left eye narrowed as he looked at Broderick and the slight note of disapproval sent a tremor of uneasiness through him and he twisted slightly in his seat.

"No. I don't have anything to do. I just want to get right on the problem and take care of it for him," he said.

"You will, Johnny. Just relax." Nolan stuffed the cigar back in his mouth and began to puff on it violently as the waiter returned with the Scotch and coffee.

Broderick eased back in his chair again and studied the length of shirt cuff showing from the sleeve of his brown, double-breasted suit. He fussed with one cuff for a moment, then looked around the room. Cops and crooks, he thought. You can always tell them because they're always looking around, always checking on everybody near them.

The room was even more crowded now and Broderick could see people waiting in the lobby. He could only see one table that was still empty. It was quite a joint, he thought. Everything in gold. The carpet, the tablecloths, the wallpaper, even the drapes. The lobby all in red, in here all gold. Very nice. Broderick knew the Owl Club was one of several speakeasies that operated openly in Greenwich Village, but it was one he had not visited before. Prohibition, my ass, he thought.

The brunette finished her number to polite applause and immediately moved into something more lively. She smiled as she sang, always showing her teeth. How can you smile when you sing, Broderick wondered. Your mouth must get sore as hell by the end of the night. But Nolan always talks with a cigar in his mouth and that must play hell with the jaw muscles, he decided.

"Not much of a voice," Nolan said. "But that's a great pair of legs. So who cares if she can sing." Nolan chuckled to himself again and looked at Broderick.

You really kill yourself, don't you, you fat fuck, Broderick thought, then returned the laugh. "Yeah, I never need somebody to sing in bed," he said.

There was a flurry of excitement near the door and as Nolan and Broderick looked up they saw Jimmy Walker making a grand entrance with Betty Compton on his arm. The captain scurried ahead and stood patiently at the table nervously toying with his tie as Walker moved slowly between the tables, stopping repeatedly to shake hands and exchange small talk. When he was closer to the table he flashed a wink at Broderick and Nolan. Betty stood at his side looking openly bored.

"The king has arrived," Nolan cracked. "But Betty doesn't look too happy, does she?"

Broderick watched Walker move gracefully between the tables, bending slightly at the waist as he spoke to people. It's like watching a dancer, he thought, allowing his eyes to follow the lines of the mayor's blue striped suit, the handkerchief set exactly right in the breast pocket, the spats an immaculate white against the highly polished black shoes. Walker was a painfully thin man, almost frail. Broderick had been surprised to see just how thin when they had once taken a steam bath together. But the clothes hid his slight build and made him seem almost athletic. Only when he extended his hands could you see how very thin his wrists were. Almost like a woman's wrists, Broderick had often thought. It was something he would never say aloud. Not to anyone. You don't do anything that might piss off your rabbi, he had told himself.

Walker reached the table with a broad smile spread across his thin, handsome face and turned to give the crowd a controlled wave as the captain seated Betty. The smile remained as he slipped gracefully into his chair.

"Chris. Johnny. How's my favorite detective?" he said, patting Broderick's hand softly.

"Just fine, Jim. How are you, Miss Compton?" Broderick smiled dutifully at the cool, honey blonde across the table, not allowing his eyes to stray toward the low neckline of her dress. Cool as an ice truck, he thought. I don't think she even sweats. "They're supposed to have quite a floor show tonight. But I'm sure it's nothing like your show."

Betty looked at him with an amused smirk. "You've been hanging around His Honor too long, Johnny. You're starting to pick up his line. Next thing, *you'll* be going into politics."

Broderick winced slightly under the sarcasm and he could tell that Betty noticed his discomfort. There was the touch of a smile on her lips now. Bitch, he thought, still smiling at her. Just like a fucking ice truck. "No, not me, Miss Compton. I like what I do just fine."

"And nobody does it better," Walker said as he took Betty's hand in his. "Johnny's left a trail of crumpled hoods behind that would fill Yankee Stadium."

"Not that many—" Broderick stopped mid-sentence as he realized Walker was ignoring him.

"Speaking of Yankee Stadium, Chris, I hear the Babe hit two into the upper decks today. I knew we should have gone out there. Listen, how do you think the public would react if we gave him a key to the city? You know what I mean, right out there at the ballpark just before a game."

"Wait until they win the pennant. Then you can give him half of Wall Street and nobody will care." Nolan was puffing away on a new cigar.

"Half of Wall Street," Walker said, an impish look on his face now. "You have big ideas, Chris. I'm saving half of Wall Street for Betty and myself. Even I have to retire someday."

Everyone laughed, except Betty Compton. She looked away from the table, scanning the crowd with a bored stare. Walker turned his attention back to Broderick.

"Now listen, Johnny. I have a little job for you. Frankly, it's a nothing job but it has to be done. And you're my boy, right?"

"Sure, Jim, you know that. Anything you want." Up to and including murder, Broderick thought. This kid's not gonna leave this merry-go-round. This is where the gold rings are.

"You know Johnny," Nolan said, patting Broderick on the back. "We can always count on him." He motioned to a waiter and ordered drinks.

"I know we can," Walker said, making Broderick wonder just how small this little job was. "It's just that it's a petty job, John, and I hate to waste a man of your talents with something like this. But then it has to be done."

"Look, nothing's too big or too small." Just tell me what the hell it is, for chrissake, Broderick said to himself.

"Be careful, faithful Johnny," Betty offered. "If it's all that petty he probably wants you to murder his mother."

Walker took her hand again and patted it gently. "Not quite that petty, dear." He turned back and looked Broderick coolly in the eye. "It's petty, John, but it's a favor that has to be done."

"You just tell me what you need and it's done."

"I knew you'd feel that way, Johnny." Walker was smiling.

"Doesn't everyone feel that way?" Betty said. The mixture of sarcasm and boredom was perfect.

Walker leaned over and kissed her cheek. "She loves me," he said.

"Again, doesn't everyone?" she said.

Nolan's face reddened. "Sure everyone does. Knock it off, will you, Betty . . . please. Somebody might hear you."

She offered Nolan a broad, false smile.

"All right now, Johnny, here's the problem. This old dame, a marvelous old lady who lives down the street from my house on St. Luke's Place—"

"Your wife's house, darling." Betty's voice was like ice again.

"My wife's house," Walker said, bowing his head toward Betty. "Well, it seems somebody broke into her place the other night and cleaned out the silver and other junk and the boys from the precinct just gave it the quick once-over. It seems they didn't know she was a big contributor to my campaign and they—"

"And a very close friend of Mrs. Walker," Betty said, smiling as she bowed her head toward the mayor.

"And a very close friend of Mrs. Walker," he patted Betty's hand without looking at her. "So what I need, is for you to pick up another detective and go over there and put on a show. You know what I mean." He was smiling again. "And of course you'll tell her you were sent by me."

Broderick looked squarely into Walker's face and he could feel the relief pass through his body. Just some old broad, he thought. Just to get the mayor off the hook with his old lady. Why not? "Sure, I'll take care of it right away."

"But make sure you take another man, right?" Walker said.

"I'll make a call for somebody right now."

"That's the boy. I really want the old lady impressed. Her name is McAvey and she's at Twenty-one St. Luke's. Call right now and see about getting somebody to go with you."

Broderick nodded and got up from his chair and moved quickly toward the lobby. He looked for the hatcheck girl, but she had been replaced by a small middle-aged woman in a colorless dress. She sure aged fast, he thought, as he moved across the lobby to the telephone booth.

Broderick dialed Headquarters and asked for the duty sergeant who handled the squad's calls.

"Sam, this is Johnny. Who's on tonight from the squad?"

"Ruditsky. He's out in a car alone," the voice crackled back over the telephone.

"Shit," Broderick said. "How about Cordes?"

"He's off," the voice said.

"Okay. Get Barney on the radio and tell him to meet me at the Owl Club, the speak in the Village. We got a job to do for the mayor so tell him to get here within fifteen minutes. I'll meet him out front. Tell him that."

"Sure. But one thing you better know, Johnny. He's got his package on. Not bad, but he's been on the sauce tonight. I could tell from his voice when he called in."

"That figures. Just tell him to get his ass here fast and to stay in the fucking car. Make sure you tell him that, Sam." Broderick hung up the phone, his face filling with anger. "Shit," he muttered. "If that bastard fucks this up I'll break his neck."

Before Broderick could get back to the table the master of ceremonies had called on the mayor to sing. Walker, insisting briefly that he was not in good voice but convincing no one, happily stepped to the bandstand, whispered to the band leader, and launched into an Irish ballad just as Broderick reached his seat.

"Everything all set, Johnny?" Nolan asked. When Broderick nodded, he added, "He's in good voice tonight."

Broderick leaned over, placing his mouth close to Nolan's ear. "Barney Ruditsky is on the way to pick me up. You tell Jimmy, okay?"

Nolan threw him a cold glance. "You better wait till he's through. He wouldn't like it if you walked out during his number. It wouldn't look good to the public."

Broderick could feel the blood filling his cheeks. Almost a bad step, Johnny, he thought. He found himself hoping Nolan would keep his mouth shut about it, and even more that Ruditsky would not get bored and come roaring in looking for him. "Sure, Chris. I didn't mean right now. I just mean in case he got tied up shaking hands or something." He sat back in his chair and listened patiently as Walker finished his song and basked in the applause.

When he returned to the table, the mayor was beaming. "Not bad for an aging politician, eh?" he said.

"You were marvelous, darling," Betty said, her exaggerated voice dripping with sugar.

"Just great, Jim. Great. The crowd loved it. Never mind what she says," Nolan said.

56

"Yeah, it was great," Broderick said.

Walker lifted his glass and offered a mock toast to Betty.

"My darling little Monk here dislikes it when I'm late," he said, using his nickname for her. "And tonight I was late."

"Tonight you had to visit your wife," Betty said, the false sugar still present in her voice.

Walker winced openly and rolled his eyes upward, then turned to Broderick. "How'd you make out, John?"

"It's all set. I got a good man and he's going to pick me up here. In fact, he should be outside right now. I just wanted to wait and hear your number." His eyes caught Betty's. A smirk crossed her lips. Had she heard him too? Christ.

"My one true fan," Walker said. "That's the boy. But you better get going and take care of this for me. Don't forget, it's Mrs. McAvey, Twenty-one St. Luke's Place. And be sure to tell her I sent you. I'll see you when you're finished, either here, or at the Central Park Casino. We have great plans to renovate the place. Make it the showplace of the East."

Broderick stood and caught an approving wink from Nolan. "I'll see you in an hour or so. Goodnight, Miss Compton. Chris."

Outside, Barney Ruditsky sat behind the wheel of an unmarked four-door sedan. Broderick walked around to the driver's side and leaned in the window. Ruditsky's constantly bloodshot eyes and red nose shone at him like a beacon. "You smell like a fucking gin mill," he said. "Move over. I'm driving."

"What the fuck's the matter with you?" Ruditsky said as the car pulled away from the curb. "Just because this is something for the mayor you gotta make a big fucking deal out of it?"

"Shut up," Broderick growled.

"So what do we have to do? And where the fuck are we going?"

"To some old broad's house a few blocks away on St. Luke's Place. She's a friend of the mayor and her joint got heisted so we gotta make her feel like the whole fucking Police Department is ready to turn the fucking city over to get her loot back."

"Boy, your buddy the mayor really gives you the important shit, don't he?" Barney was laughing.

"Just shut your fucking mouth. It's an easy job. You just keep quiet when we go in there and don't get too close to the old broad. If she smells your breath she'll faint. You let me do the talking, you understand me?"

Ruditsky did not answer. He began humming "Mother Machree" and laughing to himself as the car hurtled along the dark streets of the Village, where the converted gas street lamps did little more than cast a yellow glow along the rows of attached town houses. There were trees in front of many of the houses and the light from the street lamps produced eerie shadows as it

57

cut through the trees and played against the partially hidden buildings. They moved across Sheridan Square, where newsboys hawked the bulldog editions of the morning papers on every corner, then on into the West Village, the cumbersome Ford bouncing wearily as the streets changed to imitation cobblestones. The streets were dirty now and the Village itself changed to a collection of tenements and commercial buildings that continued until they reached Varick Street, where the area suddenly changed again into a maze of industry with large warehouses and factories looming up and hiding the quiet streets further west, streets like Barrow and Morton and St. Luke's Place, where the large brownstones of the wealthy were again dominant and the streets were clean. The unmarked car turned into St. Luke's Place and slowed behind a horse-drawn delivery wagon, then eased to the curb in front of number twenty-one, a wide, four-story brownstone, partially covered with ivy.

Broderick and Ruditsky mounted the front stoop with Broderick warning again that Ruditsky was to remain quiet and stay away from the woman.

"You check some other room out, like you're looking for clues or something, while I talk to her." He pressed an ornate, brass doorbell and stepped back. A full minute passed without any response. Behind the door he could hear a dog barking. Broderick pressed the doorbell again, and as he did an elderly woman dressed in an outlandish green dressing gown threw open the door and stood before them, her mouth open with surprise. She was holding a small poodle, the exact color of her own gray hair. The dog was barking wildly.

The woman began speaking in a dizzying rapid-fire voice. "Oh, Fifi. Be quiet, now, hush, hush, hush." She kissed the dog atop its head as she spoke. The dog strained against her arms, yapping as though it wanted to tear the two detectives apart with its diminutive teeth. Lousy little mutt, Broderick thought. "Oh, you must excuse Fifi," the woman went on. She's so upset. Ever since those terrible burglars were here. The poor darling was alone in the house with them. Are you the two detectives that Mrs. Walker said the mayor was sending by? Quiet, Fifi. Quiet. She's just so upset, you know."

Broderick started to step forward but retreated as the little dog lunged again. "Yes, Mrs. McAvey. I'm Detective Broderick and this is Detective Ruditsky. The mayor was very upset. He didn't feel the men at the precinct did everything they should have and he wanted us to come here and set things right. I mean make sure that no stone was left unturned at catching these people. So if we could come in and ask a few questions I think we can find these—er—these criminals."

With an exaggerated swing of her arm the old woman glided back into a large foyer, the full sleeves of her dressing gown fluttering like wings. The foyer was elaborate and cluttered with small tables, each holding porcelain statuettes of poodles cast in varying poses. The whole place is a fucking doghouse, Broderick thought, as he and Ruditsky stepped inside.

"Oh, come in, just come right in," she said. The dog was still barking and the woman kissed it repeatedly on the head, then placed it carefully down on the floor. At once the dog began running in circles, barking wildly. It approached Broderick, then backed off and turned to Ruditsky, who immediately stepped back. The show of concern was all the dog needed and it began to feign attacks at Ruditsky's ankles, circling him slowly, barking and growling. Ruditsky turned with the dog's movements, glaring at it through bloodshot eyes. He looked up at Broderick, his entire face now beet red, like his nose. Broderick fidgeted with his skimmer and shot back an angry stare. He could see the situation falling apart before him. Mrs. McAvey still prattled on, seeming unaware of the chaos about her.

"Of course, I don't think it was the fault of those nice young men from the precinct," she said. "They were such nice boys. I think they just didn't like Fifi and so they hurried along. The little darling can be such a bother at times. She's been so upset since the burglary. Heaven knows what those terrible people did to her." Not enough, Broderick thought. The old woman looked down at the dog circling Ruditsky. "Fifi, you stop that. You leave that nice man alone," she said.

"Oh, she's no bother, ma'am," Broderick said. "Detective Ruditsky and I both love dogs. We have dogs of our own, in fact." He gave the woman a reassuring smile.

Ruditsky stared at him, open disbelief spread across his face as he twisted to keep Fifi away from his pants cuff.

"Oh, how wonderful," the old woman said. "What kind of dog do you have, Detective?" She was looking at Ruditsky with a maternal smile.

Ruditsky began to stutter.

"Oh, it's a big sheepdog kinda dog," Broderick said. "Kind of a mongrel, but a real nice dog."

Ruditsky smiled, nodding his head at the woman.

"Oh, I'm sure it is. All animals are so sweet," she said. She looked down at Fifi, who had gotten a firm hold on Ruditsky's pants cuff. "Now stop that, Fifi."

Ruditsky began moving slowly across the foyer, Fifi still attached, growling into his cuff. "I just want to check the room for some clues, ma'am. If that's okay?"

"Oh, of course, Detective," she said, smiling. "But the silver was taken from that room." She pointed to a room on the other side of the foyer, the opposite direction from which Ruditsky was moving.

Ruditsky's face flushed an even deeper red and he nodded and changed direction, slowly dragging the poodle with him. "Thank you, ma'am," he said. "It won't take long."

"You take all the time you need," she said, smiling. "And if Fifi bothers you, you just send her right out."

I'll send the little fuck to blazes, Ruditsky thought.

59

"Yes, ma'am, I will, ma'am," he said, moving slowly into a large dining room. Once inside, Ruditsky moved from the woman's sight and shook his leg violently, sending the poodle sliding across the highly polished floor. "Take that, you little fuck," he muttered.

The dog immediately jumped back up and struck his pants cuff again. Ruditsky moved clumsily about the room, trying to shake the dog loose as quietly as possible. In the foyer he could hear Broderick interviewing the old woman. "Hurry up, for chrissake," he muttered.

"Ma'am, the silver. Can you give me a thorough description?" he could hear Broderick saying.

"Oh, yes, of course. It was my grandmother's, you know. Simply beautiful and totally irreplaceable. Each piece, the knives, the forks, the chalices, the plates, and all the serving pieces had little cherubs on them. Just so beautiful, so unique."

"How many pieces were there, ma'am?"

"Oh, well, let me see. There were twenty-four place settings, each with all the assorted knives and forks and everything. Then the chalices, the serving pieces. Oh, let me see."

Still struggling with Fifi, Ruditsky heard the old woman change the number three or four times. "Jesus Christ," he muttered. "Just count the fucking silver so we can get out of here." He pushed the dog off his pants leg but it sprang back and grabbed him again. "Get away from me, you little bastard," he said under his breath. "Get away. You're ruining a two-hundred-dollar fucking suit." He twisted away from the dog, but it jumped back, snaring the other pants cuff and began pulling at it, growling.

Ruditsky staggered and fell lightly against a carved dining room table, almost knocking over a chair. He started moving slowly away, pulling the dog with him. "Get away," he growled. "Get away, damn it or I'll blow your fucking head off." The dog refused to give up and Ruditsky dragged it toward a large front window. Gently, careful not to make any noise, he raised the window, reached down, and grabbed the struggling dog by its front legs, extended his arms out the window, and ceremoniously dropped it.

The dog let out a slight yelp as it fell, but Ruditsky quickly lowered the window and glanced back over his shoulder. Mrs. McAvey was still talking to Broderick in the foyer. Good-bye, Fifi, you little fuck, Ruditsky thought, taking a long, low breath.

He waited a few minutes, checking his trouser cuffs for damage, then walked slowly back into the foyer where Broderick was completing his interview with the elderly woman.

"I couldn't find any fingerprints," he said. "But from the description I heard you giving Detective Broderick we shouldn't have much trouble finding the stuff if those crooks try to sell it."

Broderick threw him a look of disbelief as Mrs. McAvey began to clap her hands together with delight.

"Oh, do you really think so?" she said. "It would be so wonderful if you could. Did you hear that, Fifi, the nice men say they can find our silver."

Not seeing the dog the woman began to look around her. "Fifi. Fifi! Where are you, Fifi?" She scurried about the foyer, then over to the room Ruditsky had just left. She peered inside, then rushed back into the foyer. "Fifi. Where are you? Come to Mama, Fifi. Oh, where could she have gone?" There was a perplexed look on her face.

"I think I saw her go downstairs," Ruditsky offered, suppressing a smile.

"Oh, do you really think so?" she said. She hurried to the stairs that led down to the garden level, her winglike arms flapping at the air, and called to the dog.

Ruditsky was standing next to Broderick and he leaned his head closer and whispered, "Johnny, let's get out of here."

The rush of whiskey from Barney's breath filled Broderick's nostrils and he nudged him away and whispered back, "Shut up. I told you not to talk."

Barney leaned toward him again. "Let's get out of here, Johnny."

"What's the matter with you?" Broderick whispered back. "What's the big rush?"

"The big rush is that I just threw fucking Fifi out the fucking window, that's what the big rush is."

Broderick turned to face him, his eyes widening, horrified. "You what?" he whispered.

"I just threw fucking Fifi out the fucking window."

"Jesus Christ," Broderick whispered. *"Jesus Christ!"*

"We better get out of here," Ruditsky said, a slight smile on his lips.

"What the hell did you do that for, you—you—?"

"The little son of a bitch was ruining my suit. It was either that or shoot the bastard, and I thought the gun would make too much noise."

"Jesus Christ!" Then changing to a normal voice and stuttering slightly, Broderick called to Mrs. McAvey, who was still at the stairs pleading for the dog to come to her. "Mrs. McAvey—uh, excuse me, Mrs. McAvey, but I think we should get going now and try to find your silverware." He and Barney began to back toward the front door.

"I just don't understand it," the woman said. "I can't understand where the little darling could have gotten to. But, of course, thank you for coming. Thank you so much." She walked toward them slowly, then looked back over her shoulder. "Fifi, Fifi. Oh, I'm so worried," she said.

Broderick reached back, still facing the old woman, and fumbled for the door knob. He found it and slowly eased the door open and he and Ruditsky turned to go. There, on the front steps, Fifi sat staring at them. Immediately the dog started to bark.

Mrs. McAvey rushed forward, her outlandish dressing gown flowing behind her. "Fifi, Fifi, you naughty dog. How ever did you get out there?"

"Uh, she must of run out through the door downstairs, ma'am," Ruditsky offered, stepping back away from the dog and lifting both trouser cuffs above his ankles.

"Oh, you naughty little girl," Mrs. McAvey cooed, picking the dog up and kissing it about the face and head. "You stay right here, my little darling, and don't you ever frighten me like that again."

Broderick, his face scarlet, pushed Barney out the door with his shoulder and began backing away from the old woman. "Uh, good-bye, Mrs. McAvey. I'm really glad you found Fifi. I was starting to get worried myself." He continued to back away.

"Oh, you hear that Fifi, you even frightened the nice detectives," she said, still kissing the dog's head. The dog continued to bark, straining its neck to look past Broderick to where Ruditsky now stood.

"We'll be in touch with you as soon as we learn anything," Broderick said, as he turned and moved slowly down the stoop with Barney at his side.

Inside the car Broderick's face seethed with anger. "You cocksucker! You fucking son of a bitch. You lousy drunken bastard. You got to throw the fucking dog of the fucking mayor's friend out the fucking window. You bastard. We could end up in Queens pounding a beat for the rest of our fucking lives. You son of a bitch."

Ruditsky started to laugh. "Did you see that old broad running around the house going Fifi, Fifi?"

"Shut your fucking mouth," Broderick shouted. "You stupid bastard. If we get any heat over this I'm gonna knock your fucking head off. You hear me?"

Ruditsky slid down in his seat as Broderick started the car and began to pull away. A smile slowly began to form on his face. He looked across at the hulking detective beside him. Broderick's face was still glowing with anger. Softly, Ruditsky whispered across to him, "Fifi, Fifi."

Broderick slammed the accelerator to the floor.

CHAPTER EIGHT

THE TWO POLICE OFFICERS HAD PARKED THEIR PATROL car under a tree on West Sixty-seventh Street facing Columbus Avenue. From that dark, secluded position, only a few yards from the intersection, they held a commanding view of the traffic flow along Columbus Avenue and any violation of the twenty-mile-an-hour speed limit or passing of the traffic signal could easily be observed.

The older of the two, a heavy, gray-haired patrolman in his late forties, sat on the passenger side. His cap was pulled down over his eyes and he responded in a terse but fading Irish brogue to the running commentary of his younger partner. He was too eager, the older man thought. A bit too anxious to get his name on the captain's list of favorites. He raised his cap and noted that the young man's eyes were riveted on the intersection, his muscular body straight up in the seat, ready and willing for any excitement. He'll be needin' glasses before he's thirty, the older man said to himself, thinking what pleasure it would give him to spend a tour with one of the boys he came over with twenty-five years ago. They knew how to pull a tour and save their fun for later over a few pints and a couple of lies in a good saloon, he thought.

A black Model A sedan moved slowly into the intersection trying to time the change of the traffic signal. A young man in a broad-brimmed hat was driving and there was a woman sitting next to him. The signal changed and the man looked to his left for any oncoming traffic. The streetlight caught his face and caused the younger cop to lean forward in his seat.

"Hey, that was that Crowley guy who just went by. He's one of the guys we got that message on," he said.

"So what," the older cop said.

"So I'm gonna follow him."

"Oh, come on now, bucko. It's eleven o'clock. We only got one more hour to put in before this tour ends. You're not goin' to be ruinin' the evening for me, are ya?"

The patrol car was already pulling into Columbus Avenue as he spoke, falling in one block behind the black sedan as it headed south in light traffic. It was the right distance, the young cop decided. Besides, Crowley would be paying attention to his girl friend and the traffic lights. And if they did anything good, he would be there, ready to pick up a one-way ticket to the detective division.

"Now listen," the older cop said. "Those boys in the Industrial Squad can handle their own problems. They don't need us doin' their work for them."

"We're not gonna do anything," the young cop said, his concentration fixed on the black sedan ahead. "All the message said was to keep an eye on him and report back. That's all I'm gonna do."

"Oh, sweet Jesus," the older cop groaned. "What did I ever do to deserve you for a partner? But I'm tellin' you this. Ten minutes to twelve and we go back to the station house. And I don't care if you think he's about to rob a fuckin' bank."

The young cop laughed. "Sure, sure. No problem at all. We'll just watch him for a bit. Don't worry yourself."

Crowley's car turned right on West Fifty-fifth Street and headed toward Tenth Avenue. Halfway down the block it pulled into a wide alley between two apartment buildings and came to a stop. Crowley and the young woman got out of the car, then immediately reentered, climbing into the rear seat. Down the street the patrol car turned the corner and eased to the curb, the headlights out, and moved slowly toward the alley.

Helen Walsh giggled in the back seat. Her dress and use of makeup were intended to make her appear older than her sixteen years, but the giggling reaffirmed her age. Crowley removed the broad-brimmed hat and tossed it into the front seat, checking his hair in the rear-view mirror. Then he leaned her back against the seat and began unfastening the row of buttons that ran down the front of her dress. She slipped her arms around his waist and began running her hands up along his back, allowing her forearms to press gently against the revolvers he wore under each arm. The feel of the weapons excited her and she allowed her arms to linger against them as Crowley began kissing her neck and shoulders.

64

"How come you always wear two guns, Jimmy?" she whispered, bringing one hand to one of the revolvers and tracing its shape with her fingers.

"Cause I got two hands," Crowley said. He continued to unbutton her dress and allowed his mouth to move down her neck to her chest until he was kissing the upper parts of her breasts. His other hand slid down along her leg, then, finding the hem of her skirt, started up again along the softness of her silk stocking.

"I know you have two hands, Jimmy. I can feel both of them." Helen giggled again, then began breathing heavily as he pressed himself against her. She had studied that breathing often, as Gloria Swanson's image flickered across the screen, her head tilted back, her eyes rolling slowly upward. Helen eased her head back and allowed her eyes to move upward until she was staring at the felt interior of the car's roof. "How come we can't go upstairs to your friend's apartment, Jimmy? It would be a lot better there," she said.

"We'll go there later. Right now I like it here." The dress was unbuttoned now and Crowley struggled clumsily with her panties, inching them slowly over her buttocks. "Lift up a little," he whispered. "These things are tight as hell."

She raised herself and he pulled the panties down to her knees, pulling her with them until she was almost prone on the seat. He struggled with the buttons on his trousers and slid awkwardly on top of her, twisting violently to find his objective.

"I like it here too," she said breathlessly, trying to move under his weight to help him in his search. "Let me help you," she said, sliding her hand beneath him and grasping his rigid penis.

The patrol car had pulled opposite the alley and the two cops stared out the window. Light from a distant street lamp caught the apparent emptiness of the car and the older cop turned and smiled at his young partner.

"Looks like they flew the coop, bucko. I guess you'll have to settle for an illegal parking ticket if you want to add Mr. Crowley to your list of captured desperadoes." His belly shook with laughter as he watched a perplexed look spread across his partner's face.

"They *couldn't* have gone anywhere. There wasn't time," he said. The young cop continued to stare out the window, his eyes squinting against the faint light. "Maybe I'm nuts," he said, "but I'll be damned if that car ain't moving."

The older cop stopped laughing and turned his attention back to the car. "It's the light. It's playin' tricks on your eyes."

A shadow flashed in the rear of the car, a head moving up, then down again.

"See," the young cop whispered. "They're in there, in the back seat. I'll be damned. He's fucking her in the back seat. That's why we couldn't see

65

them." The young cop leaned closer to the window. He was grinning now and his eyes were flashing with his own enjoyment of the scene before him. "Yes, indeed. Looks like we got a little action going on there. Come on. Let's have some fun and catch this guy before he gets his pecker wet."

"Aw, leave 'em alone. They ain't hurtin' nobody. Even a crook got a right to get laid now and then," the older cop said.

"Bullshit," the young cop said. "I'm gonna have some fun whether you want to or not." He swung the car door open and grabbed his flashlight off the seat. "Come on. You'll get a laugh out of it. You'll have something to tell your cronies tonight." The young man was grinning at him.

Asshole, the older cop thought. "You go play your fuckin' games if you want to. Me, I know what a bare ass looks like already." He waved a disgusted hand at his young partner and stayed fixed in his seat. I got better things to do with me time than go sneakin' up on a couple of bare-assed kids, he said to himself. Besides it's against nature to ruin the chance of a good fuck.

The young cop moved slowly around the patrol car and, crouching slightly, stepped across the street and into the alley. He could see the movement of the car clearly now and he began to laugh quietly to himself. Hurry up, sweetheart, he thought. There ain't much time left for you to pop your cork. He moved alongside the car, taking care not to step on anything that would give his presence away. Outside the rear door he could see Crowley on top of the woman. His buttocks were bared, his pants down almost to his knees, and it moved up and down with a violent thrusting that made his rectum look like a bobbing brown eye. The woman's legs were straddling him and one of her stockings had been forced down until the garter was just below the knee. He stifled a laugh, then reached for the door handle and jerked it open, turning on his flashlight with the same motion and beaming it to the back of Crowley's head.

Crowley's head snapped around. "What the fuck? . . ." His voice was breathless. He fought to see past the glaring light, instinctively pulling his trousers up at the same time. It was a full second before the shine of the badge and the brass buttons on the tunic became clear to him and then were pressed into his understanding by the outline of the cop's hat. There was laughter in the cop's voice.

"Well, well. If it ain't Two Gun Crowley." The young cop's voice rose as he shouted back across the street. "Hey, partner. Guess who we found here? Two Gun Crowley, trying to get his other gun wet." He turned back to the car. "Get out, you—"

The impact of the first shot threw him back against the wall of the apartment building. At first he seemed to be floating and it was only when he hit the wall that he heard the roar of the explosion and felt the pain spreading

66

through his chest. He never heard the second shot. His body went limp, the knees crumbling beneath him, and he slid slowly along the wall, his eyes still staring blindly into the rear seat. His mouth was open, waiting for a scream that didn't come.

Across the street the older cop bolted upright in his seat with the roar of the gunfire. He pushed the car door open and jumped out. "Kid," he shouted. "Kid." He could hear Crowley's voice shouting at the woman to get out of the car. Then a figure emerged pulling at something in the car. The woman followed, stumbling. He reached for his service revolver. The man across the street swung around to face him, his arm shooting upward. The cop threw himself to the ground as the roar of the gun came again. There was the sound of glass falling near him and the thought of the shattered patrol car window raced through his mind. He raised the gun, steadying it with his other hand as the two figures began to move away from him down the alley. The kid's in there. The woman too. The thoughts jumped into his mind instinctively. He pushed himself up and ran, crouching, toward the alley.

At the rear of the car he dropped to one knee. The sound of running echoed from the alley. He looked to his right. The young cop sat there, staring into the rear seat of the car. His flashlight lay between his legs, the glass-enclosed beam pointing upward, revealing the massive wetness that covered the front of his tunic. You stupid bastard. You damned stupid kid. He was on his feet before the thought left him, moving to the front fender of the car. Down the alley he could see the shadows of two figures running. He fired wildly. Once, then again. A trash can fell, then began rolling across the alley. The two figures came into view under a light above a side door, the man and the woman. Crowley pushed the woman toward the door and jumped in behind her. The cop fired again, this time at nothing, frustration now acting on its own.

He became aware of the noise behind him. People were gathering outside the alley. "Stay back," he shouted. "Get back from there." He ran back to the rear of the car. "One of you call Headquarters. Tell them a cop's been killed." The final word stunned him. For a moment he seemed unable to move, then he spun around and bolted toward the alley. He ran to the side door and flattened himself against the wall. The door was open. Inside, it was quiet. He jumped through the door and ran up a short flight of stairs. He was in the lobby now. A man stood in the front entrance, looking out. "You," he shouted. The man turned, his eyes widening at the sight of the police officer with his gun drawn.

"What happened? What's going on?" the man said.

"A shooting. Did you see anybody come in here?"

"A man and a woman. The man had a gun too. They ran upstairs. What's happening here?"

67

"Is there another way out from up there?" the cop said.

"No. Just the door here and the one you came in. What's happening?" The man's voice was pleading.

"What about fire escapes?"

"They're all on the front of the building," he said. "Please, tell me what's happening. I'm the manager here."

"You come with me." He grabbed the man by the arm and pulled him out the door. "A police officer has been"—he paused—"shot. The man who did it is in your building. Do you know the man?"

The manager nodded. "He's been here before. He comes to see Mr. Dunniger. He lives on the third floor."

"Front or back?" the cop asked.

"In the front. Right over our heads." He looked up, then took a step back against the wall of the building.

"How many other people in the building?"

"There are twelve apartments. Four on each floor, except the street floor. There aren't any on the street floor." The manager looked around him. People were still gathered around the alley.

"Do you have a house phone? Can you call the other apartments?"

"No. No house phone. It's a small building." He spoke the words as though offering an apology.

"Shit. Okay. Get down there with the people near the alley." He took the manager by the arm again and walked him back to the alley. "I told you to get back," he shouted at the crowd. "That's a dead cop, not a fuckin' sideshow." The crowd inched back away from the alley. He pushed the manager into the crowd, then positioned himself so he could watch both exits. He looked down at his partner. The blood was spreading across his tunic, the fabric absorbing it. He reached down and turned off the flashlight. He wanted to vomit.

Crowley pulled Helen Walsh up the third flight of stairs and stopped on the landing, breathing hard. The girl was sobbing and her face held a look of dazed shock and terror.

"Come on," he said, yanking on her arm and pulling her down the hall to a door in the center of the floor. He banged on the door with the butt of his gun. "Open the door, Rudy. It's me, Jimmy. Let me in."

The door swung open and Crowley pushed the girl past a surprised Rudy Dunniger, then moved quickly in behind her and leaned back against the wall.

"What's goin' on, Jimmy?" Dunniger's eyes flashed from the gun to Crowley's face, then back to the gun. "I thought I heard some shots, but I never thought—"

Crowley interrupted him. "I just blasted a cop."

"You what?" Dunniger's eyes widened. "No shit."

He rushed to the window and peered out, his back against the wall. Two police cars pulled to the curb. A cop ran toward them, pointing up toward the window.

"What's happening?" Crowley said.

"They're gettin' a fucking army together out there," Dunniger said. He pointed at the girl. She was huddled in a corner, sobbing. "Who's the broad?" he asked.

"We was comin' up here when this bull jumped us."

"So you blasted him?" Dunniger said.

"Yeah, that's right."

"Shit. That's fantastic." He looked out the window again. Two more patrol cars had joined the others. "It looks like we got ourselves a shootout."

Across the room Crowley emptied the spent shells from his revolver and reloaded it quickly. Dunniger rushed over to a chair where his gun hung in its new holster. He ran back to the window and smashed the glass. He fired two shots in succession, then ducked back as incoming fire smashed the glass above his head. Crowley raced across the room to a second window.

"Shit. We really got ourselves a shootout," Dunniger said. He was grinning and his free hand was pulling wildly at his crotch.

CHAPTER NINE

THE UNMARKED CAR MOVED SLOWLY ALONG EIGHTH Avenue. Cordes sat in the driver's seat drumming his fingers against the steering wheel as he guided the car through the light traffic. To his right, Johnny Broderick concentrated on the few pedestrians moving along the sidewalk, stragglers still looking for a final place to stop before going home, he thought.

He checked his watch. It was eleven-ten already. Close to the end of a dull evening that had begun with a lousy meal at the Spanish restaurant Cordes had insisted upon. Greaseball food. He would never understand how people could eat it, even if it was free.

Cordes broke into his thoughts. "Over there, on the corner, reading a newspaper. Isn't that Charlie Murphy?" he said.

Broderick scanned the intersection. A skinny man with a long pointed nose was leaning against the corner of a building, reading a newspaper. He was wearing a cheap brown suit and a large hat, the brim of which almost touched the edge of his nose. "Yeah, that's him," Broderick said. "I wonder what the old booster is up to."

"We can find out," Cordes said, easing the car to the curb.

The two detectives were standing on each side of him before Charlie Mur-

70

phy realized he had been surrounded. The shock of it made him jump. "Geez. Don't sneak up on me like that. You'll give me a heart attack." His eyes darted back and forth between Broderick and Cordes.

"What's the matter, Charlie? You got a guilty conscience?" Cordes said.

"Aw, come on fellas. I ain't done nothin' in a long time." Murphy looked at each man with wide, imploring eyes. He looked like a frightened vulture.

"Yeah, I know. It's been work, church, and home for you, Charlie, just like always." Broderick gave him a hard look.

"What do you have for us, Charlie?" Cordes was smiling, an intended contrast to Broderick.

"I ain't got nothin'. Honest. I swear it on my mother's grave."

"You never had a mother," Broderick snapped. "You crawled out from under a rock."

"Honest, Johnny. I wouldn't kid you." Murphy smiled up at him. His front teeth were badly decayed and stained a deep yellow. The sight of it disgusted Broderick.

"Don't smile at me. You make me want to puke," he said. "All right, get in the car. We'll talk about it downtown." He grabbed his arm roughly.

"No, please. Don't do that." Murphy's voice was a whine. "The last time you guys rousted me I didn't get out of there until two in the morning and some guinea kid whacked me in the head and took all my dough."

"You telling us it ain't safe near Police Headquarters after dark?" Cordes said.

"No, I ain't sayin' nothin'. Look, please. Just let me buy some tickets to the Policemen's Ball, or somethin'. There ain't nothin' I can tell you anyway."

"The tickets to the ball are expensive this year," Broderick said. There was a smirk on his face now.

"How much?" Murphy said.

"Twenty bucks."

Murphy reached into his trouser pocket and pulled out a roll of bills. He peeled a twenty from the middle and handed it discreetly to Broderick. He began to return the money to his pocket when Broderick grabbed his wrist.

"There's one problem, Charlie," he said.

"What's that?" There was a pained look on Murphy's face now.

"There's a new rule this year. You can't buy just one ticket. You gotta buy two." Broderick smiled down at him, still holding his wrist.

Murphy took a deep breath and pulled out a second twenty and handed it to Broderick. "Yeah, sure. I was gonna buy two anyway," he said.

Broderick patted his shoulder. "You're gonna love the ball," he said. "Just one thing, Charlie. The tickets aren't made up yet. We'll have to mail them to you."

"Oh, that's okay. Just give them to some needy person. Just like always."

71

Murphy was sulking and Cordes grabbed his cheeks and squeezed them. "Be happy, Charlie," he said. "Charity is good for the soul."

Back in the car Cordes and Broderick laughed as they watched Murphy scurry off down the street, glancing back over his shoulder to be sure he wasn't being pursued.

"Look at the little weasel go," Cordes said. "He's afraid he's gonna have to buy a third ticket."

Murphy moved quickly around the next corner, heading toward Broadway. He was almost running.

The one-way police radio broke into their laughter, a flat, unemotional voice coming through the speaker amid crackling interference. "All units in the vicinity of West Fifty-fifth Street, between Ninth and Tenth avenues, respond to scene. Police officer shot. Perpetrators believed trapped in building. Proceed with caution." The message was repeated twice. Cordes had the car in motion before the second message ended. It lurched across Eighth Avenue, the siren blaring, and headed north to West Fifty-fifth Street. Swinging into the cross street they could see the cluster of cars a block and a half away and they could hear sporadic gunfire, a popping sound at first, growing sharper as they drew closer. They left the car at the end of what seemed to be more than a dozen patrol cars, pinned their badges to their lapels, and moved to the cover of the buildings before working their way down the street toward a group of uniformed men gathered at the entrance of the alley.

The dead cop was still in the alley, his body covered now with a blanket from one of the patrol cars, only the lower portion of his legs protruding beneath it, the light of the patrol cars catching the glint of his well-polished shoes. Broderick stood there looking down. It was a picture every cop lived with, knowing that next time he could be the one, sprawled across some dirty alley, his face covered so the taxpaying public would not have to bear the sight of dead meat.

"What happened?" He could hear Cordes asking the question.

"It was that punk Crowley. One of my men was checking out his car and the little bastard shot him. He never even got his gun out. Now he's upstairs with a broad and some other guy. There's a lot of fire comin' from up there."

Broderick watched the sergeant as he spoke. He was young. Young for a sergeant and he was angry, the kind of anger that comes when something happens that is totally out of your control. But the anger was only in his eyes. Otherwise he seemed in control.

Crowley's name kept running through Broderick's mind as he listened to Cordes question the sergeant—the apartment they were in, how long they had been there, where the other exits were. The sergeant gave him the details of the shooting.

"Is the other guy Amberg?" He heard his own voice asking the question. There seemed to be a slight waver in it.

72

The sergeant turned to him. "I don't think so. The manager of the building said the apartment is rented to a kid named Dunniger. We got a message about both of them and some others. You the one who sent that message?"

Broderick nodded. The sergeant's eyes hardened. There was an accusation in them but Broderick ignored it.

"He's a crazy punk. We're sorry he got one of your men," Cordes said. "Who's the broad with him?"

"We don't know. Just a broad." The sergeant's voice was not antagonistic. It was calm, even.

"Can you give us two men to back us up? We'll go up and get them," Cordes said.

The sergeant barked an order to two uniformed cops and they fell in behind Cordes and Broderick as they moved along the front of the building, their backs close to the wall. Out in the street others fired up at the building from the cover of patrol cars. From above, only an occasional roar indicated the returning gunfire. But still it was there. They were still up there firing back.

Inside the lobby they flattened against the wall, their guns drawn. Cordes pointed across the lobby with his revolver to a spiral staircase off to the left. They rushed to the stairway and crouched. They started up, first Cordes, then Broderick, and the two uniformed cops, all looking up, their backs close to the curving wall. They moved slowly, stopping at each landing, then moving on. When they reached the third floor they could hear the gunfire coming down the hallway. They moved quickly down the hall and took up positions outside the door. The gunfire seemed to ease.

"It sounds quiet in there," Cordes spoke softly, almost a whisper.

Broderick took off his hat and tossed it down the hall. He leaned his head flat against the wall. He could feel the perspiration running down his forehead. Cordes was on the other side of the door. "We don't know for sure that only two of them are in there. There could be more," he said.

"It's too late to worry about that now," Cordes said.

Broderick remained flat against the wall. "Just be careful. That's all I mean."

Cordes smiled. "Be careful? Ain't you comin' with us?" He stepped back quickly and kicked out at the locked door, tearing away the frame and sending it flying open into the room. He plunged in behind it, shouting the single word, "police." The two uniformed men ran in behind him. Broderick felt glued to the wall. He pulled himself away and spun through the doorway, crouching low, his gun extended out in front of him.

Across the room Crowley was slouched down in a corner. There were patches of blood on his jacket and trousers. He had been hit several times. Dunniger stood flat against the wall, his hands stretched above his head. There was a gun at his feet and he was screaming at them not to shoot.

73

Huddled in another corner a young girl lay whimpering.

"Check the other rooms," Broderick shouted. He was still crouched low to the floor, his revolver still out in front of him.

The two uniformed men entered the kitchen, then the bedroom. They were empty. Broderick walked to a closet and carefully opened the door. Nothing there. He stood easily for a moment, then moved past Cordes to where Crowley sat sprawled in the corner.

"You punk," he said. He reached down and grabbed him by the hair and dragged him across the room and threw him against a sofa. He leaned down over him. "Where's your boss?" Crowley said nothing. He reached down and slapped him across his face. "He was in this. I know he was in this. Tell me. Tell me or I'll kick your face in." He slapped him again.

"Easy, Johnny. He ain't goin' no place." Cordes took Broderick's arm and pulled him away. "You're not gonna make a case on Amberg with this," he whispered. "So take it easy."

Broderick pulled his arm away and walked over to the girl. "Get up," he said.

Helen Walsh got to her feet. Her hands were trembling. Broderick grabbed her arm and pulled her to the sofa and pushed her down next to Crowley.

"I didn't do anything," she said. Her entire body was shaking now and she began to weep hysterically.

Broderick started to raise his hand. The sergeant and five uniformed cops rushed through the door, their guns out. Broderick's hand dropped to his side.

"You got the bastards," the sergeant said.

"We got them. Too bad they're not all dead. We should have blown their goddamned heads off." Broderick remained in front of Helen Walsh. Her hysteria continued. "Shut your mouth," he growled.

The sergeant turned to his men, pointing at Dunniger with his revolver. "Take that one and the girl out of here now. We'll get a stretcher for the other one."

"You should throw him down the stairs just the way he is," Broderick snapped.

The sergeant ignored him. "Get a stretcher up here," he said.

"Look, Sarge. You don't need us anymore. If it's okay we'll file our reports at Headquarters." Cordes was standing next to the sergeant. He nodded his agreement. "Come on, Johnny. Let's get out of this joint."

Broderick walked ahead to the elevator, Cordes several steps behind him. They waited for it in silence. When they entered the elevator Cordes handed Broderick his hat. He had left it in the hall. He looked at it foolishly. "A ten-dollar hat and I go and leave it in the hall," he said.

When the glass and metal doors of the elevator opened on to the lobby it was already crowded with newsmen and photographers. Spotting the two detectives they rushed toward them, the photographers jostling each other with their large Speed Graphic cameras. The reporters forced Broderick and Cordes back against the elevator doors, shouting out questions. They directed their questions at Broderick.

"Johnny, tell us. Did you blow Crowley away?" one reporter shouted.

Broderick grinned at the crowd, then paused to adjust his hat on his head. "Naw, boys, They're all still alive. But Crowley is shot up pretty bad. He'll be coming down on a stretcher any minute. Keep your cameras ready."

"Did you get him, Johnny?" another reporter asked.

"How many times?" a third shouted.

Broderick held his hands out in front of him. "Slow down, boys. I'll tell you all about it." The reporters crowded in closer with Broderick at their core. He joked with several of the reporters and photographers he knew. Cordes was standing behind him to his right. He seemed amused. "The first thing you should know," Broderick began, "is that I put out a request last week to have Crowley, the other guy who was arrested tonight—Rudy Dunniger—and a couple of other hoods, kept under a loose surveillance. The officer who was killed tonight—and I'm sorry I don't have his name yet—well, he was doing just that when Crowley shot him down. He was a hero, doing his job, protecting the citizens from animals like that." A reporter interrupted, asking the reason for the surveillance. Broderick shifted his feet. "I can't go into too much detail on that, because there are other people still involved who I'm keeping an eye on. Let's just say that we suspected, check that, that we had *good information* that the people we're watching are part of a gang that was planning something big. So at my request all the Manhattan precincts were asked to keep an eye on these people. It would seem that this officer spotted Crowley doing something suspicious and, being a good cop, did his duty."

"How did you get in on this, John?" a reporter asked.

"I was out, working on another case when I got the radio call about the shooting, so naturally I came right away. And when I heard who was involved I realized that I should be the one to go in and get him."

The reporters clamored for information about the shootout and Broderick went into elaborate details about working his way up to Dunniger's apartment with other officers and breaking through the door.

"Who actually shot Crowley?" a voice shouted from the rear.

"It's hard to tell, fellas. There was a lot of shooting, as I'm sure you heard. We blasted away as we went in and the next thing I knew Crowley was on the floor and Dunniger was giving up. I would guess Crowley was hit about three or four times. Dunniger wasn't hit and neither was the girl. She wasn't armed and we're not sure yet what part she played except that she was with Crowley when he killed the officer."

"Who was the first one to get to Crowley?" The question came from a small reporter close to Broderick, one he had been joking with earlier.

"Well, Earl, I guess I was." He put his arm around his shoulder.

75

"And did you show him that he was a bad boy, John?" The other reporters began to laugh.

"Earl, would I do a thing like that? Let's just say I pointed out the error of his ways." The laughter continued and Broderick raised his hands again. "Look, boys, you got your story. The sergeant will give you names and addresses when he comes down. I have some reports to fill out at Headquarters. If you need me for anything give me a call there later." He slapped some shoulders and winked at other reporters in the group as he moved through them toward the door. Outside, Cordes caught up with him and they started back down the street to the car.

"Can I have your autograph, Detective Broderick?" Cordes said.

"What's with the autograph crap?" Broderick said.

"Well, I can see the papers tomorrow. Johnny Broderick, New York's toughest cop, captures Two Gun Crowley single-handed. I just wanted to get your autograph before the crowds start to form."

"What are you trying to say, Cordes?"

Cordes stopped and put a hand on his shoulder. They were standing next to the car. "Nothing much, Johnny. But in case you didn't notice, there were some other guys up there with you."

Broderick's face reddened. "You got a mouth, don't you? Since when do you want me to talk for you?"

"You talked pretty good for yourself." Cordes was smiling and there was no indication of anger in his voice.

"Look. The important thing is that the squad gets some good ink. It gets Garfoli off our backs, right? If you're really upset about it, I'll make sure everybody gets your name when they call me later at Headquarters."

"That's okay. You know how bashful I am anyway," Cordes said.

"Oh, kiss my ass." Broderick turned away and climbed into the car.

Cordes got behind the wheel and swung the car around the cluster of patrol cars that still jammed the street. "One other thing," he said. "That big shootout when we busted in the room. I don't remember that. How you gonna explain that if somebody tells what really happened?"

"Who's gonna do that?" Broderick said. He swung around in the seat to face Cordes. "You think those two uniform guys are gonna say anything when they got a couple of good citations staring them in the face? So who's gonna talk? Crowley? Dunniger? Shit, they'll be too busy trying to save their own asses. And even if they do say anything, who's gonna believe them? That leaves the girl. Hell, you could tell that bimbo Blackjack Pershing busted into that room and she wouldn't know the difference."

"What about me?" Cordes said. "You never know. I might squeal."

"Go fuck yourself," Broderick said.

Cordes began to laugh. He pulled the car into Tenth Avenue, then looked

76

across at Broderick. "By the way you still owe me a double sawbuck," he said.

"What are you talking about?" Broderick said.

"The tickets for the Policemen's Ball. One of them is mine."

"Oh, yeah." Broderick reached into his pocket and handed Cordes one of the twenties Charlie Murphy had given him. "I forgot," he said.

"Yeah, I know. You're very forgetful tonight," Cordes said.

77

CHAPTER TEN

JOHNNY BRODERICK STOOD IN FRONT OF THE MORNING Telegraph Building, a binocular case slung over his shoulder. It was a low, dingy, brick building that had once been a cow barn. Now it had been converted into a newspaper office and the reporters who worked there claimed the rat population outnumbered the staff, although where certain editors were concerned they insisted it was often difficult to tell the difference. There was a large window on the front of the building where the front pages of several of the more spectacular editions were arranged in a circular display to surround the edition currently on the street. Broderick concentrated on that latest front page. There was a large photograph just below the fold showing two police officers carrying Jimmy Crowley to a waiting ambulance. Juxtaposed with the larger photograph were two smaller ones, official Police Department portraits, one of the slain officer and another of Broderick. The headline above the story read: "Police Capture Cop Killer in Shootout." It was followed by a subheadline naming Broderick as the leader of the police assault team that cornered the gunman.

A smile crossed his lips as he read and reread the article. The quotes attributed to him were extensive and his description of the "gun battle" had been faithfully followed by the reporter. It was good ink, the kind not easy to come by, and it would make life easier for a time, especially with Garfoli. The guinea inspector had asked for a copy of his report earlier that day. The lieutenant who had forwarded it had informed him of that. But he could read all he wanted. Broderick knew the report had been carefully written, with special care taken to praise the actions of the murdered cop, one of Garfoli's own men. It also had elaborated in detail the purpose of the surveillance he had requested. In all, it could only be interpreted as good police work, pure and simple.

He studied the photograph of Crowley again and wondered how Amberg had reacted. The arrests of Crowley and Dunniger would certainly delay any plans he had. Delay but not stop them. He felt suddenly cold despite the eighty-degree temperature that still lingered on into the early evening. Amberg remained a problem. He would have little difficulty finding other hoodlums to fill the void that had been created. The city was filled with such men; the Volstead Act and the lack of employment after the Great War had produced them by the thousands, hard young men who wanted a share of the prosperity they had been promised, many of them combat trained by the society they now opposed. And Amberg would know how to use men like that, how to promise the rewards they sought. And he was clever enough to extract a heavy price for those rewards, even if it meant open conflict with the police.

The confrontation at Lindy's returned to him. What was it he had said? He had been smiling as he leaned across the table, but his eyes had been filled with hatred, the same hatred they had held three years earlier in the courtroom. It was something about not wanting trouble, but that someday trouble might come and it would be interesting to see what happened then. *Interesting.* The dirty little bastard. He was crazy. Broderick caught his reflection staring back at him in the window and his mind raced back to that dark, dirty alley on West Fifty-fifth Street, to the blanket-draped body, the shiny black shoes protruding beneath it.

His thoughts evaporated with the wail of a siren. He swung around and watched as an ambulance emerged from the Polyclinic Hospital on Fiftieth Street. He followed it as it lumbered into Eighth Avenue, then headed north. The driver had a cigar stuck in his mouth. He could be working for some butcher shop for all he would care, Broderick thought. And some lucky bastard was about to get the benefit of his attention.

Diagonally across the street on the northwest corner of Eighth Avenue and Fiftieth Street, a large crowd milled about in front of Madison Square Garden. The marquee above the entrance of the newly built Garden announced a middleweight title fight between Harry Grebs and Tiger Flowers. Broderick looked over the fight fans he would soon join as they moved toward the

79

entrance. They were a true mixture of the city—a predominance of grubby workingmen who would fill the upper levels of the massive arena, mixing now with well-dressed society types who would dominate the more expensive seats, mingling there with the hoodlums who provided the liquor to their favorite speakeasies.

A chauffeur-driven Duesenberg pulled to the curb directly in front of the main entrance and Broderick watched as the driver hurried around the car to open the door for a tall, slender young man and his red-haired female companion. The man was in his mid-twenties and there was the self-satisfied look about him given those who simply had to be born to assume the success and authority that other men fought for each day. The driver seemed to be standing at attention. He was older, old enough to be the young man's father, and he looked foolish dressed in high boots, tan riding pants, and a matching jacket and cap, standing there awaiting the order of some snot-nosed kid.

Broderick studied the young man in the yellow glow of the street light. He was thin, unathletic, and he could easily be broken apart by the hands of a stronger, rougher man. But he was also the kind of man who could break another with a telephone call, a word dropped to the right person in the drawing room of some club. Broderick respected that kind of power—he always had—the power to inflict your will on someone else without ever having a direct confrontation. Power dealt from afar by people who didn't want to dirty their hands.

The chauffeur turned and hurried back around the car. For a long moment the young man stood there surveying the crowd. He seemed amused by the contradiction spread out before him: the workingmen in sweaty caps and well-worn shirts who had climbed out of subways and off trolley cars to mix with those who had arrived in private cars and taxis, openly staring at the women who would look at them with disdain if at all.

The redhead hung on the arm of the young man's well-tailored suit, which seemed to have resisted the intrusion of any wrinkles despite the trip by automobile. Broderick studied her long, slender body, watching her move, easily at first, then drawing closer to her companion when the crush of the shabby crowd pressed too close.

"You seem deep in thought." Johnny Cordes was suddenly standing next to him, grinning. "Been reading your press clips?" He motioned with his head to the display window behind him.

"Yeah, I read it," Broderick said. "I thought Rickard's dough might make it up for me getting all the attention the other day."

"Forget it. I'd rather have the money. What's the action anyway? You didn't explain on the phone."

"It's easy. I work here at the Garden for Tex Rickard any time there's a big event and he lets me bring in other guys if I think I might need them. All we do is take care of any trouble that comes up. You know, arguments over seats and especially any dips who are working the crowd. Tex doesn't like his rich customers having their pockets picked in his joint. That's all there is to it."

"Is that what the glasses are for?" He motioned to the binoculars case.

Broderick nodded. "I usually stay up around the second level and scan the crowd. It's harder in the winter because you get a lot of kids moving around boosting top coats and furs. In the summer it's only the occasional pickpocket or fistfight. You really don't have to do anything except maybe smooth things over if any of his concessionaires get caught selling booze. Just stay with me and after everyone is seated we'll go to Tex's office and pick up our dough. Then if he wants, we'll hang around until everybody leaves."

"That sounds easy enough. And for this we get a taste?" Cordes rubbed his thumb and first two fingers together.

"Fifty bucks apiece." Broderick put his arm around Cordes's shoulder. "Come on. Let's go to work."

They moved across the street and into the crowds, pushing their way through one of the entrance gates with a flash of their badges and positioning themselves near the concession area, just inside the ticket collection booths.

"Some crowd," Cordes said, allowing his eyes to wander along the mass of people moving between the concession stands and the ticket booths. "These two pugs have a good following. Do you have any money down?"

Broderick shook his head. "No, the odds are too heavy on Grebs. Anyway, I don't give a shit who wins."

Cordes reached out and touched his arm. "I think we got some trouble over there by the ticket booths. Isn't that Vannie Higgins?"

Broderick turned and stared at a crowd gathering in front of a ticket booth, where a chunky man dressed in a flamboyant suit seemed to be arguing with an usher. "Yeah, that's him. Let's see what's going on."

They pushed through the crowd as Higgins's voice grew louder. It was a gravelly voice, and it seemed to frighten the usher, who was glancing around the crowd for help.

"What do you keep saying no for?" Higgins growled. "I'm givin' you a C-note for two ringside seats. Isn't that good enough for you? What's wrong with my money?"

The usher stuttered, still looking for help from the crowd. "I'm sorry, sir. This is a big fight and ringside was sold out weeks ago. You'll have to try the box office again."

"Don't give me that box office crap." Higgins reached out and took the usher by the lapel of his coat. "They only got seats in the clouds. Can't you understand that?"

A heavily made-up woman standing next to him interrupted. "He doesn't understand anything. Come on, Vannie, let's get out of here."

81

"He's gonna understand." Higgins tightened his grip on the usher's lapel as Broderick pushed through the crowd behind him.

"Okay, move aside. You people are blocking the hall." He turned his attention to Higgins. "You. Let go of that usher."

Higgins did not turn. He pulled the usher toward him, staring straight into his face.

"You got three seconds to let him go and get out of here," Broderick said. He had placed himself behind Higgins, slightly to his right, his feet spread apart, setting himself.

Higgins turned and saw Broderick for the first time. His jaw dropped open and his hand fell away from the usher's lapel. But the move came too late. Broderick's right shoulder dropped two inches and his fist came up off his hip and crashed into Higgins's jaw, sending him reeling back into one of the refreshment stands. The impact sent hot dogs and soft drinks and illegal beer spewing in all directions as Higgins slumped to the floor. Broderick took two steps toward him, then stopped and jerked his thumb toward the exit. A smile moved across his face as he watched Higgins struggle to his feet and move quickly toward the exit, his girl friend scurrying along behind, then he turned back to the crowd. "Okay, the show's over. The real fight's inside."

To his left, only a few steps away, a woman in her mid-twenties stood watching, her finely etched features a sharp contrast to the crowd about her. She seemed fascinated by the violence she had just witnessed and her eyes locked on Broderick and remained there. He smiled at her and she returned the smile with her eyes. There was a tall young man standing next to her with a bored look on his face, but he stood patiently, waiting for her to move on. She lingered for what could only have been a second or two—but it seemed longer—then with a slight toss of her head she turned back to her companion.

"Come, Freddie." Her voice was soft, but there was a sense of command in it and the young man obediently took her arm and moved with her toward the arena portal.

They walked slowly into the crowd, everything about her commanding attention. She moved gracefully but with a sureness he had seen in few women. Her chin was elevated ever so slightly and it accented her long, slender neck and delicate features. She was wearing a brown silk dress covered with tassles that moved with her, and implied what lay beneath.

There was no exaggeration in the way she moved, none was needed. Everything about her seemed to draw the eyes of those about her, something that was expected but not acknowledged. Broderick took a deep breath as she disappeared into the crowd.

"I think you hurt Vannie's feelings," Cordes said. "And he left a bit of a mess behind."

Broderick walked to the refreshment stand and studied the damage. It was worse than he thought. Behind the counter what seemed like several hundred hot dogs covered the floor, fermenting there in spilled soda and beer. There was a dazed look on the concessionaire's face.

"This is like an explosion in a butcher shop," he said, shaking his head. "Who's gonna pay for this?"

Broderick shrugged his shoulders. "Just cook the hot dogs. Nobody's gonna know the difference anyway."

He and Cordes started toward the portal with the concessionaire's voice shouting behind them, "You drive me to the poorhouse and tell me to cook the fucking hot dogs. I'll call the cops. You guys better come back here."

Broderick waved his hand at the shouting voice. "Let him call the cops. That will really drive him nuts." He and Cordes laughed as they followed the last of the crowd into the arena.

Inside the portal he removed the binoculars from the case and began scanning the crowd. All seemed as orderly as possible amid the growing excitement. There was the usual gathering of hoodlums but none of the regular dips were present. He smiled to himself. The gunmen and the bootleggers were okay, but harmless pickpockets had to be watched, weeded out before they did their less violent work. He worked the glasses around ringside. She was there, seated to his right, in the third row. In profile her features were incredibly defined. Patrician, that would be the term the newspapers would use. Her nose was thin and slightly upturned, the cheekbones high, accented by the faintest touch of rouge. Her mouth seemed small and delicate, but that could be the effect of the lipstick.

He thought about the way she had looked at him. There had been no attempt to disguise her interest. It had been done openly, almost blatantly by someone accustomed to doing as she pleased. There was a monied look about her. Her clothes and the casual air with which she wore them spoke of someone used to fine things, used to them to the point that they were no longer considered important. And then there was Freddie, seated next to her, still appearing bored. There could be no question about his money, he exuded it right down to his soft, manicured hands. And she had treated him like some obedient puppy. He studied Freddie's equally patrician face. A rich little asshole, he decided.

Broderick kept the binoculars to his eyes, fingering the adjustment wheel. "Did you ever see that lady before? The one downstairs?" he said to Cordes.

"Which one?" Cordes said.

"The one who was standing there when I decked Higgins."

"There were a lot of ladies there."

"A lot of broads. Only one lady." He continued looking through the glasses. Freddie leaned toward her and whispered something. She laughed, tossing her head again with a touch of arrogance. She raised her fingers to her throat and stroked herself, still smiling, then her head turned and she seemed to look up at him. He put the binoculars down. It was too far, she couldn't see him, he was sure. But it made him feel uncomfortable, like some small boy caught looking. "Let's go see Tex," he said to Cordes.

"Why not? That's the part I came for." Cordes turned down into the portal as Broderick raised the glasses once more. She was looking at the ring now.

Tex Rickard's office was something out of a museum, much like Rickard himself, a self-made legend who'd gotten his money running a saloon and gambling house in Alaska during the great gold rush. His large, wooden desk had belonged to President Harding and lying across it was a rhinoceros-hide cane that had been given to him by Teddy Roosevelt. On the wall behind his desk was a photograph of his Great Northern Saloon in Nome, from which the wealth that now operated the Garden came. The remaining wall space was cluttered with memorabilia and citations acknowledging his public-spirited efforts on the behalf of a dozen causes. There were several pairs of tattered boxing gloves placed haphazardly about the walls and old fight posters that held special significance for him, along with the usual photographs of Tex with his important New York friends.

When Broderick and Cordes entered the office Rickard was behind his desk, seated in a chair made of steer's longhorns that looked like the throne of some African chieftain. He was nervously chewing on a soft rubber cigar holder that held a large but unlit cigar. He looked up at the two detectives as they entered, his craggy face defying any hint of his age, although Broderick suspected he was in his early sixties.

"Did you see this?" he snarled, stabbing his finger at a newspaper opened to the sports page. "Dempsey and Tunney. They signed to fight in Philly September twenty-third. Who the hell holds a championship fight in Philly? Half the fight fans don't even know where Philly is. After all I did for Dempsey and he does this to me. The son of a bitch. He was just a hick kid from a coal town when I let him fight in the Garden. In the *Garden.*" He shouted the final word as though it in itself emphasized the stupidity of the decision. Rickard stood and began pacing around the room.

"Tex, I'd like you to meet Johnny Cordes. I asked him to help me here tonight," Broderick said.

"Hello, Cordes." He turned and fixed one eye on the Spanish detective. "You the one who tossed that guy into my refreshment stand?"

"Not guilty, Tex." Cordes smiled and turned to Broderick.

"There wasn't much else I could do, Tex. The clown was roughing up one of your ushers in front of a crowd of people."

"New ushers I can get easier than fifty bucks worth of food and soft drinks," he snapped. "I don't need two big bouts in one night—that's not what I got you here for. But forget it." He reached for his wallet and withdrew several crisp bills, then opened his top desk drawer and extracted two

84

envelopes, placing equal amounts of money in each. He tossed the envelopes on the desk. "Good crowd tonight, eh?" He turned and walked to the rear wall and opened a small door that covered a window that looked out onto the arena.

Broderick walked up beside him. "Tex, can you do me a favor?"

"Sure, what do you need?" He continued to survey the crowd.

Broderick handed him the field glasses. "In the third row, to the right of the ring there's a woman sitting there—a brunette with a rich-looking guy in a blue suit. She's got on a brown dress. Do you know her?"

Rickard took the binoculars and scanned the right side of the ring, adjusting the lenses as he did so. He stopped, appraising the beautiful woman in the third row. "The brunette? The one with Freddie Wainwright?" he asked.

"Yeah, Freddie. That's what she called him."

"No, I don't know her, but I can find out. I know him, or better still, his old man. He owns a big shipping company, but the kid's a playboy, a gambler. If his father ever found out what he's up to and with who, he'd probably cut the kid off." Rickard closed the door and turned to face Broderick. "What do you need to know about her?" he asked.

"I want to meet her."

An incredulous look spread across Rickard's face. "You? Come on, Johnny, what for? She's too rich for your blood. She's part of Wainwright's crowd. Don't try to run in that league, Johnny."

"I still want to meet her. Will you find out her name for me?"

Rickard turned around and shrugged his shoulders. "If you want to make an ass of yourself I can do better than that." He sat at his desk and began scribbling a note to himself. "There's a party late tomorrow afternoon at a friend of mine's town house on East Sixty-second Street. It'll be mostly rich sports doing their Saturday afternoon drinking—and that means Wainwright will be there and she'll probably be with him. I'll arrange for you to go with me." He shook a finger at Broderick. "But don't blame me if this whole thing blows up in your puss. Meet me here tomorrow at four o'clock."

Broderick grinned at Rickard. "I'll be here, Tex. Thanks."

Rickard waved his hand at him. "Just get out of here and let me get some real work done. I got to figure a way to pay Dempsey back. This kid Tunney ain't gonna do it for me."

They left Rickard rummaging about his desk as if searching for some lethal weapon. Outside the office Cordes took Broderick's arm, stopping him.

"What's this," he said, raising his eyebrows. "You planning on entering High Society?" Cordes had his gold toothpick dangling from his mouth and it moved like a wagging finger as he spoke.

"You don't think I'll fit in?" Broderick was grinning at Cordes and himself as well.

"Oh, sure you will. Like some hooker at a church bazaar."

85

"Go fuck yourself. Let's hit a couple of joints and see what's going on. Nothing's gonna happen here." Broderick started toward the entrance.

Cordes bowed formally at the waist. "Why, of course, sir. Shall I have the driver bring the car around, or shall we walk among the peasants?"

"Let's walk. The driver doesn't like it when I take greaseballs in the car with me. He says it makes the seats oily."

"Oh, he does, does he? And how does he feel about potato peels on the floor, you shanty Irish prick?"

CHAPTER ELEVEN

H E HAD NEVER PAID MUCH ATTENTION TO THE wealthy area of the east side of Manhattan that ran from Fiftieth to Seventy-second streets between Lexington and Fifth avenues. As a cop there had been little need. Crime, the type that was attacked by the department, kept its place east of Lexington Avenue, where the tenements sat in the shadow of the Third Avenue El. Sitting in the back seat of Tex Rickard's Duesenberg he understood now why that was so. There was a subtle elegance about this part of the city that you had to study to appreciate, and it was reflected in the faces of the people who moved about its sidewalks. There were thieves here too, he mused, but not the type the city wanted to pursue. More obvious thugs stick out, they would jar the landscape; so they stayed away and avoided the one place truly worth stealing from. He smiled at the idea, the bit of official police philosophizing, as the car moved through the graciousness of Park Avenue with its carefully tended central gardens, planted to satisfy the eyes of the rich when they looked out from their towering apartments.

The driver missed his turn at Sixty-second Street, turned left into Sixty-third, and headed toward Fifth Avenue as Broderick studied the rows of brick and limestone houses that rose up five and six stories to provide the spaciousness the wealthy always seemed to need. Many still had ornately decorated hitching posts at the edge of the sidewalk, still polished and maintained from days when the horse and carriage, not the expensive automobile, served the traveling needs of the people who lived there. Many of the houses, he had been told, had the new push-button elevators that had recently come on the market, so the occupants would not have to exert themselves with stairs. He smiled to himself, thinking of the five flights he had climbed every day as a kid.

The car stopped in traffic and he looked at the carved wooden door of the house to his right, the highly polished brass and freshly swept stoop. He looked about the street and noted that not a scrap of paper could be seen, no garbage can sitting by the curb, nothing to disturb the tranquillity of the tree-lined street, or mar the quiet dignity of the houses, each standing secure, like refined old ladies with their noses pointed up in the air. The car rumbled ahead over the imitation cobblestones and turned into Fifth Avenue and again into Sixty-second Street. It was like two different cities, he thought, and Cordes's words came back to him. He fit in like a hooker at a church bazaar. But it was where he wanted to be, he told himself, as he watched two young women walk confidently along the sidewalk, their heads raised proudly, telling everyone how much they belonged to this city within the city.

It was four-thirty as Tex Rickard started up the high front stairs of the Sixty-second Street town house, his cane jabbing at each stair ahead of him as though he wanted to be sure it would not crumble underfoot. Broderick followed, smiling to himself as he watched the aging sports magnate forge ahead. Rickard had lectured him again in his office before they started out. He would make a fool of himself, of that Rickard was sure. They would serve a fine pâté and he would think it was chopped liver and try to make himself a sandwich. And he wouldn't know what to say to these people. They would talk about polo or sailing and he'd be lost. But if he insisted on making a fool of himself at least he had dressed properly. His blue blazer and tan slacks would pass the first inspection, at least. When they reached the front door Broderick was still smiling, remembering the lecture. Tex honestly expected him to be terrified. He didn't realize that he had often seen these society people vomiting in the gutter in front of high-class speakeasies and while he envied and was cautious of their power, they held no great terror for him. By listening intently and saying little Broderick found he could get through an awkward social situation. Besides, people's curiosity about *him* smoothed his way into conversation.

The heavy wooden doors of the town house were opened by a liveried butler, who greeted Rickard as a well-known guest. Inside, the house was what he had expected it would be. The foyer was dominated by a large, curved staircase, almost overpowering in itself, that rose a full two stories before yielding to an immense skylight of leaded decorative glass. Large wooden French doors faced each other on each side of the stairway, interrupted only by a gilded round table placed in the center of the marble floor. The doors to the right were open and led to a cavernous living room the size of two tennis courts placed end to end. The intricately laid parquet floors were graced with antique Orientals and held a museum quality display of Louis Quatorze furniture. Well-dressed men and women sat talking while uniformed maids moved unnoticed among them with trays of wine and hors d'oeuvres. Across the room, to the right of a large marble fireplace, more trays of food were displayed along an Irish lace-covered table, at the center of which was a stuffed peacock, its tail spread into a fan.

Broderick touched Rickard's arm and motioned toward the table. "Is that where they keep the chopped liver?" he said.

Rickard grunted but said nothing.

There were at least fifty people in the room. Occasional laughter could be heard from the sundry small groups that gathered together, talked, then drifted apart to form still other flocks of babbling conversation. To the left of the fireplace Freddie Wainwright stood with a small group of men, the same bored look that Broderick remembered from the evening before still present. He felt a moment of concern, disappointment, seeing him alone among a group of men. He scanned the various groups of chatty people, moving from one to the other like someone trying to find a friend in a crowded railway station. She was there, across the length of the room, seated on a small settee, smiling as she spoke with the young man next to her, the same two fingers of her right hand gently stroking her throat as they had the previous evening in the glare of ringside.

She turned her head and looked across the room. She was looking directly at him and for a moment there was a sense of uncertainty on her face that slowly changed to recognition. A slight smile began to form on her lips and she turned back to the young man seated next to her and offered it to him. Broderick turned back to Rickard.

"I see you found what you were looking for," Rickard said. "Let me introduce you to our host and then you can go and make an ass of yourself."

Rickard took Broderick by the elbow and walked him over to the group of men that included Freddie Wainwright. "Excuse me, gentlemen," Rickard began. "Malcolm, I want you to meet a young friend I asked to join me."

The introductions were short and perfunctory and were extended to everyone in the group. Malcolm Bainbridge was large and portly and, from the papers, Broderick knew that he kept a stable of racehorses that received far more of his attention than his Wall Street brokerage. He seemed genuinely pleased to welcome him, and his plump red face offered an immediate smile.

"It's good to have you here, Johnny. I've heard the mayor speak of you often."

Broderick returned the smile, knowing now that the others in the group would not question his right to be there. "Thank you. It's a pleasure to meet you, sir. The mayor's been known to tout your horses more than once."

At the mention of his avocation Bainbridge chortled with pleasure, then turned to the others in the group. "You see, gentlemen, I told you we had a newfound wisdom in City Hall and our friend Broderick here has just confirmed it."

Rickard left the group but still the conversation moved along easily, staying mainly on Bainbridge's love of horseflesh and his appraisals of several of the top three-year-olds he had studied at the Saratoga meeting. It was the right conversation for Broderick. He also followed the horses but he kept to his own advice and said little.

Discreetly he allowed his eyes to wander about the room. She had moved and was now standing near the cloth-covered table talking with an elderly woman. There was a break in the conversation and Broderick excused himself and started toward her. The elderly woman seemed to see someone at the opposite end of the room and hurried off as he approached. He stopped in front of her.

"Hello."

She looked up at him and smiled. There was a hint of quiet amusement in her eyes.

"You're the man who won the fight at Madison Square Garden, aren't you?"

She was beautiful, strikingly so, and she made him feel awkward. "Not exactly. I was just doing my job. The man was causing trouble."

She laughed, a slightly flippant laugh. "I agree. He shouldn't have manhandled that poor usher. Is that what you do?" She paused. "Work for the Garden, I mean?"

"No. I'm with the Police Department."

"Oh, really. What's your name, Sergeant?" Her voice was also flippant now but she was still smiling, playing games, Broderick thought.

"I'm not a sergeant. The title is detective and the name is Johnny Broderick." He smiled at her. He was committed now and ready to play her game.

"Not the Johnny Broderick I read about in the papers?" She seemed pleased with the idea, but it was still part of her game, he thought.

"I guess so. But I'm a little surprised to find out that you spend your time reading about crime." One point for me, he decided.

She smiled again, knowing now that he was playing too and fully pleased with the idea. "Oh, you'd be surprised about the things women read about today." She offered him a look of coy naughtiness, then went on before he could counter. "Well, this is wonderful. Now I understand what happened last night. It isn't often I get to see a police celebrity in action. What is it that they call you in the papers?" She paused as if trying to remember. " 'The hitter,' or something like that, isn't it?"

She caught him with that one and he felt awkward. "The beater," he said. "But sometimes the newspapers exaggerate."

"Not in your case, I'm sure. Remember, I've seen you at work, Mr. Broderick, or may I call you John?"

The game was over and she had won. She was letting him escape with the knowledge that she could do so again if she chose to. A fascinating woman, he decided.

"John is fine. But what about you? You've picked me apart pretty thoroughly. Do you intend to be mysterious?"

She laughed, genuinely this time. "My name is Mona D'Arcy and I'm being evil, teasing you this way. The woman I was talking with when you came up told me who you are. You see I asked her to find out from Mr. Rickard. Does that shock you?"

Broderick was stunned by her blatant honesty but pleased. "Not at all. He was supposed to find out about you for me."

"I know. My friend told me. It seems Mr. Rickard isn't very good at keeping secrets, is he?" She was smiling her coy smile again.

"And he gave you the 'beater' line too?"

"My friend said he seemed quite proud of you." She paused again, keeping her eyes on him much as she had the night before. "He said you're the roughest policeman in New York. Are you?"

Broderick shuffled his feet. "Never at cocktail parties."

She smiled up at him. It was a beautiful smile and he found himself wondering what he was doing standing next to her, but pleased that he was. A maid approached with a tray of champagne but Mona waved her off. She seemed to sense what was going through his mind and she looked about the room quickly.

"I think this party is boring," she said, taking his arm. "Besides, I'm hungry. Would you consider it terribly brash if I asked you to have an early supper with me? I think I'd much rather hear about you than stay here and be told about horses and sailing and things."

The offer stunned him. "Yes, I would, but I'd be happy to—"

She didn't allow him to say more. "Then consider it brash and come with me," she said.

They started across the room toward the foyer.

"What about your friend Freddie?" He asked the question automatically, still uncertain about what was happening.

"He'll understand," she said. "Freddie and I are just friends and he always understands."

He sat across from her in a small, dimly lit French restaurant, studying her closely. She was beautiful and her laughter was infectious, coming from

91

someone who did as she pleased and enjoyed herself thoroughly. He had talked far more than he normally did, concentrating mainly on his work in the department. She seemed honestly interested, although he doubted it, but still, she had put him at ease. But there was something. He felt a sense of concern several levels beyond his ability to understand, but there. And there was a sense of awe as well. Everything she did, the simplest things, seemed flawless. The way she stood or sat or held her hands. Even her laughter seemed perfected, almost practiced, never too loud, obviously genuine but controlled. She was dressed simply, but the clothes were clearly expensive, a simple off-white dress of a sheer fabric, but layered so only the suggestion of the sheerness was real. It was a loose-fitting dress, cut low in the front, and as she moved it offered the provocative hint of ample breasts. There was a matching piece of cloth tied around her head, partially obscured by the well-planned curls and ringlets, and it added a sense of elegant casualness.

The waiter had spoken only French, a fact that had sent a surge of panic through him at first. But she had handled it well, asking if he would mind if she ordered since she was familiar with the cuisine offered. He had agreed gratefully and later she had explained that she had assumed he was not fluent in French and how the waiters there often took sadistic pleasure in embarrassing people who were not. "Sometimes it's amusing to watch," she said laughing, "but we must never let them get the upper hand."

After dinner they sat drinking the remaining wine. The restaurant was getting crowded, and he was sure the waiter would want the table free. But she seemed impervious to the fact and decided she would have another bottle of wine, as though it was her right to linger as long as she pleased. The waiter seemed mildly annoyed when he took the order and when he returned she tilted her head toward him and smiled.

"*Garçon,*" she said, pointing to the bottle of wine. "My friend and I were wondering how you manage to serve wine so openly in light of the present laws." Her eyes remained fixed on the waiter and she continued to smile.

The waiter stammered, insisting in broken English that he could not understand the question.

She gestured toward Broderick and spoke as though she were introducing him to a child. "Mon ami, agent de police, le détective, Broderick." She looked at the waiter again, then motioned to the bottle of wine he had placed on the table. "Prohibition de l'alcohol, n'est-ce pas?"

The waiter began to stammer in English, insisting he was only a poor waiter and knew nothing about the management's policies.

"My, but how well you speak English," she said. She waved her hand at the wine. "Non, il importe. J'ai beau dire."

The waiter hurried away and she began to laugh, but there was a toughness in her eyes he had not seen before.

"What the hell was that all about?" Broderick asked.

92

"I'm just being naughty again," she said. "He was hovering a bit too close to the table, trying to hurry us along. So I asked him about serving wine during prohibition."

"I got that. But what about the 'agent de police' business?"

"Oh, I just introduced you as my friend the detective. Your presence seemed to have quite an effect on him. He even forgot to pour the wine."

"He was probably afraid to touch it again," Broderick said, reaching for the bottle and filling each of their glasses. He looked across at her and raised his glass. "To you. An amazing woman."

She laughed, then turned her head to the side in an exaggerated pose. "Why, thank you." She laughed again, then lowered her eyes to her glass, then back up at him. "I find you terribly attractive too." She paused a moment, then added: "Do you mind if I ask you something personal?"

"Try me."

"Well, you told me about your work for the mayor, about the strike-breaking and all and about that young Crowley man and of course I saw what you did at Madison Square Garden. Normally I'm frightened by violence. But the way you talk about it, it seems fascinating and that confuses me. You seem to enjoy the idea of it, almost as though it were really a part of your nature. But then this evening you seem so gentlemanly and perhaps because of that all the talk about violence seems acceptable. Do you really like it that much, John?"

Broderick shifted slightly in his seat, not sure how to answer. "I really never think about it that much. It's just something that happens, something I'm forced to be a part of because of what I do." He paused and watched her, trying to see if the answer was being accepted. "What I mean is that the city is filled with some pretty bad people, people who would kill you, sometimes without any reason at all. You take the average shopkeeper. Right now if a butcher wants to sell chickens to his customers he has to pay a service charge on each chicken that comes in and then another service charge on the crates they're shipped in. The same thing is true for people who sell vegetables, or clothing, or anything. And if some petty hoodlum wants a new suit, he just takes it and the tailor is glad to let him have it because he knows his store window will be smashed if he doesn't. Then you have the liquor racket and all the violence that surrounds it and the gambling and vice. There are some very rough people out there and somebody's got to sit on them or they'll take over everything. They're thugs, it's really that simple, and there are too many of them and not enough of us. If I gave them too much rope they'd end up hanging me with it. So I don't give them any. And they understand that, most of them anyway. It's probably the only thing they do understand."

Mona was quiet for a long moment. She toyed with her wine glass; the hard, deliberate look was back in her eyes. "But you really enjoy doing it, don't you?"

"You mean hurt people? No, I don't enjoy hurting anyone. It's just that sometimes I don't have any choice. Either I survive or they do."

"Come, John. You're not telling me that it's like Saint George against the dragon, or the avenging angel, are you?" She was smiling at him again, but watching him closely.

The feeling of concern that had remained beyond his consciousness returned. Perhaps this is what Rickard had meant. Two different ways of life, something he could never control because of what he was. His jaw hardened for a moment, then he forced a smile. "No. I said I never thought about it that much. How come you're being so intellectual about it all?"

Mona straightened slightly in her chair. She had challenged something within him and had touched a nerve and she hadn't wanted to. "I didn't mean anything adverse," she said. She smiled at him with intended warmth. "It's just that I find that I'm very fond of you and I want to know more about you . . . how you feel about things, so I can understand you better." Her eyes remained on him and she began running two fingers along her throat, touching herself, softly, slowly.

"Do you always touch your neck that way?"

Mona smiled. "Yes, I do. Don't you like it?"

"I like it very much. The touching and the neck."

She raised one finger to her lips. "It's a very ordinary neck."

"Really?" He continued to watch her. She did not look away. "Are you free for the rest of the evening, or do you have other plans?"

"No plans at all," she said.

"Good."

"Did you have something special in mind, Detective?"

"Yes. Have you ever been on the Staten Island ferry?"

"No." She began to laugh. "Why?"

Broderick turned and motioned to the waiter for the check, then turned back to her and saw she was still watching him. "Because we're going to sea, that's why."

"We are?" The thought of the offer seemed to amuse her.

"We are. Unless you get seasick, of course."

She laughed again. "No, I have very steady sea legs and I don't mind at all. But let's take some champagne with us. And glasses."

The waiter arrived with the check and placed it ceremoniously on the table.

"We're going to need one more thing," Broderick said.

The waiter paused. "Of course, sir." He glanced at Mona, intimidated.

"I'd like a bottle of good champagne, unopened, and two glasses that we'll be taking with us."

The waiter tilted his head and offered Broderick an incredulous gaze, shrugging his shoulders. "I'm afraid we are all out of paper cups, sir."

"What did you say?" Mona's voice was almost a whisper but sharp and the look she gave the waiter caused him to stutter again. "I, uh, said, madam that we are unable to provide paper cups. I'm sorry we just have none of these to offer."

"We didn't ask for *paper cups.*" Her eyes never left the waiter. "See here. Just bring some champagne glasses and charge them to our bill. I'm very sure if you tell the maître d' that it's for my table he won't object."

"Yes, madam, of course. Will there be anything else?"

"Just the champagne. And the glasses."

Broderick sat watching her, startled but impressed, as the waiter hurried off. Mona seemed to feel his eyes on her. She reached across the table and took his hand.

"It's infuriating when people like that try to act so terribly important." She was forcing a smile but her eyes were still angry.

He squeezed her hand lightly. "I think he got the message."

She withdrew her hand and raised it to her lips as if to suppress laughter. Her eyes softened. "He certainly did. I think we scared him half to death."

The waiter returned with the wine and the glasses and offered the bottle to Broderick for his approval, then quickly placed them in a paper bag. Broderick paid the check, leaving an ample tip, and then watched as the waiter timidly attended to Mona's chair.

She ignored him and took Broderick's arm. "And now to sea?" she said.

"And now to sea."

CHAPTER TWELVE

THE TAXI PULLED SLOWLY FROM THE CURB AND Broderick leaned toward the driver.

"I want you to stop at a newsstand at Forty-eighth and Broadway. Then you can take us down to the Staten Island ferry." He turned to Mona. "I have to see someone. It will only take a minute."

"Is it police business?"

"Sort of. The guy who runs the newsstand is an informant of mine. I check with him every day."

The taxi moved slowly through the dinner hour traffic as Mona and Broderick contented themselves with playful conversation. When the cab pulled to the curb near Danny's newsstand neither seemed to notice.

"This it?" the driver asked.

Broderick looked up, surprised they were already there. He reached for the door.

"May I come too?" she asked.

"Sure, if you want to. But it won't be very exciting."

"I'll be the judge of *that*, Detective."

She took his arm and walked, almost marching, deliberately beside him. Danny was sorting papers as they approached and when he looked up his eyes darted back and forth between Broderick and Mona.

"Hi, Johnny." He paused, staring at the woman.

"Close your mouth, Danny. There are a lot of flies around here. You trying to make time with the lady?"

Danny's face turned scarlet and he glanced quickly to each side. "Gee, Johnny, I wasn't trying to make no time, honest."

"Of course you weren't," Mona interjected. "You were being sweet. He's just a bully."

Broderick shot a wry glance at her, then turned back to Danny. "Well, if you're through staring, what do you have for me?"

"Nothin' at all, Johnny. There's nothin' goin' down, nothin' at all. Those people are layin' low since that Crowley thing, I think. But I got your papers. There's another nice item about you in Winchell's column."

"Just hold it for me until tomorrow."

"Oh, John. Let's get it. I'd like to read it," Mona said.

"Okay, if you want. Just promise me you won't start a scrapbook."

"I promise," she said. "Absolutely not."

He took the paper from Danny, then stopped. A frightened look had come over the little man's face. "What's the matter?" he asked.

Danny's eyes darted down the street. "Comin' up behind you. It's Hy Amberg and Moe Berg."

Broderick stiffened, then handed Mona the paper. "Get back in the cab," he said. "I'll be with you in a minute."

"What's wrong?" she said, turning around.

"Please. Just get in the cab."

She didn't move. He turned and watched Amberg approach. There was a crooked smile on his lips. Broderick unbuttoned his blazer, freeing his gun. The thought of a setup raced through his mind. They had him alone on the street, the two of them. If they moved to each side of him they had him cold.

"Well, well, if it isn't big, bad Johnny again. Jimmy Crowley sends his regards." Amberg's voice was cutting, snide.

"Keep walking, Amberg. A garbage truck is liable to spot you."

Amberg's eyes hardened, then he smiled again and turned to Moe. "You hear that, Moe. Johnny boy doesn't like our company. He's got a fancy lady with him and he thinks he's too good for us."

Broderick flinched at the mention of Mona. It was Amberg's way of letting him know he had him at a disadvantage. He was playing with him. His eyes moved from one to the other, watching for a moment. He could feel the sweat in the palms of his hands.

"Maybe he ain't good enough for us, Hy." Moe did not smile as he spoke. He kept his eyes on Broderick, but he seemed nervous and his neck seemed to jerk repeatedly.

"Hear that, Johnny boy. Moe here thinks that maybe you ain't good enough for us. How about that?" Amberg laughed. It was a low cruel laugh that stopped as abruptly as it started.

Mona touched Broderick's arm. "Let's go, John, please." There was an imploring sound in her voice.

Broderick heard a car come to an abrupt halt behind him. He tensed as the thought of still more attackers seized him.

"Everything okay, Johnny?" The voice came from behind; before him he could see the look on Amberg's face change. He turned. The questioning eyes of a uniformed cop met his. He felt a final fluttering in his stomach and then a feeling of calm.

"We have a couple of gentlemen here I think we should check out. They could be packing." He turned back to face Amberg and found himself fighting to suppress a smile. He felt like a cat who had just come across a trapped mouse.

"We ain't carrying nothin'," Moe said.

The two uniformed men got out of the patrol car and approached.

"Then you won't mind spreading it on that wall," one cop said.

Broderick stood behind the two officers as they forced Moe and Amberg into a spread position. Passersby stopped to watch and he thought about the humiliation Amberg would feel. The two officers finished and shook their heads.

"You sure?" he asked.

"Nothing, not even a toothpick," one answered.

Amberg turned, brushed off his suit coat, and adjusted his tie. He smiled. "It's not time yet, Johnny."

Broderick stepped forward, grabbing the lapels of his coat and pushing him back against the wall. "You listen to me, you little bastard," he whispered. "Your time's already up. You understand that."

Moe began to shout at the uniformed officers. "He ain't got no right to do that. Make him knock it off."

"Shut up," Broderick growled over his shoulder.

Amberg was still smiling but his eyes glistened with hatred. "You're right, Johnny. The time's up." He let his eyes drop down to Broderick's hands crushing his lapels, then back up into his face. "You're not gonna do anything now, Johnny. You're too smart to do something in front of witnesses." Broderick's hands dropped from his lapels and Amberg stepped away. "See you soon, Johnny." He began to laugh again.

"Count on it, punk." He spoke the words with harshness but his stomach was turning again as he watched Amberg limp back down the street pulling at his right leg. He turned and walked back to Mona, forcing a smile. "I'm sorry you had to be involved in that," he said.

Mona shivered. "What a horrible man."

"You gotta watch him, Johnny. He's nuts. Scarey nuts," Danny said.

"He certainly is. Who is he, John?" There was concern on Mona's face. She seemed frightened, vulnerable, something he had not seen in her before.

He touched her cheek. "He's nothin'. Don't worry about him." He turned to the uniformed officers. "Thanks. I'm sorry you couldn't get an arrest out of it."

"Those are two of the guys you put a message out on, right?" one cop said.

"That's right. Two of Crowley's friends." He looked at their precinct insignias, taking care that they noticed. "It was a good back-up and I'll let your sergeant know. Thanks again, fellas." He turned back to Danny. "And that's why I want you to keep your eyes and ears open," he said.

Danny nodded rapidly. "I will, Johnny. I promise I will."

He winked at the newsdealer, then took Mona's arm. "Shall we go to sea?"

She took a deep breath and offered a wan smile.

As the taxi moved south on Broadway, Amberg and Moe stood at the curb and watched it pass. Amberg raised his hand to his hat as his eyes met Mona's staring out at him. "I told you he'd be at the newsstand tonight," Amberg said. "He's there every night. I can read him like a book. And at the end of next week I close that book."

Mona could not take her eyes off the small slender man who had both frightened and excited her. "John, that man. There he is again," she said, still looking into the street.

"Don't pay any attention to him."

"I can't help it, John. I don't think I've ever seen anyone so frightening." She turned to face him. "What did he mean when he said it wasn't time yet?"

"Who knows? He's crazy. He's just got it into his head . . ." He paused. "But that's not important. He's one of those people I was telling you about in the restaurant. You shouldn't even think about him."

"But that police officer asked if he was one of the men you sent a message about. What does that mean?"

He looked at her. He didn't want to answer her questions. They annoyed him. But he knew she was only curious, the situation had frightened her, but it had also been exciting, something different, something she didn't understand and perhaps something that made him more interesting. He smiled. "I arrested him three years ago. He was just released from prison and he blames me for the time he spent there. That's all there is to it."

"No wonder you were so tense." She slipped her arm into his and tilted her head upward. "I thought it was frightening. I honestly thought he was going to attack you, he and that other thug."

"They wouldn't have the nerve, not in public anyway."

She continued to watch his reaction. "But you said he was insane. Insane people do all types of irrational things. Doesn't that frighten you?"

"Police aren't allowed to be frightened. It says so in the regulations." He laughed. It was forced laughter but he hoped she wouldn't notice. "If we let

99

people like that frighten us, we'd be walking around scared to death all the time. And besides, you saw how fast other cops were around. We take care of each other."

"I know, that was wonderful." She squeezed his arm, then paused for a moment. "But goodness. What if they hadn't been?"

He took a deep breath. "Look, he's not worth talking about." He stroked her cheek. "We were having fun until he showed up. Why don't we forget him and go back to having fun. I don't want to ruin our sea voyage talking about business."

"Of course, you're right. Our sea voyage is far more important. Let me see the newspaper now. I want to see what marvelous things they have to say about you."

He handed her the paper, then turned his attention to the street as she began to leaf through it, searching out the column Danny had mentioned. The muscles in Broderick's jaw tightened and he thought about his stomach. He wished it would stop churning.

Half the champagne was gone by the time the ferry began its return trip from Staten Island. They stood at the rail watching the bow cut the water, the sound of the waves overpowering the aft noise of the engines. Mona had removed her scarf and the wind blew her hair forward when she faced him, surrounding her cheeks and framing her delicate features. The sight of her that way excited him and he knew he wanted her, but the thought of it was also intimidating.

"It's beautiful tonight," she said. "We have stars, the skyline, the Statue of Liberty. Very romantic, Detective."

"We public servants try to please, madam."

"And you do very nicely. Now if I could only get you to become more talkative and tell me about yourself."

"There isn't very much more to tell." He raised his hand in a mock oath. "Honest."

"Whatever made you become a police officer? I'm sure you could have done anything you wanted." The amused look he had noted before had returned. He wished it had not.

"When you grow up in a slum you do whatever you can to get out." He had let the words fall heavily and it had removed the amused look from her face. He softened his next words. "It seemed to be the best thing to do. When I got out of the navy I worked for a labor leader as a bodyguard for a while, then I joined the Fire Department. After a year I transferred to the Police Department. My wife talked me into it. She thought the Fire Department was too dangerous." He laughed to himself. "Anyway, three years later I was a detective and I've been doing that ever since. I like the work."

100

Mona, disturbed by the faux pas she had fallen into, flipped her head affectedly. "And according to Mr. Winchell no one does it better."

"Walter exaggerates. He's a good friend and he tries to make me look good."

She turned her head back to him abruptly. "I don't believe that for a moment. I believe everything I read in the newspapers." She turned her attention back to the river, watching it and thinking. "John," she said finally, "what about your wife? You mentioned her. Are you still married?"

"Yes, I am. Does that bother you?" He felt a sudden sense of uneasiness.

"No. Not at all. I was just curious." She made the statement emphatically, still watching the river.

"My wife lives in Queens. I live here," he explained.

"Do you see her often?" The question was asked coldly, as though it didn't matter.

"Every few weeks. But it's not really to see her. I have a seven-year-old daughter, Suzy. I go out there to see that she's okay and to make sure they have money. In fact, I was planning to go out there tomorrow." He watched her carefully to see what reaction his words would evoke. There was none.

Mona turned back to him. "Don't you miss your daughter? Seven is a marvelous age for little girls."

Broderick was confused for a moment. He hadn't thought about missing his child for several years, although he knew he had. Especially at first. "Yeah, I guess I do. But she really doesn't like me very much. You see her mother has told her a lot of stuff that has sort of turned her against me." He lied and he felt a twinge of guilt in doing so, but it seemed better that way. "But I take care of her. She goes to a good private school and I make sure she doesn't want for anything. But things are so bad between my wife and me that I just don't go out there much anymore."

"Have you thought about a divorce."

"She's Catholic and she won't do that. Says she can't." Broderick felt suddenly uncomfortable and he knew he should change the subject. "What about you?" he said. "The head waiter at the restaurant called you Mrs. D'Arcy. You're married too?"

Mona smiled, then started to laugh. You're very good, Mr. Broderick, she thought. Very good at maneuvering out of tight corners. "No," she said. "Stuart, my ex-husband, and I have been divorced for over a year. We were married shortly after I graduated from college. Our families had been friendly for years, still are in fact, and it seemed to be the thing to do at the time. But after four years we both realized it had been a mistake, so we corrected it. But we're still friends and I kept his name because I liked it better than Mona Eatkins. Anyway, he married again and I often see him and his new wife socially. It seems odd, but I like him much more now that he's married to someone else. Since the divorce we've both continued to move in the same circle of friends, but they've begun to become boring lately." She offered him her coy look again. "Perhaps that's why I find you so attractive. You're not like any of them."

"And so now you're the gay divorcée," he said. It was his turn to look amused.

She noted the fact to herself. "Exactly." She raised her empty wine glass. "And may the gay divorcée have some more illegal champagne, Detective?"

"Certainly. The empty bottle will be enough evidence for the arrest." He poured them each champagne and they stood side by side watching the river slide past.

They were quiet for several minutes before Mona spoke. "This is beautiful, John, truly beautiful. I'm glad you thought of it. It's like a painting, or perhaps some terribly trite and romantic Mary Pickford movie."

He took her arm and turned her to him. "You're much more beautiful than she is," he said.

She raised her head and drew closer to him. He kissed her, hesitantly at first, but feeling her move against him the hesitancy disappeared. When their lips parted he looked into her face and saw only desire. He brought her to him again and she slipped her arms up around his neck and pressed her tongue against his lips, forcing his mouth to part and accept it. He continued to hold her and he could feel the excitement growing within him. He looked past her.

"The ferry's almost back at the slip," he said.

She smiled. "Good. Let's go back to my apartment, darling."

"Are you propositioning me, lady?"

"I certainly am. Do you mind?"

"Not at all."

There was a look that seemed almost like triumph in her eyes and he wondered about it.

CHAPTER THIRTEEN

THE OPULENCE OF MONA D'ARCY'S FIFTH AVENUE apartment had struck him immediately. No attempt had been made to hide the obvious wealth, only to subdue it. They had arrived at eleven o'clock and had been greeted at the door by a middle-aged maid. She had looked at him for only a moment and had seemed surprised, and after being assured that nothing would be required of her had retreated discreetly to her quarters off the kitchen. Mona had noticed the concern on his face and she had laughed and teased him, explaining that the presence of servants had to be taken for granted, much like furniture. He would have to get used to that, she had said.

But the idea had still made him uncomfortable, not only the maid's presence but also that she was not considered worthy of notice. Her background was probably like his own and for a moment he had wondered if people also thought of him that way.

Mona had offered him a brandy but he had refused. The wine they had, both at dinner and aboard the ferry, had already begun to affect him. He had never gotten used to liquor. The smell of it always evoked memories of his father, his heavyset body reeling down the street or sprawled across the kitchen table in the morning, his face next to a pool of dried vomit, his voice shouting, always shouting. *Dirty little bastard, I'll teach you to fight in the street.* It had taken years for him to learn to deal with it.

She poured herself a brandy and then a second one and he had found himself trying to remember how much liquor she had had that evening and he had decided that she drank a great deal. But everyone drank a great deal now, he had seen that. It had become expected, because it was prohibited, more so, he had been told, than it had been before, a part of the way things now were.

They had sat on a large, heavily cushioned sofa, one of two placed on each side of a carved wooden mantel, and they had talked for over an hour. She had spoken about the parties she attended, almost daily it seemed, and had wondered aloud why they had not met before. He had explained, uneasily, that he had never been part of that world and she had seemed surprised that he had said it. But he would be, she had insisted and had rambled on about the importance of meeting people who had influence. It was much like his association with the mayor, she had said, only on a personal level. But the idea had disturbed him. He had never felt comfortable with Jimmy Walker. It was something he had forced himself to do, partly out of admiration but primarily because it had been necessary to survive the pettiness of the Police Department. The idea of making it a daily part of his life was something he had never considered and he had found himself wishing she would not speak about it. They had returned to her apartment to make love, there had been no question about that, at least for him. But it had not happened and he had begun to wonder if she had changed her mind. He had retraced the evening, searching for some hint that she had. There could be no question she had decided to spend the evening with him even before he had approached her. She had been direct about it, more so than any woman he had known. She had an incredible presence about her, every movement showed it. The waiter at dinner had seen it. He had also seen the power that went with it and he had wilted. It was the same power he himself had seen so often among the wealthy, the one thing he had most envied about them, even more than their money. And it was something that was also part of her. But then there had been the confrontation with Amberg. Perhaps she had seen the fear that had gripped him then. She had asked whether he had been frightened, but he had covered that well and later she had made a point of praising him. But women of her class were taught to be charming, perhaps they were even born with that talent. It was something he had thought about, wondered about. Perhaps that had been the reason for her seeming interest in his work, a way to make him feel at ease with her. The thought of that had made him nervous, far more than he had expected, and he had found himself thinking about Tex Rickard's warning. But then there had been the ferry, the way she had reacted to him. There had been nothing false about that. She had wanted him and she had expressed it as blatantly as she had when she asked him to have dinner with her. But still they had just sat there talking.

He had reached out for her abruptly, clumsily, perhaps out of frustration

104

or the knowledge that if he did not he would not be able to do so later. But she had come to him easily, passionately, and a strange mixture of excitement and fear had gripped him, something he knew he had felt before but had not been able to place at the moment. She had whispered to him, asking him to make love to her, and had taken his hand and led him to the bedroom. He had been surprised at the ease with which she had undressed, slowly, casually, with no sense of nervousness or shame. She had stood before him in the soft light of the bedroom, her body smooth and firm, and she had taken his hands and placed them on her hips, moving them slowly toward her breasts, her breath shuddering with pleasure. They had remained there fondling each other until his own excitement had become obvious and she had looked at him with pleasure and drawn him to the bed. But he had been awkward and slow and the erection that he had fought to control had disappeared when it was finally needed and he had struggled to perform and he had failed.

They lay naked next to each other, a silk sheet draped across their bodies. Mona's head was resting against his shoulder and she was breathing quietly. He stared at the ceiling, the sense of failure overpowering. He began to speak but stopped and stroked her shoulder with his hand.

"Yes, darling?" She whispered the words and slowly began to stroke his chest with her fingers.

"It was the liquor. I'm not used to it."

She looked up at him but he avoided her eyes.

"Liquor doesn't last forever and I want you to stay here with me tonight." She began kissing his chest slowly, moving her tongue between her lips.

He could feel her hand sliding gently along his stomach almost imperceptibly, straying lower and then rising again. She lifted herself, looking down at him, her hand slowly moving to the inner portion of his thigh.

"Your body feels so wonderfully strong," she said, lowering her mouth to his as her fingers wrapped themselves deliberately around his penis. She pressed her mouth violently against his, forcing her tongue deep inside, her hand beginning to move with equal force. She moved her mouth about his face, kissing him with her lips and tongue, then down to his neck and shoulders. "John, tell me about Crowley again. Tell me." Her breath was coming fast and she could feel him growing in her hand.

"What do you mean?" He was breathing hard, feeling her move her body from side to side, rubbing her breasts back and forth against his chest.

"Just tell me about it. Like you did before. About after you caught him. Tell me about it. Tell me what happened."

His body was moving with the motion of her hand and he felt as though he would explode at any moment.

"You mean when I hit him?"

"Yes, John, yes. Tell me about it. Tell me how it felt." Her body was twisting against him and the throbbing between her fingers felt maddening.

105

He turned her quickly, violently, on her back and she felt his body move on top of her, his breath coming in heavy spasms.

"I hit him and I kept hitting him and it felt better each time. The harder I hit him the better it felt." He pressed into her with a force that moved her up along the bed. She groaned beneath his weight.

"Oh, yes, John, it does. Harder, John, harder. Keep telling me, keep telling me."

CHAPTER FOURTEEN

THE CAR MOVED SLOWLY THROUGH THE LATE SUNDAY morning traffic that jammed Northern Boulevard, trapped in the slow, methodic pace of the outer city until it reached Corona where the buildings finally began to slide away, yielding to open farmland and the occasional clusters of newly built homes. She had wanted a house in the eastern reaches of Queens because of the openness, something away from the tightly packed neighborhoods closer to Manhattan that were all too similar to the west side tenements of their childhood; something she had insisted their daughter would never know. He had tried at first, God knows how he had tried. But they had grown apart long before then and there had been nothing he could do about it.

He tried not to think about it, not because it disturbed him, but because it jarred the feelings now inside him. He had left Mona's apartment at ten-thirty. They had made love again that morning, a slow, exploring kind of love-making that had shocked him to a point of passion he had never known before. There was a lust in her that was all-consuming, transferable, and yet proper because it was done with an abandon that made it so. He had told her that he had never been with anyone like her and she had looked at him, her face soft, almost grateful, and had told him that there was nothing about sex that she did not enjoy and the thought of her saying it now and the still fresh memory of her body moving against his sent a deep satisfying chill through him.

They had eaten breakfast together at a small, glass-topped table on the terrace and the middle-aged maid, who had become Rita in the brashness of the morning, had served them with no obvious concern that he had spent the night. It was clear there had been others but it did not seem to matter and there had been easy, laughing conversation between them until she had spoken again about Amberg.

Amberg. He wished he could forget about him, about the confrontation. If he could just put him out of his mind, but he knew that would be dangerous. He had to find a way to nail him but to do that he had to wait for a mistake, an excuse, a reason that would stand up. It was crazy to have an animal like that on the street and it was even crazier not to be able to do something about it, to have to wait for something to happen before you did anything. And if it happened to you that was tough, because that was the way the bullshit system worked. But at least Garfoli was off his back, for now anyway.

When the car reached Bayside, the traffic had all but disappeared. Off to his left a man and three young boys worked in a field, a farmer and his sons probably, working even on a Sunday morning to harvest the potatoes and onions that the farms in Queens were known for. He turned into the street where her house was located, *their* house, and he noted how nothing had changed in the four weeks since he had been there, the same flower gardens in front of the same modest wood-framed houses each spaced about an acre apart, sitting quietly across from a large but unplanted field, the openness she had always wanted—her "nest" she had called it. Her nest and her Church, the only things she really needed.

The car pulled up to the gravel driveway and he could see his daughter bouncing a rubber ball against the front steps. She turned and looked at him as the car entered the driveway but she did not return his smile. She turned and sat down on the stoop, forgetting to brush it first as her mother always told her to when she was wearing school clothes or, as she was now, the light blue dress that she had probably worn earlier to Mass.

She was looking down, concentrating on the ball that moved from one small hand to the other as he approached.

"Hi, Suzy." He leaned down and kissed the top of her head. "What are you doing?"

"Nothing, Daddy."

She continued to look at the ball and a feeling of discomfort moved inside him. He changed the position of his feet.

"You could act happy to see your old man," he said.

"I'm happy to see you, Daddy." She turned her face up to him and gave him a weak smile, but only with her mouth.

She had a thin, delicate face that reminded him of his wife's many years

108

ago. He loved her very much and it was a feeling that was very strong now and he wanted to pick her up and squeeze her, but he found he could not and instead he ran his hand against her soft brown hair.

"I know you are, honey," he said. "Where's your mother?"

The child looked at the ball again and began twisting it in her hands. "She's out back working in the garden." She paused for a moment, thinking. "How long are you going to stay this time?" she asked.

Broderick took a deep breath. "I'm due back on the job tomorrow morning, so I thought maybe we could do something together. Is there anything you'd like to do, anything special, I mean?"

"Could we go for a ride in your car? All of us, I mean?" She looked up at him. Her voice had been hesitant when she asked and that same emotion was now in her eyes.

He knelt down beside her. "You like my car, don't you?"

She nodded her head, a bit embarrassed but smiling genuinely for the first time. "It's pretty. Mommy said it's a Cadillac and that it's expensive. Is it?"

"Yeah, but I got a good deal on it, so it didn't cost me very much." He smiled at her. "I saw you playing ball when I came up. You're getting pretty good."

"There aren't too many kids to play with here, so I practice a lot," she said.

He stood, still looking at her. "Look, I'll go see your mother and then we'll go for a ride, okay?"

Suzy nodded her head, still concentrating on the ball. "She's out back," she said again. He turned to start up the steps but Suzy's voice stopped him. "Why can't you come home at night, or at least every weekend?"

He knelt down beside her again. "It's the job, honey. It's like I told you before, when you're a detective you have to work crazy hours and a lot on weekends. It's what I have to do to keep my job."

"Mommy doesn't think you want to come home." She was not looking at him and her cheeks had turned pink.

He stroked her head again. "That's not true, Suzy." His voice was soft, almost hoarse. "Look, don't I take care of you both? Don't you go to that nice school? It's just that I have all these things I have to do. But I always take care of you, don't I?"

"Mommy says we don't have enough money."

He stiffened slightly but his voice remained calm. "Listen, I give you all the money I can. A detective doesn't make that much. I'm just a cop earning a salary. But I got you this house and everything. And you're not starving, are you?"

Suzy reached out and put her arms along the sides of his chest and pulled herself to him and he could see there were tears forming in her eyes. "No, Daddy," she said, holding on to him.

He stroked her head softly. "Okay then. Look I have to see your mother

109

but I'll be back in a little while and we'll go for that ride." He stood, still looking at her. Her small hands seemed to be trembling and he looked away from her quickly and started up the steps.

Inside, the front room was what it always was, neat, clean, and well ordered with hand-crocheted doilies on the arms of the heavy Victorian chairs and sofa. He walked on through the dining room and kitchen and out the rear door. Maggie was kneeling in a large vegetable garden, between rows of tomato plants, picking the last of the summer's growth. When the screen door slammed behind him she looked up, then wiped her brow with her apron and quickly adjusted a strand of hair that had fallen across her forehead.

"Hello, John. I didn't expect you to come out this weekend." She spoke the words flatly, without anger, but he knew the anger was there.

"I had a chance to get away so I thought I'd see how you and Suzy were doing."

"For a moment I thought it might be Father's Day," she said.

He didn't respond immediately but walked across the grass to the garden. She had returned to her tomatoes. "Very funny, Maggie. I just saw the kid on the front porch and I see you've been doing your usual thing, telling her what a bastard her old man is."

Maggie looked up at him, a tired sadness on her face. "Suzy's not a baby, John. She's seven. She can tell when her father has no interest in living with his family. I don't have to tell her anything."

"Then what's all this crap about not having enough money? That's a helluva thing to hear from your own kid."

Maggie smiled, then shook her head. "But it's true, John. She knows when we don't have enough money to get things. I can't hide that from her."

"Yeah, I bet." He turned his back to her. "You have any coffee on the stove?"

"Yes. But it's probably cold. I can make a fresh pot."

"Never mind." He walked across the back yard and entered the kitchen. He opened the top of the coffeepot and looked inside, then lit the gas burner beneath it with a match. Maggie came in as he was seating himself at the kitchen table and placed a basket of tomatoes on the counter across from him. The kitchen was large but simply furnished. It had the same table and chairs and battered wooden icebox they had brought with them from their small Manhattan apartment and had never replaced. Typical shanty Irish shit, he thought. There was the stale smell of previously cooked food, probably something strong that had lingered on because she hadn't opened the windows. Cabbage or onions or something like that. He looked across at her. Her back was to him and her spreading hips and heavy buttocks filled the worn housedress she was wearing. He got up and poured himself some coffee.

110

"What would you like for dinner, John? I haven't started it yet and I can make anything you want, within limits of course."

He didn't look at her. He didn't want to. "Anything you have. I don't care."

"I was going to make a roast. Is that all right?" She asked the question as if asking something else.

He ignored the implied question. "Sure. That's fine." He went back to the table and watched her as she busied herself about the kitchen, taking the necessary food from the battered icebox and beginning to prepare dinner.

They were quiet for a long time and he had poured himself a second cup of coffee when she finally turned and spoke to him.

"It's been four weeks since you've been home, John. What was the reason this time?" The question was not asked in anger. It had been building inside her and it was something she had to get out.

"I've been busy. I've been putting in a lot of extra time. If you ever read the papers you'd know that."

"I heard about some of it on the radio," she said. The way he had mentioned the newspapers had hurt her but her voice remained calm. "I wish you'd be more careful. But I also wish you'd come home at night like other men. Your daughter needs you around here and I'm getting tired of explaining to the neighbors why you're never home."

"You don't have to tell them anything. It's none of their business anyway." He wasn't looking at her. He wanted to avoid her eyes, the mournful look he knew they would now hold, like some stupid puppy that had just been kicked by its master. She could produce more guilt per look than any woman he knew.

She walked to the table and sat across from him, forcing him to face her. "That's easy for you to say, John. You don't have to deal with the problem."

He looked straight into her face, his jaw set, his eyes angry. "You can always get a divorce, you know." He spoke the words harshly and he could see the faint note of pain come into her eyes. Fuck yourself, he thought.

"That's the only solution you ever offer," she said. "And you know it's something I won't do, that I can't do. We also need money, John. We just can't get by with what you give us."

He slapped his hand on the table. "Will you knock it off? I give you everything I can. I only make four grand a year, I'm not some goddamned millionaire—and I keep almost nothing for myself. I send the kid to that fancy Catholic school you picked out for her and I keep up this stinking house. What else do you want from me?"

The child had entered the room off to their left and stood there with a puzzled, frightened look on her face. "I don't have to go to that school, Daddy. I don't, really."

111

He turned his head sharply and saw her standing there and a sickening feeling spread through his stomach. "Oh, honey. I want you to go to that school." He spoke the words softly, imploringly. "I don't want you to go to some crummy school with all these farmers out here. What we were talking about hasn't got anything to do with your school. I was just mad and I shouldn't of said that. Now go outside and play while I talk to your mother."

The child turned and walked back through the house. He waited until he heard the front door close behind her, then glared at his wife. "You see what I mean. You have to start all this crap and then the kid walks in and hears it all. That's really great."

"She's no fool, John. She knows we don't have enough money. She knows you live in a hotel and she can see the Cadillac you drive around in and the fancy suits you always have on. What do you want me to tell her, that we're poor? That we can't afford to live decently?"

Broderick got out of the chair and walked to the stove, keeping his back to her. "I have told you a dozen times, the car I got from a guy I did a favor for and the suits don't cost me a dime. I get them from a guy in my area who likes to do favors for cops. I've got a job where I have to spend a lot of time with the mayor and other city officials and I can't walk around looking like a bum."

"John, I'm not denying you those things. Just get us something too. The little money I get only gives me enough to buy material to make Suzy's clothes after all the other bills are paid. I haven't had a new dress in years. I don't even have a decent thing to wear to church on Sunday."

"So don't go to church. It's all bullshit anyway." He was speaking like an exhausted man now and his hands were braced on the stove, his shoulders slouched forward.

"That's a wonderful solution, John. What else would you like me not to do, eat?"

He turned to her, his face taking on a look of complete disgust. "You don't look like you're starving. In fact from the looks of you a little less food wouldn't do you any harm."

Maggie's face radiated anger now, her eyes held all the pent-up rage, the near hatred she had been fighting to suppress. "You're a rotten man, John. The only thing you care about is yourself. You don't even care about your child—your own daughter—and she knows it. And what do you think that's doing to her? *What?*" She shouted the final word, hurling it at him like a weapon she hoped would smash his body.

He sneered at her. "Living with you is doing enough to her. More than I could ever do, but there's nothing I can do about that."

She laughed, a breathless, sarcastic laugh. "What is it, John? Another woman, a lot of other women?"

"Shut your mouth." He leaned across the table and jabbed his finger

112

toward her face, causing her to jerk her head back. "I don't want the kid to hear you talking like that."

She seemed amused by his concern and she spoke slowly in a soft, almost exaggerated voice. "Then the least you could do is think up a good lie to tell us. Why are you doing this to us? I've tried to be a good wife to you. I stay here and I keep your home, even if you don't come to it. I take care of your child. She certainly doesn't do anything to you. You don't even telephone her. Why don't you even call? Why don't you even think enough of us to make up a lie we can believe?"

"This is why I don't come home. I'm out on the streets breaking my ass and then I'm supposed to come home to this shit? And you want me to come home to this every night? You gotta be out of your mind."

Maggie laughed. "You're risking your life? What for, John? Certainly not for me. Not for Susan. You do it for yourself, so you can be the big shot you want to be, the big Johnny Broderick with his name in all the newspapers, out having dinner with the mayor, out with his friends being the big, important man. Whether it's your work, or your women, or your friends, it doesn't matter. It's all you want. It's all you ever wanted and it's all for you. None of it's for us. Just you, you, you." Her struggle to remain calm had passed and her anger was mounting and she seemed on the verge of hysteria. She took a deep breath, fighting for control. "John, I want things the way they were. I don't want this. I want what we had when we were first married."

He stepped back from the table and leaned against the stove. He was quiet for several seconds. "What we had?" he said softly. "We had nothing. I never had anything and you never had anything. We both came from the same crummy neighborhood. All we ever had was a chance to get away from it and we did that together."

"There was more." She paused, then added, "Once." The lock of hair had fallen across her forehead again and she brushed it back. "And now we have a home in a decent neighborhood and a lovely daughter who needs a whole family. You've got a good job. It's more than our parents ever had and it could be a lot if we lived like a family."

Broderick was exhausted, tired of fighting with her. "I live the way I have to live. I can't change that."

Her voice became sharp. "John, I want you here, or I want you out. I mean it, John."

He stared at her. His face was cold, expressionless. "You got it," he said, turning abruptly and starting for the door.

"At least leave us some money, damn it. Just so we can eat next week," she shouted.

He reached into his pocket and withdrew a roll of bills, peeled off three twenties, and dropped them on the kitchen table. "Here's sixty bucks. I'll send some more out next week." He turned and walked through the dining

113

room. Maggie watched him until he turned into the living room out of sight and then she listened until the front door closed behind him. She stared down at the table for a moment, tears filling her eyes, then lowered her head into her arms and began to sob.

Outside, Broderick stood on the front porch, watching his daughter bounce a ball absentmindedly on the cement walk that led to the driveway. At the sound of his steps on the stairs she turned abruptly, her eyes questioning, but knowing.

"Are we going for our ride now?" she said.

He took a deep breath, then walked to her, bending down in front of her and placing both hands on her shoulders. "I have to go back to the city now," he said, looking down, away from the disappointment that flashed into her eyes.

"Aren't you going to stay for dinner?" she asked.

"I can't, honey. I have to get back. It's business. Something just came up, something I couldn't get out of. But listen"—he lifted her chin, which had begun to droop—"next time I'll stay longer and maybe we can drive to a beach someplace. You'd like that, wouldn't you?"

She nodded her head and he wanted to reach out and squeeze her again. He ran his hand along her cheek, then stood and reached into his pocket. He handed her a five-dollar bill. "Here," he said. "You have your mother buy you something nice. Something pretty that you can wear for me next time." He placed the money in her small palm and closed her fingers over it. "Now give Daddy a kiss," he said, leaning down next to her. She kissed him, squeezing his neck hard. He stroked her head again, then walked quickly to the car. He knew he had to get away from this place.

CHAPTER FIFTEEN

NORA ROSS CAME THROUGH THE DOOR OF MONA D'Arcy's apartment with the dramatic sense of elegance that surrounded everything she did. From the moment her foot touched the parquet floor in the small foyer her affected voice prattled on in near endless chatter. There was something about her that had always amused Mona and she seemed genuinely pleased to see her and promptly offered a drink. Nora checked the gold, brooch-type watch affixed to her dress and noted that it was well past noon and suggested martinis, provided Mona had imported gin.

"I simply cannot abide the bilge they're producing locally these days," she said.

They sat sipping their drinks, chatting about friends and the parties they planned to attend later in the week. Nora watched her closely as they spoke, expectantly, almost like some predator watching a hole in the ground hoping for something desirable to emerge. She was not a beautiful woman. Her nose was a bit too large and she was slightly underweight but there was a sense of style about her that made her seem attractive.

She stood abruptly and walked to the mantel, then turned dramatically. "You simply are not going to tell me, are you?" she said.

"Tell you what?" Mona leaned back in her chair, smiling, then sipped her martini slowly.

"About the man you left the Bainbridges' with yesterday, of course," she said.

"I wondered how long it would take for you to get around to that, dear. That *is* the reason you came, isn't it?"

"Of course it is, darling. You don't think I'd be up this early on a Sunday otherwise, do you?"

Mona laughed. "Have I ever told you that you're a terribly"—she paused—"inquisitive person?" She had almost said *nosy* but had caught herself.

Nora sniffed. "I wouldn't have it any other way. Now, for heaven's sake, *tell* me."

Mona sipped her drink again. "He's a police detective named John Broderick," she said.

"I know *who* he is, darling. Give me credit for that much. Tell me *about* him." Nora moved back to her chair and sat on its edge, waiting.

Mona walked to the liquor table. "Would you care for another?" she asked.

Nora sighed. "Yes, of course." She tilted her large nose upward, almost as though she were displaying it.

Mona refilled their glasses and returned to the sofa across from her. "We went to that lovely little French restaurant, Le Cheval Noire. You know it, I'm sure. And"—she paused again—"had a marvelous dinner."

"Darling, if you tell me about the quality of the escargot I'll simply scream."

Mona laughed again. "Then we went for a ride on the Staten Island ferry and came back here for a drink."

"The Staten Island ferry. How incredibly trite." There was an incredulous sound to her voice that made Mona laugh again. "And then?" she said with a sigh.

"Dear, you wouldn't want me to talk about personal matters, would you?"

"Of course I would. Tell me, how was he?"

"Do you mean quantitatively or qualitatively?"

"Both, damn it. Tell me all about it."

"You're not just inquisitive. You're an absolute voyeur."

"Precisely. Now go on." Nora had moved up on the edge of her chair and had no intention of moving before receiving specifics.

"He was quite good, actually." She waited, watching Nora's reaction, smiling to herself as she noted her eyebrows rise slightly. "Even better this morning." She paused again. "Actually I think he was a bit intimidated at first. I don't think he's quite used to women like us. But he overcame it rather nicely. Is that quite enough, dear?"

"Of course it isn't." Nora leaned back in her chair, partially satisfied but

116

still expectant. "He's a brute of a man," she said. There was a trace of a smile on her lips. "Tell me. Is he a brute of a man all over?"

Mona fought to suppress a smile. "Oh, we've gotten to the quantitative part, I see."

"Exactly."

"Do you want it in precise measurements or will a general description suffice?" She laughed, unable to contain herself any more. "I assure you he was not disappointing in *any* aspects." She waited, then added, "Far from it."

Nora smiled, pleased with her success. "Where do you find these creatures?" she said. "Although this *is* somewhat of a departure from the norm. A policeman. Really, dear, that is a bit much."

"I suppose it would be better if it were one of those boring little boys in our set who get passed about like tea biscuits." She stood and walked back to the liquor table. "I simply can't stand them anymore." There was no amusement in her final words.

Nora leaned forward in her chair. "You're *not* taking this one seriously, are you?"

A feeling of discomfort rose in Mona that she was forced to acknowledge but then dismissed quickly. "Of course not. I'm beyond taking any man seriously." She turned to face Nora. "That's not what they're for, darling."

They both laughed and then decided that another martini was in order. Nora walked back to the mantel, then turned, placing her back against it. "Perhaps you've discovered something new," she said. "I'll have to try it and find out. Perhaps I'll begin riding on trolley cars and find some magnificent young conductor with large brutish shoulders and whatever."

They both laughed again but Mona again felt a twinge of concern. The doorbell rang and the feeling disappeared.

A moment later Rita opened the door and Broderick stepped into the foyer, handing her his hat.

Mona got up and moved quickly toward him. "John, darling. But I thought you were going out"—she paused—"to the country."

Broderick looked into the living room and saw Nora by the mantel. "I did. I came back early." He looked at Nora again. "I should have called. If I'm interrupting you, I can call you later."

"Don't be silly." Mona took his arm and ushered him into the living room. "I'd like you to meet a dear friend, Nora Ross."

The introductions were made and Broderick noticed that this Ross woman seemed to be sizing him up, appraising him, and it made him feel uncomfortable. Then she announced that she had to leave and he felt an inward relief as soon as the words were spoken.

"But do you really have to?" Mona said.

117

"Oh, yes I must," Nora said, smiling at Mona. "I promised myself I'd take a ride on a trolley car this afternoon. I'm told you meet the most interesting people there."

There was a clever little smile on her face as she spoke and Broderick noticed that Mona seemed to be holding back a smile as well.

Nora extended her hand. "So sorry I have to run, Mr. Broderick. But I'm sure we'll see more of each other."

She hurried off with a flourish, turning again to Mona at the door. "I'll call you"—she paused deliberately—"tomorrow, I think, darling," And then she was gone.

Broderick turned to Mona. "What the hell was that trolley car business?"

"I have no idea, darling," Mona said. "She's a very strange lady. Now tell me about your visit." She guided him to the sofa and seated herself next to him. "Was it unpleasant?"

He nodded pensively. "It turned into a war. So I left."

"And your daughter? Did you see her?"

"Yes, but I'm afraid it wasn't very good for her either," he said. "That woman has a way of turning everything into garbage. I think she enjoys doing it." He turned to Mona. "I'm not going to get involved in that again. Next time I'll bring the kid into the city."

"Will she let you? Your wife, I mean?" Mona took his hand in both of hers and held it gently.

"I'd like to see her try and stop me."

There was an inward rush of satisfaction. "That sounds like a wonderful idea," she said. "You could take her to all kinds of places that a little girl would just love. The parks, the zoo, all types of marvelous restaurants. I'm sure she'd be thrilled."

Broderick nodded his head almost mechanically. "Yeah, that would be a lot better. But let's not talk about it." He waited for a moment. "Look, about coming here like this, if I interrupted you or anything, I'm sorry."

"Don't be silly. I couldn't be more delighted that you're here." She leaned over and kissed him lightly on the lips. "And I want you to stay," she whispered. "We can have a quiet supper here and spend the evening together alone. I'll even give Rita the night off."

He laughed. "You could tell that bothered me, couldn't you?"

"It didn't bother you all that much, darling." She was smiling at him.

They had a supper of cold duck that Rita prepared before leaving and they sat sipping sherry and talking. Mona told him there would be a party at a friend's home Tuesday evening and asked him to go with her. There would be a number of important people there, she explained, people he should know and who could prove useful to him in the future.

118

"You can't be the roughest policeman in New York forever," she said. "You have to think somewhat about your future."

They were in bed making love by eight o'clock, a long passionate session of multiple orgasms for each. It was something she knew he needed after the frustrations and anger of the afternoon. And it was something she wanted very much, for the first time in several months. By ten o'clock Broderick was sleeping next to her, emotionally exhausted. His sleep was fitful at first, as though something terrible, perhaps even frightening, was preying on his mind. She stroked his shoulder softly, feeling the occasional spasms that intruded into his rest.

A vulnerable man, she thought, resting her head back against the pillow and staring up at the finely etched plaster that covered the ceiling. A large brute of a man but still vulnerable. And what, in heaven's name, is he doing here? A plaything, that's what you told Nora. And that's all he should be. But is he? When he walked through that door you were happy he had come. More than happy, you wanted him there, you were pleased he had fought with his wife and delighted when he said he wouldn't stay there again, that he would bring his daughter into the city, away from her. But that's madness. Can't you just see yourself as the wife, no, never the wife, but the mistress then of a police detective. How charming, holding quiet little cocktail parties for all the other detectives and their fat frumpy little wives or their coarse little girl friends. And what delightful conversations there would be about this criminal and that criminal. My God, Mona, you are losing your mind. You've already been abused by enough men.

She rolled over in bed and took a cigarette from a silver case on the night table, lit it, and remained on her side. Why couldn't he be something else and still be the way he is. There's a coarseness about him, but that's probably inbred in what he does. He can be taught. All men can be taught, they have to be. He could even be manipulated. But what for, what would be the purpose? Leave things as they are and enjoy them. Let it remain the way it was yesterday afternoon when you looked at him and said to yourself, yes, Mr. Broderick, you'll do very nicely, you're exactly what I need. Don't change things, just concentrate on that nice hard penis of his and use it and enjoy it. Enjoy the excitement of what he does, just enjoy it and leave everything else. . . .

A sharp, almost childlike cry came from him as he twisted in his sleep. She turned to him and stroked his shoulder and kissed his back lightly. "Hush, darling," she whispered. "Hush."

119

CHAPTER SIXTEEN

HIS FAT SERGEANT, HIS SECRETARY, STOOD IN FRONT of the desk waiting for a chance to speak. Garfoli looked at him and felt disgusted. The buttons on his uniform blouse were straining against the flesh beneath, fighting to hold in the results of his daily gorging on pasta, he thought.

"Will you please get a blouse that fits you? You look like some circus clown in that thing," the inspector snapped, absentmindedly brushing his own brass with his sleeve.

"Yes, sir." The sergeant shifted his feet nervously. There was a notebook in his hand and he put it behind his back as though he had decided it had been a mistake to bring it.

"What have you got there?" Garfoli asked.

"It's the notes I've been keeping on Broderick, Inspector. I was going to go over it with you, but if you're busy . . ."

"What have you got?" Garfoli shut him off abruptly, then watched as the sergeant began leafing through the book, licking his thumb before he turned each page. A disgusting habit, he thought. But fitting.

"Well, sir," the sergeant began, drawing himself up.

"Never mind the formalities. Just *tell* me." He was almost sorry now he had ever agreed to let him keep tabs on Broderick.

120

"On Friday he met Johnny Cordes, he's another detective assigned to the Industrial Squad, outside the Garden and then the two of them went in. They didn't pay, I mean, they just flashed their shields and walked right in. And he did roust a cheap hood named Vannie Higgins, but Higgins was roughing up an usher and Broderick only hit him once, so I guess you couldn't make nothin' outta that. Then later they went up to Mr. Rickard's office, the guy who runs the Garden, and they're there for a while and they leave." The sergeant took a deep breath. "Now the next day, that's Saturday, in the afternoon Broderick and Rickard met at the Garden again and then they went in Rickard's car to this big house on Sixty-second Street. There seemed to be a party going on. Well, Broderick, he stays there for a while and then he leaves with this rich-looking broad, I mean, lady, and they go to this real expensive French restaurant." He looked down at his notes, searching. "The Chevy Nower, or something like that.

"Well, they ate there and he paid the tab. I checked with the guy who runs the place afterward. He paused a moment, studying his notes. "Oh, he ran into a hood named Amberg and a buddy of his and he and two uniformed guys patted them down but nothing happened. It looked to me like he was just showing off for the lady. Then they go to the Staten Island ferry and they go across and they come back and there's a little kissing and stuff and then they go back to this woman's apartment. Her name's D'Arcy, Mona D'Arcy, and she lives in one of those flashy places on Fifth Avenue." A slight smirk appeared on the sergeant's face. "Well, he didn't leave that night. He stayed there until the morning and then drove out to see his old lady and his kid. Then he comes back there and he spends the whole night again."

Garfoli stared at him, his mouth open. "Did you stay out in front of that apartment all night, Saturday and Sunday?"

"No. I slipped the night doorman a deuce and then I checked with him the next morning. He never left on either night." The sergeant closed the notebook. He was smiling, obviously pleased with himself.

Garfoli leaned back in his chair and allowed his hands to fall loosely in his lap. "Is that it?" he asked.

"Yes, sir," the sergeant said, nodding his head.

Garfoli took a deep breath and was quiet for nearly a minute before speaking. "Well, you really got him, didn't you? He was probably moonlighting at the Garden and, of course, nobody in the department does that, do they? And you got him fucking some rich woman and we know that cops never fuck anybody except their wives, don't we? And you got him going to a party and paying his bill in a restaurant. So far the only thing he's done out of the ordinary is pay his fucking restaurant bill. Maybe we could suspend him for that. What do you think, Sergeant?"

The sergeant's face had paled and his lips moved for several seconds before the first words came out. "But, sir, I thought you wanted to know what he

121

was doing. I thought that maybe for spending the night with that woman, that maybe we could get him for co-co—"

"Cohabitation," Garfoli said.

"Yeah," the sergeant said hopefully.

"Do you really think he's not smart enough to have that woman say that she hired him to guard her apartment because she was afraid it was going to be robbed?" He raised his voice. "And do you really think that *I'm* stupid enough to drag some wealthy woman into a department trial involving shit like that?"

"No, sir."

"Then what were you thinking about?" Garfoli got out of his chair and began pacing his office. "I thought I explained to you I want to get him taking a bribe, knocking somebody around who he arrested, somebody small who hasn't done anything serious enough to deserve it. *That's* what I want."

"Well, he didn't do none of that, sir."

Garfoli turned and pointed his finger at the sergeant. "But he will. He will."

"Yes, sir, I know he will. And when he does I'll know it."

Garfoli sank back into his chair. "I wonder," he said. "I really wonder. But keep watching him. Just don't waste my time with nonsense." The sergeant turned to go but Garfoli stopped him. "No, maybe you better waste my time with everything. He might do something that you won't recognize and that I will."

"Yes, sir, everything."

The sergeant moved quickly out of the office and Garfoli sat at his desk rubbing his palm against his forehead. Jesus Christ, he thought. How do we ever catch anybody with morons like that on the force. But at least somebody was watching Broderick and that was the only way he was going to get caught. At least he had him lying low for a while and that was something. No new complaints had come in about him. He and his buddies in the Industrial Squad were staying in their own area. But that was only temporary. They were greedy men. He studied the brass on his tunic again, debating whether it was clean enough and decided it was, then began pacing again. He returned to his chair and lit a large cigar, taking care to be sure it was drawing properly. Maybe he should assign some other men, he thought. No, he decided. That would attract too much attention.

CHAPTER SEVENTEEN

MONA WAS SMILING TO HERSELF, INWARDLY PLEASED about what might lie ahead as he guided the Cadillac north along Madison Avenue. He had refused to tell her where they were going this evening, only that they had to be there by nine o'clock and that if she had enjoyed the Grebs-Flowers fight, she would enjoy this. He had warned it would be seedy and rough and had suggested she wear dark clothing, preferably something she wouldn't mind having soiled and the thought of it all, along with the mystery had only added to her excitement. It was one of his surprises, like their "sea voyage" on the Staten Island ferry and, without question, another glimpse at this world of his that she found so fascinating.

As the car continued north past the eighties and nineties and gradually moved into Harlem she began to glance at him nervously, and when it finally pulled to the curb at Lenox Avenue and One Hundred Forty-first Street her mouth had become a small circle of surprise.

"Here?" she asked.

He looked at her and grinned. "Trust me," he said.

She smiled weakly. "But where?"

He motioned his head toward the dingy front of a small sandwich shop and through the filthy plate glass window she could see that the counter was filled with poorly dressed black men of varying ages. The expression on her face showed the discomfort and distaste the idea of entering the greasy door held for her. He laughed.

"I'm not taking you to dinner there," he said. "The joint's a front. In the back room there's a cockfighting arena. That's where we're going. I'm sorry about the area, but the niggers control this action. It's an old southern thing that goes back to the slave days. My partner, Cordes, introduced me to it a few years back. Seems the Spanish are big on it too, especially in South America and the Islands. But you don't have to worry, not while you're with me. I don't like being around spooks either, but there'll be a lot of whites in there too. The guinea hoods like to bet on these fights."

"You can bet?" she said, her expression changing now, the excitement of the entire idea, the cockfight, the betting, now taking hold. "Is it legal?" she asked, almost giggling.

He raised a finger to his lips. "If you don't tell, I won't," he said.

The men seated at the counter looked at them as they walked through the front door, then quickly turned their eyes away, back to the greasy food that would offer less trouble than a white cop, and probable indigestion was far better than that. Up ahead a fat black man dressed in a flamboyant pin-striped suit and wide-brimmed hat waddled toward a rear door. When he reached it he glanced casually over his shoulder and saw Broderick moving toward him and immediately spun on his heels and started back down the narrow aisle. The fat man was only a step away when Broderick's left hand shot out and grabbed the knot of his bright yellow necktie, twisting it sharply until the black man's eyes bulged in his head.

"Fat Louis. Why you running away all of a sudden?" Broderick said, loosening his grip.

The fat man coughed as his breath returned, then smiled at Broderick, the single gold tooth set in the row of ivory glistening under the light. "I wasn't goin' no place, Johnny. I'm jus' movin' roun' seein' what's doin'. How you been?"

"None of your business," Broderick said, returning the smile. "You mean you weren't goin' back to watch the cockfight?"

"Cockfight? No kiddin'. They got cockfights here?"

Broderick began to twist the knot of the necktie again.

"Okay, Johnny. Okay, it's jus' dat I don't *need* no aggravation, if you knows what I mean."

"This isn't a raid, Louis. The lady and I are goin' back there as spectators. And I just bet you could help the lady pick out a few winners. Unless, of course, you're in a hurry to go someplace. But then I just might have to bust some of your numbers runners tomorrow." Broderick's smile was almost benevolent.

Louis returned it, then turned his gold tooth to Mona. "Beautiful lady, Fat Louis is about to make you a wealthy woman," he said.

124

The cockfight pit was circular, surrounded by a three-foot wooden wall both to protect the spectators and contain the birds. The diameter of the dirt-covered fighting area was ten feet and the walls that surrounded it were splattered with the dried blood of previous battles. Behind the wall chairs had been placed for the more honored spectators and behind them was a wide elevated platform with a railing, where the less respected aficionados could jostle each other for favored positions. The cocks were kept caged in a separate room and brought out two at a time by their handlers and paraded before the spectators so bets could be decided.

The birds were smaller than Mona had expected but she was fascinated by the aggressive darting movements of their heads, the way they would glare and crane their necks and strain against their handlers' grasp when another cock came into their line of vision.

"They seem to hate each other," she whispered to Broderick.

"They just love to fight. They're bred for it," he said.

The first fight featured two birds that were easily distinguishable, a white and a reddish brown. The handlers emerged from the rear room, their birds held firmly, the four-inch-long steel spurs that would later be attached to cocks' legs held in their own mouths.

"Why do they do that?" Mona asked. "Hold those strange-looking things in their mouths, I mean?"

"Those are the spurs that go on the birds' legs. That's how they fight, they kick at each other with the spurs. Their own aren't long enough and a fight would take too long without the artificial ones. They cut deeper—they're sharp as razors—and the loser bleeds more and weakens faster."

"Do the losers always die?" Mona asked.

Broderick smiled at her. "Usually, but not always. If a handler sees his bird has no chance and hasn't been hurt too bad he can pull his bird out. But usually it's too late anyway. They're tough little devils and even when they're hurt bad they fight like hell. Besides, if a handler pulls his bird out the people who bet on it could get mad."

"But why do they put the spurs in their mouths, it seems so disgusting?"

"That's the way the handlers let the betters know there's no poison or drugs on the spurs," Broderick explained.

"An if one of dem handlers starts noddin' off to sleep all of a sudden, he gonna wake up with a part of hisself missin'," Fat Louis added.

Mona giggled at the thought of which "part" Fat Louis was undoubtedly referring to and then asked him which bird she should bet on.

"You bets the brown bird, beautiful lady. You in Harlem now an dat poor white sucker don't have no chance at all."

Mona looked at Broderick, raising her eyebrows.

"Bet like Fat Louis says," he advised. "He knows his birds." He leaned toward her and whispered. "He'll also know which fights are deliberate mis-

125

matches, which birds are being tossed in to be killed off because they were hurt too bad the last time out to ever be any good again."

"Why would they do that?" Mona whispered.

"Those birds are expensive, especially the good ones with good breeding lines, so the owner has some friend of his bet against his hurt bird and he can win enough to replace him in his stable."

"Isn't there anything that's completely honest anymore?" she whispered.

"Of course not. It wouldn't be any fun if things were honest." He winked at her. "Besides, then I'd be out of work, wouldn't I?"

Behind them raucous shouting of last minute bets filled the air as the two handlers poked their birds at each other, raising the fighting spirit of each to a fever pitch. Mona leaned forward, her hands against the protective wall, her eyes riveted on the two birds. Broderick reached out and took her arm.

"Lean back a little," he said.

She did but was forward again as the birds were released, screeching and flailing at each other with wings, beaks, and spurs. Her head jolted back and her hand moved quickly to her face and as as she withdrew it she saw the blood staining her fingers and she was suddenly pale.

"It's from the birds," Broderick said quickly. "That's why I told you to stay back and it's why I told you to wear clothes you didn't care about."

She placed her hand on her breast, feeling her heart pound as he wiped her face with his handkerchief.

"For a moment I thought I'd been cut," she said.

"Just chicken blood," he said, smiling at her. "Now you've been initiated."

She laughed, partially at herself and partially in relief, then looked back into the pit, sitting well back in her chair now. The breast of the white bird, the one she had bet against, was stained red and it seemed to be moving more slowly, it's head beginning to sag almost imperceptibly. Mona leaned forward again and blood splattered against the sleeve of her dress but she remained.

"It's winning," she said, bouncing in her seat. "The brown one is winning. Get him, get him."

Within seconds the white cock began to sag to its right side, its right leg no longer functioning, its right wing scraping against the dirt, trying vainly to keep itself upright. Blood now dripped from the beak, adding to the already soaked white feathers on its breast. The brown bird strutted closer, pecking occasionally, almost as though trying to decide if another blow from its spur was needed. The handler of the white bird moved in and pulled the dying cock from the fight.

"We won," Mona said, clapping her hands like a child who had just found victory in her first game of tag.

The handler of the white bird held it by its feet and carried it off, the battered cock's wings fluttering in the final throes of death as its brown killer strutted about the pit almost seeming to acknowledge the approving shouts that engulfed it.

Mona's gaze was fixed on the brown cock and she smiled and applauded it politely. "He was wonderful, wasn't he?" she said, her eyes remaining on the bird. "Look at how he walks," she said, looking at Broderick now. "I don't think I ever really understood what the word 'cocky' meant until now, not completely anyway. He walks like you do," she said. There was a smile on her lips as she said it and her eyes were warm.

There were nine other fights and Fat Louis offered three more suggestions, all of which were winners. The remaining six contests left Broderick and Mona to their own resources and only two proved to be the right choices. Even so, Mona's excitement seemed to mount with each fight and even the oppressiveness of the humid, airless room, the growing stench of blood and feathers did not lessen it.

It was past eleven when they stepped back through the door and into the luncheonette, the pervasive smell of the greasy food filling their nostrils. Outside on the street the air seemed cool and fresh and Mona clung to his arm and breathed in deeply.

"Oh, that was fun," she said. "Those cocks are just marvelous."

"How much money did you win?" he asked.

"About fifty dollars, how about you?"

"Nearly two hundred," he said.

Her eyes widened.

"I bet a little heavier than you did, but the same birds each time."

"My God, if I had only known about this when I was a little college girl. What a marvelous way it would have been to pick up extra pin money."

Broderick laughed to himself. Yeah, he thought, and those wouldn't have been the only cocks you would have run into if you trotted your little white ass up here alone.

Inside the car he suggested a stop at the Cotton Club. "It's just down the street," he said, "and Josephine Baker is playing there tonight, if you feel up to it."

"I would have loved to if I didn't smell and feel like a chicken coop," she said. "Do you mind if we just go back to my apartment?"

She moved close to him and pressed against his arm as he drove south. When the car halted for a traffic light at Ninetieth Street she reached up and kissed him, forcing her tongue deep into his mouth, her hand sliding to the inner portion of his thigh and moving upward, groping almost desperately.

"If you keep that up I'll never make it back to your apartment," he said.

"Don't make it back," she said, her mouth still against his, her hand feeling the suddenness of his swelling. "Just stop somewhere, please."

He turned the car into Eighty-ninth Street, not waiting for the light to

127

change, and pulled to the curb at the first darkened place he could find. He had been fearful earlier in the day, fearful because of his initial failure that first evening together. It had been the liquor he had told himself and it had not happened the next time. But still there had been doubts. Now there were none as he slid away from the steering wheel, feeling her move against him, her lips and tongue against his mouth as her hands pulled her panties from beneath her bloodstained dress.

He remained sitting and she mounted him that way, raising and lowering herself as she rocked back and forth in the same motion. Her first orgasm was almost instantaneous and no sooner had it ended than the second began and her mind, almost mesmerized by the shudder rising through her body, seemed to wander. She thought of the birds in the blood-spattered pit and of the penis pressing inside her and suddenly she was a young girl again, a young girl receiving her first riding lesson and for a moment she almost wished she had a riding crop in her hand.

CHAPTER EIGHTEEN

THE LITTLE MAN WAS BUSY INSIDE THE NEWSSTAND, opening the stacks of bound packages that held the bulldog editions of the city's major newspapers. He did not notice when the powerfully built man in the tuxedo arrived, nor even now as he stood at the counter watching him, the impression of a revolver showing only slightly under the lightweight summer fabric of his white dinner jacket. When he lifted a stack of papers and swung around to place them on the counter Danny saw the man for the first time; his jaw dropped open with surprise.

"Jesus," he said. "What are you all dressed up for? You going to a wedding or somethin'?"

Broderick grinned at him. "I'm going to a party. At least you didn't ask me if I was working as a waiter someplace. I got your message. You have something for me?"

"You bet I do, Johnny." Danny leaned across the counter in a gesture of unnecessary confidentiality. They were alone. "I know where Amberg is staying," he whispered. He watched a smile spread across Broderick's face. "He's staying at the Manhattan Hotel. Him and Moe Berg and his girl friend are staying together in a small suite. I don't know the room number but I know they're there. Two different guys checked on it for me." Danny returned the grin now.

"Good boy, Danny. Good boy. I owe you for this one." Broderick dug a hand into his pocket, but Danny lifted his hands, stopping him.

"You don't owe me nothin'. I saw that creep the other night and how he tried to make you look bad in front of that lady. And I got somethin' else for you too." He paused, noting Broderick's curiosity grow. "He's got himself two new guys. One's name is Carmichael, the other one I don't know. But they both just got out of stir and the story is that they're planning to pull something this week, some kind of heist. A friend of mine heard them talking at a speakeasy over on Ninth Avenue."

"You know what the job is?" Broderick leaned forward, then eased back as Danny shook his head.

"But it's gonna go down soon, that I know for sure," he said.

"That's good enough. That's beautiful, Danny. I'll be all over his ass starting tomorrow." He withdrew a twenty-dollar bill from his pocket as Danny waved his hands indicating he did not want it. "You take it or I'll hit you in the head," he said. "And you lay low. If that maniac finds out you tipped me off he'll come after you. You close up the stand and stay home for a couple of days. I'll pick up the tab for any business you lose."

"Johnny, he ain't gonna find nothin' out." He glanced quickly to each side.

"You do what I say." He pointed a finger at his nose. "I don't want anything to happen to you. If what you say is right it'll only be for a couple of days. Get somebody to take over the newsstand if you want, but I don't want to see you here, okay?"

"Okay, okay." Danny tried to look annoyed by the request but his pleasure over Broderick's concern showed in his eyes. "So tell me about the party," he said. "You goin' with that lady you was here with."

"That's right. I'm taking your girl friend out. You mind?" He watched Danny blush. "We're going to her uncle's house on Sutton Place. The old boy owns a hat factory in Brooklyn. You didn't know I traveled in those circles, did you?" He was grinning at Danny but also at himself. He did feel like a waiter dressed that way and he only hoped no one could tell the tuxedo was a rental.

Danny grinned back at him. "Pretty soon you won't even talk to me anymore," he said.

"If Amberg finds you I won't be able to, you remember that." He pointed his finger at Danny again, then winked and walked back to his car.

Danny watched him as he drove off. He was pleased with himself and he thought again about Amberg and how Johnny would get him now. But there was also a feeling of uneasiness and he quickly made the sign of the cross. Johnny could get hurt going after him and he would be partially to blame. He hoped that would not happen.

William Eatkins's home on Sutton Place was almost as overpowering as the

Bainbridges' town house. There were large French doors in the living room that opened on to a terrace overlooking the East River. At the extreme right of the terrace there were steps leading down to a large private garden where drinks were being served when they arrived. It was a small, intimate group made up mostly of Eatkins's business associates and from the outset there was little doubt that Mona was a favorite of her uncle. He had taken her aside almost immediately for a long, private talk and had seated her next to him at dinner, taking special care that everything was to her liking. The other guests had also paid special attention to her, in deference to her uncle, he thought. But she was very much the princess at the ball and he felt awkward playing Prince Charming in his rented dinner jacket.

The news about Amberg still preyed on his mind and the realization that it would soon reach a climax only added to the growing tension. Throughout dinner he fought to keep his mind on the casual talk about trips abroad and the summer's activities on Long Island and on the Jersey shore that were now coming to a close. But it had been difficult, and on one occasion when a question had been directed at him he had been forced to excuse himself and ask that it be repeated.

The dinner was sumptuous. Maids moved along the table with trays of food and he found it awkward manipulating the serving implements from the side and at first he had been afraid he would hit one of the trays with his shoulder and send it crashing to the floor. Mona looked at him, smiling, throughout the dinner between conversations with her uncle and the other guests, and he noticed that her uncle watched the display of attention closely. At one point the conversation turned to the growing labor problems that most of the city's businessmen were facing and Eatkins, alluding vaguely to Broderick's experience in that area, asked him if he thought it could be stopped.

The question stunned him at first, not having expected to be drawn into that kind of conversation, and his answer surprised him even more because he could not remember having thought about it in those terms. He told Eatkins simply that *anything* could be stopped provided enough force was used but that he doubted the force could be maintained because of the political pressures it would produce. He mentioned the general strike that had paralyzed Britain the previous May and how the law the British government had passed making general strikes a national crime was already an admitted failure. The discussion was cut short by Eatkins's wife, who insisted that the dinner should not be marred by talk about "those dreadful people who want more money for less work" and who, she was certain, were being directed by "those equally dreadful people in Moscow." Her words produced polite laughter but also ended the discussion and Broderick found he was grateful that it had. He had answered the question with a certain degree of authority, he felt, but if asked to elaborate he was afraid he would make a fool of himself. He had also noted the look of interest his remark had produced in Eatkins. It had betrayed neither agreement nor disagreement, simply a curiosity about the person who had made it.

After dinner Mona took his arm as they returned to the living room and whispered to him that everyone *simply adored* him. How she could tell such a thing baffled him. They were a cold, calculating lot and, beneath the charming exteriors, left him feeling as though he was swimming in a pool filled with piranha. But she had been right about the importance of knowing these people. They could be valuable. They were the real power in the city, the people that even the mayor sought to please. He had once thought that the Industrial Squad's work against the labor unions was simply a moneymaking proposition for the Hall. But it was more than that, he now realized. It was a way to curry favor with the people who controlled the city, the people of wealth who provided the money for political campaigns, who could arrange loans from banks and make jobs available in industry if an election was lost.

Standing next to Mona he found himself thinking of the man he had arrested in front of the Goldspan Building. Johannes, a frightened little man whose eyes darted about like a trapped animal, one of those "dreadful people" that Mrs. Eatkins didn't want discussed at her dinner table, and he wondered if he and the others had any idea about the kind of power they were trying to fight and how easy it was to have them crushed with a simple telephone call. Only a different kind of power allowed them on the streets now. Arnold Rothstein's money. And he would exact his price too.

Mona guided him to the terrace and below, in the garden, he could see the servants removing the outdoor furniture that had been set up earlier for cocktails. It was a sultry evening but the breeze from the river was soft and steady and the lights from the homes and factories in Queens were providing their nightly display for those who could afford to stand on the right side of the river and watch it. It was a final irony that the people living there, many of them involved in those labor battles, would provide subtle comfort to the people they fought by simply turning on the lights in their homes.

Off to the left the lights of the Queensboro Bridge added a beauty to the river and he could remember nearly twenty years ago when it was being built, how he and his friends would sneak aboard the Third Avenue El to travel uptown and watch the men working high above on the steel girders. They had heard stories about the men who had died when the Brooklyn Bridge had been built and they had gone to this new bridge to watch them plunge to their deaths. But no one had ever died, at least not while they were there. So they had contented themselves with a swim in the filthy waters of the river and the only death they ever saw was Charlie Sweeney's, the skinny kid from down the block who had been swept away by the current and whose body had never been found.

132

"I always loved this house," Mona said, interrupting his thoughts. "I came here a great deal as a child, especially after my father died. I always loved how peaceful the river was, how gentle."

"It's not that peaceful," he said. "The current gets pretty bad, especially at high tide."

"I know. We often sailed up it on the way to Long Island Sound in the summers and Uncle used to remark how easy it would be to lose control in Hell's Gate if you weren't a good sailor." She laughed, remembering. "I always asked him to let me take the wheel but he never would. I think I was a bit of a tomboy then. He used to tease me that if he had any children he would want them to be boys just like me."

"I haven't seen many boys like you," he said.

"Well, that's because I changed, darling. I found out how much more fun it is being a girl." She turned to him and the breeze from the river caught her hair as it had aboard the ferry. "How do you like Uncle?" she asked.

"He seems fine. He seems to like you a lot. You're his favorite niece, aren't you?"

"I'm his only niece," she said. "There are no other children in the family. I think he was a bit disappointed when I divorced Stuart. He was hoping for a grandnephew, I think, an heir to his hat factory, a new king of the chapeau. He takes it all quite seriously, you know."

"I would too, if I owned a hat factory," he said.

"My Lord. I can't quite see you as a hatter, although I'm sure you'd make an excellent one. Can't you just picture it? The famous John Broderick strolling through his factory in an open gate collar, casting a disapproving eye on the employees who, of course, would begin to work furiously when they saw him coming."

"Afraid I'd shoot them," he said.

"Oh, no. There wouldn't be any gun, heavens no. Just a withering gaze. Uncle says that's all that's ever really needed."

"I'm very good at withering gazes," he said.

She laughed. "I know you are. I saw you give one to that evil little man the other night."

He tightened at the mention of Amberg. He was like a nightmare that kept returning whenever he relaxed. "I don't think a withering gaze is enough for people like that," he said.

"No, I suppose not," she said. "But still you do it magnificently. Come to think of it you might not make such a bad hatter after all. And think of all the free hats you'd get. I've been trying to get Uncle to start a women's line for years, but the silly man insists that men's hats are more profitable."

"Did I hear you discussing my lack of business acumen again?" Her uncle had come up behind them.

133

Mona turned and lifted her head in mock defiance. "You certainly did. If you had taken my advice long ago and manufactured women's hats you'd be far richer today."

"I would have been serving dinner tonight, instead of eating it," he said.

"You see," she said to Broderick, "he has no respect for my opinion."

"I have great respect for your beauty and charm, my dear. I don't need your opinion." He smiled at her feigned display of umbrage. "I merely came out to suggest you join the others for brandy. Will you forgive me long enough for that, my dear."

Mona remained cool, teasing him. "I'll try," she said.

"Good. Why don't you go inside and join your aunt while Mr. Broderick and I talk. I'd like a chance to get to know him."

"Oh, so I'm being dismissed, am I?"

"Precisely, my dear. Now run along." He watched, amused, as Mona continued her act.

She tossed her head defiantly. "Don't let him bully you," she said to Broderick. "He loves to bully people." She nodded to her uncle, then moved off through the terrace doors.

"An imp of a girl," Eatkins said. "But that's one of the reasons I'm so fond of her." He took Broderick's arm and led him along the terrace. "Let's take a walk in the garden, if you don't mind."

Broderick assured him he did not and then descended the stairs into the courtyard below. It was an English-style rose garden and the flowers were still in bloom, filling the air with a fragrance so strong that it reminded him of a funeral home.

"Mona tells me that you two just met at the Bainbridges' last week," Eatkins began. "I hope you don't mind my speaking to you, but you see she has always been like a daughter to me and I'm deeply concerned about her welfare."

"I understand and I don't mind at all," Broderick said.

"Good," Eatkins said, leading him to the rear of the garden well out of hearing range of the terrace before he stopped. "She spoke to me about you yesterday when she called to say you would be joining us tonight. In point of fact, she didn't offer a great deal of information. You might say I drew it out of her. The personal information, I mean." Eatkins stroked his white moustache as he spoke. It was like Mona's habit of stroking her throat, Broderick thought.

"You mean the fact that I'm married," Broderick said, deciding he would not fence with this man.

"You're direct. I like that, John." Eatkins's face was pleasant, friendly, but his eyes were cool and hard, a man used to frank conversations. "Of course I understand that you and your wife do not live together and I'm also modern enough to realize that such things do happen and that other relationships do develop during those periods when married couples are living apart. But, as I said, Mona is very dear to me and although you may not be aware of it she has suffered a great deal already due to a rather ruinous marriage and a number of subsequent relationships that I don't believe were good for her."

"I've asked my wife for a divorce," Broderick interrupted. "Not because of Mona, but because it's what I want." He spoke the words almost roughly. He wanted to tell Eatkins to mind his own business but decided against it.

"That's comforting to hear, John, and your being a gentleman I was sure that was the case." He paused, studying Broderick. "But that's not the cause for my concern. Mona seems unduly attracted to you. I found that to be the case when we spoke and even more so observing her reaction to you this evening. I say 'unduly' only because of the short time you've known each other and for no other reason. I suppose she finds your life exciting, perhaps even romantic. But if the association continues, and I assure you I have no objection to it doing so, I feel there are some things you should know about her. Mona is the spoiled child of a wealthy family. She's a lovely child and I adore her, but I also hold no illusions about her. She is accustomed to fine things and expects them and there's no reason she should not. We are a wealthy family."

"And you feel á cop couldn't provide those things," Broderick said. He did not like the tone of the conversation, the near condescending look of Eatkins's smile.

"No, it's not that at all, John. Mona can well afford to provide for her own indulgences and there is little question she will always be able to do so. The point I'm trying to make is that these indulgences and the fact that they have always been so easily available have been the root of her difficulties. Stuart D'Arcy was a pompous little fop. I never really questioned his masculinity but, to be frank, I was never quite certain of it either. Following their decision to divorce there were, and still are, a string of rather useless young men, if you know what I mean. And I'm afraid the entire experience has been somewhat disappointing to Mona and more than a little disheartening. She's a good child, John, a good person. But she's a spoiled child and she becomes easily hurt if things don't go precisely the way she wishes them to. What I'm suggesting is that you be understanding of her and try not to disappoint her as the others did. I know this can be difficult for a self-made man such as yourself.

"You know, I consider myself somewhat of a self-made man. When I took over the family business it was close to failing. I turned it around. Later I joined those who were lobbying for this nation's involvement in the Great War, which I also believed was in the best interest of the country. When that involvement came, I secured large contracts for military hats and the business grew far beyond what anyone in the family had ever dreamed. So you see I understand a man like you and I appreciate the values you must have.

135

But enough of that." He placed his arm on Broderick's shoulder and began walking with him slowly about the garden.

He was a persuasive man, Broderick thought. Tall and angular with a bearing about him that was authoritative, and he could see him as Mona had abstractly described him before, moving among his employees commanding increased work by his presence, a silver-haired figure of doom if he chose to be, someone who knew how to use his power over people.

"You know I was quite impressed with you earlier this evening," Eatkins continued. "When you were asked if you felt the labor problems we're all facing today could be stopped, you said you didn't think so. I, for one, agree with you, although most of my business colleagues are not in agreement with me. I don't believe in stopping the inevitable." He stopped and smiled at Broderick. "But I do believe in subverting it if it's in my interest to do so. Mona tells me that she feels you might one day be lured away from police work. Is that so?"

The statement stunned him and he wondered where Mona had gotten the idea.

"I haven't really thought about it. But I suppose if I suddenly came into a great deal of money I might decide there were better things to do than get shot at."

Eatkins chuckled. "Yes, I suppose that does become a bit frightful from time to time." They began walking again. "You know there will be a great future in labor, from the management side of course. There will be a need for men who know how to deal with these people forcefully, men who can instill respect and who will know how to cope with the violence that is sure to occur from time to time. The secret to business in the future, I believe, will not be in stopping unions from forming, although we certainly must resist to a certain degree whenever possible, but rather in bringing them to heel, in finding ways to *encourage* their leaders to see things from the viewpoint of the employer. It's not that difficult a task, but the type of executive who exists today has never been forced to face up to that, and frankly he's the type of person who detests dealing with the average workingman. So far he's been able to deal from a position of arrogance, which is not always a position of power, and I'm afraid it may be too late to teach him differently. So the situation will soon call for a new type of executive, one who specializes in these problems and who can deal with them forcefully and, yes, at times brutally if necessary. Someone these people can understand and fear. Fear even more than the people who run the company. And it will also allow those in the other executive positions to remain aloof from the problems and appear, at least, to be uninvolved. This, of course, will then make it possible for those other executives to make compromises without any loss of prestige when compromises are needed to insure continued production. Do you understand what I'm driving at?"

"Completely," Broderick assured him. "But why tell me this?"

136

"Again, direct and right to the point. Good." Eatkins was smiling at him but there was no joy in the smile, and the whole conversation was beginning to confuse Broderick. "The reason is simple, John. You could be exactly the kind of man who will be needed in that type of position. With proper guidance, of course, but without question precisely the kind of man men like myself will *need*. I'd like you to think about that, think about it seriously and then perhaps we shall talk again one day. I can tell you that the financial rewards for such men will be significant." He paused, then smiled again. "May I ask you how much you are paid for the rather hazardous work you do?"

"The salary is four thousand dollars a year," Broderick said.

"You say that as though one could reasonably assume there were other benefits." Eatkins smiled knowingly.

"I think you could say there are other benefits." Broderick returned the smile. This man did not like him and the feeling was mutual, he decided.

"Good," Eatkins said. "That shows initiative. But I assure you the men involved in what I was speaking of will become men of enormous power and their incomes will match that power in time. You see power, not money alone, is the key to having what one wants in life, John. But I'm sure I don't have to explain the importance of power to you. So enough of this. We should return to the ladies and we'll speak of this again, won't we?"

"Certainly."

Eatkins smiled with satisfaction as they started back to the house. "I think you and I will get along very well, John. Very well, indeed."

The conversation in the massive living room had reverted back to the subject of travel when they returned but Mona quickly freed herself and asked him to join her under the guise of showing him her uncle's art collection.

He wanted to ask her what was going on, why she had suggested he might want to leave his job, but he decided to wait. He wasn't annoyed with the idea, just overwhelmed. He was disturbed that she had done it without asking him, but only slightly, only the reasons not the fact bothered him.

"Did you and Uncle have a nice chat?" she said, as they studied a painting at the far end of the room.

"He told me all your secrets." He wasn't looking at her; he kept his eyes on the painting, awaiting a reaction.

"What secrets?" There was a trace of nervousness in her voice.

"Like the time you got picked up shoplifting and that time in college when they found a naked man in your room."

"You bastard." She could not keep a slight smile off her face. "Are you going to tell me what you talked about or not?"

"Or not." He continued to avoid her eyes, fully enjoying his dominance of this new game.

"John!" She stamped her foot lightly.

137

"You can't always have your own way, Mona." He looked down at her foot, amused.

"Why not?"

"I think I'd like to have some brandy." He turned and gazed absentmindedly about the room as though trying to see where the liquor was kept.

"You don't drink that much. You told me so."

"I lied."

She stamped her foot again. "Then I just won't speak to you. Besides, I don't like your tuxedo."

"I'm sorry about that," he said, still fighting a smile. "The waiter I borrowed it from said it was almost new."

"John, you didn't?" she whispered, her eyes wide, almost horrified.

"Well, I cleaned off all the gravy stains."

She spun on her heels. "You're a double bastard," she whispered, her back to him. She was smiling now, pleased by this newfound ability to overpower her verbally.

"This is a very nice painting." He had cocked his head, appearing almost professorial.

"It's more than nice, you Philistine, it's an original." Her voice was cool and affected.

"What's a Philistine?"

She grabbed his arm and squeezed against it. "Oh, John, *please.* Tell me what you talked about."

His suppressed amusement emerged. "Just some labor stuff," he said, laughing.

"But what about it?" She had felt a surge of excitement when he said it and now wanted more.

"It was just more about what he asked me at dinner."

"Is that *all?*" There was a sudden sinking feeling.

"Well, he did kind of hint that it might be a good thing for me to get involved in."

"He did? Did he say anything about his company?" She was eager now and could not hide it.

"What he did say is that you told him I might be lured away from the Police Department. What made you think that?"

She felt caught and she was uncertain how to extract herself. "All I meant is that anyone could be lured away from something if a better offer came along." She tried to take on a detached air but she knew her lie was obvious.

He did not press her. He didn't want her to know that the seed Eatkins had planted had taken root almost immediately, but he was curious about her reasons. "I was very flattered he thought I could do something like that," he said.

"But you could, John." She was emphatic and she caught herself. "You're a

138

forceful person and that's the secret of success in business. All the rest is just a bit of polish that comes with exposure."

"You're not ashamed of what I do, are you?" He was smiling, trying to appear amused, but the question was serious.

She felt herself tighten again. "Of course not, darling. You can do anything you want. I promise you I won't mention it to him again." She lied, urging caution on herself. "But it is nice that he was that impressed with you."

"Yes, it is. He made it sound very attractive. But if I ever turned in my gun I'd probably walk with a tilt."

Her face brightened, pleased that he had been tempted. "We could put a weight in your other pocket to straighten you out," she said.

"I think you'd have to."

When they joined the others, Mona was beaming. There was a brightness in her face that seemed to radiate satisfaction. She had put the evening together carefully and it had been a success. She had been worried at first. He was not a sophisticated man and she had wondered if he could handle himself with the people there. He had been uncomfortable at times, but that was to be expected. And his tuxedo *was* a disaster and the bulge from his gun had been obvious, too much so. But she would speak to him about that later, or better still, help him buy a new one. She frowned for a moment. No, it was worth it, she decided, dismissing a momentary doubt. And it would be exciting to see what developed. She would simply be subtle, that would be best, and when she was ready her uncle would do as she asked. And so would John.

She had to coax him to spend the night. They had returned to her apartment at midnight and he had explained that he had to be up early the next morning to begin a surveillance and would have to change his clothes, but she had promised to see that he was and he had agreed to stay.

She watched him remove the tuxedo and said, not unkindly, that she planned to burn it while he slept.

He stood before her naked and laughed, extending his arms. "I'll look cute walking to my car like this. I hope your doorman isn't a fag."

She extended her hand, urging him toward the bed. "You'll be too used up to do anything about it even if he is." He stepped toward her. She swung her legs over the edge of the bed and stopped him in front of her and began running her lips along his stomach. "But just in case," she said softly, "I intend to show you that a woman can do anything a man can."

CHAPTER NINETEEN

IT WAS ALMOST NINE O'CLOCK WHEN HE RETURNED TO his hotel room. They had not awakened early as they had planned and he was annoyed with himself, although not as much as he normally would have been. Inwardly he was pleased with the new turn his life seemed to be taking. The conversation with Eatkins the evening before had produced new ideas, possibilities that had never before crossed his mind. He had toyed with the prospects driving back to his hotel and even now, as he removed the tuxedo and prepared to climb into the shower, the thought of a large office and a secretary catering to his whims dominated his thoughts.

Broderick pulled the shower chain and listened to the pipes gurgle as they prepared to loose a cascade of water on to his head and shoulders. The water spilled out and spread over his face, forcing his eyes to close. It was tepid and he blindly adjusted the mixture. Despite the late August heat the increased warmth of the water felt soothing and he remained there longer than normal, allowing the heat and rising steam to surround him until it began to impede his breathing.

He opened the bathroom door to let the steam-covered mirror clear as he worked his shaving brush furiously in its mug, building a thick white lather. Even the straight razor felt good against his face; the short scraping sounds seemed rhythmic and forceful. The men involved would have power and money, that was what Eatkins had said. The true kind of power, not the kind that came from a badge or a pair of brass knuckles. The kind that Chris Nolan and Jimmy Walker had. No, even more than that. Even they catered to the kind of power Eatkins was talking about. Sure, they might screw them occasionally like they screwed Goldspan, but that was only temporary. That was just playing the odds until somebody raised the ante and changed the tempo of the game.

He rinsed the razor and smiled at himself in the mirror as he wiped the remaining traces of lather from his face. He really didn't think Eatkins wanted him, but it was obvious that Mona did. It was all a bit strange. Maybe he could even have a title and his name painted on the door of his office. The other guys would shit if they saw that. He laughed at himself and walked to his closet and began surveying the row of suits. The gray pinstripe and a nice conservative tie. He would begin to tone down his dress, be a bit more conservative, more businesslike. He looked down at his gun on the night stand next to the bed. It would be hard to give that up, if he ever decided he should, it had become almost a part of him. There was a sense of comfort feeling it against you, feeling its weight tugging against your belt: a bit of instant lightning that gave you an edge even if you never had to take it out of the holster. But he wouldn't need one, it would be that simple. He wouldn't be doing the things that made it such a comfort and that sometimes made it a problem in itself. He remembered what the old Mick who trained him had said, how the gun sometimes makes the problem, how somebody who's scared will shoot if they think you've got one. But, Jesus, who the hell would do the job without one? Besides, the department said you had to. It was a regulation.

Mona said she would put a weight in his pocket to keep him from tilting. Mona. That was the other plus. Everything Eatkins had hinted at and Mona too. He looked into the mirror on the inside of his closet door and nodded at the rugged good looks that stared back at him. Or was it just the opposite? He could have just as easily meant it that way. He hadn't thought of that before. Keep her happy, that's what he had said. Keep her happy and there's a lot in it for you, kid. But what the hell difference did that make. He wanted her whether all the other stuff went with it or not, and it was far from certain. He had never met a woman like her. Every time he was with her he felt like he had the world by the balls. Every time he looked at her he felt as though he was going to come busting through his trousers. She was unbelievable. She did things to him he had only gotten from high-priced hookers, the exact reason he went to those hookers in the first place. And she loved it. Jesus, did she love it. Christ, he could feel himself starting to grow just thinking about it. . . . His pocketwatch was next to the revolver. He picked it up and opened it. Nine-fifteen. He was an hour and fifteen minutes late for his tour. Fuck 'em. He'd make up an excuse if anybody asked. He slipped into a stiff white

141

shirt and selected a solid maroon tie from the tie rack. Solid ties with striped suits, that's what Walker had once told him. He adjusted the tie carefully, trying to get the effect without the benefit of trousers or a suit coat. He sat on the edge of the bed and pulled on his socks and attached the edges to his garter straps, taking care the ribs were lined up evenly. The telephone gave two abrupt rings. He stared at it. The long slender shaft ending with the mouthpiece at the top made it seem as though the instrument was staring back at him. It sang out again in two short, insistent blasts. It could be the lieutenant wanting to know where the hell he was. If it was, he could book off sick, telling him he had been too bad off even to call. The telephone rang again. He reached out, grabbing it with both hands, and lifted the receiver from its cradle and placed it to his ear.

"Yeah, who is this?" he said.

Cordes's voice crackled back at him. "Johnny, wake up. It's Cordes."

"I'm awake. What's the matter, you miss me?"

"It's after nine. You must of had a good night last night. But you better get your ass moving. We got a bad stickup in a jewelry store on West Forty-eighth just off of Fifth. The owner's shot up so bad we can't even move him. We're hoping he's gonna come around and talk before he croaks. You better get over here." Cordes's voice was easy and matter of fact.

"What's the big rush? Is the brass on the way there?"

"No, but some witnesses described the guys who pulled it off. One of them was big and from what they said it might have been Moe Berg. I thought you'd be interested."

"I'll be there in ten minutes." He slammed the receiver down and shoved the phone back on the night stand. For a moment he felt glued to the bed. Amberg. He had forgotten all about it. He was supposed to start surveillance this morning but he had not gotten up and his mind had been all fucked up with everything else. He jumped from the bed and began yanking on his trousers, then threaded the holster through his belt. He would have been right behind them. His mind went blank, then rushed back. And he would have been alone and right in the middle of it when they came out. God watches over us, his wife always said. This time he couldn't argue with her. Thank God, he hadn't told anyone about the surveillance he had planned.

He was still pulling on his coat as he went through the door and began running down the hall. He jabbed his thumb repeatedly against the elevator button. Below he could hear the doors slide shut, the motor engage, and the almost painful groan of the cables as it began to rise. Five floors and it seemed like forever. When the doors parted the skinny pimple-faced kid who ran it gave him a stupid smile.

"Good morning, Mr. Broderick," he said.

"Never mind the good mornings. Just get this thing moving," he snapped.

The boy grinned foolishly. "It only goes at one speed," he said.

"I said, move it." The boy's face paled and he pushed the door as hard as

142

he could, then slammed the operating handle to the down position. Broderick moved his feet nervously, listening to the car rumble down. Finally it eased to a stop and he bolted through the door sideways, not waiting for it to open completely, and ran across the small lobby and out into the street. His car was parked illegally in front of the building and there was the usual ticket on the windshield that would have to be fixed. He grabbed it off the windshield, cursed, and shoved it into his pocket. The engine struggled, then coughed to life and the car lurched forward.

The traffic was still heavy and he leaned on the horn, swerving in and out, slowing at traffic lights and then racing across. It was maddening and his anxiety to be free of it made it worse. Near the intersection of Fifty-second and Fifth a horse-drawn ice truck lumbered along, squarely in the center of the street. He leaned on the horn and the sudden blast caused the horse to jump forward, then rear in fright. The driver struggled to control it, pulling it to the right, and Broderick whipped the car around it and turned left into Fifth Avenue, gunning the engine. When he pulled to the curb at Forty-eighth Street he could see the patrol cars clustered in front of a small store four or five doors down the street. He climbed out of the passenger side and moved briskly toward the cops gathered on the sidewalk, flashing his shield at one who stepped toward him with his hand raised.

Cordes was standing just inside the door and there were two uniformed men at the rear of the store listening to Barney Ruditsky question two civilians, a man and a woman. A man in a white jacket, a doctor he guessed, was kneeling next to the body of an old man while the other men dressed in white stood next to a nearby stretcher. The old man was on his stomach. He had been hit at least twice in the chest with a heavy caliber weapon and he could see the exit wounds clearly in his back, the gaping holes in the torn fabric of his coat holding bits of flesh covered with dark coagulating blood.

"You look great," Cordes said. "You better watch out when the coroner gets here. He might not know who the corpse is."

"Is the old guy dead?"

"Just about," Cordes said.

"Did he say anything? Could he identify anybody?"

"He never came to, not yet anyway."

The doctor walked toward them. He was young but he looked tired and it made him appear older than he was.

"How is he?" Cordes asked.

"I'm amazed he's still alive. He should have been dead by the time he hit the floor. If we even tried to move him we'd rupture anything that's left inside his chest." The young doctor shook his head. "But it won't be long now, minutes, maybe less."

"Can he talk?" Cordes asked.

"Every minute or so he groans, but I don't think he's really conscious. But try, if you want. You can't hurt him any more than he is already." The doctor motioned to the ambulance attendants and they picked up the stretcher and began moving it toward the door. "I'll stay until he goes, but he's going to be the coroner's baby, not mine."

Cordes moved over to the body with Broderick behind him. He knelt down, placing his face close to the old man. He looked up at Broderick, who knelt down quickly beside him. "I think he's dead," Cordes said.

"Bullshit," Broderick said, pushing Cordes aside with his arm. He leaned down next to the body, his face no more than six inches away from the old man's. There was a small pool of blood next to his mouth and still more trickled slowly from his lips. His eyes were slightly parted and they stared lifelessly at the floor. The sour smell of death rose from his mouth, the odor of the drying blood and vomit that was still trapped in his throat. Broderick tried not to breath. "Who did this to you, old man? Did you recognize him?" He waited, placing his ear close to the old man's mouth. A drop of blood fell from his lip and he could hear it strike the small red pool on the floor. "Yeah, yeah," Broderick said. He nodded his head slightly, then looked up at Cordes. "He said it was Amberg. He said he recognized him from his picture in the newspapers."

Cordes knelt down next to him. "What the hell are you talking about? He's deader than hell," he whispered.

Broderick stared at him coldly. "He is now, but he wasn't a second ago. You were wrong. He was still alive and he said it and I'll swear to it in court."

Cordes tilted his hat back on his head. "Hey, Johnny. This is pretty rough," he whispered.

"I said I asked him and he answered me. What's the problem? The doctor said he might talk and he did. That's all you have to worry about."

"Okay, okay. If you say so. I didn't know you wanted to get rid of the punk that bad. If they ask me I'll say I heard you ask him but couldn't hear the answer." He spoke the final words emphatically.

"I heard him. That's enough."

Ruditsky walked up to them. "You guys want to talk to those two witnesses?" he asked.

"I do," Broderick said. He stood quickly and walked across the room with Cordes and Ruditsky following behind.

The man and woman stood at the rear of the store. Both seemed nervous and the woman was trying not to look at the body on the floor but her eyes kept returning to it, then darting away. They were both middle-aged. The woman was short and stumpy, the man only slightly larger, and he was fumbling with his hat, moving it in a circular motion between his hands.

"Excuse me," Broderick said. "I understand you were both outside when the men came out."

"How is he?" the woman said, her eyes moving back to the old man and then retreating again.

144

"He just died," Broderick said. He let the words fall heavily, giving them the maximum effect.

"Oh, my God," the woman said. "Why did they have to do that?"

"They're killers, lady. That's why we have to get them. Next time it could be somebody in your family." He paused, letting his words sink in, looking from the woman to the man. "Can you tell me what you saw?"

"There were three of them," the man said. "One was big, I mean really big. He was about as tall as you but even huskier. The other two were thinner, about average." The woman nodded her head in agreement.

"The big guy, what was his face like?" Broderick asked.

"He was ugly," the woman said. "His face was sort of flat. I mean his nose seemed to be pushed in, sort of flattened against his face."

"And he was so big he looked like he didn't have a neck," the man interrupted. "You know, like his shoulders started from under his ears or something. He was frightening. He had a gun. So did the other two."

"What did the other two look like?" Broderick said.

"I can't remember," the man said. "I couldn't take my eyes off the big one."

He looked at the woman but she only shrugged, indicating she could add nothing more.

Broderick looked from one to the other. "The old man identified one of the others before he died. He was positive. He had seen his picture before. I'm going to pick him up now and I'd like you to look at him later. I'm sure if you saw him again you'd recognize him, wouldn't you?"

"Oh, yes," the man said. The woman nodded her head emphatically. "Then you know who did this?" the man added.

"No question about it," Broderick said. "But we'll still need your identification."

"Oh, I will," the woman said. "This is terrible."

"Good. Detective Ruditsky will take you down to Headquarters." He turned to Barney. "I don't want them to see any pictures or anything. I want to wait until we bring them in so we can get a positive identification."

Ruditsky nodded, then glanced, bewildered, at Cordes. Cordes looked down at the floor. Broderick thanked the man and the woman, then took Cordes by the arm and walked to the center of the store.

"They'd identify Jesus Christ after that little speech," Cordes said.

"You bet your ass they would. Have you got a list of what was stolen?"

"No idea," Cordes said.

"It doesn't matter. It's probably been fenced by now anyway. Let's go get Amberg."

They left the store and climbed into Cordes's unmarked car. Cordes turned to him.

"I suppose you know where he is, too?" he said.

145

"The Manhattan Hotel on Eighth Avenue," he said.

"You're fucking unbelievable. If I didn't know better I'd think *you* stuck up the store just to nail the little creep."

"I would have if I'd thought of it," Broderick said.

The car moved slowly across town through the traffic. Broderick stared out the window feeling his stomach tighten. "We'll call for some uniformed back-up outside the hotel," he said.

"I was wondering about that," Cordes said. "I didn't feel like going in there alone, especially if it *was* them and there are three guys waiting there for us."

Broderick watched the traffic ahead. The car moved forward slowly but deliberately, bringing him closer to the confrontation he had known for weeks would have to take place. Then it would be over, he thought. Once and for all the little bastard would be put away. They'd fry his ass in the electric chair for this and he would be rid of him. He'd ask for a large back-up, he decided. Go in there with a fucking army and if he did anything they could blow him apart right there. He almost hoped that he would. It would be simpler, easier that way. No chance of any slipups. But everything was set now anyway. Those people would identify him no matter what. Cordes was right, they'd identify Jesus Christ if they saw him sitting in Headquarters with handcuffs on. The only trick now was to get him there. Taking him wouldn't be easy, nothing was easy about him. He took his watch from his vest pocket and opened it. It was ten-thirty. They'd be back in the room holed up if it had been them. They wouldn't want to be out on the street. If it hadn't, they'd probably be there anyway. Maybe they'd even still be asleep. He'd get a passkey from the front desk, just in case. But if they were asleep it could screw things up. Some smart lawyer would say that proved they didn't do it. But Gillie would be in bed with him and he could say they were screwing when he found them. That would explain it. And if he went for a gun he could blow his fucking head off right there in bed. But it had to be them. The description matched Moe, a gorilla with a flat face; ugly, the woman had said. He paused, a feeling of uneasiness spreading through him. Amberg's leg. They ran out of the store, that's what the man said. Amberg's limp. It would have been noticeable if he was running. You can't hide something like that. He would have to make sure the witnesses didn't see him walk. He'd have to be sitting down when they identified him. There was no point in confusing them and even if some lawyer tried to make something out of it later it wouldn't do any good. They'd be so convinced by then it wouldn't make any difference. The papers would make heroes out of them, he would see to that, and it would make them even surer, so sure they'd be ready to pull the switch themselves. The car came to a halt in the heavy traffic and Cordes leaned on the horn. There was no rush now, Broderick thought. Everything had to be done slowly and easily and carefully. He was too close now and it was no time to get careless. In a couple of hours it would be over and one big problem would be gone. He could breathe easily again and his head wouldn't be constantly filled with that madman. He took a deep breath. It was true, the little punk scared him and he could feel a sour taste come into his mouth as he admitted it to himself.

Cordes lit a cigarette and the smoke wafted across the car and filled his nostrils, leaving him with a sickening feeling in his stomach.

"You have to smoke that damned thing?" he said.

Cordes glanced across at him and smiled. "You're getting a little edgy, aren't you?" he said.

"You know I hate the smell of those things."

Cordes tossed the cigarette out the window. "If it makes you feel better it's gone," he said.

Broderick stared out the side window. He *was* edgy and that wasn't good. You made mistakes when you let yourself get too tight; he knew that. They were a block away now, the car had just crossed Broadway. He took another deep breath.

"We better call for the back-up inside the lobby, just in case they come down," he said.

Cordes nodded. "It shouldn't take long for them to get guys there. But you're right. We better get some idea from the desk clerk whether they're in their room or not."

"If they're not there we can stake the place out and wait for them," Broderick said. That would even be better, he thought.

"How'd you find out he was staying there?" Cordes asked.

"I've had somebody checking on them. In fact, I just found out yesterday. The same guy also told me they were planning a job." He looked across at Cordes to see how he had taken the additional bit of information. He seemed impassive. "That's why I know it was them. It had to be."

"It's their style," Cordes said. "It's the kind of stuff they've done before." He looked across at Broderick, then back at the street. "Look, Johnny. It doesn't matter to me. He's a piece of shit and he ought to be off the street anyway. You just shook me up talking to that guy when he was stiff like that. It was kind of weird. Thank Christ it wasn't a broad. You might have screwed her."

Broderick was forced to laugh himself. It felt good. It broke some of the tension.

"That's your department," he said. "You're the great Latin lover. At least that's what you're always telling me."

"I don't know," Cordes said. "You're in with all those High Society types now. How'd you ever make out with the broad you asked Rickard to set you up with?"

Broderick's mind rushed to Mona. "Beautiful," he said. She was probably

147

still sleeping. She had hardly stirred when he got up. She had just muttered something about being sorry she hadn't gotten up. But she might be up by now, sitting and having breakfast on the terrace. He should be there too, he thought. He should be any place but where he was, where he was going to be in a few minutes.

Cordes pulled the car to the curb on Forty-fifth Street on the side of the hotel. "There are three exits," he said. "There's this one on Forty-fifth, another side entrance on Forty-fourth, and the main one on Eighth. But the elevators and stairs all come down into the lobby, so we shouldn't have any trouble keeping an eye out for them while we wait for support."

Broderick nodded. The sour taste was back in his mouth and he did not feel like replying.

Cordes withdrew his revolver and checked the cartridges in the cylinder. Broderick did the same. The palms of his hands were sweating and as he put the gun back in its holster he placed them on his knees and rubbed them discreetly.

"You ready?" Cordes said.

Broderick nodded. The children's refrain: "Ready or not, here I come," ran over and over in his mind.

CHAPTER TWENTY

INSIDE THE HOTEL, THE LOBBY WAS ALMOST DESERTED. Two men sat in overstuffed chairs reading newspapers, and across from them an elderly woman repeatedly glanced at the front entrance, waiting—hoping—for someone to arrive. A young couple walked slowly through the lobby and out the main entrance. They were followed by an elderly man with a cane who stopped momentarily at a newspaper stand, studied a collection of coins in his hand, and then hurried out without buying anything. They had placed themselves just inside the lobby near the Forty-fifth Street entrance and had carefully studied each person. To their left were the banks of elevators and beyond them a staircase that led to the upper floors. There would be a rear staircase too and they would have to station someone there, but for the moment the most they could do was concentrate on the main exits to make sure no one slipped by.

Across the once plush carpet the desk clerk and cashier stood behind a large wooden counter busying themselves. There were several deep scratches along the face of the counter from the careless handling of baggage and it was clear the hotel had seen better days.

They crossed the lobby to the front desk. The clerk had turned his back to them and was placing mail and messages in a large bank of pigeonholes, each bearing the number of a room. Broderick rapped his knuckles on the counter and the clerk looked over his shoulder, then returned to his task, ignoring him.

"You," Broderick snapped.

The clerk turned. He looked at Broderick as though being forced to gaze upon something distasteful. "*Just* a moment, *sir,*" he said.

Broderick pulled his shield from his pocket and held it out to the clerk. "Get your ass over here *now,*" he said.

The clerk took a deep breath expressing his annoyance, then put down the stack of mail and messages and moved to the counter. He walked like a woman. "Yes," he said.

"Hyman Amberg. What room is he in?"

The clerk took another deep breath. "I'll have to check the registry as soon as I get a chance," he said.

"And I'll have to break your goddamned neck," Broderick said. He had given the clerk a look of near total fury.

"Room 412," the clerk said quickly.

"Is he in?"

The clerk drew another impatient breath. "Really, it's hard for me to—"

"I said, is he in?" Broderick's voice had become a growl now and it forced the clerk to take a frightened step back.

"I think so."

"Are you sure?"

"Yes, sir, I believe he is. I haven't seen him go out."

Broderick felt his stomach sink. "But he could have gone out, right?"

The clerk seemed confused. "Yes, sir—I suppose he could have. But I believe he's in his room now. He called down earlier for some newspapers."

"Give me your passkey," Broderick ordered.

"I'm afraid that's against the rules. I'll have to—" He stopped abruptly as Broderick reached across the counter and grabbed him by the shirt.

"Maybe you don't believe what I told you."

The clerk fumbled with a drawer in front of him and quickly produced a key with a heavy wooden block attached to it. He gave Broderick a nervous smile. "I guess you don't want me to announce you," he said prissily.

Broderick released him and took the key. "You go within two feet of that phone and I'll break both your arms," he said.

The clerk glanced at the telephone as though trying to judge his distance from it. "Yes, sir," he said.

Broderick turned to Cordes, "You better make that call now," he said.

Cordes nodded and moved around the counter. He walked past the clerk, then turned quickly toward him. "Boo," he said, causing the already frightened clerk to jump backward. He picked up the telephone and gave the operator a number.

Broderick placed his back against the counter and concentrated on the elevators and the staircase. It was quiet, almost deathly so. The door to one of the elevators slid open and he stiffened. A bellhop, who looked like a born thief, stepped off and walked cockily into the lobby, whistling. It was quiet again. Broderick allowed his eyes to move slowly about the lobby. One of the men who had been reading a newspaper stood and began walking to the rear of the lobby. Broderick watched him. There was nothing familiar about the man, but he was walking stiffly, too stiffly. Amberg should have someone watching for the police. Even if he hadn't been involved in the stickup, he should have someone watching his back. He had always been careful in the past.

Broderick moved quickly across the lobby and came up behind the man. He grabbed his arm, holding his shield out in his other hand. "Excuse me," he said.

Without warning the man yanked his arm free and bolted toward the exit. Broderick threw his body forward and raced after him. Within ten feet of the door he lunged, sending his shoulder crashing into the middle of the man's back, the impact sending them both hurtling to the floor. In an instant Broderick was on his knees straddling his back and his fist slammed into the man's ribs and then smashed the back of his head, forcing his face brutally against the floor. He grabbed his right wrist and jerked it behind his back. "Move, cunt, and I'll break it off," he growled.

Cordes had scrambled over the counter and raced toward them. He drew his revolver and leveled it at the man's head. "What do you have?" he said.

"I don't know. Check him."

Cordes kept his gun behind the man's ear and worked his free hand along both sides of his body. He pulled the right side of the man's coat away and yanked a .45 caliber automatic from a holster. "He ain't no boy scout," he said.

"Check his wallet." Broderick said, jerking the man's arm up again until he groaned in pain.

Cordes pulled his wallet from an inside pocket and began looking through it. "His drivers license says he's Michael Carmichael from the Bronx."

"Carmichael. He's one of Amberg's goons. I got his name from my snitch." He jerked the arm up again. "Talk to me, you prick," he said.

"I got nothin' to say to you," Carmichael snapped back.

Broderick slammed his wrist up under his shoulder blade. Carmichael shouted in pain.

"You can fuck yourself," he groaned.

Broderick pulled him up by the wrist and hair and Cordes quickly cuffed his hands behind his back, then shoved him back toward the counter. The other man who had been reading a newspaper and the elderly woman were on their feet now, staring, their mouths open. The bellhop hurried toward the counter. Cordes withdrew his shield and held it up, motioning for calm.

151

Broderick grabbed Carmichael by the scruff of the neck and marched him to the counter. The clerk stared at them, his face pale.

"You ever see this slob before?" Broderick said.

The clerk began to stutter.

"He never saw nothin'," Carmichael said, keeping his eyes on the white-faced clerk.

Broderick's fist dug into his stomach, forcing him to knife forward over the counter.

"I seen him before," the bellhop said. He had weasel eyes, like the thief Broderick knew he had to be.

"He's one of Mr. Amberg's associates," the clerk snapped, shutting off the bellhop with a sense of authority.

"That's right," the bellhop countered. "He's been hanging around here for the last week."

Six uniformed cops came through the front entrance. Broderick turned and stared at them in disbelief. He looked at Cordes. "That's all they sent?" he said.

Cordes shrugged. "That makes eight of us. Two down here and four to back us up upstairs. Jesus, Johnny, there's only two of them up there, three at the most if they had somebody driving. What do you want—an army?"

"You bet your fucking life I want an army. Call for some more. Tell them we got a prisoner."

Cordes shook his head and went back to the telephone. When he completed the call he walked back to Broderick. "They're sending two more cars, one to take the prisoner and one to stay with us. The desk sergeant sounded like he thought I was nuts," he said.

"Fuck him," Broderick said. "I don't intend to get my ass blown off just because some slob sergeant doesn't want his sectors thinned out."

"Well, you got 'em, so we better get to work," Cordes said.

The lobby was cleared before the other men arrived and the guests in the rooms on either side of Amberg's were called and asked to leave quickly and quietly. Cordes located the rear stairs and placed one of the uniformed men there, while stationing a second behind a pillar in the lobby that held a commanding view of both the elevator and the main staircase. He pulled Broderick aside.

"I think we ought to use the stairs," he said. "I don't like the idea of stepping out of the elevator and not having any cover."

Broderick nodded his head. His palms had begun to sweat again but he knew that wiping them off would do little good now. He did so anyway. "Maybe we should send two of the uniformed guys up first to check out the stairs," he said.

"Come on, Johnny. They'll tell us to go fuck ourselves if we ask them to do that. And I wouldn't blame them."

152

"Okay, okay. I just don't like the way this feels. There's something we should be doing that we haven't," he said.

"What?"

"I don't know. I just feel it, that's all."

They started slowly up the stairs, Cordes, then Broderick, followed by the six uniformed men. The staircase moved upward in a gradual but continuous circle, opening on to each floor, then moving on—the same carpeting, the same continuous pattern of wallpaper, all of it making it difficult to gauge how far they had gone. Halfway up the staircase Broderick felt his legs growing heavy and it surprised him that the few flights of stairs he had traveled had put a strain on his body. When they reached the fourth floor Cordes raised his hand for them to stop. It did not seem as though they had gone far enough but when he looked into the hallway Broderick could see that the room numbers were in the four hundreds. They were there.

Amberg's room was at the far end of the building. The hall was quiet; nothing could be heard behind the succession of doors as they made their way down. One of the uniformed men had been left at the stairs and another was sent ahead to take up a position at the far end of the hallway. Cordes waved the four remaining men in uniform past the door to Amberg's room and had them flatten against the wall.

Broderick's temples were pounding with his own pulse and he rubbed his fingers against the left side of his head, hoping to make it stop. His right hand gripped his revolver tightly, the index finger resting heavily on the trigger guard, ready to jerk inward with the first sound.

Cordes leaned his head against the door. The buzzing sound of quiet conversation filtered back through the heavy wood and he looked back toward Broderick, nodding his head and smiling.

He stepped back quickly, the sound had come closer and he motioned Broderick to move back against the wall. They both flattened against it, trying to become part of it. Broderick felt his finger press lightly against the trigger and all his strength suddenly seemed to move to that point. He removed it, instinctively.

They could hear a voice behind the door now, muffled but strong. Cordes raised a finger to his lips. The doorknob began to move and they pressed even harder against the wall.

Slowly the door began to open and Moe Berg's voice became clear. "It won't take long, Hy. I'll get some bagels and stuff and be right back."

Moe stepped from the room, still looking back into it, then pulled the door closed behind him. Halfway into his second step down the hall he stopped abruptly, his eyes riveted on the man in uniform standing at the top of the stairs. Cordes's gun pressed behind his ear.

"One sound, slob, and your brains go down the hall ahead of you," he whispered.

"I hear you," Moe whispered back. He raised his hands and placed them on top of his head.

Broderick moved around him quickly and yanked his gun from beneath his coat. Moe stared into his face. His eyes were cold and calm but his neck had begun to jerk uncontrollably. A slight smile formed on Broderick's lips. They had them cold now. They could push the big slob in ahead of them and Amberg would never have a chance to react. He whispered Amberg's name and motioned toward the room with his head. Moe closed his eyes and nodded.

"Who else?" he whispered.

"Just the broad," Moe whispered back.

Broderick pushed the barrel of his revolver up under Moe's chin and threatened him with his eyes.

"That's all. Just the broad," Moe repeated.

Cordes grabbed him by the arm and stood him before the door as Broderick pulled his hands behind him and locked them there with his handcuffs. He leaned his chest against the wall and slid the passkey into the lock, turning it slowly. Cordes pushed Moe forward against the door, forcing it to swing open.

Amberg was on the sofa reading a newspaper. He glanced up and saw Moe's face. "What's the matter, you forget something?"

Moe's body hurtled into the room, propelled by Cordes's hand. Amberg jumped in his place, then froze. Cordes and Broderick leveled their guns at his head. Behind them there was a maze of blue uniforms.

"What's going on?" Amberg's eyes remained fixed on the weapons pointed at his head. He was transfixed, unable to remove them from the barrel openings.

"Move and I'll feed you to the dogs, Hy." Broderick's voice was hoarse, but there was a deep pleasure in it that was unmistakable.

"You'd like it that way, wouldn't you?"

Broderick's hand tightened on the revolver. "Nothing would make me happier, punk." He was smiling now.

Cordes moved quickly around the sofa and pushed open the bedroom door. A squeal came from inside and within seconds Gillie rushed out ahead of him, dressed in a flimsy nightgown.

"What's happening, Hy?" Her voice was high and frightened.

"Shut up," Amberg said. He leaned back against the sofa and smiled at Broderick. "You guys got a lot of nerve busting into my room like this. You want to tell me why?"

Broderick stepped toward him, returning the smile. "Just a social call," he said. His right hand swung forward, the barrel of the gun slamming against the side of Amberg's head and sending him sprawling to the floor. "You're under arrest, creep."

154

Cordes moved quickly to his side and took his arm. "Take it easy, Johnny."
He pulled his arm free and struck out with his foot, catching Amberg in the ribs.

Cordes grabbed his arm again. "That's enough, Johnny. I mean it." There was a threat in his voice and Broderick did not resist it.

Amberg twisted his body and stared up at Broderick, his eyes glaring through the pain that covered his face.

Broderick turned away and stepped toward Gillie. She moved backward as he approached. "Get dressed, bitch," he snapped. "And leave the door open."

Gillie spun and ran into the bedroom. She turned and looked back at him. He was in the doorway, watching her. "You gonna watch?" she said.

"Yeah, I'm gonna watch." His voice mimicked her own and she spun around and began removing her nightgown.

"What's the fucking roust for?" Amberg's voice screamed behind him.

"Murder, punk. This time you bought the whole trip." Broderick's voice was calm and he was smiling, watching Gillie's naked body struggle to find clothes while keeping her back to him.

"Murder, shit," Amberg screamed back. "I didn't kill nobody."

"You killed an old man in a jewelry store on Forty-eighth Street," Broderick said, still watching Gillie. "He gave me a deathbed statement. And guess who he named as the guy who shot him?"

"Deathbed, shit!" Amberg screamed. "I was here. I never left this fucking room today, and Moe and Gillie will swear to it."

Broderick turned and looked back at him. He was on his knees now and Cordes was holding on to the back of his collar. "Then you got nothing to worry about. If the jury believes that scum instead of me, you get off." He smiled down at him. "But of course we know Moe was there too. And I'm sure the D.A. is gonna bring up Gillie's old record as a hooker."

"I was never a hooker." Gillie's voice came indignantly from the bedroom.

Broderick turned his head to her. She had spun around and her heavy breasts were still bouncing with the movement. He looked at them and she turned her back to him quickly. "Too bad," he said. "You should have been." He turned back to Amberg. "This time you're finished, creep. By the way, I like you on your knees. You look good that way."

Amberg struggled to his feet, still unsteady from the blow to the head. He was screaming again. "You lousy bastard. You set me up again. I'll kill you for this. You were gonna be dead by the end of the week. Dead. You hear me? Dead. No matter where they send me I'll still kill you."

Cordes slapped him across the face. "Shut your fucking mouth," he said.

Broderick walked slowly toward him. "Nice of you to tell all of us that. How you were planning to blow away a cop. It'll sound nice for the jury, stupid."

155

One of the uniformed men took Amberg's wrists and handcuffed them behind his back. Broderick reached out and pinched his cheek, then walked behind him. "Let me make sure these are tight enough," he said. He reached down and squeezed the handcuffs, pressing the sharp-edged metal into his flesh.

"You cocksucker," Amberg shouted.

Broderick walked around in front of him. "Naughty, naughty," he said. His knee drove up into Amberg's groin, lifting him on to his toes. His body buckled and fell to the floor like a bag of wet laundry.

"He deserved that one," Cordes said, looking down at Amberg writhing on the floor.

"Get him out of here," Broderick said to one of the uniformed officers. "We'll meet you at the precinct in a little while. I want to talk to the bitch." He turned slowly and walked into the bedroom.

Gillie had a dress on now and she looked at him angrily. "What's the matter, didn't you see enough?" she said.

"Shut up and sit down," he said.

She backed up cautiously and sat on the edge of the bed. Cordes walked in behind him.

"Close the door," Broderick said.

"Hey, wait a minute." Gillie was frightened; she watched Cordes close the door behind him, her eyes darting back and forth between the two men.

"Just shut up. I just want to talk to you," Broderick said. "If you're a good girl, nothing's gonna happen to you."

Gillie moved up along the bed away from them. Her face was uncertain. "You promise?" she said.

Broderick pulled a chair away from a dressing table and straddled it facing her. "It looks like we're gonna have to charge you too, honey. It could have been you driving the car," he said.

"I wasn't driving anything. I don't even have a license," she said.

Broderick laughed. "Don't say that or we'll have to give you a summons for that too."

"Look, I was asleep in this room. I didn't even come out until you came in," she said.

Satisfaction spread across Broderick's face. "Then you don't know where Hy was this morning, do you?"

"He was here," she said.

"How do you know that?" Broderick snapped back.

"I could hear him out in the other room when I woke up." She was still watching them nervously. "And he came back in here right after I woke up."

"What time was that?" Cordes asked, sticking his gold toothpick into his mouth.

"I dunno. About nine-thirty, I guess."

156

"What's the matter, you stupid bitch, you can't tell time?" Broderick stood menacingly and Gillie cringed back on the bed. "I'm tired of her fucking lies, let's lock her ass up," he said to Cordes.

"Give her a chance," Cordes said. He sat down next to her and put his hand on her shoulder. "Look, honey. We know they pulled that job this morning and now the only question is whether you were involved or not."

"I wasn't involved in anything," she pleaded.

"You're a fucking liar," Broderick said, sitting back in the chair. "I don't know why the hell we're trying to help you."

"What do you want me to say?" She was pleading again.

Broderick smiled at her. "I want you to tell us how Amberg and Moe and this guy Carmichael went out this morning and how they all had guns with them. You don't have to know where they went, just that they went out. Understand?"

"He'll kill me if I say that," she said.

"He's not going to kill anybody," Cordes said. "His ass is going to be locked up for good. The only question now is whether you're gonna be locked up too."

"He'll get out and he'll kill me," she insisted.

"Look," Broderick said. He was speaking softly to her now. "He's going straight to the electric chair this time. I'm gonna strap him into it myself. So is Moe and so is this new guy Carmichael." He looked at her, trying to appear sympathetic. "And so is anybody else who was involved."

"I wasn't involved in anything. You have to believe me." She was begging now.

"We want to believe you. All you have to do is sign a statement telling the truth, just like we said, and there's no problem. And if you're worried about him, somebody will stay with you all the time he's on death row." He smiled at her now. "I wouldn't mind staying with you myself," he added.

"I don't know what to do," she said, twisting her hands together. "He'll have somebody else kill me if he can't get out."

"We can give you some dough and setup in another town. That's no problem. You could go to Miami. Who's going to know you in Miami? Or you can go any place you want. If the department won't spring for the dough I'll give it to you myself. I promise."

She looked at Broderick. "Would you really do that?" she asked.

"You name it and you got it," he said.

"And all I have to do is sign a statement?"

"And then testify in court," Cordes said.

She grimaced. "I don't know if I could do that," she said, twisting her hands again.

"Look," Broderick said sharply, "it'll be a lot harder if you're the one on trial."

157

She sat there, letting his words sink in. "He wasn't very nice to me anyway," she said finally. She looked at Broderick. "You know he used to slap me around a lot."

"Well, he's not gonna slap you around anymore, Gillie." Broderick's voice was soft, compassionate.

"And nothing is gonna happen to me?" she asked.

"You're just gonna be an innocent kid who was led astray," Cordes said.

She looked at him. "I used to be innocent," she said.

Cordes laughed. "I know, honey. Weren't we all."

CHAPTER TWENTY-ONE

GILLIE SAT ON A CHAIR IN A SMALL, DUST-FILLED office of the Midtown Precinct. She was still nervously wringing her hands and with every sound she turned quickly to see what had caused it. Cordes sat across from her, behind a desk, striking out awkwardly with two fingers at the typewriter before him. In one corner, leaning back so each of his shoulders rested against a different wall, Broderick stood dictating the "statement."

It was a clear, simple statement, one that even Gillie would be able to remember. She had awakened around eight-thirty as Amberg and the others were leaving the hotel room. She had not been told where they were going and had no idea there would be trouble until the police arrived shortly before eleven. Amberg had returned sometime after nine-thirty and he and Moe Berg had remained in the outer room, talking. They had seemed pleased about something, but she had never been told what it was.

The statement was innocuous; it was intended to be so. The times had to be approximate and not appear as though she had been keeping a stopwatch on Amberg's movements. She would simply establish that he was not in his room when the killing occurred. The deathbed statement and the two witnesses would take care of the rest, and together with Amberg's previous record no jury in the world would believe anything he said to dispute it. The fact that the statement was innocuous was the one thing that gave it strength. Broderick smiled to himself. He had not spent all these years in the department without learning how to prepare a statement that would be difficult to challenge in court.

He walked across the room and pulled the statement from the typewriter and read it carefully. Turning it around, he placed it on the desk in front of Gillie, then laid an open fountain pen beside the single sheet of paper.

Gillie stared at it, biting her lower lip. Her hands did not move from her lap. She took a deep breath. "Do I really have to?" she said, not looking up.

"No," Broderick said. "You don't have to do anything."

She looked up at him hopefully. His eyes told her what she wanted to know. She picked up the pen and scratched her name under the last sentence. "What happens now?" she asked Cordes, who in turn glanced up at Broderick.

"You're free to go if you want. Just stay in the city," he said.

Gillie turned pale. "I thought you were going to protect me," she said.

A pained look spread across Cordes's face. He was still looking up at Broderick. "We did promise, Johnny," he said.

"Sure, if that's what she wants, that's what she gets. Can you arrange it?" Cordes nodded and Broderick offered Gillie a warm, sympathetic smile. Cordes was right. They had to keep her happy, at least until the trial. "I just wasn't sure you wanted us around," he said. "I thought maybe you had enough of cops for one day."

She seemed reassured. "I'm glad Hy didn't kill you," she said.

Broderick laughed, feigning bravado. "Me too," he said. He paused, still curious. "When was he going to do it? He said something about this week."

Gillie shrugged as though they were talking about something that lacked consequence. He felt his stomach tighten and he had the urge to slap her across the face.

"All I know is that he said you'd be dead by the end of the week and then he could go on and do other things." There was a foolish, innocent look on her face.

"Did he say how he planned to do it?"

"No. He never talked about that. Only that it was going to be in front of a lot of people." She paused, thinking about the wisdom of continuing. "He said a lot of crazy stuff. About how you were going to know, just like those guys in prison who are going to the electric chair know, and how people would watch." She paused again, deciding she had gone far enough. "Just stuff like that. I guess he was crazy." She searched Broderick's face for some sign of approval. There was nothing.

He picked up the signed statement, folded and placed it in his breast pocket. "I'll check on you later," he said, then to Cordes: "You make the arrangements, then meet me upstairs so we can tie up the loose ends on this thing."

"What loose ends?" Cordes said. "You practically got this guy buried already."

Amberg sat in an interrogation room, his hands still pinned behind his back with handcuffs. Barney Ruditsky and a uniformed man were perched on the edge of a small table against the far wall. No one spoke.

When the door to the room opened Amberg's eyes filled with hatred. The door closed as quickly as it had opened. Broderick had counted on that look of crazed hatred and Amberg had not disappointed him. He turned to the two people standing in the hall with him, motioning with his head back to the room behind the closed door. "That's the man?" he said. It was a question, but it was also a positive statement. It was intended to be. The middle-aged woman hesitated for a moment, as though waiting for the man with her to speak first.

"It sure looks like one of them," the man said. "Is that the man that poor guy in the store identified"—he paused—"before he died, I mean?"

Broderick winked at him. "I'm not supposed to tell you that. We don't want to influence you, you know."

"I'm sure," the woman said. "He has the same mean look on his face. Is he dangerous, I mean, could he hurt us?"

"Not anymore, lady. Not if you both identify him and let us keep him locked up." He looked at the man, waiting. The woman also turned to him.

"Well, I'm sure," he said. "There's no question about it."

The woman smiled, "I am too," she said again. "We're both sure."

"You're good citizens," Broderick said, trying to sound as official as possible. "One thing, though." He waited for effect. "The newspapers will probably want to know the names of the witnesses. You know, sort of as an inspiration to other citizens. But I don't have to give them your names if you want privacy. Being interviewed, and all that." He shook his head, indicating the distastefulness of it all.

"Oh, I don't mind," the woman said.

"I guess I don't mind either," the man added.

"Good. We like to try and have good relations with the press." He put his hand on each of their shoulders. "Now there's just one more thing I want you to do. In the next room we have the two other men. Just a quick look and we'll be finished. Is that okay?"

They both agreed, and the procedure was followed again, with equal success. But something different also happened. When the door opened there had been a look of recognition on both Moe and Carmichael's faces. They had been there, Broderick now knew. But Amberg had not recognized the people. He remembered Danny's words. Two new guys, one named Carmichael and another whose name he did not know. There was someone who had been involved who was still out there. Hiding now, maybe even on his way out of town. He had nothing to fear from him, and if he brought him in he might even help Amberg. But still he had to know who he was. He went back to Gillie.

"I don't really know," she said. "All I know about him is that his name was Joe and he wasn't around very much. I don't think Hy liked him. And I think Hy made *him* nervous. He was a little guy and sort of slimy."

"It doesn't matter," Broderick said. "I don't think he was involved. It doesn't fit. You forget all about him. Understand?"

"Sure. Anything you say."

Broderick went back to the interrogation room, Cordes with him; he had finished the arrangements for Gillie. They had gotten her a room in a Greenwich Village hotel and the district attorney had agreed she should be protected, although Broderick knew the brass would not be happy with the expense. They never wanted to spend money, especially if they thought it meant easy duty for a cop.

When they entered the interrogation room Ruditsky and the uniformed man were still there. They sent the uniformed man out and Broderick pulled up a chair and placed it directly in front of Amberg. He sat down and leaned forward, resting his hands on his knees. Amberg stared straight into his face. He seemed calm, too calm.

"Oh, you're in serious trouble now, Hyman," Broderick began. "We know all about it. We know about you and Moe and Carmichael. We even know about your friend Joe." He turned to Cordes, "What's his last name?" he asked.

"I forget. I got it written down downstairs," Cordes said.

Amberg did not respond. The ploy had not worked.

"Those people who looked in before? They were witnesses to the Forty-eighth Street thing, Hyman. And they identified you as one of the men." Broderick's face was impassive.

"Everybody makes mistakes," Amberg said. "I told you, I was in my room with Gillie."

"Oh, yeah, Gillie. I almost forgot." Broderick reached into his breast pocket and withdrew the typed statement. He looked at it for a long moment, then turned it and held it up for Amberg. "Seems like Gillie remembers it different."

Amberg's eyes darted across the five terse sentences, then began again, his face growing darker with each second that passed. "So the lousy little bitch is gonna help you set me up." His voice was quiet, in total contrast to the fury that filled his eyes. "I'll kill her just like I'm gonna kill you. I'll kill all of you bastards. There ain't no place you can hide. I'll get every one of you."

162

Broderick leaned back in his chair, grinning. "The only thing you're going to get is the hot seat, Hyman. And the last thing those beady little eyes of yours are ever going to see before they cover your head is going to be me sitting there looking at you and smiling." He leaned forward again, bringing his face close to Amberg's. "And then they're going to pull that big switch and fry you until you look just like the nigger you are. And while they're putting you in a box I'll be on my way to that nice little steakhouse in Ossining to celebrate the fact that you're on your way to hell."

Broderick's body lurched backward. Amberg's head had moved like a snake's and the saliva he had spat had caught him squarely in the face. He bounced off the back of the chair and came forward with all his weight, his right fist coming straight from his shoulder. The initial punch ripped the skin above Amberg's left eye and sent him reeling to the side. But even before his body could fall from the chair the left hand followed with surprising speed, hitting him squarely in the nose, crushing it and forcing his body back, chair and all, to the floor.

Cordes jumped off the table and threw his body into Broderick's chest, grabbing him with both arms.

"I'll kill him," Broderick shouted.

"You already did," Cordes said. "He's as good as dead already. Think about it. This isn't the place—it's trouble."

Broderick's body eased. Amberg lay on the floor laughing through the blood that now streaked his face.

"I'm gonna kill you, Broderick. I'm gonna get out and kill you. You can count on it. And I'm gonna kill you slow. You're gonna die looking at *me*. I'm gonna shoot you in the belly and stand there and watch. It's gonna take hours. Hours, I tell you, hours."

Ruditsky reached down and pulled him to his feet. "You like to spit," he said. He spat in Amberg's face and threw him back against the table. "You move and *I'll* kill you," Ruditsky warned.

The door to the interrogation room opened. Garfoli stood there in full uniform, the brass buttons and gold shield glistening in the light. He looked around the room. His eyes were those of a rigid commanding officer, but there seemed to be a slight smile forming on his lips. Then he seemed to catch himself. "What is this all about?" he demanded. He directed his question at Broderick almost as though the others were not present.

"We were interrogating a murder suspect," Broderick said.

"Since when is interrogation synonymous with a brutal beating?" Garfoli snapped.

"He attacked Detective Broderick," Cordes said.

Garfoli nodded, then walked across the room to Amberg and looked behind his back. "That must have been a neat little trick, especially with his hands cuffed behind his back," he said.

"They weren't cuffed then. We just cuffed him," Ruditsky said.

Amberg began to laugh. Garfoli spun around and jabbed a finger at him. He was still a cop and nobody laughed at other cops. "You shut up," he snapped.

He walked over to Broderick and he could see the anger in his face, an anger now directed at him. To a degree it was deserved. He accepted that.

"I don't think you understand, sir," Cordes said.

"No, I don't, Detective. Why don't you and Detective Broderick explain it to me right now in the captain's office." He turned to Ruditsky. "You lock up the prisoner."

They followed Garfoli down the stairs to the main floor, past the court-styled desk of the desk sergeant, and across a large open area to a door just to the left of the main entrance. The inspector did not knock. He opened the door that bore the simple title, Commanding Officer, and walked inside.

The captain stood immediately, surrendering his position of authority to the superior officer and took a chair at the rear of the office. There was a smug look about him. He had remembered the directive issued to all precinct commanders almost two weeks earlier and had contacted the inspector as soon as he learned Broderick was interrogating a prisoner in the building. It would mean that he had earned favorable points with the chief of patrol.

Garfoli assumed his rightful position behind the large wooden desk, removed his cap, and dropped it on the blotter in front of him. He folded his hands and looked up at the two detectives standing before him. "Now explain," he said.

"We took off the cuffs because the prisoner had complained they were too tight. A young uniformed man put them on and in the excitement of the arrest he just did it too hard," Cordes began. He had noticed a slight change in Garfoli's expression with the mention of a patrolman, one of his own men.

"Go on," Garfoli said.

"Then the prisoner attacked Detective Broderick and he defended himself. He only hit him twice, just enough to get him under control."

Garfoli turned his attention to Broderick. "You must hit pretty hard, Detective. The man was pretty badly banged up."

Broderick did not respond.

"You said he was a murder suspect. Tell me about it."

"He and two other men were involved in a holdup at a jewelry store on West Forty-eighth Street this morning. They killed the store owner." Cordes spoke matter-of-factly, almost as though reading from a report. He knew it would impress a man like Garfoli whose only real involvement in police work now was in reading the reports filed by subordinates.

"And you're both *sure* he's one of the men?" Garfoli had begun drumming his fingers on the desk. It was a tactic he had used before, one intended to show his growing impatience and designed to make those standing before him nervous.

Cordes smiled. "We sure are, sir. Detective Broderick was able to get a deathbed statement from the victim and we located two witnesses who positively identified the three men we arrested. We caught them in a room in the Manhattan Hotel, less than two hours after they pulled the job, with the assistance of men from this precinct. One other thing you should know, Inspector."

Garfoli looked at Cordes. A sickening feeling was beginning to grow in Garfoli's stomach. He was losing this round too, he could feel it happening. "What?" he said.

"When we arrested the prisoner he stated, in front of a number of officers, that he had been planning to kill Detective Broderick." He watched Garfoli's jaw tighten. "So, you see, when he attacked him later we all had reason to believe he might be trying to carry out that threat."

Garfoli leaned back in his chair, turning again to Broderick. "And why would this man want to kill you, Detective?"

"I arrested him three years ago for armed robbery, sir. He just got out of prison and he still carries a grudge for that previous arrest." Broderick's voice was flat, concealing the disgust he felt for the man seated before him. He forced his face to remain expressionless.

"I see." Garfoli folded his hands again. He looked back at the captain. His face seemed confused. He too recognized that no charges could be filed. But there was also no need to surrender to these two thieves, Garfoli told himself. He was still an inspector and they were just detectives. "It seems odd to me that with three of you there you couldn't subdue the man without nearly beating his brains in." He looked up at Broderick. "But then that seems to be your style, Detective."

"I suppose I should have waited to see whether he killed me or not, sir." Broderick could not withhold his disgust any longer and the sarcasm was more than obvious.

Garfoli was inwardly pleased. He stood behind his desk. He was equal to Broderick in size and far more so in authority and he intended to use both to his advantage. "I don't like your attitude, Detective. In case you've forgotten, you happen to be addressing a superior officer who is raising some serious and totally justified questions."

"Yes, sir," Broderick snapped back.

"I had been willing to accept your explanation, but now I think some further inquiries are in order, especially since this arrest also involved people under my command." He was covering himself. He knew he had to have authority to investigate a detective without causing strife with a fellow superior officer. He walked around the desk, placing himself directly in front of

165

Broderick. He lowered his voice. "I don't like you, Broderick. I don't like the way you operate. And I'm going to check out every detail of your story, and if I find one single hole in it I'm going to bury you in that hole. Do you understand me?"

The veins in Broderick's neck were bulging. "Completely, sir."

Garfoli folded his arms in front of his chest. "Good." He let the word draw out slowly. "Now, are you finished with the prisoner and your reports?"

"Yes, sir," Cordes said.

"Then I want you both to get out of my precinct. Is that understood?" He returned to his chair and watched them file out of the office, then spun the chair around and faced the captain. "Shit," he said.

Out on the sidewalk Broderick stood next to Cordes, his fists clenched, his face livid with anger. "That guinea bastard. That fucking guinea bastard." His voice was a low growl.

"Don't let him bother you," Cordes said. "He can check that story out until he's ninety-four and he's not gonna find anything wrong with it." He took Broderick's arm and began walking him down the street to his car.

"It's not this. It's him. He's after us for something else. Somehow we cut in on him and he wants us for *that*. This is just an excuse. He's going to keep on us until he gets us for something."

"What are you talking about?" Cordes said.

"I told you about it a couple of weeks ago. When he called me into his office and started giving me a whole bunch of bullshit. I don't need any more problems, especially from that son of a bitch."

"So do something about it. You got friends."

Broderick stopped and turned toward him. "You're right. It's time to cash in a few debts with Chris Nolan. I'll go see him tomorrow." And then there won't be any problems, he added to himself.

CHAPTER TWENTY-TWO

J OHNNY BRODERICK WAS FEELING COCKY, COCKIER than he had felt in weeks, and as he walked along Broadway even the soot-filled gray skies could not dampen that feeling. All about him the noise was chaotic; the rush-hour traffic was in full flower and the blasts of the automobile horns and the angry shouts of motorists who wanted to be somewhere else played like some insane concerto. It sounded beautiful. It was alive, vibrant, and it guaranteed that the world would be there tomorrow and would be even better than it had been today.

The meeting with Chris Nolan four days ago had certainly helped. Nolan had laughed when he had told him about Garfoli. "I'll have somebody talk to that stupid wop," he had said. Now, only four days later, the lieutenant had informed him that all the reports Garfoli had requested had been returned "without comment," and to celebrate he and Cordes had gone to the Toledo and had shaken down the guineas again and it had made him feel wonderful. It had been difficult over the past few weeks. He had avoided making many of the regular collections because he had been convinced that Garfoli was hiding behind every lamp post, and he had been forced to rely on the money Cordes and Ruditsky had brought in and it had made him feel like a thief, not doing his share. Now, with money in his pocket he had earned himself, everything seemed right again.

He was still dressed conservatively, still playing the businessman role he had decided to assume until he made up his mind about the future, and he studied his reflection in the passing windows with satisfaction.

His shoulders swayed as he walked. He caught himself and began an amused self-lecture on how that would have to stop. All cops walked that way. It was an indelible mark that allowed you to spot them a half a block away. The weight of the badge and gun, an old-timer had once told him, the weight of each making you swagger from side to side. It was not far from the truth, it simply required a different understanding of the word *weight* to be properly understood. Within minutes he caught himself doing it again and shook his head. You're going to have to learn how to walk all over again, he decided.

He stopped at the intersection of Forty-fifth Street, waiting for the traffic light to change. He took his watch from his pocket and opened it. It was five-thirty, and he was fifteen minutes late. He could hurry but he did not want to. Even the hot, damp air felt good pressing into his lungs and he wanted to savor it. He looked to his left and far down the block he could see the marquee over the north entrance of the Manhattan Hotel. He inhaled deeply, feeling the humid warmth engulf him from within. Even Garfoli was off his back now and there was nothing to worry about. He was on top of the heap and ahead was even a better mountain, complete with elevator.

Halfway up the next block he caught himself swaggering again. "Stop it," he said aloud. A woman walking near him gave him a concerned look, and he quickly offered her a long, lewd wink that set her feet in motion, scurrying ahead of the maniac she had stumbled across. He followed her for a full block until he reached the tearoom where Mona would be waiting, and each time she glanced over her shoulder he winked again, throwing her transmission into an even higher gear.

He pushed his bulk through the revolving door of the tearoom and found himself amused again. It was a genteel establishment, new to him, but one that wealthy old ladies would choose for afternoon tea, exactly the type of place in which Mona would feel comfortable sitting and waiting. He did not see her at first, but she was there, sitting at a small table placed discreetly behind a row of potted palms, a cup and saucer and pewter teapot set out before her. There was something queer about her as he approached, a look of confused concern that seemed out of place with the surroundings. He sat across from her.

"What's the matter? You find a mouse in your tea?" He was grinning like a schoolboy. He could not help it.

"I've been reading your press notices," she said. Her eyes seemed almost hurt.

"It can't be that bad." He was still grinning at her.

"It is for me," she said, handing him a folded newspaper.

He took it and read quickly. It was a full account of Amberg's arraignment that morning, and the reporter had outdone himself reporting the screaming threats he had made, promising again that Broderick was going to die. No effort had been spared to make the account as chilling as possible.

"It must have been a slow day for news," he said, dropping the newspaper on the table.

"I suppose you're just delighted that some madman has promised to kill you." She looked away from him, annoyed.

The thought of another madman jumped into his mind, this one pursuing a woman up Broadway, his eye blinking in a wild, lustful frenzy. He laughed. "Of course I'm delighted. Didn't you know that I planned a new career? I'm going to be the toughest angel in heaven."

She picked her gloves up from the table and threw them in her lap for emphasis. "You're very funny, John. How do you think I feel reading something like that?"

He picked up the paper again and feigned a quick rereading of the article. "I don't see where the little creep said anything about killing you," he said.

"That's *all* you have to say about *this*, this insanity?" She had raised her voice, and she looked around quickly to see if it had been noticed.

He leaned forward, speaking softly. "Look. That crippled little dwarf was brought to court in chains. They keep him in the maximum security wing of the Tombs. He couldn't get out of that place with ten sticks of dynamite. After his trial they're going to take his crazy little butt and drop it in Death Row in Sing Sing, and that's no crackerbox either. Then some morning they're going to strap him in and fry his insane little brain until it looks like a burnt piece of hamburger. And you want me to worry? Mona, Hy Amberg is dead. He's already in his grave and he knows it. The only difference is that he hasn't stopped breathing yet. And that's only a matter of time."

She stared at him for a long moment, letting his words sink in, reaching desperately for some answer. "But what about his friends?" she finally said.

"He hasn't got any friends. All his old friends are locked up and they're going to end up the same as he is. And anybody who isn't has no interest in doing anything for a dead man. It's not their style, believe me."

"But he could hire somebody." Her voice was insistent, not wanting to give in to his obvious logic, afraid to do so.

"I hope he does. They'll take his money and laugh all the way to the nearest speakeasy. Who do you think is going to take on a cop-killing for somebody who's already dead and buried? The odds are all wrong. Nobody with the guts to do it is stupid enough to back a sure loser. Hy Amberg will just have to wait to meet me in Hell. That's all there is to it."

She took a deep breath and began toying with her teacup. "Then why is Danny so upset?"

"Danny? Where the hell does Danny come into this?"

169

"That's where I got the newspaper. He was upset about it too."

Broderick looked up at the ceiling. "Jesus, Mary, and Joseph. That's all I need, the two of you deciding I don't even know my own business." He pointed a playful finger at her. "The next time you see your boyfriend you tell him that if he doesn't keep his mouth shut I'm going to stop letting him make book on the side."

"Oh, be quiet. He just cares about you. We both care about you, although I'm beginning to wonder why."

"Because I'm so gorgeous. You keep telling me I'm gorgeous."

"That's with your clothes off," she whispered. "With your clothes on, you're absolutely dreadful."

A crazed look spread across his face. He reached up and began unloosening his tie. "That, madam, can be corrected."

She began to laugh. "Stop it, you fool. There are people in here who know me."

"But do they *really* know you?" He widened his eyes in mock madness.

"Stop *it*," she whispered, glancing about her.

He straightened his tie and leaned back in his chair. "You stop and I'll stop. Deal? It's either that or you drink your tea with a naked detective sitting across from you."

"I surrender," she said quickly. "Besides, I see no point in arousing all these ladies with your lovely beefy body."

"Good. And speaking of beef, I could eat a steak the size of this." He held his hands apart as though holding each end of a football. "How about an early dinner?"

"I'll do anything to get you out of here," she said.

When they came through the revolving doors the rain was hitting the sidewalk in dime-sized drops. He ran to the curb and hailed a cab, then pushed her in ahead of him, struggling to keep them both as dry as possible.

"The Homestead. Ninth and Fourteenth," he told the driver, then leaned back and gave her an impish look. "Another minute out there and you would have looked like a drowned rat, madam."

"There is only one rat in here"—she smiled—"and he's wearing big, flat feet."

The canopy over the entrance to the Homestead sheltered them from the rain and the rich, dark paneling that embraced them as they entered made it seem impossible that it had been raining at all. It was a room imbued with warmth, and the greetings of the owner turned maître d' were like that of an old friend, replete with complaints that Broderick's last visit had been too far in the past.

Mona was pleased by both the greeting and the restaurant. It was one with which she had not been familiar and when he had given the address to the driver she had shuddered inwardly, realizing that the location was in the

170

heart of the city's meat district. But the image of burly men chewing on steaks was far from what she had found. The restaurant was masculine but with touches of solid good taste. The dark paneling was covered with fine oil paintings and in the center of the beamed ceiling of the main dining room there was a large skylight of intricate stained glass. The only flaw she found was the stuffed heads of four antlered creatures that had been placed high on the walls, guaranteeing them a commanding view of every course that would be served.

She glanced casually at each. "Are those previously dissatisfied customers, or were they formerly part of the bill of fare?" she asked.

"The owner likes to think of himself as a big game hunter," he said.

"Really. What, in heaven's name, are they—deer?"

"A little bigger than that. The two behind you and the one to your left are elk. The one behind me is a moose."

She studied the animal behind Broderick's left shoulder. "He's an ugly brute. I'm not sure I'd care to have him looking over my shoulder while I ate."

"I won't worry unless he asks for a bite."

"If he does, darling, I'm leaving immediately," she said.

They continued their playful banter as they looked over the menus. It had become part of their way with each other, part of the warmth that had developed during the preceding week. She had noticed the change that had come over him, the greater ease with which he now seemed to approach things. She was beginning to feel comfortable with him and he with her, she thought, and even more importantly he seemed to be at ease with himself, lacking the inner turmoil she had sensed at first.

"They've raised the damned prices again," he said, his brow furrowed as he studied the menu. "The steaks are sixty-five cents now. The last time I was here they were four bits."

"Fifty cents, darling," she corrected. "Stop trying to sound like a hoodlum."

The image of his swaggering shoulders returned with a mixture of amusement and annoyance. "Some habits are hard to break. But I'm trying," he said.

"Johnny!" The sound of his name came from behind, the voice strong and commanding, and he knew immediately who it was. He rose from his chair as he turned to meet the warm smile of Jimmy Walker and the smug boredom of Betty Compton.

"Hello . . . Jim." He had paused, catching himself. He had almost said "Boss," a term he sometimes used to please the mayor. But he would not use that word in front of Mona, and Walker had not seemed to notice the hesitation. Quickly he greeted Betty Compton and then introduced them to Mona.

Walker's eyes sparkled immediately. There was nothing he liked more than a beautiful woman and he always seemed at his best in their presence. An awkward pause followed and Broderick ended it by suggesting that they join him. Walker accepted graciously, but insisted they would have to be his guests. The situation sent a wave of uncertainty through Broderick. He had been left no alternative and the mayor had taken command at once and he knew now that he would have to make the best of it.

Mona felt total ambivalence. She had never had the pleasure of the mayor's company and the idea aroused a degree of curiosity. But she had also looked forward to a quiet evening alone. It was Betty Compton's air of resigned dissatisfaction that quickly changed her feelings. She would thoroughly enjoy deflating her obvious pretentiousness, of gently exposing her as the social unequal she so certainly was. She had heard quiet gossip about the mayor's show-girl companion but she had not expected the false sense of importance.

Jimmy Walker continued to exude his never-ending charm and explained that he had slipped away from City Hall early so he and Betty could enjoy dinner together before her appearance that evening.

Mona seized the opportunity and offered Betty Compton a warm smile. "Are you in the theater, Miss Compton?" she asked.

Betty Compton's eyes widened. "Yes, I am. I have been for some time," she said.

"That must be terribly exciting. I would love to see you perform. John will have to get us tickets. What theater are you appearing at?" Mona could feel the woman's blood turn cold.

"The Imperial," she said, her voice icy and aloof. "But Jim reserves two seats for every performance. I'm sure he could arrange for Johnny to have those tickets."

"Of course," Walker said. "You stop by the office and I'll take care of it." He turned to Mona. "You'll love the show. Betty is marvelous."

"I'm sure we shall," Mona said. "I've always admired those who have the inclination to perform in public."

"And what do you do, Miss D'Arcy?" Betty Compton sought quick retaliation.

"Oh, nothing quite as exciting as you, I'm afraid. Some occasional charity work, but far too little of that. At least that's what I'm told."

The feminine combat had not escaped Walker and he watched Mona closely. "Your name, D'Arcy, seems familiar," he said. "Do I know your family?"

"I believe so," she said. "But D'Arcy is my former husband's name. I believe you know my uncle, William Eatkins. Eatkins was my maiden name."

"Bill Eatkins, of the hat company," Walker said. "Yes, indeed. I know him well. He's been very supportive, although I secretly believe he's a Republican."

172

Mona laughed. "He certainly is. But above all he's a businessman." She watched Walker's reaction. It was veiled but his underlying sense of understanding was unmistakable. She had established herself with this man and with that, Broderick, as well, she decided.

Walker tilted his head toward Broderick. "I didn't realize you were traveling in society these days, John," he said.

Broderick flushed and seemed to grope for an answer and as Mona watched him she felt a sinking hope that he would respond well. Betty Compton denied him the chance.

"But we haven't seen Johnny in several weeks, Jim," she said. "Apparently you haven't had any of your important errands for him." She turned to Mona. "Jim has a way of attaching great importance to the most ridiculous things at times and then everyone else has to treat them as though they thought they were important too."

The humiliation had been administered thoroughly. Mona felt as though she had been slapped and forced herself to return Betty Compton's laughter, using it as a shield. Broderick sat there appearing oblivious to what was being said, not even trying to defend himself, not even aware that he should, and she wished she could reach out and shake him.

"I'm afraid Betty doesn't think any of the duties of the mayor are very important," Walker said. "But Johnny and I both know how important some things are that seem insignificant to others."

Walker had saved him. The tactful diplomat, she thought. He had done what John should have been able to do for himself. Instead, he had sat there like the lackey this show-girl had made him out to be. And still he sat there looking completely out of his element. She was not certain whether it was the fact that it had happened or that it could happen that so upset her.

They ordered dinner and the conversation turned to idle chatter. Walker raised the newspaper account of Amberg's arraignment and was lavish in his praise of men forced to engage in police work, given the type of criminal that now populated the city. But even that failed to inspire Broderick to any degree and she noticed that the bravado he had displayed earlier with her was now missing and that his remarks, at best, were self-effacing. She fought to salvage something for him, speaking of the casual approach he seemed to take toward dangerous situations. But it only made things worse.

Walker began a long story about an adventure he had with Broderick, a story that was obviously one of his favorites and one he told with great satisfaction. It ended with Broderick arresting a hoodlum in the presence of the mayor and some friends and it was obvious that he had performed on command. Even the laughter that followed the story, laughter that Broderick shared, left him sitting there very much the court jester basking in the approval of his personal king. It gave her a sick feeling, being forced to sit and watch his display of weakness. She had found weakness in every man she had known. But she had not found it before in him, and now it was there.

At seven-thirty Betty reminded the mayor that her first curtain was half an hour away and a hasty departure was begun. Mona quickly declined an offer to drive uptown with them, explaining before Broderick could speak that they planned to visit friends not far from there. The thought of any continued conversation appalled her and she needed time alone, time to escape the humiliation of the evening.

The mayor's departure also marked the disappearance of Broderick's reticence and with it the establishment of her own. The transformation was overpowering and she watched him, amazed by the difference, and she wondered if it was just this one man, this politician, who produced what she had witnessed. She had seen him with others far more imposing than the mayor. Her uncle, his business associates. He had been ill at ease but he had not been subservient. It was maddening.

He suggested dessert but she merely shook her head and said nothing.

"You're very quiet all of a sudden," he said. "Is something wrong?"

Her eyes rose to meet his and by the change of expression she could tell that he could see the disappointment she felt so deeply.

"What is it?" he asked.

"I just found their company very unsatisfying," she said.

"I'm sorry. There wasn't much I could do. I had to ask them to join us."

"It had nothing to do with their joining us. I was just very upset by the way you let them treat you." She watched his face. He understood what she was saying; he had simply hoped she would not notice. His subservience had been a conscious thing, she knew that now and as such she also knew it could be corrected.

"I do work for him. He can control what I do and where I do it. I don't necessarily like it, but it's true," he said.

She listened to his words, to the hollowness in his voice, and her anger began to fade, replaced by a sadness that bordered on the maternal. She reached across the table and took his hand, feeling the size and power of it, so totally juxtaposed with the hurt that had now settled in his eyes.

"John, I care about you. And because I do it hurts me to see someone like that manipulating you as though you were a marionette. You're too good a person for that."

"You've got him wrong." He paused, hearing the lack of conviction in his own words. "He's been good to me. And believe me, it doesn't hurt to have the mayor pulling for you. The Police Department is political. It's very political."

"Then perhaps you just don't belong there. You should be dealing with that man as an equal, not someone who has to perform for him on command. You're better than that. Believe me, John." She was speaking softly but her voice was strong and confident.

"Look. No cop is an equal of the mayor. It just doesn't work that way. He runs the city and I work for it and there are a few thousand cops who would trade places with me tomorrow if they could."

She squeezed his hand. "You didn't hear what I said, John. Perhaps you shouldn't be in the Police Department any longer. There is no reason why you have to be. You certainly don't need the danger." She smiled. "And I promise I'll provide all the excitement you need."

His face broke into a grin and his eyes brightened with the release of tension. "And what should I do, become a kept man? Come to think of it, I always wanted to be a kept man."

"That has some definite possibilities, but I'm not sure you could survive spending twenty-four hours a day alone with me. You might waste away. You'd certainly lose a great deal of weight." She sipped her coffee, still watching him over the edge of the cup. "There is something you could consider." She paused, gauging his reaction. "My uncle spoke to you about possibilities in private industry. There is that."

"There's a big difference between 'possibilities' and a job. Your uncle just said we'd talk again some day. I can't slip in my papers on that."

" 'Slip in your papers?' What, in heaven's name, is that?"

"Retire," he said.

"Oh. Hoodlum talk again."

"No, just cop talk."

She sat back, her fingers rising to her throat; stroking it. "Why don't you talk to Uncle again?" she said.

"He hasn't asked me. Besides it's a very big step." He did not want her to know yet how much he had been thinking about it.

"You mean you're not sure it's what you want." Her voice was sharper and there was a hint of disapproval in it that was intended.

"No, it's not that. I just don't want him to think I'm looking for anything." He twisted slightly in his chair, recalling the conversation with Eatkins in his garden, the questions about his marriage, about his feelings toward Mona.

"That's silly," she said. "If he hadn't been interested in you he never would have raised the subject. He is too much of a businessman for that, I assure you."

"Well, I'd still rather wait for him to contact me, or at least until I see him again. I'd feel more comfortable about it that way."

"Well, if you won't mention it to him, I shall." She waited for his reaction. There was only a slight shrug of his shoulders. "I'll be seeing him later to-night, anyway."

"Tonight? I didn't know you had plans to go there."

He seemed confused and she had to keep herself from laughing. "I simply forgot to tell you, darling. My aunt called this afternoon and asked that I stop by this evening. She's having a party and wants me to help with the guest list.

But as long as I'm there I'll speak to Uncle about you."

"Do you really think that's such a good idea? I'd hate to have him think I was putting you up to something."

She brushed away his concern with a toss of her head. "My uncle knows me far too well. The last thing he would ever assume was that someone was forcing me to do something I didn't want to do. He's tried that often enough himself."

Broderick folded his hands nervously. "Okay, you do what you want to do. But you have to understand that I'm not promising anything. He may not offer and I may not accept even if he does." He was sure it would more likely be the former and he knew he did not want to fail again in her eyes.

"You don't have to promise anything, darling." She smiled at him sweetly. You just have to do it, she thought.

CHAPTER TWENTY-THREE

THE YALE CLUB STOOD LIKE A STONE FORTRESS, STARing omnipotently across Vanderbilt Avenue. It was a rigid building with barred windows on the ground floor that made it seem implacable, an aging dowager quietly waiting for her sons to emerge from Grand Central Station after a wearisome trip from New Haven. There was a sense of near absolute power about the exterior, and the large flag with its massive white "Y" emblazoned on a field of blue hung above the entrance with a touch of patrician indifference that seemed altogether fitting.

He had been there once before, four years earlier, when two of the club's members had been robbed as they left this private fortress. There had been a celebration, he recalled, the twenty-fifth anniversary of the club, and it had been an occasion duly noted by two of the city's more enterprising young thieves.

Standing before the building now Johnny Broderick remembered his impressions of the massive gothic lobby that had seemed then like the interior of some castle he had read about in books as a child. It was something the average person was never allowed to experience, he had thought then, a place reserved for those born to it. The people who ran the club had not been pleased when he arrived four years ago and he had been admitted with a sense of distasteful necessity and then asked to question the victims in an out-of-the-way office so the other members would not be disturbed. Now he was back again, as a guest this time, and he wondered if the reception would really be any different.

Eatkins's secretary had telephoned his office at ten and had extended the luncheon invitation in a purely businesslike way. He had been staggered by the call, not so much because he had doubted Mona's ability to arrange it, but because her uncle's response had come so quickly. It made him wonder if it was due to her influence or the old man's interest in him. He really didn't care, but he felt certain it wasn't the latter.

The gothic majesty of the lobby was unchanged; if anything it was more overpowering than he had remembered. Inside, an elderly black man dressed in a dark suit and tie took his hat and directed him to the reception desk where an officious little man greeted him with a warm but questioning smile. Even the mention of Eatkins's name did not seem to alter the clerk's demeanor, and after a quick check of the leather-bound book set before him he explained that a table had been reserved in the Tap Room on the third floor and that the book indicated Mr. Eatkins had already arrived. When Broderick asked directions to the elevator a small smile appeared on the clerk's lips and he immediately regretted having asked. It was the tip-off that he'd never been invited before, he thought, and the clerk picked up on it immediately. They were such intimidating little bastards, these people. They never missed the chance of letting you know you were no better than they were.

The clerk had soured him, and the feeling sank deep inside as he rode the elevator to the third floor. The four men who had entered the elevator with him had not helped: Their casual sense of assurance and practiced, near Anglified manner of speaking only made the feeling more ingrained and the glances they had given him made him sure they also knew he did not belong there.

His entrance to the Tap Room added to the mood. As he was led across the room he could see Eatkins seated at a small corner table and he sensed a look of wry amusement on his face as though he was considering how he would later explain his strange guest to other members. The feeling did not change when Eatkins rose and extended his hand. There was no obvious sign of embarrassment; he was smiling. But there was something about his manner, something that made Broderick feel that the older man was enjoying his discomfort. He wondered if that was why he had chosen this place, to let him see exactly how much he did not belong.

"John, it's good to see you again," Eatkins said, gesturing toward the chair opposite him. "Can I offer you a drink? We don't observe prohibition here. Each member is allowed to keep his own stock. It circumvents the law."

Broderick declined and Eatkins asked him if he had been to the club before. He explained the robbery four years ago.

178

"Oh, really? I was here that evening, but like most of the members I never knew about it until several days later. It was quite a celebrated event and there was a great deal of discussion later about the wisdom of building the club so close to Grand Central Station, the criminal element that seems to hang about such a place and all that. But of course I don't have to tell you about criminals, do I?"

"I've had a certain exposure," Broderick said, not quite sure how else to answer.

"Yes, I noticed you had quite a bit of excitement the day after you were at my home. What was that chap's name you arrested?"

"Amberg," Broderick said, smiling to himself. He had never thought of Hy Amberg as a "chap" before and he could picture Eatkins saying "my dear chap" to him and suddenly finding a gun shoved under his nose.

"Terrible thing killing that shopkeeper," Eatkins went on. "But I suppose you get used to the violence after awhile." He smiled benignly across the table.

Broderick nodded and returned the smile. The inane nature of the conversation was annoying him and so was Eatkins's condescending attitude. The man did not like him. He was being polite. The waiter interrupted them with menus and Eatkins quickly ordered a simple sandwich, explaining he ate little at lunch. Broderick did the same, not because he would not have preferred something else, but because the menu held little he wanted to eat. When the sandwiches arrived he was surprised to find the crusts removed from the bread and even more that the bread itself had been buttered. Butter next to meat was something he never would have considered and as he bit into it he was surprised to find it even passably palatable.

Eatkins refused to get to the point; he contented himself with a detailed explanation of the virtues of the club: its excellent squash courts, exercise rooms, but most of all the camaraderie that existed there and the inestimable value it provided in a business sense. He went on to lament that members, "all graduates of Yale, of course," were not able to have corporate memberships and what obvious benefit that would be if it were allowed. The point, though made in an offhanded way, was not wasted on Broderick and he sat back trying to hide the anger that was building. He decided to let Eatkins finish his subtle lesson about keeping one's place.

The old man noted the change—he could see it in the younger man's eyes—and he seemed to hesitate for a moment.

"Well, enough about the club, John," he said, his eyes becoming sharper, more direct. "You have to forgive an old university war-horse. It seems one never quite gets the ivy out of one's veins and any opportunity to wave the old banner is just too great a temptation."

"Yes, I feel the same way about East Twenty-third Street," Broderick said.

179

There was no mirth in his voice and none was intended. A puzzled look swept across Eatkins's face but only for a moment, then he caught himself and forced a laugh.

"Very good, very good indeed," he said, his eyes also lacking any sign of amusement. "But we should get to the point, shouldn't we?"

"If there is one," Broderick said, smiling again. "I just thought we were having lunch." He was playing detective with him now and enjoying it.

"Certainly we are," the old man said. He was embarrassed by the remark but he hid it beautifully behind a controlled patrician facade that Broderick was forced to admire. "But there was a business matter I also wanted to discuss with you. A matter we discussed briefly once before, if you recall."

Broderick nodded, refusing to commit himself further.

"I suppose you're aware that Mona made a point of discussing this matter with me?"

Broderick could feel his stomach suck in. The question had been too direct and he had not anticipated it. The old boy was playing fast and loose and he thought he would have made a good stand-up boxer in his day, never allowing himself to be pushed into a corner by a brawler. He decided to play it his way; he had no idea what, if anything, Mona had told him. "She mentioned last night that she planned to talk to you, but I didn't have any idea she planned to do it so soon. She's been talking to me a lot about it lately."

"Mona does things"—he paused—"hurriedly. Sometimes impetuously," he said, allowing his eyes to take on a far-off glow as if remembering her past eccentricities. "But she has a good business head." He added the last sentence almost too quickly, Broderick thought, as though scotching any implication of criticism.

"I'm afraid I haven't had a chance to see that side of her."

"No, you wouldn't, of course," Eatkins said. "But you said something a moment ago that puzzles me. You said she had been talking a great deal recently about our previous conversation. Exactly what did you mean?"

Broderick leaned forward as if offering to share a secret. It was an old cop trick and Eatkins fell for it, leaning forward as well. "She seems to think I should do something else than police work. Maybe it's the danger, I really don't know. But she talks about it a lot." He was feeding the fish now, trying to see how hungry he was.

"Then I take it you're not particularly interested? On your own, I mean?"

"I'm interested in everything. It's just not something I'm pushing for. It's like placing a bet. The morning line is one thing, the price before the game starts is something else."

Lines appeared in Eatkins's otherwise smooth face and he began to stroke his moustache deliberately. He had hoped the man would be looking for something, but realized now that he was clever enough to wait to be asked.

He had overlooked the fact that someone involved with the police would be used to playing things close to the vest, never soliciting but always open to suggestion. He sat back in his chair. He too knew the value of a good poker hand. "I had hoped I had stimulated you with our earlier conversation," he began. There was a slight note of sarcasm in his voice. Then it disappeared. "Mona is right, you know. There are great benefits in business." He waited, but Broderick failed to pick up on the suggestion. "Tell me, have you given any thought to our conversation?"

"Some. But like you said, I've been busy with my own work lately, so most of it has come from discussions with your niece. The idea is very interesting, but I thought you were talking in a general way when you spoke about the opportunities. I didn't take it as any kind of offer."

"No, you were correct. I don't make offers rashly. But I have thought about it and apparently so has my niece. But, being a businessman, I like to know the degree of someone's interest before making an offer." Eatkins raised his coffee cup to his lips, keeping his eyes on Broderick across the lip of the cup.

"You make it hard for me. It really depends on what you have in mind."

Eatkins folded his hands in front of him for a moment, then unfolded them and picked up a spoon, holding it between his fingers like a ruler. "Let's not fence any longer, John. What I have in mind is someone to handle labor matters on an executive level. The position will pay between twenty and twenty-five thousand a year. Let's say twenty-five thousand, why bicker? A smart man could find other fringe benefits as well. I've taken the trouble to do a bit of research on you. It's something I do with all prospective employees, so please don't be offended. You live exceptionally well for your income, so I must assume you've found fringe benefits of your own to supplement that income. That is admirable. Labor relations, I believe, will also provide those opportunities. Gambling, for instance, exists in every factory and for the large part is ignored unless it interferes with production. It's a way of keeping one's workers happy, even if it also happens to keep them poorer than necessary. But it doesn't have to be ignored, if you understand my point. The main thrust of the position will be to see to it that the employees at that level work for the least amount of money possible and for the longest hours possible. We also hope to curtail demands for improved working conditions. That will mean private agreements with the people who eventually come to positions of authority in the unions and these agreements will have to be made by men who can deal with these people, speak their language, and make whatever arrangements are mutually beneficial. This is what I would be offering if things work out as they appear to be at this moment." Eatkins sat back and waited, still toying with his spoon.

"I think you lost me on the last part," Broderick said.

181

Eatkins smiled. "I don't think so, John." He watched Broderick's eyes and found he was right.

Broderick's jaw tightened. "You're talking about Mona and me," he said.

"It is a family concern. I'm sure you understand that, but of course there would be a contract to afford a certain degree of protection in the event, well, shall we just say in case the infatuation faded."

Broderick stared at him and then forced a smile. "You know you're real cute, Mr. Eatkins. You make me an offer out of one side of your mouth and then out of the other side you let me know you really don't want me to take it."

Eatkins sat back in his chair and stared, unmoved, across the table. His own features were firm now, all traces of the false friendliness having disappeared. "Go on, Mr. Broderick," he said coldly. "You have the floor now."

Broderick pushed his coffee cup aside and placed his forearms heavily on the table, folding his hands in front of him. He had played the obedient puppy the previous night at the Homestead and he had done it in front of Mona without even realizing it. He had no intention of repeating that performance. "You bet I'll go on," he said, smiling again. "What bothers you is Mona's interest in me. I'm sure you've tried to do something about it, but it obviously hasn't worked out too well for you. Well, that's too bad because I'm interested in her too and I intend to keep things that way."

"Bully," Eatkins said, his voice dry and sarcastic.

Broderick ignored him. "Now you just told me about the job. But what you talked about mostly were all the illegal things I could and would be doing. Now that's a strange offer to make to a police officer, isn't it?"

Eatkins removed a cigarette from a gold cigarette case and methodically tapped the end of the cigarette against the case. "I wasn't aware that illegalities concerned you. As I told you, we have looked into your background."

"If you're making charges, I think you ought to make them to the police commissioner. I don't like being investigated, Mr. Eatkins. You know a little time could be spent looking up your ass too." Broderick's voice was still calm but his folded hands were now tightly clenched.

"What a quaint turn of phrase, Mr. Broderick. Why don't you get to the point." Eatkins lit his cigarette and blew a shaft of smoke out above Broderick's head.

"The point is that the bullshit stops, that's all. As far as the job goes, I really don't care how you run your business. You and I both know that the days of the old Homestead Strike are over. You can't win by muscle alone anymore. Sure we can roust pickets, but it's not like the old days in the steel industry. They just don't stay rousted any more. As far as buying off the labor leaders goes, what the hell do I care?" He looked at Eatkins as though he were watching someone who was comical. "Just don't think you invented the

182

idea. It's been going on for a while." Eatkins began to speak, but Broderick raised his hand stopping him. "Now, you talked about gambling and working conditions. Gambling, I'm not even going to talk about, Mr. Eatkins. Because as far as I'm concerned it doesn't even exist. And your working conditions are your business. You can have another Triangle Factory fire for all I care. I learned a long time ago that you're either part of the people who have the money or you're part of the people trying to get it. I grew up on the wrong side of that game and I decided early on that I didn't like it there. That's why when I go out and roust the kind of people I came from it doesn't bother me a bit. And that's why people like you don't bother me either. Because you need men like me. We make things work for you."

Eatkins tapped the ash from his cigarette into an ash tray. "Very eloquent, Mr. Broderick. What you fail to mention, however, is that while we do need *people like you*, we don't need *you* personally. We need someone like you. Someone with your . . . shall we say . . . merits."

"Then find him." Broderick began to push his chair from the table.

"Just a moment, John," Eatkins said, stopping him. "Why don't we declare a temporary truce?" Broderick shrugged his shoulders and Eatkins drew a long breath before continuing. "I have no interest in making my niece unhappy, for reasons that are very much my own. I don't particularly like you and I don't approve of you for her, but that's really a moot point, isn't it? You could do the job I want and I might even have hired you myself." He smiled faintly, more to himself than at Broderick. "Perhaps not at the salary discussed, but I still might have hired you. So your working for the company doesn't really upset me *that* much. But your relationship with my niece does."

"If you're suggesting I could have the job and keep you happy by dropping her, forget it."

Eatkins's face became strained and he suddenly looked tired, older. "That's not what I'm suggesting and I certainly don't want you to convey that to her. In fact, I prefer this entire discussion remain between ourselves."

"Don't worry. I won't talk out of school," Broderick said, enjoying himself now.

Eatkins crushed out his cigarette and quickly lit another. The conversation had taken an unfavorable turn and he needed time to regroup his thoughts, to regain some advantage.

"There is one thing that bothers me greatly," he began.

"What?"

"Your family, John. When we spoke before you mentioned plans for a divorce. Speaking purely as an uncle, may I know just how those plans are progressing?"

"I don't think it's any of your business," Broderick spoke the words without anger.

183

"I disagree. I do have Mona's interests at heart and I feel it's a fair question."

Broderick felt his stomach tighten. Several answers flashed through his mind and were rejected as quickly as they appeared. "It's difficult to say right now," he answered. "My wife is Catholic and the word 'divorce' isn't really in her vocabulary."

"What about an annulment. I'm told those can be arranged for certain considerations?"

"You mean if the price is right."

"Even religion is run by businessmen," Eatkins said. "Have you considered that?"

"I don't think it'll be necessary. If my wife knew there was someone else, somebody specific, I think she'd give in. But Mona and I haven't discussed marriage, that's something you should know."

"No, I'm sure you haven't and I assure you she's given me no such indication either. But let's just say I see the flowering of a relationship that seems to point in that direction. Mona is ready for another marriage. She's bored and has been for a long time now and you seem to have ended that boredom. By the way, I compliment you for that. It's no small feat."

"Are you telling me marriage is part of the deal?" Broderick grinned at him and watched Eatkins's facial muscles tighten.

"Of course not." Eatkins's voice had grown cold again. He had struggled for an advantage and had lost it. "Family is very important to me, both in the business and out of it."

"And when you're in the business being part of the family has certain advantages," he said. His smile was almost a smirk now and he could see the unhappy effect it produced on the older man.

"Always direct, aren't you, John? Let's just say that merit is always rewarded, no matter *whom* it comes from. And merit is something I expect from anyone who works for the firm."

Broderick laughed. "Mr. Eatkins, you don't have to tell me that you don't want me as part of your family. But I promise you one thing. If it ever does happen I'll never call you Uncle William."

"I'd be eternally grateful for that, John."

"As far as the job goes, I'd like some time to think it over, if that's okay."

"Of course. Why don't we say a month and set October first as a time for decision, and if you decide favorably we can discuss whatever contract will be needed and plan to have you aboard whenever you can work out the necessary details with the Police Department. Is that agreeable?"

Broderick nodded almost absentmindedly. There was still something unspoken. It was almost as though Eatkins wanted to tell him something more but had decided against it. There was an aloofness about the man, something he had also observed in Mona, as though each of them were out of the same

184

mold. But of course they were, he told himself. A sudden feeling of concern passed through him; he needed time to think about this, to feel his way a little more so he was sure he knew what he was doing. It all seemed simple, almost too simple, and that bothered him.

"You seem deep in thought already, John," Eatkins said, drawing him back.

"There's a lot to think about."

"Yes, there is. Changing one's life is always a difficult step, no matter how attractive that change may *seem* to be."

Broderick rubbed his chin, then reached for his pocketwatch and noted the time. "I better get back to work or I may need your job." He smiled across the table. "Right now I don't."

"I understand that," Eatkins said, rising and offering his hand. "But we'll be seeing each other again soon, I've no doubt of that. And thank you for joining me on such short notice."

"It was my pleasure," Broderick said. "I really mean that."

Eatkins watched him leave, noting the slight swagger of the man's shoulders as he walked. The expression on his face remained rigid; he seemed drawn, as though he had been forced to endure something he knew was a mistake. He motioned to the waiter and ordered more coffee. He would take some steam before he left, he decided. It was always soothing. Then he would finish the day's business, perform his family duty, and also see if he could salvage something out of it all. A friend, an old schoolmate from the same class, came over and joined him, and part of the growing tension was abated by idle conversation. The old school tie nonsense still provided a place to hide from the realities of life that were beyond control, he told himself.

Later, in the steam room he thought about it all again. Control was not completely lost, not yet. There were matters that could be discussed subtly, it was simply a question of technique, of choosing the right approach to the situation. Situation. My God, what a polite word. It was snobbishness pure and simple, but it was a snobbishness he firmly believed in, one that had always been a part of his world and that he was certain should be maintained. There were too many things going on in this world today that forced one to change one's way of thinking, of living. The whole idea of unionism was descending on them like a poison for which there was no antidote. It could be handled, he was sure, by the subtle manipulation of the lesser minds who would operate these abominable organizations. He saw that even if most of his friends did not. Accommodation, not senseless battle that could only lead to a humiliating surrender, that was the key. A maintenance of control and with that control a maintenance of total power. The reality of it settled on him and with it a certain degree of comfort. A man like Broderick could indeed be useful in the future. He had the same plebeian mind that this new opposition would have and because of that he would know exactly how to

185

deal with them—with the proper direction, of course. There was nothing wrong with that part of it; it made perfect sense from a business point of view. But God, not at twenty-five thousand a year and certainly not as a member of the family. The thought of it was enough to make him ill.

Outside the club Eatkins decided to walk, to give himself time to think. When he tired of walking he would take a taxi, he decided, and he told his driver to return home. He turned into Forty-fifth Street and then again into Madison Avenue. Perhaps he would walk the entire distance, he thought. Perhaps he would need that much time to sort out his thoughts.

CHAPTER TWENTY-FOUR

MONA SAT IN HER APARTMENT WAITING FOR HER uncle to arrive. The luncheon had taken longer than she had anticipated and while she was certain that was to her advantage the idleness it had produced had been annoying. Their conversation the evening before had been brief and to the point. She had asserted her rights simply but pleasantly and despite some argument he had agreed to "pursue" the matter. It was the word *pursue* that now caused her some concern. She had not taken notice of it then and perhaps she should have. Uncle was sly, he always had been, especially in his manipulation of the family. She had seldom questioned his decisions, but then why should she? The business was a success and the money was simply there and there was never a reason to concern herself with it. But now she wanted something and she intended to have it. She crossed the room to the liquor table and poured herself one of the martinis she had mixed earlier. It was well after three o'clock and he should have arrived by now. She tapped her foot against the floor impatiently. He had said he would come and if his plans had been changed he would have called. Or was it simply his way of asserting his authority as head of the family? She doubted it, but she could not be sure. She had never forced an issue with him before and because of that there was no way to anticipate his reaction.

She had returned to her comfortable perch on the sofa when the doorbell finally rang ten minutes later and she remained there, allowing Rita to answer it. When her uncle strode, smiling, into the room she rose and walked to him, extending her cheek for him to kiss.

"For a moment I thought you had abandoned me," she said.

"Never, my dear," he said, handing his hat to the waiting Rita.

She walked to the liquor table, then turned. "As you can see, I've become an afternoon drinker. May I offer you a martini?"

"I'd love one," he said, walking up beside her.

She handed him a glass, then returned to the sofa and watched, waiting as he selected a chair opposite her.

He tasted the drink. "Delicious," he said. "We should have you working at the club. Or at least giving instructions to the barmen. Sometimes I think they steal the good gin and replace it with the bathtub variety." He laughed at his own little joke.

"And tell me, darling, how was luncheon?"

He paused, taking another drink, still gathering his thoughts. The walk had done little but form an outline for him. "It seems we may soon have your young friend working for us," he said.

She interrupted him, her voice crisp but not angry. "What do you mean, we *may?*"

"We agreed he should have some time to think the offer over, that's all. I think that's a sensible thing, don't you?" His voice was calm, gracious, almost patronizing.

Mona noted each quality of sound, each nuance. "Exactly what did you offer him, Uncle?"

"The position we discussed at a more than ample salary."

"Precisely how ample, darling?"

"Twenty-five thousand. I think you'll agree that's more than generous considering today's market."

Mona turned her head to one side, indicating her approval. "And what did he say?"

"Well, I wouldn't say he jumped at it." He raised his hand stopping the objection rising in her throat. "But he did express interest—and I believe a genuine interest. I have no doubt he'll accept it." He chuckled. "He'd be a fool if he didn't."

"Then why the delay?" She was studying him closely, watching for the truth he was not going to offer.

"Mona, dear, it's a big step for young Broderick. He's being prudent and that is certainly to his credit." He drained his glass, then rose and walked to the liquor table, asking without need if he could help himself to another.

She watched him, waiting for some telltale flaw. "You said that *we* agreed he should have time to think it over. Exactly whose suggestion was it and

188

how long a waiting period was agreed upon? You know I do intend to speak to him about it, Uncle William."

He turned and looked at her as though she were still a little girl trying his patience. But there was no point lying to her; it would only push the problem into the future. "I suggested the time period, partially because of his hesitancy—but only partially. And we merely delayed a final decision until the first of next month." He raised his hand again, halting her objection, then continued as he returned to his chair. "I said 'partially' because I still feel the decision is unwise and I also want *you* to have time to think it over. And I also believe it would be fairer to Broderick as well."

She stamped her foot and the gesture seemed absurd from a sitting position. It almost forced him to smile.

"I have never, ever asked for anything involving the company," she snapped. "And the first time I do you immediately throw obstacles in front of me."

"I am not placing *any* impediments in your way. I am only suggesting that after a suitable period if you still want me to find a position for your young man, I shall. I set it at one month, but believe me I wish it were far longer and I am still hoping you will see the reason in that and allow it to be extended further. It wouldn't be difficult to find reasons to do so, reasons that would in no way offend him."

"No!" Her voice was sharp and her eyes flashed with anger.

"Mona, I do run the company and I do believe I should have something to say about its operation."

She stared at her uncle. "I had hoped it wouldn't be necessary to remind you that *I*, like you, hold one-third of the stock and that without my support it is quite possible that the other stockholders would have chosen someone else to fill that position. And I honestly feel my support is worth some, *small* consideration."

Eatkins's face reddened with anger. He had known the point would be raised eventually but anger now suited his purpose. "I think, my dear, that my business experience would allow me to win any proxy battle. But I must confess I never expected this type of pressure from someone I treated like my own child."

"Oh, save the heartfelt speeches, Uncle. If father hadn't left me his share of the stock you wouldn't have given a damn about me. That doesn't make me angry. That's the way our lovely little family has always been."

He allowed his features to take on what he hoped was a look of crushed innocence, and held the look for a long moment. "It hurts me to think you feel that way," he said.

"Please stop it," she said. She extended her hand, holding out her glass. "Please get me another drink if you must play the wounded uncle." She had turned her eyes away from him and kept them away until he returned with her drink.

"Will you tell me why you're so anxious to have him in the company? Do you intend to marry this—this detective?"

"I have no idea what I plan right now," she said. "I only know that I'm extremely attracted to him and I very much want to see if there is more to him than simply being a detective."

"And this is your way of finding out?" He offered her an incredulous look. "Do you really think that's quite fair, either to the company or to him?"

"I don't understand what you're talking about. The company can certainly afford one more executive, and based upon what you told him about expected union problems it would probably turn out to be a good investment."

"Quite probably. Perhaps not worth twenty-five thousand a year, but the idea itself is sound enough." He settled back in his chair and brought his glass up in front of him, holding it with both hands. "And what about the degree of fairness to him?" he added.

"I don't understand your point," she said, returning his soft, all-knowing look.

"Well, my dear, we will be asking Broderick to give up his career in the Police Department, won't we? Now let's suppose that your infatuation with him fades. It has been known to happen. Or let us say that Mr. Broderick fails to get a divorce and is thereby unavailable. This certainly might alter your attitude, isn't that so?"

"Uncle, I have no idea if I want to marry the man. Perhaps we'll live in sin. This is 1926, you know. The Puritan age is well behind us." She offered him an unpleasant smile.

"I won't even comment on that remark," he said. "Let's just continue on with the all too reasonable premise that your relationship one day might come to an end. Do you think you'll then want Mr. Broderick working for *our* company?"

"I have no idea what I'll want in the future. I'm not a crystal ball gazer, darling. I merely know how I feel now and what I want to find out. I don't see why we have to go beyond that, anyway." She had crossed her legs and was nervously swinging her ankle back and forth.

Eatkins watched her. He had made a dent in the armor, how much he could not be certain, but at least it was some degree of progress. He stood and closed the physical distance between them, sitting next to her on the sofa.

"My dear, all I'm suggesting is that we show a little patience for the good of everyone involved, not the least of all Broderick himself. I'm sure if you think about it you'll agree."

"I'll agree to no such thing," she said, looking straight ahead. "He's being

190

offered a marvelous opportunity and there's nothing wrong with that. If he left the company, for whatever reason, he'd certainly get another position. He'd benefit from it, no matter what."

Eatkins drew a deep breath. "I can see you've made up your mind and there's no point in trying to change it. Will you at least go along with the October first date and, in fairness to him, give him a chance to think it over?"

"Yes." She snapped her head around and avoided looking directly into his eyes. "But he isn't going to change his mind. I assure you of that."

No, but perhaps you will, he thought. "I have no doubt about that, my dear," he said, patting her hand. "As I said, he'd be a fool not to take advantage of the situation, especially if he believes the relationship with you can be a lasting one. I myself have great doubts about that."

"Why should you?" she asked coldly.

He wanted to tell her the reasons he knew to be true, but decided against it. A picture of Broderick's obvious inability to fit in at the club would only anger her now, perhaps even produce a few belittling phrases about the pompousness of his generation. At best it would solidify her resolve. Better to leave her with her own doubts, he decided.

"I suppose I shouldn't have any doubts. I suppose I really have no right to them at all," he said. "But to be frank I can't quite see him as a member of the family. There is a slight question of breeding and, to be honest, our Mr. Broderick simply doesn't have it. Certainly you see that."

"I see nothing of the kind," she said. "What he doesn't know he can learn."

"My dear, there are some things one just doesn't learn after a certain age. There are things one is raised *with*, taught to believe in through a host of experiences. You have only to look at the *nouveau riche* to see how true that is. It could take years to add even a slight polish to Mr. Broderick."

"Don't be such a snob. I really couldn't bear a diamond-in-the-rough speech." She exhaled heavily.

"Well, I certainly hope you come to your senses. I don't relish the thought of one day presenting some Twenty-third Street barbarian as the husband of my only niece." He had become annoyed and had lost the control he had hoped to maintain.

Mona stood abruptly and walked to the mantel, then turned on him, her eyes flashing her own anger. "No one has asked you to present anyone to anyone. And if you weren't so pompous about your social position you'd realize that my interest in finding out more about the man's capabilities are precisely what *is* needed to avoid any embarrassment whatsoever."

The accusation he had hoped to avoid cut into him. "I think *pompous* is a bit strong. I'm simply expressing precisely the doubts you yourself are trying to rid yourself of. Why else your little experiment?" Their eyes met, each as hard as the other's, each unmoving. He broke the deadlock with a gesture, lifting his hands toward her, palms upturned. "But why should we fight? Perhaps you're right. Time will tell in any event. There's no need for us to war with each other. You'll have your way. . . ."

"It's my right," she said, still not wanting to end the battle, still suspicious of him.

"No one says it isn't. And I will support it completely." He motioned her to him, beckoning with the upturned fingers of his hands. She walked to him and placed her hands in his. "You promise?" she said.

"You have my complete word on it." He stood and placed his arms about her in a paternal hug. "If not, you can offer your voting stock to the highest bidder."

She drew herself back and looked up into his face. "I will, you know," she said.

"I have no doubt about it, my dear. No doubt at all." He stepped away. "But now I must go. Consider everything settled."

She walked him to the door as Rita quickly retrieved his hat, then dutifully disappeared. As he opened the door she reached out and touched his arm, stopping him. "Thank you, Uncle William," she said.

A partially suppressed laugh rose in his throat. "Do the perpetrators of blackjack assaults usually thank their victims?" he said.

"Only when they're people of breeding," she answered.

"I see," he said, offering her a farewell smile as he turned away. But William Eatkins was not a happy man.

The closing of the door left her satisfied but it also made her aware of a deep-seated fear. Mona walked briskly back into the living room and poured the last remnants from the martini pitcher. She looked at the small watch pinned to her dress. It was past four, twenty minutes past. John was due in an hour and a half and she had already had more than enough to drink. She drained the glass quickly, then marched into her bedroom. She would bathe, relax, and then change for the evening. She was right no matter what his concerns were. It was the correct step, the necessary step, and it would be a successful one. There was more man in him than the simple fops she had previously surrounded herself with, more of what she wanted in a man. A man. God, she thought, he might even be the first one she had known. She stood before the mirror turning slightly to each side. And she certainly was a woman—there was no question about how much she enjoyed the fact.

Rita entered and was sent off into the bathroom to begin drawing her bath after first laying out a dressing gown on the bed. When she returned minutes later Mona was wearing the dressing gown and she stopped in front of her.

"Yes, Rita. What is it?"

"It's about Mr. Broderick," she said.

"What about him?" The question had drawn her from her thoughts and the sudden mention of his name by Rita confused her.

192

"He left some clothing here from last weekend, madam. I just wondered what I should do with them. I've had them cleaned, it's just . . ." She paused, embarrassed.

Mona laughed. "Put them away, dear. We'll keep them here." And perhaps more very soon, she thought.

Inside the mirror-lined bathroom Mona stripped off her dressing gown and paused for a moment, studying herself closely. She smiled, pleased with what she saw.

CHAPTER TWENTY-FIVE

BRODERICK NARROWED HIS EYES AGAINST THE BRIGHT morning sun as he stepped through the rear door of City Hall. It was hot and his body felt heavy, his movements slow, almost ponderous, as he descended the stone staircase and started toward Park Row along the wide, curving walkway that ran between City Hall and the Tweed Courthouse. The sunlight cut through the heavy foliage of the surrounding trees and sent flashes of light and shadow across his face and the summer heat seemed to press against him, slowing his progress. Near the end of the walkway a young man had set up a small puppet theater and was busy entertaining the handful of people who had stopped to watch the sidewalk performance. Broderick stopped at the edge of the crowd and watched the man's nimble fingers move the marionettes comically about the stage. There was a tin cup set out before the makeshift portable stage but it held only the few coins he had been able to cajole from the small crowd. Several snickers rose from the audience and as Broderick watched the wooden caricatures, helpless against the manipulation of the strings, he felt a repressed anger rise in his throat. He stepped forward, his back to the crowd, and displayed his gold detective's shield.

"You're going to have to move this out of here, Mac." His voice was flat, without emotion. There was a groan from the crowd and he snapped his head

194

toward them. "And you people better move along too. This isn't the theater district."

The crowd began to scatter slowly and the puppeteer, a tall, slender man, stood quietly with an imploring look on his face. His two marionettes dangled limply in front of him, appearing to have collapsed with the slackening of the strings.

Broderick watched the young man's lack of movement. "I mean today, not tomorrow," he said.

The young man took a deep breath. "Look, Officer, I'm just trying to make a few dollars. Things haven't been going too well."

"They're going to go worse if you don't move." Broderick stepped toward him and placed his foot on the stage as though preparing to push it over; then he leaned forward, resting his forearm on top of his knee.

The puppeteer forced a weak smile. "You know I spoke to the other officer, the one in uniform, and he said it would be okay as long as there wasn't too big a crowd." The young man looked at him hopefully. "If you ask him I'm sure he'll tell you."

Broderick felt the blood rush to his face and he wanted to reach out and grab the man. He looked briefly to his left toward City Hall. His voice remained calm. "He's a patrolman and in case you didn't notice, I'm a detective. And *I* told you to move. Now if you want I can bust up some of your puppets to show you I'm not kidding."

The young man threw his hands up in front of him. "Okay, okay. I get the idea. I guess you just don't like puppets."

A slow, unfriendly smile crossed Broderick's face. "I love puppets, kid. I just don't like the people who play with them."

The walk back from City Hall did little to help his mood and his face was still dark and angry when he returned to the squad room. Cordes greeted him cheerfully and then sat back in amused silence as he watched Broderick settle behind his desk and stare antagonistically at the unfinished reports spread out in front of him. Across the room Ruditsky sat with his forehead cupped in one hand, nursing a hangover. Broderick looked at him with disgust.

"In case you haven't noticed, Ruditsky's dead," Cordes said.

"Fuck you," Ruditsky said, bringing his other hand up to his forehead.

"Fuck both of you," Broderick said. He began to shuffle a handful of the reports.

"Wonderful," Cordes said. "I got one partner who's dead and another one who's already at the wake."

Broderick pushed his chair away from the desk and stamped across the room to the lieutenant's private bathroom. Inside he loosened his tie and filled the basin with cold water and began splashing it on his face. Cordes came in behind him and leaned against the wall.

195

"Bad time at the Hall, babe?" he said.

"You ever hear of a good time with those cunts." He picked up a folded towel from a shelf above the basin and pressed it against his face.

"You want to talk about it?" Cordes said.

"No." He snapped out the answer without thinking, then took a deep breath and turned to face Cordes. "That cunt Nolan called me down there to ask me why I'm spending so much time with a society broad. I don't know who the fuck he thinks he is." He threw the towel in a hamper next to the basin. "Then he tells me that somebody saw me having lunch with her uncle the other day and he wants to know if I'm doing any labor deals with him."

"So what's bothering him? Is he worried that you're moving up in society, or is he just afraid he might lose a few bucks?"

"Who the fuck knows." Broderick straightened his tie and ran his fingers through his hair. "He's just letting me know that I better stay in line, that I better be a good boy. And I just sat there with my finger up my ass."

Cordes looked at him closely, surprised by the sudden tone of self-disgust. "How'd he know about the lady?" he asked.

"We ran into the mayor and his blond bitch at a restaurant a few nights ago. Then I guess Nolan heard about the uncle and figured something was up."

"Is something up?" Cordes held his hands apart to show his lack of concern. "Not that it matters to me, I'm just asking."

"Not the way he thinks." Broderick paused, deciding whether to go on. He chewed on his lower lip and stared at Cordes. "The uncle wants me to leave the job and come to work for him. He's talking a lot of bucks."

Cordes let out a low whistle. "So what's the problem? Tell Nolan to go fuck himself. Then take the money and run like a thief."

Broderick sat back on the edge of the basin. "I'd like to, believe me, especially after today." He shook his head, angry at his inability to sort out his own thoughts. "It's more complicated than that," he said at length. "The old man, the uncle, doesn't really want any part of me. He wants me like he wants *shit* in his living room. But Mona wants it and it seems the old man is going to do whatever she says."

Cordes seemed confused. "So like I said, what's the fucking problem?"

"It's a lot of little things. Petty shit. There's my wife for one thing and what I do about getting rid of her."

Cordes raised his eyebrows. The thought of getting rid of a wife did not strike him as a small thing. "You mean that's part of the deal, dumping your old lady?"

"No." Broderick hesitated, thinking. "But it could be a problem later. I'd like to take care of it first, but I can't do it just like that." He snapped his fingers for emphasis.

"You mean you think things might fall out from under you later if you couldn't get rid of her." Cordes stated the possibility more as a fact than a question.

Broderick shook his head, looked down at his shoes, and then back at Cordes. "I'm not really worried about that. Things are good between Mona and me and I don't think she'd let go that easy. Besides, I *want* to get away from my old lady, I've wanted to for a long time now. It's just a question of talking her into it. Maybe an annulment. Some way she can keep those fucking priests happy."

"But if it didn't work out it could be trouble, right? I mean after awhile, if you couldn't talk her into it?"

"Yeah, sure, I guess that could happen. But I know I can work it out. It's just gonna take a little time. Besides, I decided the other day that I'd start taking a good look at Mona's uncle, get something on him. Sort of insurance against something happening six months or a year from now. He's not the most kosher guy you ever met." A slight smile formed on Broderick's lips. "Once I had it, the old bastard would never get rid of me. And it's there, I'm sure it's there. Whether it's some broad he's got stashed away or some crooked deal he's pulled."

Broderick paced the length of the bathroom as Cordes continued to watch him. Then he turned and jabbed a finger at the air. "The thing that's *really* eating at me is that everything is happening all at once. I don't have time to think anything out. Everybody is pulling at me to do one thing or another." He began gesturing with one hand and then the other. "Mona wants this; her uncle wants that. My old lady wants, Nolan wants. Shit, I just got rid of Garfoli sniffing up my ass trying to find something that doesn't smell right and after this talk with Nolan this morning I'm not even sure I can still count on him to keep the heat off." He let out a deep breath. "Look, I know none of it's all that bad. I *know* that. It's just that there's too much going on all at once and when it all comes together I feel like I'm choking."

Cordes stared at him with a half smile. "So what do you *want*, babe?"

Broderick paused and then returned the smile. "It's like you said. I want to take the money and run like a fucking thief. But I need a little time."

"So move slow and easy. Big deal. Just don't let anybody push you. Shit, I should have your problems." Cordes walked over and squeezed Broderick's cheeks between his thumbs and index fingers. "You know what your real problem is?" he said. "Ever since you started sucking on rich tit you haven't been out with the troops. You need to blow off some steam and you're not gonna do *that* at some Park Avenue dinner party."

Broderick shook his cheeks free and grinned down at the shrewd-eyed Spaniard. "What have you got in mind, some greaseball orgy?"

"It wouldn't hurt you, hump. You might find out what real fucking is like. But you probably couldn't handle it." He put his arm around Broderick's shoulder as though ready to impart some great secret. "What I got in mind for *you* is maybe a day at the track, followed by a little action around town. Maybe we could even get you a horn honk from one of our old friends on Broadway, a class tuba player. We could even do it today."

Broderick waved both hands back and forth rejecting the offer. "Not me. I'm not going to the track today. I got too many people watching my ass now. The way my fucking luck is running I'd sit right in back of Nolan and Garfoli. And they'd probably be holding hands."

Cordes had taken on the air of a street corner huckster. He squeezed Broderick's shoulder. "So we don't go to the track. Listen, we'll do this. We'll go up to Houston Street and grab an early bite at Katz's. Then we'll go to that speakeasy around the corner, the one with the wireroom in the back. We're overdue to make a collection there anyway, so we'll make it and then play the nags with their money." His voice turned serious. "Listen, I got to get Ruditsky out of here anyway. If he doesn't get a hair of the dog, the fucker really *is* gonna die."

"What do we have to take him for? I can't stand that bastard anymore." Broderick began to pull away but Cordes grabbed his arm, stopping him.

"Look, you're just pissed off because he threw that fucking mutt out the window. What's the matter, you losing your sense of humor? Some day you'll think back on that and piss your pants laughing."

Broderick fought to keep a smile from his face. "I should have broken his fucking neck," he said.

"Yeah, yeah," Cordes said. "Look, call your girl friend and tell her you're gonna be tied up on some big case all night and let's get out of here before the lieutenant shows up and finds some work for us. We can fill in some phony shit on our schedules and get the hell out of here."

During lunch Broderick began to wonder if Ruditsky might not really die after all. The noise in the cavernous delicatessen was deafening, the clatter of dishes and shouted orders seemed endless and each new wave assaulted Ruditsky like a punch to the head. It was only later, at the speakeasy, that he began to revive and then only after he had thrown down his second jigger of bootleg whiskey. The speakeasy was in a small, musty basement room, with a second room behind it that housed the betting parlor. Ruditsky seemed completely at home. For several years now Broderick had suspected that Barney was never completely sober, but like most drunks simply moved between stages of withdrawal and renewed drunkenness with only severe hangovers separating the two. He reminded him of his father.

To Cordes's surprise Broderick agreed to drink with them, although neither made any attempt to keep up with Ruditsky, who threw his drinks down as if he were watering a dying plant. Cordes watched him with incredulous mirth.

"You know, if Barney ever broke his hands the bootleggers in this town would go broke," he said at length.

"No, they wouldn't. He'd just learn to drink it out of a saucer like a fucking cat." Broderick said.

Ruditsky looked from one to the other, offering each a false smile. "I'm just getting my heart started again," he said.

"Barney, your heart isn't going," Cordes said. "You've been dead for two years. You just haven't sobered up long enough for your body to realize it yet."

Broderick started to laugh, already feeling the effect of his second drink. Ruditsky sat nodding his head, knowingly.

"Two big fucking experts," he said. "A wine-slopping greaseball and a teetotaling mick. I don't know why either one of you ever became cops."

"We never learned how to pick locks and we couldn't figure out any other way to steal," Cordes said.

Ruditsky's coarse laughter ended in a wheezing cough and he took another drink before speaking. "I told you before, it ain't stealing. What we do is limit the profits of the criminal element and thereby reduce the effects of crime on society."

"Listen to *him*," Cordes said. "He sounds like some fucking professor. Reduce the effects of crime on society. No shit, Barney, is that what we do?"

Ruditsky pursed his lips and nodded his assurance.

"Well, in that case I suggest we call the manager of the wireroom out here and proceed with our daily fight against crime. Would you agree with that gentlemen?"

Ruditsky nodded solemnly.

"Yeah, but make sure that prick understands that he better not try to beat it out the other door like he did a couple of weeks ago," Broderick added.

Cordes formed a circle with his thumb and index finger and then motioned the waiter to their table. "You go back there and tell our friend Harry that Johnny Cordes and two associates are here to see him." He reached out and held the waiter's arm for a moment. "And tell him that if he goes out the back door like last time the three of us are going to break the arms of every guy working the board and telephones back there."

The waiter stared into Cordes's smiling face, then shot quick glances at Broderick and Ruditsky. He drew a deep breath and shrugged his shoulders, then walked quickly toward a door at the rear of the room. Thirty seconds later, a short, balding man in shirt sleeves waddled toward their table. There was a stub of a cigar clenched between his teeth; he looked unhappy.

"You know you boys don't have to send messages back to me like that. It's embarrassing," Harry began. "I always do the right thing. You know that."

"Listen, you fat prick," Broderick said, "the last time I was here you beat

199

it out the door so fast you left a cloud of dust. I thought you were fucking Tom Mix."

Harry held out his hands, palms up, pleading innocence. He was sweating, but he always seemed to be sweating, even in winter. "Johnny, I left before I ever knew you was here. I'd never try to pull that on you. There's no percentage. We both know that."

Cordes smiled at the fat man. "Don't pay any attention to him," he said. "He's in a bad mood; he just wants to break somebody's arm. But I'll tell you what I'm gonna do. I'm gonna let you make a double payment just to prove that Johnny's wrong and then to show what nice guys we are, we're gonna spend some of it right here on your booze and your horses. How about that?"

Harry squeezed his eyes shut and nodded.

"If he was really sorry, he wouldn't charge us for the booze. I think Johnny's probably right about him," Ruditsky said.

Harry kept his eyes closed and continued to nod his head. "The drinks are on me," he said. He looked at Ruditsky. "You sure you don't want me to give you a couple of winners too?"

"I can do that all by myself, fatso," Ruditsky said.

Harry nodded again. "Okay, fellas. I got to get back to work. Suddenly the day ain't so profitable anymore. Enjoy yourselves. Come back and check the tote board when you're ready."

"Yeah. You enjoy yourself too, Harry," Cordes said, watching the sweaty fat man waddle back toward the wireroom. "We'll see you again next week." He looked at Ruditsky and then Broderick. "Fighting crime is really a bitch, ain't it?"

"Just work, work, work," Ruditsky said.

A few minutes later Cordes was counting the money that had been delivered in an envelope by one of Harry's employees.

"Is it all there?" Broderick asked.

"Two hundred bucks," Cordes said. "I suppose we better give the lieutenant his taste this time."

Broderick nodded. "Yeah, we better. He knows Harry."

"You know, that always pisses me off," Ruditsky said. "The split only goes one way, *up*. It ain't right. The guys above, they make their own collections too. But the splits still only go up. We never see any of the dough they take in and I bet it's plenty."

"Why don't you file a complaint with the P.C.," Broderick said. "Tell him we'll unionize if the payoffs aren't divided fairer."

"Yeah, Barney," Cordes added. "You could head the pickets and carry a sign that said 'no payoffs, no work'."

Ruditsky's face suddenly brightened and he leaned forward grinning. "Shit, I forgot to tell you what I heard about the P.C. the other night," he said.

200

"What?" Cordes said. "He wants to join our union?"

"No. Shut up and listen." Ruditsky leaned forward even further until his chest was hanging over the table. "Last night," he whispered, "I ran into this guy I know who works in the commissioner's office and he said there's a fucking war going on up there. You know how the commissioner is supposed to get his envelope every Friday, right?"

Broderick and Cordes nodded.

"Well, every Friday the blank envelope is left on this small table outside the P.C.'s office. Shit, there must be twenty, thirty grand in it, maybe more; his split of everything collected in all the precincts. Well, according to this guy the commish always leaves it there until he and his driver leave. And of course he makes sure he's the last one to leave every Friday so nobody sees him pick it up. Like it's a big fucking secret or something. Well, last Friday he comes out and there's no fucking envelope. But it was there earlier. He saw it there. And right away he knows somebody's fucking goniffed the loot. Some smart fuck just came along and said to himself, there's the fucking house in the country and the new car and *plop*, dropped the envelope in his pocket."

"You mean somebody robbed the commissioner's dough?" Cordes rocked back with laughter. "Fucking beautiful," he shouted.

"So what did he do?" Broderick said.

"This guy said he called in every fucking boss in the building. He was in a fucking rage. He still had to split with the Hall and now there was no fucking money. His driver told my friend that he was shouting how he wanted a fucking investigation and the bosses kept trying to tell him how he couldn't do that, how word might leak out, and how they'd all look like a bunch of assholes."

Tears were streaming down Broderick's face. He was on his third drink now and could no longer control his laughter. "It's terrible," he said, almost choking on the word. "You can't trust nobody anymore."

"That's what the fucking P.C. said," Ruditsky screamed.

Cordes rocked back in his chair so hard he almost tipped it over. Patrons at the bar had turned to look at the three men guffawing like schoolboys. Broderick pulled a handkerchief from his pocket and began wiping his eyes.

"I love it," he said. "I just wish I could be there when the prick goes in and tries to tell Chris Nolan how somebody stole the envelope."

"The guy who stole it ought to get the Medal of Honor," Cordes said.

"He ought to get the medal and a free blow job every day for the rest of his life," Ruditsky said.

"From the commissioner," Broderick said.

Cordes took a deep breath to control his laughter. "What do you think Nolan will do?" he asked.

"He'll tell him to go visit his tin box and come up with the money," Broderick said. "Fuck him, he can afford it. Did you guys ever stop to think how much dough there is at that level?"

"I can't count that high," Cordes said.

"You bet your ass you can't." He looked knowingly at each of them. "How many pinball machines do you think there are in the city?"

"I dunno. A couple of hundred thousand," Ruditsky said.

"Easy," Broderick said. "You know anybody who has any free machines?"

"They're not supposed to," Cordes said.

"And they pay a buck a machine a week, right?"

Ruditsky and Cordes nodded.

"And that's just pinball machines, which is small shit. We're not even talking about prohibition, speakeasies, gambling, prostitution, or any of that stuff. And then you got labor contracts. Look at what Rothstein gave for just six months of free time in the fur district. And how many deals do you think there are that we never hear about?"

"Thousands," Ruditsky said.

"Well, at least hundreds," Broderick corrected. "Then you got stuff that doesn't even involve the department. New buildings, new roads, repairs, inspections, violations of fire laws, all kinds of licenses. Shit, if you're high up in politics in this town and your party is in office it's like you discovered a fucking gold mine. Christ, you even got to pay somebody off to run for office. You got to pay somebody off to be a judge, a fucking *judge*."

"It's disgusting," Ruditsky said. "You can't trust nobody any more." He began to giggle again.

"Fuck the lieutenant. I ain't givin' him his hundred bucks," Cordes said. "Where do those guys *keep* all that money?"

"I dunno," Ruditsky said. "But I tell you, when I retire I'm gonna buy a fucking shovel and start digging in their back yards."

"Yeah. You'll discover a fucking tin mine," Broderick said.

"Naw, they don't do that," Cordes said. "Only dumb cops do that. They buy up city property where a new road or a new building is going in and they put it in their old lady's name, or their girl friend's or their Great-aunt Tizzie's. Or they get some prick at some brokerage to buy stock for them under the table. Then the taxes get paid in somebody else's name and they're home free."

"The fucking thieves." Ruditsky was pouting over the injustice of it all as he poured everyone another drink. "It's not fair. We get our asses shot at and our heads punched and they get all the heavy gravy."

"Hey, we ain't doing all that bad," Cordes said. "We've been taking in about three months salary every month, with no taxes and free meals and free suits. We're not starving."

"Yeah, but that's still only about twelve grand a year. How often do *we* get a deal like the Rothstein thing. Shit, I bet those guys get those things all the time. We ought to start shaking the tree a little harder," Ruditsky insisted. He threw his drink back and poured another.

"Don't get fucking greedy," Cordes said. "How many guys do you know knocking down sixteen grand a year with only four of it on top of the table?"

"Cordes is right," Broderick said. "Garfoli's already pissed off with us, probably because we pushed his gumbas too hard."

"Fucking greaseball," Ruditsky said. "You can't trust nobody anymore, not even a fucking cop. Christ, most of my dough goes to my fucking bookie anyway." His eyes suddenly brightened again. "Speaking of bookies, we probably already missed the first race sitting here shooting the shit. I'm gonna check out the tote board." He pushed his chair away from the table.

"Make a list and bring it out," Cordes said. "If we all walk in there they'll think we're raiding the joint and Harry'll have a fucking heart attack."

Cordes sat back, smiling at Broderick. "You feeling better, babe?" he said.

"Yeah. I loved hearing about the P.C. What a pair of balls that guy had. If I knew who he was I'd kiss him."

"I got somebody else for you to kiss." Cordes pushed his chair back and stood. "I'm gonna check with the office and make up some more lies and then I'm gonna call some old friends of ours and have them join us here. A couple of good flute players."

"They got musicians cards?" Broderick said.

"Guaranteed certified," Cordes said, winking at him.

"Look, check for me and see if Mona called. I just left a message with her maid."

"Fuck you," Cordes said. "You can get along without rich tit for one night."

Cordes and Ruditsky returned at the same time, Ruditsky waving his sheet of selections before him.

"I got it. I fucking got it," he said. "In the third, Barney's Baby. How can it fucking miss? And it's fifteen to one."

"Barney's Baby. Fuck you," Broderick said. "What else you got there?"

Ruditsky handed over the sheet and watched as Broderick and Cordes shared it, each picking a different horse.

"I told them to turn on the radio out here. Harry bitched, but I persuaded him." Ruditsky was grinning foolishly, already filled with liquor.

Cordes wrote each of their selections on a slip of note paper, folded some money inside it, and handed it back to Ruditsky, who had been designated the runner by a two to one vote.

"It'll keep him more sober, running back and forth like that," Cordes said, as they watched the grumbling detective rush back to the wireroom.

"Nothing is gonna keep him sober. I think he was born drunk," Broderick said.

When Barney's Babe came in Ruditsky's scream almost cleared out the bar. Harry came running in from the wireroom and stood ashen-faced at their table, sweating even more than usual.

"What the hell happened?" he said. "I thought somebody got murdered out here."

"Barney's nag came in. A fifteen to one shot," Cordes said.

Harry squeezed his eyes shut again. "What else you guys gonna do to me today?" he moaned.

"You just behave yourself," Broderick said, pointing a not too steady finger at him.

"And send over some more booze. We got some ladies joining us later." Cordes added.

"That's what else you're gonna do to me. You're gonna send me to the poorhouse," Harry said.

By four o'clock Broderick was sitting in his shirt sleeves, his skimmer perched awkwardly on his head, his forearms on the table supporting him.

"What the hell should I do?" he mumbled to Cordes. "I gotta do somethin' soon, don't I?"

"What's he talking about?" Ruditsky said.

"None of your fucking business," Cordes said.

"You know I'm gonna give you all jobs some day," Broderick said. He stared down at his hands. His eyelids had grown heavy and he began to blink. "All of us, we'll all be fucking executives with secretaries," he said.

"Can I be your secretary, honey?"

The voice came from behind him. He had not seen the two women approach the table and he turned toward them and grinned.

"Jeanie, baby. Of course you can," he said. "Who's your friend? She can be Cordes's secretary."

The slightly plump blonde, named Jeanie, smiled down at him, shaking her head with amusement over his condition. "This is Maggie," she said, nodding toward her brunette companion, then looking at Cordes. "My other friend couldn't come," she explained.

"Maggie is my old lady's name," Broderick said, ignoring her words to Cordes. "She's a bitch. I hope you're not a bitch."

"I promise," the brunette said, wiggling her shoulders.

Two more chairs were pulled to the table and the two women eagerly attacked their first drinks. The blonde, Jeanie, had positioned herself next to Broderick and she looked at him and shook her head again.

"I thought you didn't drink," she said.

"I don't," Broderick said. "They corrupted me."

"They sure did," Jeanie said. She reached down and squeezed his genitals. "I hope you can still get it up."

Broderick held up his left forearm and grabbed it at the center with his right hand. "Like a goddamned horse," he said. "Just like a goddamned horse."

Maggie giggled. "What's all this you were saying about secretaries? They giving cops secretaries now?" she said.

Broderick raised his index finger to his lips, indicating secrecy, then tapped his nose lightly. "Can't say too much about that. Big business. Big deals. You know, corporate stuff. Debentures, mortgages, writs of habeas prickus." He began to giggle.

"Where's my broad?" Ruditsky said.

"She couldn't come," Jeanie started to explain.

"He couldn't make her come, anyway," Cordes said.

"She found out you were a Jew and she knew you'd have a small prick. She knows Jews get their pricks cut off," Broderick said.

"They don't get their pricks cut off," Ruditsky insisted. "You fucking stupid micks don't know anything. They just get the foreskin cut off."

"Same thing," Broderick said. "You got a small prick."

"Who's got a small prick?" Ruditsky said, fumbling with the buttons of his trousers and finally exposing his penis.

Maggie leaned across the table and giggled. "You got a small prick, Barney," she said.

They all collapsed with laughter, all but Ruditsky, who sat glaring at the brunette.

"I'll stick it in your ear and you'll hear it coming," he said.

"That's all right, Barney," she said. "I got small ears." She pulled back the tufts of hair around her ears.

Laughter engulfed the table again and this time even Ruditsky was forced to join in.

The gales of drunken laughter drew the attention of the people at the bar again and a tall, slender man with a flushed face ambled over to the table. Ruditsky quickly buttoned his trousers.

"Hey, pally," the tall man said, placing his arm on Cordes's shoulder, "you boys sound like you're having a great time."

Cordes turned in his chair and looked up into Scratch McCarthy's bloodshot eyes. He still had his press card dangling from a safety pin attached to his lapel from an earlier assignment and he wore the affable grin of a reporter expecting a free drink.

"Get the fuck out of here, Scratch," Cordes said. "You ain't given *me* a scratch in six months. The only person *you* write about is your buddy Broderick. So don't call me 'pally,' you prick. Broderick's your pal, not me."

Broderick stretched out both hands. "Scratchy darlin', you haven't had my name in the paper for weeks. Don't you love me anymore?"

205

"I love ya, Johnny." McCarthy's eyes flashed between the two women before returning to Broderick. Without asking he pulled up a chair and joined them.

"Don't pay any attention to Cordes. He doesn't understand that you don't write about greaseballs in white men's newspapers." Broderick sat back and grinned drunkenly at Cordes.

"We should never let you drink, you big Irish clown. You lose respect for your betters," Cordes said.

"Yeah, and he makes fun of people's pricks too," Ruditsky said.

Broderick waved both hands at them, then turned back to McCarthy. "Scratch, me darlin'," he said, affecting his best west side brogue, "I ain't seen you socially in months."

"Not since McGrath's funerals," Scratch said.

"You sure you're a reporter?" Jeanie said.

"Of course he is," Cordes said. "He's not much of a reporter. But he's a reporter. You can tell by his deep pockets. His fucking hand can never reach his fucking money."

Scratch feigned displeasure, then turned to the blonde and smiled. "I'm a rose among daisies, I assure you," he said.

"Then how come you said McGrath's 'funerals'," she countered. "What happened, he died twice?"

"No, he only died once, God bless him. But he got buried twice. Well, not buried really. But he had two funerals and two wakes."

"That's crazy," Jeanie said. "I think you're all loaded."

"No, it's true," Cordes said. "It was probably one of the great Irish funerals of all time, both of them."

"So what did he die of?" Jeanie said, wrinkling up her nose to show she believed none of it.

"A broken heart," McCarthy sighed.

"He died of a stroke in a speakeasy," Ruditsky said.

"Same thing," McCarthy said. "He had already paid his tab."

"Oh, I think you're all crazy," Jeanie said.

"No, it's true," Broderick said. "Scratchy, tell her the story."

"Well, he died, you know," McCarthy began. "But he must of known it was coming because a few weeks before he made a bunch of us promise that when he died we would make sure that he had two wakes and two funerals. One for his old lady and his kids here in Manhattan and another one for his girl friend up in New Rochelle." McCarthy poured himself a drink and drank it. "Well, then he died and so we had to do it. So we had the wake with his wife and kids and then we took the casket to the church and the cemetery and we had the funeral. Then we all stopped back at his wife's place and paid our last respects. After awhile, we left there and we went back to the cemetery and the hearse had come back like we told it to and we snatched the coffin and drove it up to New Rochelle. And then we had another wake with his girl friend and another funeral. He even had two high masses. My God, he must be a helluva saint up in heaven today." McCarthy bowed his head in mock solemnity.

"But that's against the law," Jeanie insisted.

"No, it wasn't," Cordes interrupted. "The mayor went to both funerals and the medical examiner signed something to make the transfer of the body legal and we gave him a police escort both times. How fucking legal can you get?"

Maggie, who had listened to the story wide-eyed, sniffed back tears and then took another drink. "How romantic," she whispered.

"Yeah, and now there's an empty fucking grave in the Greenlawn Cemetery that his old lady's gonna put flowers on every fucking Christmas," Ruditsky said.

"Don't speak ill of the dead," McCarthy said. "He was a great man."

"I ain't speaking ill of the dead," Ruditsky insisted. "It was two of the best fucking funerals I ever went to. Especially when his girl friend got drunk afterward and gave everybody a horn honk." He leaned back in his chair and shouted, "What a fucking tuba player."

The scream brought Harry running out of the wireroom again, but when he saw where the noise was coming from he turned on his heels and rushed back inside.

Broderick leaned on the table again and stared at Cordes. "I got to make up my mind, Johnny," he said. "What should I do?"

"Take the money and run like a fucking thief," Cordes said, slamming his hand on the table.

Maggie leaned over and put her arm around Broderick's neck. "What are you talking about, honey?"

"I'm gonna get married," Broderick slurred.

"You're already married," she said.

"I know," he said, pausing to figure out the next sentence. "But I'm gonna get married again. If McGrath can get buried twice, why can't I get married twice?"

"Because your prick's too small," Ruditsky said.

"No, it's not, Barney," Maggie said, reaching down and squeezing Broderick again.

CHAPTER TWENTY-SIX

HALFWAY DOWN THE LONG HOT DREARY CONCRETE and steel corridor known as the fifth floor maximum security wing of the Tombs, Hy Amberg sat with his back to the cell door, hunched over the scraps of note-filled papers he had pieced together in secret. His eyes moved slowly over the large childlike script, pausing occasionally as if trying to decipher his own hand, then moving on again and again, reading and rereading, his body rocking slowly to the rhythm of his mind.

8:00 A.M. Tour changes. Four for four, unless somebody sick.

8:10 A.M. Head count. Two counting, two still at post.

10:00 A.M. Coffee. Two leave, two stay, fifteen, twenty minutes at most.

10:15 or 10:20 A.M. Other two leave, first two stay. Still fifteen to twenty, no more.

Noon. Lunch. Same as coffee, except longer. Full hour. Only two on.

1:00 P.M. Same. Full hour. Only two.

He studied the final notation on the first page: "1:00 P.M. Same. Full hour. Only two." The "full hour, only two," heavily underlined in pencil. He continued on through the other pages, noting the remaining timetable of the changing shifts of guards, the all so regular periods for coffee, lights out, prisoner mess, exercise, the clockwork created by dull daily routine that imprisoned the keepers and the kept alike. Alongside each notation a row of checks appeared, each marking a day when the routine was repeated without change. Check, check, check, check, check. Never a variation. Like a clock hanging over the entrance of a bank, banging out each minute with the assurance it alone was correct, no matter how many other clocks offered a different assurance in all the other banks and schools, railway stations, and whorehouses. *They* were his clock now, the only one he needed. And the court was his calendar, working in reverse, marking points that left days in between, the days in which things could happen. And soon he would arrange for his divining rod and it would reach out and settle all the scores. He began to laugh softly, his body still rocking. His mind was pure now, purged of all the doubts that came when the steel door slammed shut, locking him in again as he always feared it would. He had paced the cell for days like an animal in a zoo, tearing at himself. So wrong, so completely wrong. He understood that now. His clock was moving, banging out the time, his time, just the way he wanted it to. *Give me liberty or give me death.* He laughed, thinking of the skinny teacher who had pronounced those words so heavily, the same teacher he had smashed in the face on the last day they ever let him go to the school again. He looked down at the notes again, shuffling them quickly until the first page reappeared again. *1:00 P.M. Same. Full hour. Only two.* He placed a large star next to it and he began to laugh again.

"Amberg. On the gate."

The voice came from behind him, harsh and authoritative. His body stiffened and he crammed the notes and pencil inside his shirt.

"Yeah, what is it?" He didn't turn.

"You got a visitor. On the fucking gate."

He slid his feet off the bed and turned, looking up at the skinny young guard. "Can I go pee-pee first?" he said.

"You can fuck yourself. Either you want the visit or you don't. I could give a shit."

He stood. "I'll hold it," he said. "Who is it?"

"I ain't your social secretary. They sent a message up that you got a visitor. That's all I know. Hurry up. I'm supposed to be having my lunch."

"What time is it?"

"One o'clock. Any other fucking questions?" He swung the door open and Amberg stepped out.

"I'm sorry about your lunch," he said, fighting his own smile.

They moved in tandem down the corridor and past the office where the guards spent most of their time, locked in safely behind a heavy wooden door. Through the glass upper half of the door he could see the two guards there now: one, an old man, the other, heavyset and younger. Only two. Two up, two down. *One o'clock. A full hour.* He began to whistle as they waited for the elevator, counting the time it took to ride up from the first floor. About two minutes, he guessed as the door slid open, exposing the bored face of the old man who ran it. It went down without a stop. A minute and a half, he estimated. The old man took his time starting up. The door slid open again and they faced the red brick wall of the elevator waiting area. They turned right and then right again, pushing their way through the swinging doors that opened into the main reception hall itself, divided in half by a low steel gate that separated the moving prisoners from the rows of desks used by the prison clerks. They turned left and walked across the reception area, stopping in front of a locked steel door.

"On the gate," the guard snapped.

Another guard appeared, a large key in his hand. "Who you got?" he said.

"Amberg, from max," the first answered.

The second guard checked a sheet of paper, then nodded and opened the gate. "The middle table. You got ten minutes. Keep your hands behind the wire."

Amberg walked across the gray dimly lit room, his eyes fixed on the grinning man who was in the center of the long wire-divided table. Sammy had promised Dunniger he would come to get his instructions and he had. He was Dunniger's friend but he had obeyed the indirect order without question and now he sat there grinning, sure a piece of pie would be his for doing as he was told. Amberg slid into the seat opposite him and looked to each side. Other prisoners sat to his right and left but they were far enough away to insure privacy.

"Sammy, thanks for coming. Rudy told me you were a good man."

Sammy's grin widened. His teeth were rotting in his mouth. "When Rudy told me you had something for me to do, that was enough for me. You just tell me what you got in mind and you got it."

Amberg leaned forward, clasping his hands in front of him like a man in prayer. Despite his sharp, angular features, his face seemed soft, composed, almost saintly. "It's a small thing, but the rewards are going to be big. I'm going on a vacation, Sammy, and you're gonna book the reservation for me."

"What do you need?" Sammy asked.

"There's a guy in Harlem named Henry. He runs a little pawn shop on One Hundred and Twenty-fifth and Lex called Ace Pawn. But his real business is selling special merchandise from the back room. Merchandise that goes bang, okay?" He watched Sammy nod his head like some jack-in-the-box that had just popped out and was still vibrating. "You pick up one of those things, something small but in a heavy caliber, and you bring it here."

"Here?" Sammy looked around the room as though he had been asked to slash his own wrists.

"Not here, here," Amberg corrected. "Here, outside the building." He watched the confusion continue to spread across the man's face. "Outside, there's an alley that leads to a coal yard. You know the one I mean?" Sammy nodded. He was talking to him like a child now, trying to insure against any possible error. "In that alley there's a row of trash cans up against the wall. There are five of them. You wrap the merchandise in a piece of white cloth and put it on the top of the crap in the second can. The second one from the front of the alley. You got that?"

Sammy nodded again, but the look of assurance that had been there before was missing now. "But what if somebody spots me?" he asked.

Amberg felt his plan slipping away. Sammy was afraid, and frightened people made stupid mistakes. He winked at him knowingly. "The trash cans are toward the front of the alley. You keep the package under your coat. You walk down the street with a paper bag with a doughnut in it and when you get near the alley you take the doughnut out and start eating it." He winked again, emphasizing the cleverness of the plan. "Then you got this paper bag, see. And you look and you see the trash cans, and being a good citizen you walk over and you toss the bag in the can. What could be more natural. And with your back to the street nobody sees nothin' when you drop the other package in and then you go on your way like any other guy on his way to work."

"Yeah, but what if there's somebody in there?"

"You do it in the morning, day after tomorrow, at eight-thirty in the morning. The only time there's ever anybody in the alley is after nine. That's when the work crews go there." He smiled. "And that's when my guy picks up the package. He brings it in—you don't have anything to do with that, okay?"

Sammy nodded. "What do I do then?"

"Then you make sure you come back with a car and park near the alley at one o'clock, no later. You'll only have to wait ten minutes, we'll be out by then. Ten minutes, that's all it's gonna take." Sammy still seemed uncertain and Amberg watched him closely, trying to find some way of assuring himself that he would not just walk out of there and then run like a frightened rabbit. "You know, this is gonna mean big dough for you. More than you ever dreamed of." Sammy's eyes brightened immediately. "After we lay low for a while we're gonna take off for Canada and I'm gonna set up a sweet little racket there shipping booze back into the States. And you, you're gonna become my man here in New York. You know what that's gonna mean, don't you?"

Sammy blinked, confused again. "Yeah, but I thought all that stuff was all sewed up?"

"Didn't Rudy tell you? I already got it all taken care of," Amberg lied. "Before I took that lousy fall I made all the deals. Now it's just a question of me getting out of the country and everything can go right ahead just like I planned. But look, if you don't want in, we just get somebody else. It's just that Rudy told me you were the right kind of guy, the kind of guy we could use."

"No, look, I want in, I just like to be careful, I like to know what I'm doin',

211

that's all." Sammy was nodding his head, playing the jack-in-the-box again, reassuring himself as well as Amberg.

"That's good," Amberg said. "It's good to be careful. We wouldn't want you in if you weren't that way. We only get one shot at this so it's got to be right. Now tell me what you're gonna do."

"It's a cinch. I go to this pawn shop at Lex and a Hundred and Twenty-fifth and I see this guy Harry—"

"Henry," Amberg corrected, feeling his stomach tighten.

"Yeah, that's what I mean, Henry. And I buy the merchandise, something small but heavy, and I wrap it in a white piece of cloth and bring it to the second trash can and leave it at eight-thirty day after tomorrow. And I do the thing with the doughnut. It's a cinch, no problem."

"And the car, don't forget."

"Sure. One o'clock on the nose. I park it near the alley and you'll be out in ten minutes."

"Now listen, if it's eleven minutes or even twelve minutes, you stay, right?"

"Sure. You don't have to worry about me, Hy." Sammy looked at him closely. "But, Hy, you guys are in maximum, right? It ain't easy to get out of there."

"Easier than you think." Amberg grinned. "I got it all figured out and believe me it can't miss. Once I get the merchandise inside, I'm home free. Those clowns got Rudy and Moe Berg right on the same tier with me. We'll go out of there like we were a fucking army. I've seen where they keep their pieces locked up and all we got to do is grab one of the guards and we'll have everything we need. These clowns don't carry their guns inside so there won't be any trouble. We'll walk out of there like we owned the joint, understand?"

A crooked smile began to form on Sammy's lips. "You make it sound easy."

"It is easy. And when it's over you're gonna be walking around with a broad on each arm and a wad of dough in each pocket. And nobody is gonna be any the wiser."

"That's it, Amberg. Time's up."

The guard walked up behind him and placed his hand on his shoulder. Amberg winked at Sammy again. He would do it, he was sure now. "So listen, you tell my brother there ain't nothin' to worry about, okay?"

"Sure, I'll tell him. And I'll be seeing you again soon," Sammy said.

"Listen. I said, time's up," the guard snapped.

"Sure, sure," Amberg said. "This place stinks anyway."

"You don't like it here you shouldn't bump off old guys in jewelry stores," the guard said.

"That was a bum rap. It was a lousy setup."

"Yeah, I know. We got almost a thousand guys in here on bum raps. Ain't

212

you heard. Everybody's innocent." The guard laughed at his own joke as he led Amberg back to the gate, opened it, and pointed to a wooden bench. "You sit there. The guard who brought you down ain't through with chow yet. You wait there like a good boy. And don't cause no trouble or you end up in solitary."

Amberg sat at the end of the bench and leaned back against the wall. I'll be like a fucking angel, he thought. I'll be so good you'll think I'm one of those boy scout kids. He began to laugh to himself. But two days from now, sweetheart, and you're gonna shit your pants just thinking about Hy Amberg. He thought about the visiting room again. There had been no office in there, no secure area where the guard could have safeguarded a weapon. There had also been no alarm that he could see. It was a place they did not expect trouble because everybody was locked in there, and when things were locked these people felt safe. It was the way their minds worked. He closed his eyes and allowed his mind to wander and his face became smooth again, almost peaceful. It would all go just as he had planned. Ten minutes after they were out they would be in New Jersey. They would go to the small hotel in Newark that he had used before when he was running.

But this time he wouldn't be running. This time he would be waiting; just a few days to let things cool down and then he would be back. A few days to let Broderick sweat, to sit and think about him out on the streets again. Everytime he turned a corner he would wonder if he would be there, ready to spread his brains out on the street. All cops were afraid of that. You could see it in their eyes. Even when they tried to hide it, it was still there, hidden somewhere in the back of their minds, eating away, making them wonder if the day was coming, if it was already there. They moved around big and tough but their balls were sweating all the time because they were part of a world that didn't want them and they knew it. And Broderick sweat more than most, he had seen that too. He sweat because he knew there must be a hundred guys who wanted to see him dead, guys he had slapped around, guys he had set up.

Amberg's hands closed into fists, the fingers pressing into the palms until the knuckles grew white and the fingernails dug into his palms. The muscles in his jaw began to jump and his lips drew together into a thin line. Nothing else mattered now, only Broderick and then Gillie, if there was still time for that. There was little hope of reaching Canada, he knew that, he felt it deep within himself. Broderick had pronounced the death sentence in that stinking room and he had felt the truth of it each time his fist hit him. But Broderick's own death sentence would also come true. And he would let the world know about it after it was done, it was important to do that, to show everybody that he had won. Canada was still possible, but only just possible. Every cop in the country would want a piece of him. They would want it for the same reason that every cop was always afraid. If you kill a cop and you get away

213

with it, then none of them are safe and they want to be safe, safe in their fucking beds at night, safe when they walk down the street. Broderick liked to be safe. He had come for him with a dozen men, playing the odds, making sure everything was in his favor, slapping him around when he was hand-cuffed, kicking him like some fucking dog. But he had spit in his face and he would spit in his face again, this time while he was lying there with his guts hanging out, knowing he was a dead man, a piece of garbage lying in the street waiting for somebody to put dimes on his eyes. The newspapers had played him up so big, but this time it would be him, Hy Amberg, that they'd write about; about how he kept his promise and killed Johnny Broderick. He could still see him that night on Broadway when he had been with the rich broad and the fear in his eyes when he thought the odds were against him. He was dogmeat and he knew it and his balls were dripping with sweat. Then when the odds changed he was the big man again, the big tough cop that his asshole newspaper buddies wrote about, Johnny "the Beater" Broderick.

He touched his left cheekbone, feeling the slight tenderness that was still there from the weight of Broderick's right fist, even though it was more than a week old now. The eye had been closed for four days and his balls had hurt even longer from where he had kicked him. He had pissed blood for the first two days and it had scared hell out of him watching his own blood pour out of his prick that way. He pounded his fist down into his leg. The next time it would be different. It would be done right. No more screaming like he had done in court, just slow and easy, everything planned out to the last, no mistakes this time. He had to decide where and when. There had to be people, people to see it happen, it was important that it be done that way. "Witnesses to the execution," he said aloud, then caught himself and glanced around to see if anyone had heard. But first you have to get out. Sammy would do it. The kid was too hungry, too fucking hungry and greedy not to take his shot at making a big score and it was too simple even for him to fuck up.

The trustee was set. He had been given promises too and he would get the gun to him during the exercise period and then it would be set. He had his clock, a clock that never changed. Tick, tick. Everything nice and neat, just like the fucking army, everything done by the numbers. He had seen it, watched it. They had laid it out for him nice and neat. Their own stupid system would provide him with everything he needed, the routine, doing everything according to the routine, the one flaw and he had spotted it. He was a fucking genius at organizing things, he always had been. They thought they had everything worked out so good. The doors were locked and they had the keys and that made everything jake. Two days from now and they'd all see how fucking smart they were, how good their fucking routine was, how a smart guy could take it and shove it right up their ass. He laughed softly, closing his eyes again and resting his head back against the wall.

Around the corner he could hear two clerks talking in low, muffled tones. One of the clerks had been a fat, red-faced little mick; he had noticed him earlier. That red face would turn as white as a sheet in two days when he shoved a gun into it. He would shit in his fat little pants when they walked out of that elevator and told them that they were taking a fucking vacation. No, don't bother to send up for our bags, we'll send for our things later. He giggled at the thought of actually saying it. I know we reserved the rooms for a longer stay, but we find we must move on. Yes, you'll have to forgive us, but you see I have an appointment to kill a fucking cop and I simply can't be late. Maybe he could do it with an English accent. He squeezed his knees together and giggled again. Oh, it was going to be beautiful. Just walking out of maximum security. They'd go after the warden's balls, the fucking newspapers would chew his ass. And they'd put *his* picture on the front page and they wouldn't forget to remind everybody that he had sworn to get Broderick, had sworn it in court before God and everybody. And Broderick would read it and he'd fucking well remember.

He'd dream about it and he'd sweat bullets. He'd think about it when he got up in the morning and when he went to bed at night, when he ate and when he held his prick in his hands to piss. It was just like he planned, maybe even better than he planned. And he would get to Canada. He was a fucking genius. He could do anything now and nobody could stop him. Oh, it would feel so good to get that gun in his hand, just to feel it there. He would get a bigger one later to kill Broderick with. A .45 maybe, something that would blow him apart, put a hole the size of his fist in his belly, right below the belly button so it didn't kill him right away, and then he would spit in his face just before he blew his fucking brains all over the street. He felt himself starting to sweat with the excitement of it all. It would be better than fucking, better than a blow job. He would come in his pants when it happened, maybe even before it happened, when he saw him standing there scared shitless, knowing it was coming and knowing there wasn't a fucking thing he could do about it. Oh, Jesus, it was going to be beautiful. All of those other guys, Legs Diamond, all of them would just be punks next to him. And if he made it to Canada he'd be a fucking legend. Maybe he'd even have his face changed, have one of those operations and come back and piss on Broderick's grave, send the police commissioner a fucking postcard, just to remind him he was still walking around and that all his dumb fucking cops couldn't find him. Postmarked from New York. It would drive him out of his fucking mind. Send one to the newspapers, too, so they could tell everybody how Hy Amberg was laughing at them all, laughing in his fucking beer. It was all there, laid out so perfect and there was nothing that any of them could do about it.

A chill rose along his spine. But what if Sammy screwed it up? What if the trustee got nabbed before he got the gun to him? Everything would be out the damn window then. They'd stick him in solitary and make sure nobody

215

could get near him. Once they got him back to Sing Sing, on Death Row, there'd be nothing he could do.

He thought of the death house, of when he worked there, that little room painted with that light green paint and the church pews they, had put in for the assholes who came and watched guys get their brains fried. They were sick bastards all of them. Some of them puked afterward, that's what the guards had told him, left their suppers there on the floor after they smelled the guy burning. He remembered the first time he saw the chair, how funny it looked, not like a real chair at all, with no real back to it, just a couple of pieces of wood, like slats. And the straps attached to the arms and legs, the whole thing sitting there on a metal plate and the scuff marks on the plate where guys' feet had kicked out for the last time and the marks on the arms where their fingernails had dug into the wood when the juice hit. And that's what that bastard wanted for him. He said he was going to be there to watch, how he'd sit there and laugh when they pulled the switch. If anybody had a right—

"All right, Amberg, let's go."

He opened his eyes and found the guard staring down at him. There was a spot of gravy on his shirt. "Oh, is it two o'clock already?" he said.

"That's right, get moving." The guard's voice was gruff, cocky.

One P.M. *Same. Full hour. Only two.* He laughed to himself. I love your system, asshole, he thought. Everything by the numbers. "How was the chow? The stuff we had at eleven-thirty was really bad."

"We don't eat the shit they feed you. You think we're crazy?" He pushed Amberg ahead of him and they turned into the reception area.

Amberg looked to his left. The fat clerk was sitting at his desk shuffling papers. Oh, I hope you don't stay home sick two days from now, he thought. I want to see that fat little face turn white. I bet you'll shake all over like jelly and then pee in your pants a little. They passed from the reception area and turned toward the elevators. The old man was sitting on a stool in the small waiting area and he looked annoyed as they approached, realizing that he would be forced to get up and put the elevator in motion. Too bad, old man, Amberg thought. We'll see how upset you are in two days when I shove a gun in your fucking mouth. All of them, they were all the same. The people behind the bars were shit because they had the keys. Just like the animals in the zoo. Everybody could be big and brave and stand there and laugh at the fucking lions because they knew they couldn't get through the fucking bars and bite their fucking heads off. He'd like to slap the shit out of all of them right now, show them how big they were, how tough. But he had better plans for all of them. In two days everybody would know what they were, when he walked out of their jail like it was nothing.

The elevator rose slowly, the gears groaning as they pulled the weight upward. He would have to remember to listen that day, to make sure it was

216

working. He couldn't risk the stairs, it would be too dangerous. Wouldn't that be a bitch, he thought, if the elevator broke down? Everything would have to be set back until it was working again. He'd have to reach out for Sammy again and the delay would probably scare him off. Jesus, don't worry about those things, he told himself. You'll drive yourself nuts. Nothing's gonna go wrong, not this time. Everything is gonna go just like you planned.

The elevator door swung open and ahead lay the corridor and the rows of cells. They passed by the small office. Three guards were inside. The hour's over, he thought, just like the clock says. He passed Dunniger's cell. He was sitting on his bunk staring at him, his eyes full of questions. Farther down was Moe's cell, but he wouldn't pass it, it was beyond his own. But he didn't want contact with them now; he wanted nothing that could draw any concern from the guards. He could talk to both of them at the evening meal in a natural, easy way. Let the guards sleep on. They had the keys, they were in control, they had nothing to worry about.

He listened to the sound of his leather heels clicking along the concrete floor, the sound of the guard moving behind him almost like an echo. There was a firm determination to the sound, he thought, something that was moving ahead and could not be stopped. He liked the sound and he let his heels fall more heavily, emphasizing it so the cadence was near to someone marching. Even the sound of his bad leg, throwing the cadence slightly off rhythm, felt good to his ear. His sound. His. He stopped abruptly before his cell door, turning to face it while the guard worked the key into the lock. His face froze. There was a man on the top bunk. He had had the cell to himself before and now there was someone there.

"What's this?" he said.

"You got company. What's the matter, you expected a private room?"

He turned on the guard, his face angry. "Nobody said nothin' about this."

The guard looked at him as though he was crazy. "You think we got to ask your permission, or somethin'. Get in there and shut up." He swung the door open, but Amberg remained bolted to the floor. "Get in, I said."

He moved through the door hesitantly; he could feel the trembling begin in his legs and then spread up into his hands. He stared at the man in the upper bunk. He was lying there as though dead, his eyes blankly fixed on the peeling paint of the ceiling. He was big, bulky, but he looked like he was dead. Amberg sat on the lower bunk and looked up at the impression in the mattress, the cloth pushing through the small interlocked wire rectangles that supported it. He could even be a cop, a plant, anything. Or he could be nothing, just another stiff locked in a cage. But he wasn't part of the plan, he was something new, something different that he hadn't counted on. He slid back on the bed until his back rested against the wall and drew his feet up in front of him. He propped his elbows on his knees and began rubbing his temples with his fingers. Should he talk to him, find out about him. It would

217

be natural. He could even be friendly with him if he had to. Or he could just keep his mouth shut, ignore him for the next two days, shut off any attempt he made to talk. But it didn't look like he wanted to talk either. His body didn't seem to move, the impression in the mattress didn't change, almost as though he had been planted there and was waiting to take root. He was quiet, like somebody who had done time before, somebody who had his own problems to live with and didn't need anybody else's to mix with it. And he *was* in max, that meant something. But it could mean a lot of things, a major rap if he just came in, or maybe trouble on another tier, a fight or something like that. Or he could have been a stoolie who somebody said they would get and who the bulls were trying to protect. Whatever he was, none of it was good because he wasn't part of things the way he had worked them out.

The big man stirred, causing the bunk to shake under his weight. His legs dropped over the side and his body followed, slipping down to the floor in a smooth easy motion. He walked over to the toilet, unbuttoned his pants, and let them drop to his ankles and sat. There was a cigarette in his mouth now and the smoke rose steadily and then spread into curling wisps. Amberg lit his own cigarette to kill the smell he knew would come. He had spent years locked up smelling other men's shit, guarding his commissary, making sure his soap and candy bars and cigarettes were safe. He had seen men cry when their stuff was lifted, tough guys, guys who would cut your throat on the outside, crying like fucking babies over a bar of soap. But he had more to protect. He had his notes and in two days he would have the gun. If he got friendly with this stiff he might decide to get curious, start watching him or sit around on his bunk wanting to talk—and talk was something he didn't need, not now.

He slid to the middle of the bunk and lay back, propping his head against the doubled-over pillow and stared down over his shoes out through the bars. The man was behind him to his left and he wanted to be sure their eyes did not meet when he returned to his bunk; he wanted to avoid any excuse for conversation, even recognition. He had heard him complain to the guard, there was no way he could not have, so he would accept the way he ignored him, unless—unless he was a plant . . . or a fool. He could hear him finishing now, hear him pulling up his pants and then the sound of the toilet flushing, the chain that hung from the water box above it banging up against the wall again and again. Out of the corner of his eye he could see him return to the bunk, then pull himself up, the bed shaking from his weight. He sat there for a moment, his legs hanging down over the side, the gray prison pants pulled halfway along the calves of his legs. A large scar ran down the back of one leg and from the width of it where it met the edge of his pants, he guessed it probably continued on up. A wound from the war, he thought. Another asshole hero who had bled for his country and now found himself locked up. He hadn't noticed any limp when he walked so it probably wasn't that bad.

218

He noticed limps; it seemed he had always noticed them and all the names, the taunts, the catcalls he had grown up with always came back to him each time he did. But nobody said those things anymore. They knew better, he had taught them to know better and he was still teaching them, teaching them about Hy Amberg and what it would mean if you crossed him. And in a few days he would teach them all again.

He took a long drag on his cigarette, held the smoke deep in his lungs and then opened his mouth and let it escape slowly on his breath, like steam rising from a lake on a cold morning. Canada would be cold; in a few months it would get incredibly cold and it would bother his leg. But he could hide in Canada, he had been there before and he knew if he kept to the English-speaking parts no one would pay any attention to him. He could go to Kingston, just across the border from Watertown, or farther east to Brockville, which was only a hundred miles or so from Dannemora. They had a chair at Dannemora too, one of the four they kept going. Four chairs, no waiting.

A chill rose along his body thinking of the one at Sing Sing, the one Broderick had dusted off for him. He looked up at the impression in the mattress the man above him made. You'll be a part of it, buster, he thought. You don't know it yet, but you're going to be a part of it and some day you'll even tell people how you were in a cell with Hy Amberg when he was making his plans, lying there figuring the whole thing out, setting it up for everybody to see and how if Johnny Broderick had only known what was being planned for him then, how he would have shit in his pants, knowing there was no way he could stop it. A low laugh rose in Amberg's throat and then stopped. His mouth spread out to each side and his lips parted almost unnoticeably. He was smiling out into the empty corridor where the noise from the other inmates carried in a steady, even din. He didn't hear the noise. His mind was playing its own symphony and he was both the orchestra and the audience.

CHAPTER TWENTY-SEVEN

SITTING BEFORE THE VANITY MIRROR SHE SEEMED IN-
credibly delicate. The dressing gown she wore was almost transparent and the
outline of her soft nakedness beneath it was a pale shadow. He sat on the bed,
the pillows propped up against the headboard, watching her. The soft silk
sheet was pulled up just below his waist, covering his own nakedness and
beneath it he could still feel the warm satisfaction that lingered from their
love-making. She used the hairbrush deftly with quick, knowledgeable
strokes, returning the soft curls that fell away during the pleasant violence of
the struggle that had just ended. He liked watching her. It gave him a sense
of comfort knowing he was there with her. That she wanted him there and
would continue to want him there because they were good together. There
had been doubts, but they were vanishing, for both of them, he thought.
Everything was laid out before him, all the things he had wanted and had
never really considered. It had just happened. He had reached out and taken
it for himself and she had not objected. She had wanted it too. She had
wanted him too.

She looked up from her brushing and smiled at him. "Are you keeping me
under surveillance, Detective?" There was a teasing familiarity in her voice
that came whenever she was happy. He had noticed that about her.

"Always," he said, keeping his eyes on her.

"Is that necessary?" She looked back in the mirror but her voice still held laughter in it.

"It's not necessary. I just like to," he said.

"Like to what?" Her hand was adjusting the position of the curls, her fingers moving delicately against each, cajoling them into place.

"Like to look at you," he said.

"Some people would consider that voyeurism. Isn't that against the law, being a peeping Tom, I mean?"

"You forget, I am the law."

"Not for long, darling. Soon you'll be part of the business world and you won't be able to get away with things the way you can now. What are you going to do then?"

"I haven't agreed to take the job, yet."

His voice had a joking quality in it and the words did not disturb her. She continued to look at herself in the mirror. "You will, darling. Even Uncle William thinks you'd be a fool not to. He told me so."

"Did he tell you how much he wants me then?"

"Of course he did."

"He didn't tell me that." His voice had flattened out, thinking of her uncle and the feeling he had left him with.

She noted the change but still avoided looking at him. "Of course he didn't. In business you're never supposed to let someone know how much you want them. He said you reacted much the same way, so obviously you know how that little game is played."

He remembered the contest. He hadn't done badly, he thought. He had played it the way it should have been played. But he knew he hated that silver-haired old bastard, and he knew the feeling was mutual. There was still something unspoken between them. But still, like she said, that *was* the way the game was played. No, he hadn't done badly at all.

"Well, until it happens—if it happens—I'll keep on looking."

She turned and stood, then walked slowly toward him. "Have a closer look," she said. She moved deliberately, affectedly, swaying her hips slightly in a vague imitation of whoreishness. She stopped in front of him and mimed the chewing of gum, cranking her hips to one side at the same time. "See anything you like, mister?"

He reached out and spread the dressing gown open with his fingers. "Not bad. A little skinny, maybe, but not bad."

She swung her hand out, brushing the top of his hair. She put her hands on her hips. "I suppose you'd prefer something plumper?"

"There's more to hold onto then," he said, ducking as her hand swung out again. "But the guineas say the closer to the bone the sweeter the meat. I guess I just haven't experimented enough."

She threw her head back in mock laughter. "Oh, no," she said. "You're a

221

virtual virgin. The virgin detective. John 'the virgin' Broderick. I'll have to tell that to your newspaper friends. Perhaps they'll use it next time instead of 'the beater.' I wonder what all your criminal friends would say to that." She changed her voice to a low, gruff rasp. "Watch out, Max. Here comes da virgin."

He reached out and pulled her toward him, forcing her to put her knee against the edge of the bed to keep from falling on top of him. "I'll take care of this virgin business right now," he said.

"Again?" she said, widening her eyes. "My, aren't we feeling frisky tonight." He pulled her down against him so her breasts were brushing his face and began running his tongue slowly along them. "Again," he whispered.

"Yes, again," she said. She began to breathe deeply and pressed herself against his face. "I want you. I want you all the time." She began running her fingers through his hair, pressing his face forward against her. "You're so different now. The last few weeks. It's been as though I never knew you before."

He slid her down next to him and they made love slowly, gently. The clumsiness and uncertainty of earlier days was gone now and the tenderness of his touch drove her into an immediate frenzy and she closed her eyes and smiled, enjoying the pleasure of it.

They lay quietly next to each other without speaking. She was turned toward him, her head resting against his shoulder and her breath was soft and slow, a prelude to the sleep that was creeping into her. Behind her a faint light filtered through the gauzelike curtains that covered the double windows, and beyond them, far across Central Park, the illumination from the distant buildings glistened with a faint warmth. He reached up and turned off the light on the night stand, then allowed his hand to fall gently on her naked shoulder. She stirred slightly under his touch and kissed his shoulder, in her sleep he thought at first.

"It's so good, John. Isn't it good?" Her voice seemed sleepy, distant.

"It's everything I want," he said, almost surprised by his own candidness.

"It never has to change. I don't want it to. I want it to stay like this between us, always." She had pulled herself even closer to him and he could feel the outline of her body.

He stared up at the ceiling, still feeling her and his mind began to race with the need to resolve those parts of his life that now interfered with what he wanted.

"I'm not pressing you, John," she said, seeming almost to read his thoughts. "I know you have to work things out for the sake of your daughter."

The thought of his child stumbled into his mind. He had not thought of her at all, not as part of it. The strange, sad little girl. He wished she wasn't like that, wished it didn't matter to her. It would make everything so much simpler and then he would even be able to develop some kind of understanding with her. He would be able to spend time with her then without feeling as though he was slapping her face each time he left.

"I guess she's the only real problem," he said. "I just don't know what to tell her."

"It's better not to tell her anything," Mona said. "Children understand things in time. All they really have to know is that they're loved."

He nodded, but said nothing.

"John, I'm not going to force you away from your family. They don't even have to know about us if you don't want them to." She stared across his chest, avoiding his eyes, and her words came slowly, carefully spoken. "I want you here with me. In time, your wife will understand and she'll accept the idea. And you'll be able to care for them. Your future is so bright now."

"Your uncle and I talked about that a little," he said. He could feel her body stiffen slightly.

"You did?" she said. The stiffness had transferred itself to her voice, almost imperceptibly.

"Nothing in any great detail. I think he just wanted to be sure my intentions were honorable." He laughed and stroked her arm again.

"Did you tell him I didn't want your honor, just your body?" Her answer was light, but the touch of concern still carried in her voice.

"That would have curled his moustache. I just told him I wanted to get a divorce."

The feel of her body changed again. He could not tell how but he knew that it had.

"Is that really what you want?" Her voice and her body were both expectant now, awaiting the reply.

"It has to be that way. It's just her damned religion. That's the only thing stopping it. Your uncle said something about an annulment, about how it could be bought. I never thought you could buy off a church, but I suppose you can. You can buy off every other damned thing these days."

"Do you think she'd accept that, an annulment I mean?"

"I don't see why not. It doesn't break the rules of her religion. Those goddamned priests. They fill people's minds with such crap. Everytime you turn around you're doing something you're not supposed to."

There was a trace of disgust in his voice, hidden partially by the soft way he was speaking, but it sent a tremor of happiness through her. "But you were raised as a Catholic, weren't you? I never asked but I just assumed it, with the Irish name and all."

"When my mother was alive she made me go to church. But after she died the closest my old man ever got to it was the gin mill down the street. I went for a while, I guess, but those priests were murder." His mind rushed back for

223

an instant to the thick Irish voice drifting through the thin black curtain of the confessional, a voice that had damned him to hell so many times that his body always shook before he entered.

"Were you that bad as a little boy." She was changing the subject intentionally now, pacing herself. "You probably kept sneaking up on the rooftops with little girls."

"It wouldn't have been so bad if you just had to tell them what you did." He smiled thinking about it. "It was the questions they asked. How many times you did something. How many different people. What you did, even how you did it."

"You mean they asked you for details?"

"They asked you everything. Christ, if I hadn't been so scared I probably would have gotten all hot and bothered again just talking about it that way. It wasn't anything, just kid stuff, but sometimes I used to think that was the way they enjoyed it themselves, because they couldn't have a woman, or anything."

"I don't know," she said. "I've seen some priests give some pretty lustful looks, especially at cocktail parties."

"Yeah, I bet they do." The disgust was back in his voice again. "But you ask them to bend one of their rules and they'll send you straight to hell on the next trolley car."

"But you said an annulment wasn't against the rules." She was back to the subject now, faster than she had intended but he did not seem to notice. She ran her fingers along the hair on his chest, stroking him, distracting him from the quiet urgency in her voice that she did not want him to notice. Her eyes were still averted but they were firm, staring across the room at nothing in particular, her mind too intent on every nuance in his voice.

"The only problem is that it takes time. I want things to happen fast, so they can be over with once and for all. Maybe money will make a difference to her. She's always after it, trying to get more than I have." He lied, remembering how little he had ever given the woman. Not a bad woman. Not bad at all. A million men would think she was perfect. But she was not what he wanted. She hadn't been that for years.

"You'll have money soon, John." Her voice was even softer now, the words deliberate and cautious. "And if you ever need a specific amount for a settlement, Uncle can advance it. It's something the company often does for its executives." Her mind toyed with the idea of offering her own money as well but she rejected it as quickly as the thought came to her. She would not take the chance of frightening him, she decided. And she would also not take the chance of offering him too much. Not until she was sure, and she knew she was not. There was still a great deal to prove, to find out about, even though she was speaking as though there wasn't and would continue to act that way.

224

"I wouldn't want to take any money from him, not right away anyway. I don't think he trusts me very much."

"If he didn't trust you, John, he wouldn't be offering you a position of responsibility. Besides, darling. I can vouch for you."

"You never know. You might wake up some morning and find I've stolen the family jewels. You know what they say about crooks and cops. They both work the same side of the street." He squeezed her shoulder to assure that he was only joking.

"I'm afraid they're all locked up in a safe deposit box," she said. "You'll just have to settle for me." She pulled against him again, knowing her body would emphasize the value of the offer.

"It's all I want, kid."

"You're all I want too, John. I want things to stay like this between us and if they change I just want them to change for the better."

He kissed her hair and allowed his eyes to close, thinking how he had what he wanted now after years of not even knowing what it was he had been after. It was Mona and the life he could have with her. Nothing would stand in the way of it. Nothing really could, he was sure of that; and if something did it would not remain there for long. He would see to it. He listened to her breathing, his eyes still closed. He could feel her breasts rising and falling. She was asleep now, he thought.

But Mona was not asleep. Her mind was still playing and replaying her own thoughts. But she was content with those thoughts, at least for now.

CHAPTER TWENTY-EIGHT

THE BAR OF THE BROOKLYN HEIGHTS SPEAKEASY WAS dimly lit and through the thin walls came the occasional rumble of traffic moving across the Brooklyn Bridge. It was midnight and there were only a few customers scattered along the bar and at the handful of battered tables behind it. Two stools down from where Sammy sat a well-worn blonde toyed with the drink set before her. He had noticed her when he had entered almost an hour ago and he had decided she was probably a hooker plying her trade among the dock workers who dominated the neighborhood nightspots. Inside his belt he could feel the package Henry had delivered earlier that afternoon, a short-barreled .38, small but heavy, just like the man had ordered. He knew he should have left it in his room, but the rent was overdue and the landlady had a habit of poking around for any loose change she could put her greedy fingers on and he had decided it would be safer to keep it with him. Besides, he didn't like to come to the neighborhood joints unprepared. The dock workers carried their hooks with them, stuck in their pockets or hanging from the loops sewn on to the shoulders of their jackets. He motioned to the bartender for another drink and watched as he poured it, making sure it was a fair one. The drink was right and he motioned the bartender toward him with his head.

The bartender placed his heavy forearms on the bar and leaned across, no particular degree of curiosity showing in his eyes.

"The broad, you know her?" He motioned with his eyes toward the blonde.

"Never saw her before," the bartender whispered back.

"A working girl, you think?" Sammy offered him a slight grin, exposing the decay that spread out from between his two front teeth.

The bartender shrugged. "Who the fuck knows. She ain't from no convent, that's for sure."

Sammy nodded knowingly, then looked to his right again trying to size up the availability of the woman. She was over thirty, he guessed, and she bore the marks of more than one war, somebody who had been knocked around more than once, but who seemed ready for it again if the opportunity arose.

"Hey, can I buy you a drink," he said down the bar. "If you ain't waitin' for somebody, I mean."

The woman looked at him, then shrugged her shoulders. "I'm not waitin' for anybody." She looked at the bartender. "I'll take another one of those things you call Scotch," she said.

The bartender came over to her and poured the drink. "Sorry it ain't imported, honey," he said.

"It's not even distilled." She picked up the glass and raised it toward Sammy. He stood and walked toward her. "I guess you're gonna join me," she said.

"Just for a friendly drink. You mind?" He exposed the decay again.

She shrugged and he slid on to the stool next to her. "I figured there was no sense in both of us drinking alone. Right?"

She gave him a sideward glance, eyeing him up and down. "I was watching you before and you looked nervous," she said. "Was it because you wanted to talk to me?" There was a toughness about the way she carried herself that could have been taken as a veneer except that it came off her like steam rising from a sewer on a cold morning.

"I just got a lot on my mind," he said. He waited, then drew himself up on the bar stool. "I got some important stuff to do in the morning."

"Yeah. Like what?" Her voice was intentionally skeptical, intended more to dismiss his bravado than draw him out.

"I can't talk about it. But don't worry, you'll hear about it." He showed his rotting teeth again and raised his glass to his lips.

She laughed. "Everybody I meet these days is about to do something big that I'm gonna hear about."

He bristled under the rebuke, one of the thousands he had received for as long as he could remember. His dark face grew even darker and his eyes became cold. A small lock of his strawlike hair fell on to his forehead. "This you'll hear about," he grumbled.

227

"Look, honey, I didn't mean anything." She reached out and brushed the strand of hair back off his forehead. "I just got a funny sense of humor. If you say it's important, then it's important." She drained her glass as though it was water. "Can I have another?" she asked.

"Sure, why not." He motioned to the bartender and watched him as he poured the drink full, then drained his own and watched again as he refilled the glass.

She turned to face him, crossing her legs as she did and observing that he took care to note them. "You want to tell me about it?" she asked.

"It's something I can't talk about."

"Oh, it's like that." She grinned. "I hope you're not gonna be a naughty boy."

They both laughed and she leaned back thrusting her breasts out as she did. His eyes moved to them immediately.

"Well, you ought to get to bed and get a good night's rest then," she said.

"But I ain't sleepy." He leered at her.

"Who said anything about sleep?" They both laughed again and she looked at him closely, somewhat revolted by his rotting teeth but not enough to pass up the opportunity.

"You got any ideas?" he said.

"My place ain't far from here. We could get a bottle and go there and relax."

He ordered the bottle, paid for it, and then stood. She reached out and touched his arm. "There's only one thing though, honey." She looked up into his eyes, begging sympathy. "I'm a little behind on the rent and if the landlady sees me coming in with somebody she's gonna want it in the morning. She's an old bitch." She pouted effortlessly.

"How much is it?"

"Just five bucks," she said. "I really hate to ask you."

His mind jolted at the amount. "That must be some place you got," he said, watching as she shrugged again. He counted quickly. He had twenty-three dollars in his pocket, only three of it his own. The rest belonged to a friend of Dunniger's, who had given it to him to make the purchase. They would need some money tomorrow, but not that much, he decided. Besides he could always claim that Henry overcharged him for the gun and nobody would know the difference. He grinned at her. "Sure, honey. Why not?" He pulled out his money and extracted a five-dollar bill.

She took it and looked at him coyly. "Let's go," she said.

A mile away Hy Amberg lay in his bunk staring at the mattress above him. He was satisfied that everything would go well now and the occasional tremors of doubt were dismissed easily and he was sure that Sammy by now had the one final item that would make all his plans a reality. If he had known that at that same moment Sammy was explaining that item to a blond prostitute he would have flown into a violent rage. But he did not know and sleep gradually crept into him as the thoughts of the man he would soon kill slipped away.

Five miles north Johnny Broderick slept quietly, his arm draped over the naked shoulder of Mona D'Arcy. He was dreaming of an office and a secretary and in his dream he was smoking a large cigar and its presence confused him. He did not smoke.

Across the East River in Queens another man, Louis Lorch, also slept in a small, sparsely furnished apartment. Lorch had been tossing about his small cotlike bed for most of the night, his sleep-filled mind returning again and again to a battle he had fought almost eight years ago in France.

Sammy left the blonde's apartment at four o'clock and it was only then that the fears he had put off throughout the day returned. The meeting with Henry had been a disaster on his part. The sleazy little pawnshop operator had not wanted to do business with him and he had had to mention Amberg's name to force him into the sale. It had been wrong, he knew that. It was information that could be sold to the police, and he was sure after meeting him that Henry was not beneath working both sides of the street. Then there was the blonde. He had said too much to her as well, bragging about his Big Plans for the next day and letting her see the gun. She too would now have something to sell and she wouldn't be the first whore to work deals with the cops on the side.

He turned the corner and walked down to the river, needing time to think. Off to his left the Statue of Liberty shone in the darkness and the sounds of the first tugboats of the morning drifted back to him as they worked their way out to the anchorage off the eastern tip of Red Hook. He could show up at one o'clock and the cops could be waiting for him. It was something that was more than possible now. They could even be there at eight-thirty when he dropped off the cloth-covered package, but that was less likely. He could do neither and be safe. Safe until later when Amberg found somebody else and decided to repay him for running out on him. No matter which way he turned now he felt like a loser and the feeling both angered and frightened him. He had felt that way all his life and deep inside he knew there was full justification for it. He turned and walked the six tenement-ridden blocks that led back to his rooming house, trying not to think about it anymore. It was four-thirty now and he still had three and half hours before he had to leave, if he decided to leave at all. There was a doughnut shop close to the subway at Borough Hall and he could buy them there and eat all but the final one on the ride to the Canal Street stop. He could even postpone his decision until then, he thought, and if he decided not to go through with it he could simply stay on the train and continue on away from his fears.

It was eight-thirty when Sammy climbed out of the subway into the already humid warmth of Canal Street. Even then the street was alive with the Chinese tradesmen who always seemed to fill the area, always working their street stands and their shops, which never seemed to close. He hated the Chinese, the strange smells that came off them, the odd foods they ate, the pigtails and skull caps that some of them still wore. He didn't like the fact that he could not understand what they were saying and he remembered the stories he had heard as a child, how they were all plotting against the white people and would rise up some night and kill everybody in their beds with meat cleavers.

Sammy struggled through the ambling crowds of Chinese and turned south on Centre Street and began walking the remaining blocks to the Tombs. He glanced about him as he walked, looking for any unusual number of police moving in the area and with each step the weight of the gun wrapped in white cloth and tucked into the belt beneath his coat seemed to grow heavier. At Leonard Street he turned left and walked along the side of the Tombs, moving steadily toward the alley halfway down the block. There were no signs of police anywhere in sight but the fact comforted him only slightly. As he passed the entrance of the prison he took the final doughnut from the bag he carried and bit into it nervously and began crumpling the bag in his free hand. He was only ten feet from the trash can now and if there was no one in the alley he would toss the bag and the package in the second can. He would do that. That much he had decided. Whether or not he would be back at one was a question he had still not resolved.

Inside the heavy steel door that marked the main entrance to the Tombs Louis Lorch looked out through the small, square peephole and watched the man walk past eating a doughnut. He had awakened late that morning and had missed breakfast and seeing the man bite into the white powdered doughnut had reminded him of the fact and had made him wish he could leave his post and satisfy that hunger. As the man passed from view Lorch turned and resigned himself that he could not. His post at the main gate had no relief until noon and then only for an hour. He would be hungry until then, he knew, and there was nothing he could do about it.

It was half an hour later when Lorch again returned to the door, this time to open it for the morning work crew who picked up the trash in and around the exterior of the building. The five men, accompanied by two guards, each dragged a canvas bag behind them which they would use to gather up the refuse along the street. There, three of the inmates and one of the guards moved along the sidewalk, gathering the refuse that had collected during the night. The two remaining inmates and the second guard moved on to the alley that led to the prison coal yard, there also to pick up scattered refuse and to carry five trash cans out to the curb to await collection. When the work crew returned twenty minutes later one of the inmates carried a gift tucked inside his shirt. When Louis Lorch closed the door behind him he thought again about how hungry he was.

CHAPTER TWENTY-NINE

O N THE TERRACE SEVEN FLOORS ABOVE FIFTH AVENUE the breeze moving across Central Park cut the morning humidity, leaving behind the pleasant warmth of early September. From the heavy stone railing that enclosed the terrace the monstrous double-decker buses could be seen lumbering down the avenue taking people to the offices and shops where they would spend the day. It was eight o'clock, and as he stood there looking down Johnny Broderick realized he would be late for his tour. It had become almost a habit now. In the past two weeks he had been late at least seven times and he had taken pleasure in the fact that it no longer mattered to him. He would work with Cordes today, fulfilling a contract the squad had received from the Hall and he knew Cordes would cover for him. He smiled to himself. None of it mattered now; he was only going through the motions, counting out the time, checking and rechecking himself as he had learned to do years before.

Behind him he could hear Rita setting out the silver coffeepot and cups on the glass-topped table, the sound of her starched uniform rustling with each movement.

"Beautiful day, isn't it?" He kept the back of his lightweight blue serge suit to her, contenting himself with the view of the park below.

"Yes, sir, it is." Her voice was pert and high pitched and it made her sound younger than she was. There was a pause and he knew she was standing still. The rustling sound had stopped. "Would you care for eggs this morning, sir?" she asked.

"Yes, that would be nice." His lips parted into a smile and he breathed in deeply, feeling his chest expand against his suit coat. Out in the park a police officer ambled along one of the paths twirling his nightstick the way every rookie was taught and took so much pride in during his first years on the force. He would miss the camaraderie if he did leave. He had learned to depend upon it without even knowing he had. There was something special between men who risked their safety together, very much like the military, he guessed. He had never seen action during the war; his post in the navy had been a safe one, but he knew it was the same. He watched the cop continue down the path and he knew if he saw him suddenly in trouble he would rush from the building and go to him, just as that cop, or any other, would come to him. It was really the secret of their power, more than the badge or gun. Just the fact that they protected each other, because they had to, because it was the only way to survive.

Survival. He hadn't thought in those terms for over a week now and it felt good to know it had not been necessary. He breathed in deeply again allowing the warm air to fill his lungs. Below, a trolley car rumbled down the center of the street, its bell clanging at the cars that crossed back and forth in front of its path. The trolley man would be cursing a blue streak, he thought. He could almost hear him grumbling about his right of way and how everyone in New York ignored it, including the cops. Everyone in the city grumbled about something, but none of them would live anywhere else. And why should they? Where else could somebody grow up in a filthy slum and stand like he was now, looking down at it all with the world by the balls?

It was fifteen minutes past nine when they finished their breakfast together and he left the apartment and walked down the hall to the elevator. The door of the elevator slid open at almost the same moment that Louis Lorch unlocked the heavy steel door of the Tombs to allow the work crew to make their way to the street.

Broderick chatted with the man operating the elevator and in the lobby he stopped to talk to the doorman who he had learned to call by his first name. When he stepped through the front entrance of the building he breathed deeply, then turned and began walking south on Fifth Avenue. He had left his car at Headquarters the night before and he decided he would walk several blocks before grabbing a taxi to take him on his way. He walked slowly down the street. The swagger that had marked his movements in the past was missing now and he moved easily, enjoying the morning. He watched the other pedestrians on the street, each moving at a similar pace, none in any particular hurry to reach their destinations. There were no businesses along this part of Fifth Avenue and the people who moved along the

233

sidewalk at this hour were not pressed for time. They were people who enjoyed their leisure, people who could afford to enjoy it. The few who were on their way to offices had no time schedule to worry about, no one who could determine what hour they should arrive at work. It was a different life, one he knew he wanted despite any claims that he had not yet made up his mind. It was just his usual caution. It was the way he had been taught to be, a cautious cop watching for the things that could bring trouble.

Johnny Broderick, the cop, he thought. The words seemed to go with the name. He had become used to the idea and now all of it was ready to change. It would be hard to think of himself as something else. It would also take getting used to. He felt the weight of his gun on his right hip and wondered if he would actually have trouble keeping his balance without it. Old cops that he knew, those who had retired, he recalled again, still carried their guns. Perhaps he would too, in the beginning at least. There was only one more decision to make now and he knew he would probably make it before the day ended. He had thought it would be the hardest, but he knew now it would not.

CHAPTER THIRTY

HY AMBERG WAS STRETCHED ACROSS THE LOWER bunk in his cell. Through the barred door the cacophonous din of the Tombs filtered into the ten-by-eight floor enclosure. Amberg did not hear the noise. His mind was four blocks north of the Manhattan jail, in a car parked on Centre Street across from the main entrance of Police Headquarters. Within a few days he would be there, a pistol resting in his lap, waiting for Johnny Broderick to step out on the street swaying those cocky shoulders as he walked. Even now he could see the look in Broderick's eyes when he found himself in front of that gun, that last moment before six bullets ripped into his face. It was the last thing he would ever see, the gun and Hy Amberg laughing at him.

He sat up abruptly, his eyes dancing with his own thoughts. Slowly the sounds of the six-story city prison forced their way back into his consciousness. Steel banging against steel, radios playing one against the other, the curses and the low murmurs of too many conversations taking place at once, the leather heels of the guards moving along concrete corridors.

It was oppressively hot. The September heat hung throughout the jail, remaining in each cell like a gluey mist. The back of Amberg's prison uniform was saturated and drops of perspiration slid down his thin, angular face. He lit a cigarette, then reached into his shirt pocket and removed a watch.

Quarter to one, almost time. Fifteen minutes and then it would be there, he thought. By then half the guards would be eating.

He reached under his pillow, turning his back to the cell door to keep out unwanted eyes, and withdrew a .38 caliber pistol. He stroked the barrel, feeling the reassuring hardness of the blue-black metal. He cocked the hammer slowly and rotated the cylinder gently between his fingers. Soon this gun would get him out of there. Then it would kill Johnny Broderick. He could almost feel the power of the revolver jumping in his hands as it burst to life. He would send the gun to the mayor with a note. A present for Jimmy Walker, the gun that blew Johnny Broderick's head off. A smile that was close to a sneer crossed his lips. They would still be talking about it on Broadway twenty years from now.

Amberg slid the pistol back under the pillow. He got up from the bunk and walked to the cell door. Looking to his right he could see Moe Berg standing behind a cell door a few cells down the tier. He smiled at him and Moe returned the sign with a nod, his flat face emotionless. To his left Amberg could see Dunniger also waiting. He was grinning with his mouth open like some stupid dog waiting to be fed, and he would soon start playing with his prick, Amberg thought. He winked at him. It's almost dinner time, kid. Almost. He turned and walked to the bunk and took out his watch. Five to one. He reached under the pillow and removed the revolver, quickly sliding it through an unbuttoned opening in his shirt and into his belt.

He stood and rested his arm on the upper bunk where the large, muscular man, naked from the waist up, was sprawled across it. His eyes were closed.

"I got a little job for you, punk," Amberg said.

The man on the bunk did not move.

Amberg waited, staring at him. "I said I got a job for you." He reached out and slapped him hard across the shoulder.

The large man jumped to life, turned on one elbow and stared into Amberg's face. "You got a job for nobody. You go fuck yourself."

Amberg stepped back from the bunk, still looking the man in the face. He opened his shirt slightly and exposed the handle of the gun.

"Me and some friends are taking a little vacation from this joint. We're gonna do it now and you're gonna help us, or else."

"You're outta your fucking mind," the man said.

"I said we're doing it now," Amberg said. His voice was soft and there was no sign of emotion on his face. "All you have to do is call the screw. You're gonna be very excited and when he comes you're gonna tell him how I just collapsed on the floor and you don't know why 'cause you didn't do anything to me. But you're gonna look a little guilty. I don't think that'll be too hard." Amberg's face broke into a smile, "And if you don't do it right I'm gonna use this on you before he can even get the door open." He patted the gun

236

beneath his shirt. "Remember they can't burn me twice so I got nothin' to lose. You understand, tough guy?"

The man lay back on the bunk and stared at the ceiling. "I understand. You just make sure that you slug me before you leave. I'm due out of here next week and I don't want to get the axe for being part of this bullshit."

"You just do it right and you won't have any problems."

"Listen, big shot. I'll do it and I'll send flowers to your funeral. You don't have a chance in hell of pulling this crap off."

Amberg patted his shirt again. "Just watch me, jerk. Get off that bunk and get your ass to the door."

The large prisoner eased himself up slowly and slid down from the bunk. He looked at Amberg, then walked to the cell door. Amberg dropped to the floor, pulling his knees up to his chest, and began to moan in pain. The inmate began to shout for the guard. His voice was loud and there was a realistic note of concern in it.

An older guard with white hair rushed up to the cell door, "What the hell is going on here?" he growled.

"I dunno. This guy in here with me, he just keeled over. I think he's got a heart attack or something."

The guard stared hard into the prisoner's face. "What happened to him?"

"Look, I dunno. I didn't touch him. He just fell over and started breathing funny."

The guard looked past him for a moment, staring at Amberg on the floor of the cell. He could hear a low moan coming from him, then he turned and looked down the hall. "Hey, Charlie, get over here. We got trouble with one of the sweethearts in this cell." He turned back to the large inmate and he could see he was sweating. "You move over to the far wall, right next to the crapper and you keep your back flat against the wall," he said.

The prisoner obeyed immediately, stepping lightly over Amberg's body as the second guard reached the cell door and looked in.

"What's wrong with him?" he asked.

"I dunno," the first guard said. "This other clown said he just keeled over."

The older guard took a ring of keys from his belt and opened the cell door. Both men stood in the doorway for a moment, each holding billyclubs in their hands. The older guard moved forward first, the second staying close behind. When he reached Amberg the older guard bent over and prodded his shoulder with the billy. A low groan rose from Amberg's lips. The guard bent closer, pressed the club hard against Amberg's shoulder and began to turn him over. Suddenly his body lurched backward, his back slamming against the wall. Both hands rushed to his face where the side of Amberg's gun had caught him.

Before the second guard could move Amberg was on one knee pointing the gun in his face. "One move, cocksucker, one sound and I'll spread your fucking brains all over this tier."

Amberg got to his feet and pushed the older guard with his knee. He tumbled over on his side, falling at the feet of the other guard. There was blood streaming down his face from a deep gash above his eye. "Now pick him up and move," Amberg said. "We got two other cells to open."

Amberg bent down and picked up the keys the older guard had dropped and moved quickly out behind them and locked the cell door. Then he turned and looked back at the inmate inside the cell.

"Sorry, pal, but I can't take you with me like you asked," he said.

"You rotten bastard," the inmate shouted. "I hope they blow your fucking head off."

Amberg laughed as he pushed the two guards down the corridor to Moe's cell. Other inmates were shouting encouragement now and several were asking to join the break. He could feel the power surging through his body and he wrapped his fingers tightly around the handle of the gun and tapped his finger gently against the trigger. One squeeze and anybody he chose was dogmeat, human garbage.

Amberg shoved the older guard against the door of Moe's cell. He handed the keys to the younger one, whose lips were now trembling uncontrollably.

"Open that cell," he ordered.

The guard fumbled with the keys, then finally pulled the door open. Moe grabbed him by the shirt and threw him up against the wall. He pushed the older guard out of his way, swung the door behind him, and locked it.

"All right," Amberg said, pushing the older guard back down the corridor. "We got one more cell to open."

Further down the corridor they could hear Dunniger's voice urging them on. When they reached the cell he was still babbling. "Beautiful, Hy, beautiful. F-u-c-k-i-n-g b-e-a-u-t-i-f-u-l. Let me out of here so I can kill that screw." He was yanking violently at his crotch.

Moe reached his arm through the bars and grabbed Dunniger by the shirt.

"You don't kill nobody, stupid. Not till we get more hardware from his office." He turned to Amberg. "Hy, you sure you want to take this nut with us?"

"He goes. Now both of you shut up. And leave your prick alone," he snapped at Dunniger.

Moe unlocked the cell door and Dunniger jumped out. He grabbed the guard by the hair and pulled him down the corridor. At the end of the tier they crowded into the small cubicle that served as an office. Dunniger, still holding the guard by his hair, spun him against a large wooden desk.

Amberg placed his gun against the guard's ear and the older man swayed back and forth on unsteady legs. "Give us your guns, screw. And all the ammunition you've got," Amberg said.

The guard pulled open a deep desk drawer and stepped back slowly. "That's all there is," he said.

"You wouldn't try and play games with us would you old man?" Amberg pushed the gun hard against his ear and cocked the hammer.

"That's all there is in here. Honest." His voice trembled and for a moment Amberg thought he was going to faint.

Dunniger jumped forward and dug both hands into the drawer, coming out with three handguns and three boxes of ammunition.

"Three .38s, Hy. And plenty of ammo," he said.

Amberg took one of the guns and handed it to Moe. "Make sure it's loaded," he said.

Moe opened the cylinder and nodded that it was.

Amberg reached out again and took a second gun from Dunniger. He turned to the guard and smiled. "Thanks, Pop," he said as he brought the gun crashing down on his forehead, grinning as the older man crumpled to the floor. "Okay, let's go."

"Let me plug him first," Dunniger said, his body twisting with anticipation.

Amberg took him by the arm. "Yeah, sure, stupid. And why don't you pull the alarm while you're doing it?" He pushed him toward the door. "We get the elevator. When the door opens we just push the guy running it back inside and he takes us right down to the first floor. If you have to do any shooting you do it down there, not before."

On the first floor Guard Louis Lorch looked out through the small window in the solid steel front door. It was cloudy, he thought. It would probably rain before he got off work and he would get soaked walking to the trolley. Should of brought a coat, he thought. The paper last night said it was going to rain today. Now he'd have to have his uniform pressed again.

Lorch turned away from the door and took a few steps into the reception area. He was a large man, well over six feet, with a frame amply covered with muscle, although he seemed slender. In the center of the reception area a fat, red-faced clerk named Murphy sat at a small desk reading a magazine. There was a door behind him leading to the warden's office, but it was closed. Another door to his right led to the guards' locker room and in front of the desk was the swinging door leading to the cellblocks. Lorch turned and walked back to the front door, again looking out the small window. Still no rain, he noticed. But it would come, he had no doubt about that. He walked back into the reception area and stopped at Murphy's desk. He was about to speak to him when the door to the cellblock suddenly swung open. Turning, he found himself facing a small slender prisoner holding a gun in each hand and behind him were two others, who also had guns.

"Give us the key to the front door or you're dead." Amberg's voice was steady and hard.

Behind him Dunniger began to shout, almost hysterically, "Everybody get their hands up. Hands up or you're all dead."

Lorch was frozen for a second. Where had these people come from? How did they get guns? This was crazy. They were just going to take his keys and walk out the front door.

"In a pig's ass," he muttered under his breath, shooting both heavy arms straight out in front of him, taking Amberg by surprise, hitting him squarely in the shoulders with each hand.

The force of the blow threw Amberg back into Moe and Dunniger, and Lorch bolted quickly to his right, dropping low behind Murphy's desk and scrambling toward the door of the guards' locker room. As he reached the door he heard the explosion of three shots and he threw his weight against the door, smashing it open and propelling his body inside. Lorch jumped to his feet, pulling his keys from his trouser pocket as he did and ran to his locker. Inside, he knew, was his only protection, his service revolver, stuffed into a holster on the top shelf. Frantically he fought the locker open as two more shots exploded in the reception area.

Lorch yanked his gun from the holster and ran across the narrow locker room, flattening his back against the wall alongside the reception area door. Next to the door was the alarm. He reached up to press it but it sounded before he could, set off by another hand, and he flattened back against the wall again as it clanged in his ear, filling the entire first floor with deafening sound. But what the hell do you do now, he thought.

Before the words finished tumbling through his head the door to the locker room burst open again and Murphy staggered in holding his bloodstained stomach. He sank to his knees, his normally red face now pure white.

Lorch grabbed him and pulled him back against the wall.

"Stay here. Don't try to move," Lorch said. Outside, another round of gunfire filled the reception area as Lorch stepped over Murphy's outstretched legs and slid along the wall to the door.

He eased the door back two inches, then three and four. Across the reception area in the doorway of his office he could see the warden down on his knees, his pistol out on the floor in front of him; his chest was covered with blood. Lorch began to ease the door back even further when another shot erupted and he saw the warden's head snap back against the door frame, a spray of blood spattering the wall beside it. The warden's body spun off to the side and crashed to the floor, and Lorch could see the back of his head, little more now than a mass of dark wet hair twisted around a bloody hole. He pulled the door open and moved his hand holding the gun out the opening.

"Get the key," someone was shouting. "He's got to have a key."

He saw one of the prisoners run toward the warden's body and bend over it. Lorch leveled his gun at the prisoner when gunfire exploded again sending splinters of wood flying from the door frame near his head. He jerked back instinctively, still watching the young prisoner near the warden's body. At the sound of the gunfire the prisoner turned suddenly and began firing toward the locker room. Lorch pulled back hard and stumbled over Murphy's legs and fell backward on to the floor.

"Hurry up, for chrissake. This place is gonna be crawling with cops," a voice shouted in the reception area.

Then another voice: "I got it. I got it."

Lorch struggled to his feet. He could hear footsteps running and he jumped toward the door and eased himself into the opening again but the room was empty now and as he stepped out he stared down at the warden and for the first time he realized that he was trembling.

Outside the Tombs, Amberg, Berg, and Dunniger ran toward the alley that separated the two wings of the prison. There were two police cars moving down the street already, their sirens blaring, and in the distance more could be heard. Twenty feet away a car bolted out of the alley, Sammy behind the wheel, his eyes staring straight ahead.

"You rotten bastard. Come back here. Come back here," Amberg was screaming.

The first patrol car skidded sideways and jerked to a halt and four uniformed cops began to pile out.

Moe grabbed Amberg by the arm. "In the alley. In the alley," he shouted.

The three men ran into the alley, turning and firing as the police crouched behind the patrol car. There was no way out. The alley was a dead end, leading only to a mound of coal stored in a central courtyard.

CHAPTER THIRTY-ONE

THE OWNER OF THE CAFE D'ORO WATCHED BRODERICK from behind his cash register, more with sadness than bitterness, and thought again about his own special problem. He was a short, heavy, round-faced man, who now in his fiftieth year had become bald and paternal. He had come from Italy eleven years ago and after nine years of hard work had finally realized his dream, a small coffeehouse on Grand Street in the heart of Little Italy. If only they had told him, the friends who he had depended upon, then he would have moved a block further east. He ran his fingers against the waxed tips of his moustache and looked at Broderick again, shaking his head.

Broderick was unaware of the owner's mood as he sat there musing about his wasted morning. Since leaving Mona's apartment he had been chasing down leads on a labor organizer who was stirring up the garment district. But he found nothing to use against the man and he looked up at the clock on the wall and noted it was twelve-fifty, past the time Cordes should have met him. Perhaps he had found something, but he doubted it, and, suddenly smiling to himself, he realized he really did not care. He had made up his mind. He had actually decided days ago but had refused to acknowledge it, never allowing the reality of it to register. Now he had and he wondered why he had let it drag on so long. On the weekend he would go to Queens and tell his wife, offer her the choice of an annulment, which he was now sure she would take. He smiled to himself, thinking of the priests she would be seeking to please, with whom she would want to remain in good standing, the same men whom he now believed would agree to an annulment as long as the price was right. The irony of it all amused him. Everyone and everything had its price, even among those who set the moral tone for thousands, millions. He had always understood the power they had over people's lives; he had lived with it since childhood. He had been inside the residence of the archdiocese and had seen the power of their wealth, but he had also believed that they knew little about the life that existed outside the safe, comfortable confines of their residence. He had assumed that they lived placidly in their comfortable rooms with Saint Patrick's towering behind them and remained blissfully ignorant of how the world really functioned. Now he knew he had been wrong, even about them.

"What are you doing? Don't you know thinking can give you a headache?" Johnny Cordes's voice came from behind, filled with laughter, and Broderick's thoughts evaporated with it.

He looked up at the slender Spaniard and found himself inwardly pleased by his grinning face. Cordes was one of the things he would miss about the job, one of the few things, he decided.

"You look like the cat who ate the canary, kid. What happened? Did you come up with something good on our friend?" Cordes was still grinning at him as he sat across from him at the small, round table.

"I didn't find a damned thing and I couldn't care less," Broderick said.

Cordes eyed him shrewdly and he pulled thoughtfully on his long, slender nose. "That's a nice attitude. You're going to love it back in uniform, counting sea gulls on Staten Island."

"I'm going to love it in civies," he said, grinning.

The corners of Cordes's eyes wrinkled with pleasure. "You made up your mind?"

"You bet your ass. At the end of the week I slip in my papers and they can kiss this paddy good-bye."

Cordes reached across the table and slapped Broderick's arm. "Well, it's about time, you big dunce. I was beginning to wonder if you were really as stupid as I always said you were. I wish I could be around when you tell Nolan and all the others to go fuck themselves. It's the best news I heard in a month, two months maybe."

"You want some coffee, hump?" Broderick asked.

"Coffee, shit," Cordes snapped. "We're gonna celebrate today. For starters I'll take you to lunch and I'll even pay for it. Did you tell your rich lady yet?"

"I called her about an hour ago."

"Well, when we stop back at the office you call her again and tell her that your friends are taking you out and to expect what's left of your body very late tonight."

Broderick shook his head. "I don't know if I can handle that again. It took me three days to get over our last celebration and I'm still checking my prick to see if Jeanie left me with any presents."

"You'll survive." Cordes grinned. He looked around the room and noticed that the owner of the shop was smiling at them. He leaned across the table to Broderick. "I suppose that being the big business executive you didn't bother collecting here today," he said.

Broderick shook his head.

"Well, unfortunately, I'm still a working stiff and can't afford to be that generous." He pushed himself away from the table and walked to the cash register. The small, heavy man smiled knowingly and quickly withdrew two dollars from the cash drawer and handed it to him with a smile. Cordes pocketed the money and grinned at Broderick. "From now on you don't get your share," he said.

The owner watched them file out the door and fondled the tip of his moustache again as the smile disappeared from his face. The two dollars a week did not bother him; he paid the Blackhanders so why not the police, and besides it was worth it to remain open seven days a week, he told himself. But still he wished his friends had warned him. Then he would have opened his shop further away from Police Headquarters. He would make much more money if he had, he thought. He wouldn't be paying for the coffee habits of half the Police Department.

Outside, Broderick and Cordes ambled along Grand Street, quietly appraising the young Italian girls who stood along the street talking while others moved in and out of the small shops. They were safe here, Broderick thought, as he plucked an apple from one of the many pushcarts that lined the curbs. No one bothered these girls, although many would like to and probably would if they paraded this way through other neighborhoods. It was simply not worth getting an ice pick in the back from some crazy Sicilian who thought his honor had been ruined because someone had rolled in the hay with his daughter or sister. He watched one young woman walk with deliberate sensuality ahead of them and he smiled to himself, realizing how those young girls understood the facts of life of their neighborhood, how they knew they could give off the most inviting looks and know they were never going to be asked to deliver on their promises.

He was still smiling to himself about this neighborhood he had known so long as they started up the marble stairs of Police Headquarters. Halfway up the stairs the main doors ahead of them flew open and a group of uniformed men rushed out and Cordes grabbed one by the arm as the others pushed past them.

"What the hell is going on?" he demanded.

"Jailbreak at the Tombs," the young cop snapped.

Broderick felt his stomach tighten and for a moment he was unable to draw a breath. "Who got out?" he said, hearing the words as though they were coming from someone else.

"Nobody knows yet," the cop said, pulling away from Cordes. "Three guys. They shot the warden and some other guy and now they're trapped outside in the coal yard."

Broderick watched the officer run toward a waiting patrol car and behind him he could hear Cordes's voice, but the words seemed to run together and only the sound of him speaking was distinguishable.

"Come on, Johnny, we better go." Cordes was pulling on his sleeve and he heard himself suggest that they get a car, but the voice did not sound like his own.

"Forget the car. It's only four blocks and we can run there faster than we can get through the traffic."

He felt the firm yank of his arm as Cordes moved past him down the stairs and headed south on Centre Street in long loping strides. He moved after him, feeling his feet strike the pavement, as the sound of sirens seemed to come suddenly from all directions. He had heard sirens moments earlier, he realized, but had paid no attention, knowing instinctively that sirens were part of the city, with its fires and ambulance calls, knowing that it was something to be expected, like rain every fourth or fifth day. Now the sound was different and it seemed to beat into his head and against his chest and his feet seemed to strike the pavement with the rhythm of each separate wail. His breath came in short gasps even though he had only run half a block and he tried not to think about Amberg but the thought kept rushing back to him. There were hundreds of men in the Tombs, he told himself, hundreds.

They moved quickly along the sidewalk, cutting into the street when the crowds of shoppers became too thick, and he watched the rows of tenements with their stores and restaurants at street level slip past. People stopped to watch the two men running, one behind the other, thinking, he told himself, that one was probably chasing the other because of some insult. He should stop and explain to them, he thought, knowing instantly how ridiculous the idea was. But why was he running? He was through with it all now; he had decided that hours ago and still his feet were moving toward the last place he wanted to be.

When they crossed Canal Street into Chinatown the crowds became thicker and they stayed in the street moving as fast as they could between the traffic and parked cars and pushcarts. In the distance they could hear the muffled popping of gunfire, the sounds seeming to become more distinct with each stride, and at the corner of Leonard Street they turned east and saw the cluster of police cars jammed around the entrance to the alley a block away, the bodies of the cops moving up and down behind the cars as they jumped up to squeeze off a shot, then retreated quickly to avoid any returning gunfire. Broderick and Cordes ran up behind the cars, staying as low as possible. They spotted a captain behind a car closest to the entrance of the alley and they moved in quickly and crouched next to him.

"Who you got in there, Cap?" Broderick asked.

The captain looked back over his shoulder. "Three prisoners. Somebody named Amberg, some kid named Dunniger and another guy named Moe Berg," he said, turning his attention back to the alley and shouting orders to four cops trying vainly to work their way toward the entrance.

"You sure?" Broderick said. His voice sounded almost like a plea, and he felt as though a fist had struck him in the chest.

"That's what they tell me," the captain said. "Anyway, whoever it is, they got one helluva good position in there. The only way in is the alley and they have that big mound of coal for cover and the only window that looks out in there is no good. You can't see them from it unless they stand up. And they ain't standing up."

"What about the roof?" Cordes asked.

"The overhang slants down just enough to cover them. Besides, there's a shed in back of the coal mound with a metal roof and it's perfect cover from above," he said.

"How much ammo they got?" Cordes said.

"We don't know," the captain said. "One of the guards in there said they got at least a couple of boxes, maybe more."

"Shit," Cordes said.

"You sure it's Amberg?" Broderick asked again, his voice hoarse, almost a whisper. "Did anybody see him for sure?" The captain stared at him for a moment as though trying to understand the strange tone in his voice. "Not our people. But a guard identified him. And another one said it was him who shot the warden."

"How bad is the warden?" Cordes asked.

"Bad as you can get," the captain said. "They shot him all to hell. They got another guy too who doesn't look like he'll make it either."

Cordes leaned back against the car and stared straight ahead. Broderick didn't have to ask what he was thinking about. He knew. If they hadn't set Amberg up—if *he* hadn't set Amberg up—the warden would be going home to dinner tonight just like always. That's tough shit, he thought. Nobody gets any guarantee for a full ride and it wasn't his business anymore, it simply wasn't. He inched closer to Cordes.

"If he was out on the streets he would have killed somebody else by now," he whispered.

"But he wasn't out on the streets and he didn't kill somebody else. He killed that fucking warden," Cordes answered.

246

"Okay. That's the way it works. There isn't anything we can do about it now," Broderick whispered.

Cordes turned to face him, still squatting. "Yeah? Well, the way I see it, you and me put him in that coal yard and you and me have to get him out."

Broderick stared at him, his stomach tightening. "You're outta your mind. You see anybody getting in that alley? Every time somebody tries to go in he comes running out like his ass was on fire."

Cordes moved away from the captain, grabbing Broderick by the lapel of his suit and pulling him with him. "Johnny boy," he whispered. "I went along with you setting that little bastard up and I know you have big plans, but you better go along with me on this, or I'll see that everybody knows what a rotten bastard you really are. I'm not going to let some cop get blasted because of what we did. You understand me?"

Broderick looked into his face, still not believing what he was hearing. But he knew Cordes would do it. The crazy Spaniard would get moralistic about the whole thing, and it could cost him everything he wanted. All they had to do was wait. They'd run out of ammunition sooner or later. But he knew Cordes would not do it that way.

"I still think you're out of your mind. But you're not giving me much choice, are you? Just one thing. We take them dead, at least Amberg, and we end this thing once and for all." He was glaring at Cordes and he knew he hated him right now and probably would for a long time.

"If they fight we take them dead," Cordes said. "And it sure as hell looks as though they're going to. You know Amberg will." He eased himself up behind the car and pointed toward the alley. "See those trash cans? We each take one of those and we keep them in front of us for cover and we move down the alley, one on each side, pushing the cans in front of us."

"Oh, that's great," Broderick said. "Who the fuck do you think we are, Buffalo Bill and Jesse James?"

"No, you're Buffalo Bill," Cordes said, jabbing his finger against Broderick's chest. "I'm Wild Bill Hickok. Amberg, he's Jesse James." He grinned coldly and moved back toward the captain.

"Captain, we're gonna try something. You have your men give us cover, plenty of cover. Tell them to shoot straight down the alley. Right down the middle of it. Johnny and I are gonna be moving down the sides against the walls. And for chrissake tell them to shoot straight." The captain nodded and Cordes looked back at Broderick. "Okay, Johnny boy, let's do it."

Cordes, with Broderick a few steps behind, moved along the cars making sure they were clear of the gunfire from the alley, then rushed forward until they were alongside the building, slowly moving up to the entrance of the alley. Behind them the captain was shouting orders to his men. The cops stopped firing and waited for the two detectives to get in position.

At the entrance to the alley Cordes dropped into a crouch, then darted

247

halfway across, threw his body forward, and rolled to the other side. A burst of gunfire came from the courtyard but Cordes was already on his feet, safe on the other side. He looked back at Broderick and then flattened against the wall waiting for the gunfire to subside.

Broderick's mind was spinning. Going into that alley was madness. He'd let Cordes force him into it. But he still didn't have to go. There was nothing in the book that said a cop had to put himself in unreasonable danger. There were dozens of cops here right now, right out in front of him hiding behind cars. Nobody was forcing them to go up that alley and get their guts splattered all over the walls. Even the captain was safe behind his car, and when his men had gotten close to the alley he had pulled them out. He could just walk away, just like the other cops had. Who the hell could blame anybody for not committing suicide?

He looked at the cops peering out from behind the cover of their cars, ducking their heads down at every sound of incoming gunfire. They seemed a hundred miles away. No fucking heroes there, he thought. And why should there be? For a lousy four grand a year. The thought exploded. But you have a lot more at stake, a helluva lot more, he remembered. And you'll have a lot of fun spending it when that crazy little fuck in there blows the top of your head off. There's no reason to go in. Just walk away. Those crazy bastards in there aren't going anyplace. Sooner or later they got to surrender or die. There's no other way for it to end.

He looked out at the assault force again. You walk away and Cordes stays, he thought. That will make great conversation all over town. Like the time two years ago when that rookie cop who didn't know who you were knocked you on your ass in that Brooklyn precinct. You talked your way out of that one. A lucky punch, you told everybody. They held you back and then the young kid apologized. It was bullshit, but it got you out of it.

Broderick looked down the street. The reporters and photographers were being held back at the corner of Centre Street. They sure as hell won't miss Johnny Broderick walking away. Fuck them. You don't have to die for them either. Just get your ass out of here.

"Johnny," Cordes's voice broke through his thoughts. Broderick looked across to him. The gunfire had stopped. "Let's go," Cordes said.

Quickly they both slipped into the alley, staying close to the walls, and moved up, crouching, behind the rows of trash cans that lined each side. Behind them they could hear the captain's voice and the sound of police gunfire exploded at their backs.

Slowly they began to ease their way up the alley, pushing the trash cans in front of them. Broderick could hear the bullets zipping by in both directions and he had the insane thought that there was so much lead flying around this alley that it was certain the bullets would smash into each other.

There was a dull thud against the front of the trash can concealing him,

248

then another and another. He looked across to Cordes. They were almost at the end of the twenty-foot alley now. "They know we're comin'," he shouted.

"Yeah, I can see the welcome mat already," Cordes shouted back.

They reached the entrance of the courtyard; the coal mound was thirty feet away now. Broderick pulled his gun from its holster and the revolver almost slid out of his hand. He put the gun down in front of him and wiped his hand on the side of his trousers and saw how the heavy coating of sweat had left a large, wet patch. Cordes had pushed his trash can about three yards ahead and was firing toward the coal mound. Broderick inched his way up so he was parallel to Cordes, then squeezed off two quick shots. The gunfire intensified from behind the mound. Bullets slammed against the trash can and Broderick now simply stuck the gun out and fired without looking. Maybe they'd run out of ammunition, he thought, wondering how much they could really have. Then an unpleasant thought gripped him. Shit, we don't have that much either. He touched the leather bullet case on his belt. Twelve there and three left in the gun.

A voice came from behind the mound. It cut into Broderick like a knife. He didn't have to think about who it was.

"Is that you, Broderick?" the voice shouted. "Keep coming, tough guy. I got a big present here for you."

Broderick could feel the sweat pouring out of his body and he put the gun on the ground and rubbed his hand against his trousers again.

"Come out, Hy, and bring your playmates with you. You don't have a chance. Sooner or later you gotta lose this one. Play it smart." Cordes's voice rang out clear and firm.

"Johnny Cordes. Is that you Johnny Cordes?" Amberg called out. "You got your toothpick with you?"

"It's me, Hy. You comin' out or not?"

"Sorry, Johnny. I got this present I got to give to Broderick and I can't come out until he gets it. You there, tough guy?"

"I'm here," Broderick shouted back. He was surprised at his own voice. It sounded firm even though his stomach felt like jelly.

"Then come get your present." Amberg started to laugh. It was a high, chilling laugh and Broderick remembered that day at Lindy's, the day he had warned Cordes about Amberg, how unpredictable he was. He should have let him take care of Amberg then. He shouldn't have stopped him. They wouldn't be here now if it hadn't been for that.

The gunfire erupted again and Broderick and Cordes returned the fire, intermittently pushing their trash cans ahead. Broderick was counting each shot he fired. It was like sand running out of an hourglass. Except this time, when the sand ran out you couldn't turn the glass over and start again. They were only twenty feet from the coal mound now. Suddenly, out of the corner of his eye, Broderick saw Cordes's body leap backward. When he looked he saw him squirming to regain his cover behind the trash can. Instinctively he fired a quick shot to cover him. More sand gone.

"Johnny. You okay?" he called out.

"Yeah," Cordes called back. "Just the shoulder. It's only a scratch. I'll cover you."

Broderick continued to look at Cordes. There's no fucking way out of this now, he thought. Slowly he pushed the trash can forward. Bullets smashed against it and off to his right he heard Cordes firing cover. Suddenly the gunfire from behind the mound stopped. Everything was quiet there. He looked out from behind the trash can and fired one shot and across from him Cordes fired three more. No gunfire was returned. Broderick crouched behind the can, paused, and reloaded his gun. Just twelve bullets left now.

He looked across to Cordes. Cordes motioned him forward with his head. Broderick took a deep breath and he could feel the vomit rising to the back of his throat as he jumped out from behind the can and raced toward the mound as Cordes's gun slammed away. Broderick dove forward, rolling his body over and over until it hit the side of the mound. He jumped to his feet and flattened his back against the black coal and froze there, fighting to breathe. Cautiously he inched along the mound until he reached the point Cordes had been approaching, then with a quickness that surprised him he darted to the rear of the mound, his body crouched low, his gun held out in front of him. There, seated on the ground in front of him, were Moe and Dunniger. Their guns were on the ground and he froze, straightened up, and stared down at them.

"Don't shoot, Johnny. Our guns are empty," Moe said.

Broderick was confused, his body frozen, stunned. The expectation of a brutal confrontation and then the sudden absence of it had left his mind numb and his head seemed to spin for just a fraction of a second. Then his senses jumped back to him and he glanced about nervously.

"Where's Amberg?" he said.

From the side of the mound to his left, the side he himself had first been approaching, Amberg suddenly appeared, a gun in each hand, both pointed at Broderick's head.

He slipped along that side as I came around this one, his mind told him, and now I'm standing here caught like a fool. Like a fucking fool.

"Here I am, tough guy," Amberg said. He looked at Broderick's hands. They were trembling and his face was a mass of perspiration, and he felt as though he was about to urinate in his pants. "Keep shaking, tough guy, 'cause here comes your present."

Amberg began to laugh and the sound of it left Broderick frozen, unable to even look away. The barrel openings of the two revolvers seemed to grow larger and the laughter seemed far off and then he heard the click of the hammer falling. The sound slammed against his ears like cannon fire, then slowly faded, and there was a different look on Amberg's face. It seemed to

250

happen in stages, a look of fear, then frustration, then anger. He heard another click, then another and another and as he came back to himself he realized that Amberg was frantically pulling the triggers of both guns and they were both empty.

His body moved for the first time in seconds and he raised his gun, feeling the heaviness in his arm as it leveled at Amberg's head. "Good-bye, punk," he heard himself say, his voice still shaking as he squeezed the trigger and felt the pistol jump in his hand as Amberg's head flew backward into the red mist that sprayed out behind him, a single dark hole in the center of his forehead.

Dunniger jumped to his feet, his face white with rage. "You murdered him—you murdered him," he stammered.

Broderick turned to him and stared blankly into his face. "He committed suicide," he said. "And so did you." He swung the gun to face level and again it exploded in his hand. The bullet struck Dunniger in the mouth and sent him flying back as though someone had picked him up and dropped him.

Moe started to get up, then stopped halfway, leaving himself in a crouched position. He was staring into Broderick's face, his neck twitching violently. Broderick turned the gun toward him.

"No, Johnny, no," he said. His voice was almost a whisper.

Broderick pulled the trigger as Moe twisted his body in a final effort to escape and the bullet smashed into his temple, cartwheeling him sideways onto his shoulder. His feet hit on the coal mound and Broderick watched as his body slid gradually down, pushing his face along the soot-blackened ground.

Broderick stood there, the gun still out in front of him, as Cordes stumbled around the coal mound, his own gun raised.

"Johnny!" Cordes shouted. "Johnny. For chrissake answer me. Are you all right?"

Broderick turned slowly and lowered his gun. "Yeah, I'm fine," he said.

"Why the hell didn't you answer me?" Cordes said. "When I didn't hear anything I called to you but you didn't answer. Then I heard the first shot and I called again. Christ, I thought they got you when you still didn't answer." He looked about him, staring down at each body. "But I see you got them."

Broderick's head snapped up and his eyes bored into Cordes's. "No," he said. "They killed themselves. They each used the last bullet in their guns to kill themselves. They didn't want to be taken alive. There was nothing I could do."

Cordes stared at him, mouth opened. "Johnny, you ain't gonna try to sell that story, are you?"

"That's what happened. I got no choice." His mind was clicking off probabilities, accusations.

"Okay, Johnny. If that's the way you want it that's what happened. I didn't see it, but I heard it, if that's what you want."

Broderick looked off to his right and his eyes suddenly were frozen to one spot. It was a window in the Tombs. The only window back there the captain had said. In that window now he could see the face of an elderly black man. There was a look of complete terror on the old man's face. You can only see them from that window when they stand up, the captain had said. And they ain't standing up, he had said. Broderick kept his eyes on the old man's face and he felt the terror he saw there transfer to his belly, then the old man suddenly disappeared from the window as though he had fallen through a trapdoor.

Cordes turned around and looked over his shoulder. "What the hell you looking at?" he said. "Are you okay?" He kept his eyes glued to Broderick's face.

"Nothin', nothin' at all," Broderick said. His mind had frozen, then he turned to Cordes, trying to find the words he knew he had to speak.

They stood there for a moment as police in uniform rushed into the area, their guns drawn. It was too late now.

"What happened?" a cop said.

"They killed themselves when they saw Broderick coming," Cordes said.

Broderick looked at Cordes. Everything is moving too fast, he thought. He looked down at Amberg. He was on his back, his eyes staring blindly at the sky. Under his head a pool of blood inched its way outward. A sense of long-awaited relief moved across Broderick's face. At least that's over with now, he thought.

"How's your shoulder?" he heard someone ask Cordes. "You okay?"

"It's nothin'. I'll be fine," Cordes said.

"You better let these guys take a look at you," Broderick said. "I'll see you out on the street. I have to get out of here."

Broderick turned away and walked around the coal mound. Cordes followed a few steps, then stood and watched as he walked out toward the alley, his gun hanging loosely at his side. Fifty feet away, at the entrance of the alley, Cordes could see the reporters and photographers being held back by uniformed cops.

CHAPTER THIRTY-TWO

THE INTERIOR OF THE HOTEL ROOM WAS DARK WHEN he opened the door and he stood in the doorway waiting for his eyes to adjust to it before closing the door behind him. He wanted it dark; the light coming through the window would be enough. He walked across the room and sat on the edge of the bed, placing the package he had brought with him on the night stand. His hands were trembling. They had been trembling for over an hour now. He got up and walked into the bathroom for a glass, then returned to the bed and opened the package and filled the glass half full with bourbon. He drank a third of it in one swallow and coughed against the harshness of the liquor attacking his throat. He drank again to accustom himself to the taste and he suddenly felt as though he would vomit but he fought it off.

There was a large mirror on top of a dresser across from where he sat and the window where the light came in was behind him. The effect made his image look like a very large black square, a spector he found disturbing to look at. He drained the glass and then refilled it. He propped the bed's two pillows up against the wooden headboard and stretched out, half sitting, his eyes staring blindly at the door through which he had entered. The room seemed even smaller in the darkness and he had to fight off the sensation of it closing in on him. He drank again, concentrating on the darkness, trying to keep any thoughts from his mind. The telephone rang but he ignored it and the ringing continued. The clerk downstairs had seen him when he arrived and would continue to ring until it was answered. He reached out and picked up the phone and placed the upright portion against his chest and brought the receiver to his ear. He did not speak and after a moment he heard Mona's voice repeating his name.

"Yeah. I'm here," he said. His voice sounded tired and distant and for a moment he was not sure he had spoken.

"Oh, Johnny, are you all right?"

"I'm fine." His voice was stronger now but the words were clipped and short. He thought he heard her shudder but he could not be sure.

"I heard about it on the radio and then when you didn't come back to the apartment I thought you might be hurt. They said an officer was wounded but they said it was Johnny Cordes, the friend you've spoken about." She rattled the words off, running one thought into the next, unable to stop herself.

"No, I'm all right. It was Cordes, but he's okay too. It was nothing serious, just his shoulder—"

"Why didn't you call? I was so worried, I—"

He interrupted her in return. "There were a lot of papers to fill out, a lot of bullshit. And then I just needed to be alone. I didn't even think of calling. I just couldn't think about anything else. I'm going to stay here tonight. I think it's better that way. I can't help it." It sounded as though he was apologizing, he thought, but that was not how he meant it and he realized he wasn't sure how he meant it. He just did.

She was silent for a moment. "Oh, John, are you sure? I could come to your hotel. It might be better to be with someone. Or you could come here, whichever you prefer. I've been calling you for hours."

"No. No. Look, it's nothing bad. Honest. I just have to be alone. You're going to have to understand this once. I'll call you tomorrow and we'll meet after work." He did not wait for her response. He could hear her voice as he placed the receiver back in its cradle. He slid the telephone back on the night stand and poured another drink. At least she didn't mention the three of them, he thought. He had answered too many questions already and he was tired of hearing his own voice explain it all away. Even Garfoli had been asking questions. It was his job because uniformed men had been involved but it had still been upsetting seeing him there.

But there had been praise too and Cordes had backed him up. There had even been talk of a commendation, a medal maybe. His head was spinning, the thoughts running together; they seemed to come two and three at a time. He squeezed his eyes shut and shook his head. He took another long drink. That fucking nigger. That fucking old nigger. You do everything by the book your whole life. You check. You make sure. You cover your ass and then for one minute you don't watch your back and your ass is up for grabs. Why

254

didn't you look? He rubbed his forehead with the back of his hand and realized for the first time that he was sweating. Sure, Amberg had a gun, no problem there. And Dunniger, he was moving toward you screaming. Nobody would fight that one very hard either. But Moe Berg, fucking Moe Berg. He was begging and the old man had to see him. If you only looked first. And then you told Cordes it was suicide because you knew the guns were empty. And that's when you see the nigger. He drank again. You could of changed the story, put bullets in their guns and Cordes would have kept his mouth shut, covered for you. No. You don't do that. You don't expose yourself, not even to a friend, not even another cop. You don't put yourself in anybody's hands that way, you brazen it out. But you still got that old nigger. Damn his fucking ass. Too fucking stupid not to look out a window when guns are going off. But maybe he didn't. Maybe he looked later. No, the look on his face. He knew, he saw. He shit when *you* saw *him*. But niggers keep their mouths shut, especially the old ones. They don't care when white people kill each other. They're probably glad when it happens. He won't say anything.

The telephone rang again and he looked at it in disbelief. Mona, he thought. Still worried about him. Or upset about the way he cut her off. He picked it up.

"Hello."

The voice came strong and gruff into his ear. "Johnny. It's Chris Nolan. Great job today, kid. The mayor is really proud of you. Is everything okay?"

He was befuddled for a moment, then answered, "Yeah. Everything's fine. Thanks, Chris."

Nolan went on as though the answer really didn't matter and wasted no time getting to the point of his call. "Look, Johnny. There's one small problem." He waited, allowing the words to sink in. "It seems some of our enemies are going to push for an investigation of the whole thing. You know, how these guys got their guns inside and all that. They want to embarrass the administration, pure and simple. The problem, John, is that they want to investigate *everything.*"

"What does that mean, Chris?" He could hear the apprehension in his own voice, and when Nolan hesitated he knew he had heard it as well.

"It means they also want to go into how they died and all that. You'll probably be a witness. You and Cordes." He waited again and then continued. "We hear they're talking about trying to get some new kind of test approved. It's something that was just developed where certain experts claim they can take a bullet and tell what gun it was fired from. Something called 'ballistics.' It's something I never heard of before, probably a lot of bullshit." Nolan waited for a response but none came. "Johnny, did you hear me?"

"Yeah, Chris. I heard." There was silence again. "That might not be so good, Chris," he said.

"I didn't think so, kid." Broderick could hear him expel his breath. Cigar

255

smoke blowing into the phone, he thought. "I talked to one of our people in the coroner's office just in case and he's going to make sure the bullets turn up missing."

Broderick could feel a sudden release of tension. His body was drenched in sweat now and he could feel it along his chest and back and suddenly he realized he had to urinate.

"Good," he said. "Thanks, Chris."

"That's no problem, Johnny. We can take care of that easy. But one thing I have to know is whether or not anything could turn up that would embarrass us." His voice had become intentionally stern. He softened it to a conversational tone again. "The committee that investigates will have our people on it too. We'll control it, you can be sure of that. Right now we plan to take one of the guards as our patsy. We have this one named Lorch and it seems he can accept a great deal of criticism on the grounds of cowardice. Seems he ran away when these inmates broke out and we can argue that the whole thing could have and would have been stopped if he hadn't. But we *have* to know if anything else could turn up. Anything we *don't* know about? How about it, Johnny?"

"No, there's nothing," he lied. "And if anything does come up it won't be anything I can't handle beforehand. When is the hearing going to be?"

"They want it in the next couple of days, but we're going to stall them until sometime next week, on the grounds that the prison people have to have time to finish their own investigation before they start answering questions. The press will buy it. We'll tell them we need time to get the goods on the people responsible. The warden, God rest his soul, may have to take a bit of posthumous criticism too. I don't think we can avoid that. My big worry now is any surprises. I want you to be sure, Johnny. You have to be sure. We don't want to embarrass the mayor, right?"

"I'm sure, Chris," he lied again. "You can count on me. You know that."

"Okay, kid. We *are* counting on you. And don't forget how proud Jimmy is of you. Get some sleep now."

The telephone went dead but he continued to hold it in his hands, hearing individual words Chris Nolan had spoken replay in his mind. He rose suddenly, dropped the telephone to the floor and rushed into the bathroom. He vomited, his stomach heaving violently. Kneeling before the toilet he wondered where it had all come from. He had not eaten since breakfast.

"Don't embarrass the mayor," he mumbled as he wiped his face with a towel. And what about your ass, he thought. More than that, what about your future, all the plans, everything? He walked out of the bathroom, his legs feeling rubbery beneath him. He poured another drink and looked at it, wondering if it would send him rushing back into the bathroom. He sipped it and decided it would not, then took a longer drink and sat on the edge of the bed. The telephone was still on the floor and he picked it up and returned it to the night stand. No more calls. He looked across at the dresser and saw himself in the mirror. The light in the bathroom was still on and the room was no longer hidden in darkness. He studied his face. He looked as though he had aged five years. The old black man returned to his mind.

"One problem, just one problem," he said aloud.

He would have to get to the old man, talk to him, make sure he kept his mouth shut. Maybe get his ass out of town. But he couldn't go to the Tombs and ask about him. He couldn't do anything officially and draw attention to the old nigger. Somebody would mention it when the committee started nosing around. Somebody would say, "Oh, yeah, that cop who was involved in the shootout, he was here talking to our old nigger." Shit. He rubbed his fingers into his temples. His head was throbbing and he wanted to sleep. He needed to sleep and then he could think. But he had to get things in motion. He couldn't wait. He had to move quickly before someone else did. He opened his watch, turning it so it caught the light. It was early, only nine-thirty. He could do it and still sleep. It was an easy job for anybody who knew his way around, anyone but him. Any bullshit story would get the old nigger's name and address. Danny could do it. The little fuck knew people everywhere and he would keep his mouth shut, he'd believe anything he told him—he'd think he was helping in another investigation and he'd go off in his pants just thinking about it. He went to the bathroom and washed his face and straightened his tie in the mirror. No matter what you do you're not going to look much better, he thought. But maybe the air would help. He hoped it would.

His car was parked in front of the hotel. He climbed behind the wheel and sat there. The liquor had taken its toll; he wasn't used to it and he rolled down both windows, hoping the rush of air would clear his head. The Cadillac's large engine roared to life and he pulled it slowly from the curb and pointed it toward Broadway.

It began to rain, slowly at first and then in a torrent, challenging the abilities of the windshield wipers. He rolled up the windows and kept the speed of the car down, not trusting his own reflexes, too aware that his nerves were far from steady. A car behind him blasted its horn and he jumped in his seat. Anger rushed through him and he wanted to stop the car and jump out and throttle the driver who had frightened him. He accelerated but the rain combined with the additional speed made it impossible to see and he slowed the car again. A red traffic light brought him to a halt and he watched several people run across the street, hurrying to reach shelter on the other side. One was a young black man and he found himself wishing it was the old man he wanted to find. A slip of the clutch and the problem would be over, he thought. It might even be worth the trouble it would bring. The light changed and he moved forward. Danny's newsstand was only four blocks away now but the traffic was slow because of the rain. His head still throbbed and he wished he had remembered to take something for it. He had even forgotten his hat, something he never did. One old nigger and you're falling apart, he told himself. He thought of Eatkins sitting in the Yale Club, calm and relaxed, and he wondered what he would think if he saw him now. He wondered what Mona would think and he shook his head, driving the thoughts from his mind. He would take care of it, just as he had told Nolan he would. Ballistics. What the hell was he talking about? It didn't make sense, but he decided he would ask about it at Headquarters. Someone there would know. There were people in forensic who kept up on all the new technical bullshit.

The car turned south on Broadway. He was two blocks from Danny's stand and he kept to the right, inching along in the snarl of traffic. There were cars parked and double parked alongside the newsstand. The early editions of the morning papers had just hit the streets and the horse players were moving in for their copies, trying to find out if their bookies owed them or not. He waited for a place to open, then pulled the car to the curb. The rush for papers continued and he decided to wait it out. He wanted to talk to Danny alone, without any extra ears, innocent or not. There had been one too many mistakes already and there was no point in trying for two. He sat in the car feeling like a criminal who could not afford to be seen. The thought amused him in a sick way, forcing him to think again about the coal yard and the faces of the three men just before they died.

But they were criminals, he told himself. Rotten bastards who would have killed him if they had the chance and he was only doing his job, nothing more. He felt suddenly cold even though he was sweating in the cooped-up car. He knew no one would accept that argument, except perhaps a few of his friends, and even they would shake their heads over the clumsy way he had gotten himself in a jam. He panicked, that's what they would say, and a professional isn't supposed to panic.

He slid across the seat and wiped the moisture from the window with his forearm. The crowds at the newsstand were dwindling now but there were still too many. He leaned his head back against the seat and waited, watching the sheets of rain cascade along the windshield. He looked at his watch again; it was ten minutes to ten. He closed his eyes, telling himself that he could not fall asleep, not there. He would sleep soon, but only after he had taken care of things.

Five minutes later the rush for newspapers had ended and he opened the car door and ran to the shelter of the newsstand overhang. His hair was soaking by the time he crossed the short distance between the car and the squat little newsstand hut. Danny looked up at him and grinned, then automatically glanced around to see who, if anyone, was nearby.

"You look like a drowned rat," he said. "The newspaper guys should see you now. They really gave you a splash. Jesus."

258

Broderick started to speak but Danny interrupted him, unable to control himself. "You gotta take a copy of every paper," he said. "Jesus, one is better than the next. Christ, listen to me. I didn't even ask how you were, or how Cordes is. Jesus, that must of been something."

"We're both okay." He stopped, not sure how to begin, and watched Danny gather each of the morning papers and begin piling them in a stack in front of him.

"Oh, you gotta see this one, in the *Mirror*. They make you sound like a one-man army or somethin'. The *News* is almost as good, and wait till you see—"

"Danny, listen to me for a minute. I need a favor."

Danny looked at him, surprised. "Sure, anything. What do you need?"

"We think maybe we know who smuggled the guns in to those guys," he began, making the story up as he went along. "But we don't want to go through any official channels; we just don't know who we can trust over there. So what I want to do is find out the name and address of the guy we suspect so I can talk to him alone."

"You don't know his name even?" Danny looked at him, bewildered.

Broderick knew the story sounded phony and he struggled to make it work. "All we know is that it could be an old nigger who works there. I figure they probably only have one nigger working in the whole place, certainly only one old one. So I need you to try and get me his name and address without anybody down there finding out that it's me who's looking for it. Do you know anybody at the Tombs, somebody who could do it and keep it quiet?"

Danny's face broke into a broad, self-satisfied smile. "Sure. I know some guys who are trustees. They could get you one of the fucking cells and carry it out to you and nobody would know nothin'. They could get this easy. When do you need it by?"

"Yesterday. But I have to have it by tomorrow night at the latest. Can you do it that fast?"

Danny was still grinning; his head was cocked to the side as if Broderick was foolish to even ask the question. "No problem," he said. "I'll have what you want no later than six. You want me to bring it to you, or you want to come here?"

"I'll come here," he said. "But you have to be sure. It's important to me, okay?"

"I promise you, Johnny. You got nothing to worry about, I swear it."

Broderick breathed deeply and he could feel the tightness in his face grow slack. "Good boy, Danny. I'll be here. Now look, I'm bushed so I'm going to take off and get some sleep. But I'll be here tomorrow at six sharp." He turned to go but Danny's voice stopped him.

"Johnny, the papers. Don't forget them."

He picked up the stack of newspapers and smiled weakly at Danny. The rain had eased and he walked back to his car, tossing the newspapers on the

259

seat beside him. The Cadillac's engine roared to life again and he pulled away from the curb.

When he reached the hotel he dropped the newspapers into a trash can and walked wearily inside to the elevator. The last thing he wanted was to read the reports of the afternoon. It was the first time he could remember ignoring his own press clippings.

CHAPTER THIRTY-THREE

ONA D'ARCY STOOD AT THE CORNER OF FORTY-third Street and Broadway. There were two small packages under her arm and she held them tightly against her as she glanced expectantly up and down the street. She was wearing a light blue summer dress that would have been sheer were it not for the layers of tassels that covered it. It was a dress designed to move with the person who wore it and Mona knew how well it worked for her. She wore a scarf folded into a thin band across her hair, giving her the same air of casual sophistication she had shown on the first night Broderick had seen her. She wanted to achieve the same effect she had then. It worried her that he had remained away the night before.

She looked at the broochlike watch pinned to her dress. It was nearly six o'clock, the time he had asked her to meet him in their brief telephone conversation that afternoon. It had been a strange conversation; he had seemed distant and nervous and she had told herself that the shootings had simply taken their toll. But still she worried about it.

It was a mild evening. The rain the night before had brought an end to the stifling humidity that had hung over the city for days and she did not mind waiting for him that way. She would make it a happy evening for them both and she would help him overcome the effect of the shootings. She still found it hard to believe. She had read the reports in the newspapers again and again and still she could not quite visualize it. The articles had been grotesquely descriptive as though the reporters had been there writing it all down as the bullets flew back and forth. They seemed to enjoy the gory details and it was almost as though one writer was trying to outdo the next with the dramatics of his report. Normally she would not have read them but his decision to remain away had forced her to read each account to try and find some reason. She had wondered what it had been like to come upon three men who had killed themselves that way. Certainly he had seen death before. She assumed all police officers did. It was part of their job. But perhaps no one ever really became used to it, she had told herself. It was the only explanation she could think of.

He came upon her from behind, from Forty-third Street, and she jumped when he touched her arm without speaking. When she turned she reached up immediately and kissed him on the mouth, surprising both of them by the suddenness of the act.

"Oh, John. Since I spoke to you today I've been going mad waiting to see you." She could see she had embarrassed him but she did not care.

"Yeah. Boy, you know you're going to get us both arrested doing this in the street." He glanced around and was forced to smile at the boyishness of his reaction.

"If you can arrange for us to be in the same cell I'll do more than just kiss you." She spoke the words as though they were a challenge.

"I'm afraid it doesn't work that way," he said.

"That's a pity." She slid her arm into his and they started to walk along Broadway.

"What's in the packages?" he asked.

She stopped and turned to him. "I completely forgot about them," she said. "I stopped and bought you a new necktie. And I got one for your friend Cordes also. How is he?"

"He's fine," he said as they resumed walking. "I drove him home from the hospital this afternoon. It was just a flesh wound but they kept him overnight just to be safe. In a week or so he'll be back at work as good as new." The recuperation period would keep Cordes away from the hearing. He was pleased that it would. The investigators would have to content themselves with a written statement and that would mean that no one could challenge his corroborating story. "Cordes will like that. He likes to think of himself as a sharp dresser."

"Well, you get to pick the one you want first," she said. "His present was just an afterthought." She pressed herself against his arm.

He was forcing himself to keep his mind on the conversation but it was difficult. Danny was just up the street now, inside his newsstand, and it was time to see him. He had hoped Mona would be late so he could see him first, alone. But she had been early and there had been no way to avoid her.

"Don't ever tell Cordes he was an afterthought," he said. "He also thinks he's quite a lady's man."

"Well, this lady is only interested in one detective," she said.

They continued on slowly and she tried to keep a conversation going between them. He was still distant. She could sense it. But she could also tell that the distance was not directed at her. It was simply there, brought on by what was bothering him. She would avoid any discussion of the shooting, she decided. And later she would help him forget.

Broderick came to a stop ten feet before they reached the newsstand. "I have to see Danny for a minute. You don't mind, do you?"

"Of course not. I think he's adorable. He might even be able to steal me away from you." She laughed at the idea.

He turned quickly and left her there and walked up to the newsstand. Her mouth dropped slightly. She had not expected to be abandoned on the sidewalk that way and she decided it must be his confused state of mind.

Danny was alone and Broderick stared at him eagerly. "Did you get what I asked you to get?" he asked.

The little man winked at him beneath the brim of his floppy workman's cap. "Sure I got it," he said, obviously pleased with himself. "I had it by three and I tried to call your office but you were out. I wrote it down for you." He reached across the grimy counter and handed Broderick a slip of paper. "His name is Leroy Johnson and that's his address on East One Hundred and Thirty-fifth Street. You were right. He's an old geezer. My man at the Tombs said the employment record has him listed as sixty-three. But you know those niggers, you can never tell how old they are. Most of them don't even have birth certificates. They just get hatched at home." Danny laughed at his joke.

"You sure the address is right?"

"No problem," Danny insisted. "My friend got it right out of the office. And he only started working at the Tombs a month ago, so he still ought to live at the same address." Danny looked past Broderick and grinned. "Hi, Miss Mona," he said.

"Hello, Danny."

Broderick turned, hearing her voice right behind him. He had expected her to wait for him away from the newsstand where he had left her. "You shouldn't sneak up behind me like that." His voice was sharp, sharper than he intended, and he saw immediately the effect it had on her.

A slight flush came to her cheeks and her own voice became haughty and defensive. "I wasn't sneaking up behind you, John. I just wanted to say hello to Danny. You know you left me standing in the middle of the sidewalk."

"I'm sorry," he said. "I'm just edgy, don't pay any attention to me." He wanted to get her away from the newsstand quickly. There was no problem in her hearing about the old man. He knew he could explain away any questions that came up and he knew she would have no interest in an old

Negro anyway. He had just not expected her to be there; it was another lapse on his part and it annoyed him.

She looked away from him and smiled at Danny, trying to recover some of the dignity she felt she had lost. "How have you been, Danny?" she inquired, not really caring what the response was.

"Just great," the little man said. "Did you read all the stuff about Johnny?" he asked.

She was immediately sorry she had spoken to him. The little fool had brought up the subject she wanted to avoid and she sensed Broderick's body tense slightly at the mention of it. She assumed it was the unpleasantness of what he had been through. She smiled in acknowledgment and tried to change the subject. "It's such a beautiful evening, so much cooler. It's a shame you have to stay and work."

Danny followed the ploy. "Awe, I don't mind," he said. He spoke to her shyly but behind his eyes there was a resigned lustfulness that only a woman would notice. The thought of it amused her.

Broderick stirred, shifting his feet impatiently. "Look, Danny, thanks again," he said. "I owe you one." He took Mona's arm lightly. "We better get going if we're going to have an early dinner," he said.

She said good-bye to Danny and they started up Broadway again. They did not speak for over a minute. Broderick was trying to formulate his thoughts, trying to find the right words to explain away his sudden rudeness. She had decided to let him speak first.

"Look, I'm sorry," he said finally.

"Johnny, what happened yesterday must be tearing you apart," she said, pressing against his arm again. "That's why I've tried to avoid talking about it."

Even the vague reference to it sent a feeling of unpleasantness through him. There was still something he had to do that night and he had not mentioned yet that he would be leaving her early. Now it would have to wait before he told her. They would have dinner first, he thought, and allow things to quiet down. He could feel a slight, almost unnoticeable trembling in his hands. He felt as though he was being pulled at from all sides, that decisions, actions were being necessitated outside his own ability to control them. He hated the feeling, the sense that he was being manipulated, forced to take steps he would never have considered. He slipped his hand into his pocket and felt the piece of paper Danny had given him, but it only added to his anxiety and he withdrew the hand quickly.

"Why don't we find a small place around here where we can get a good steak?" he said.

"Anything will be fine with me. A nice quiet little place would be marvelous." She paused a moment. "I didn't mean to upset you, John. It's the last thing I wanted to do."

"You didn't," he lied and smiled at her. "You were right. It was just yester-day and all the nonsense you have to go through when something like that happens. All the reports. They have to have everything on paper; it's the way their minds work, I guess, and I'm really not that good at it."

They walked along quietly and then turned left into Forty-ninth Street.

"John?" she said. "Who is Leroy Johnson?" She was still holding his arm and she felt him stiffen when she mentioned the name and at once she was sorry she had asked him.

"He's nobody. He's just an old man I have to talk to." He smiled at her again but only with his mouth.

"I'm sorry, John. I'm not trying to pry, honestly."

"No. Don't be silly. It's just that it's really nothing. He's just somebody who I think I can get some information from about a case I'm working on. I just don't feel like talking about business. I've had enough of it today."

"Of course you have," she said. "And I'm bringing it all back like a silly fool." She was irritated with herself and she meant what she said. "You know I do believe I'm starving," she said, changing the subject deliberately. "Let's find someplace quickly so we can relax and have a good meal."

They picked a small French restaurant on Forty-eighth Street, across Eighth Avenue, after she pointed out on the menu displayed outside that they served a steak au poivre. It took a little convincing on her part—the idea of a brown sauce and green peppercorns was not his idea of what should be done to a good piece of beef—but she swayed him after some teasing that he should abandon his meat and potato mentality about food.

It was a small, quiet restaurant and he was relieved to find that the waiters spoke English, recalling the first dinner they had together where everything was ordered in French. He reminded her of it and joked that she could have fed him anything that night and he would not have known the difference. They ordered and she joined him in the steak au poivre to ease his concern, even though it was not a favorite dish for her. She preferred more delicate food and a salmon mousse would have been more to her liking, but she intended to make the evening pleasant for him at all costs.

It was seven-thirty when they finished dinner and sat comfortably full with their coffee before them. It would not be completely dark for another hour and he was in no hurry. He wanted it to be dark when he went to Harlem, and he only hoped the old man was not in the habit of staying out late. He wanted to find him and take care of things as quickly as possible. She would be upset when he told her; he had no doubt about that, but there was little he could do about it.

"John," she said suddenly, "have you given any more thought to when you'll leave the department. After yesterday I'm more convinced than ever it would be best for you to do it quickly."

"I've thought about it and I couldn't agree more." He watched her face light up as he spoke the words and he was glad he was making her happy. It would make it easier later, he thought.

"Oh, that's wonderful. We can tell Uncle tomorrow and then start planning to get away. When will you tell your superiors?"

"I can't do that until next week," he said.

She seemed confused. "Why? I don't understand."

"There's going to be a hearing about the escape. Some politicians are going to try and make a big deal out of it to try to embarrass the mayor." He said it simply, trying to hide his own concern.

"But what does that have to do with you?"

"They want to investigate everything and so I'm going to have to testify. Everybody who was involved in any way will have to."

"But why would that stop you from resigning?"

"It's just that if I suddenly resigned before the hearing they might try to make something out of it. You know how politicians are. They don't care who they go after as long as they get something out of it for themselves. So I'll just wait until it's over and avoid any chance of trouble."

"I still don't understand," she said. "What possible kind of trouble could there be? You were the hero of the entire thing. All the newspapers said so." She was looking at him intently, remembering his nervousness and wondering if this, not what had happened at the Tombs, was the cause of his uneasiness.

"There won't be any trouble," he assured her. "I'm just a careful person and I know what kind of people I'm dealing with. If they even hinted my leaving had something to do with it, it would raise doubts and they would get the kind of publicity they're looking for. Believe me, I know what I'm talking about. I've seen guys like this play their dirty little games before. Besides, what does another week matter? Then we'll tell your uncle." He paused, biting his lower lip, then continued. "Look, there's something I wanted to ask you. This thing the other day and all the publicity. Do you think something like that would upset your uncle and make him change his mind about wanting me around the place? It was kind of violent."

She laughed. "Of course not. Don't be silly. You were doing your job and you did it magnificently. If anything, it would make him proud of you. Why he probably has been bragging about having lunch with you the other week. Besides, darling, the only kind of publicity that ever hurts in business is the scandalous type, and you certainly couldn't call what you did scandalous."

He smiled weakly. "No, I suppose I am being silly," he said. He sipped his coffee to avoid saying anything further. Scandal. The word had never come to his mind, but that was exactly what it would be if questions were raised. But there was only one way questions could be raised now. Even if they were, he would survive them, he was sure of that. No one would take the word of an old nigger against his and Cordes's, a frightened old nigger to boot. But it

266

would create a stir and the newspapers would run with it; it was something they would never pass up.

He listened to her voice prattle on aimlessly about the trip they would take and he smiled occasionally to make her feel he was really listening. A hardness had come over him. The line of his jaw was firmer and his eyes had become cold and determined. He sipped his coffee slowly, stealing a glance at the watch pinned to her dress. It was eight o'clock now and in a few minutes he would leave and do what he had to. Then everything would finally be resolved. There would still be the hearing but he was sure Nolan would take care of that. They were professionals at those games and they would not take any chances and let it get out of hand. By the time the hearing took place they would have their sacrificial lambs lined up. He remembered the one time he had visited the slaughterhouse on the east side, watching as a steer with a bell led the others down a long chute. They had followed it innocently right to where the big Pollack had waited with a sledgehammer, never suspecting anything was wrong until the sledgehammer hit them right between the eyes. He wondered what guards were being readied for just such a walk right now. The one who ran away, Nolan had said. At least he had it coming, he decided. The dead warden. What a great way to be remembered. "God rest his soul," Nolan had said, cutthroat bastard that he was. And maybe even some others. No, the hearing would not be a problem. He would worry until it was over, but he was sure they would have everything under control. They would probably even take credit for it in the end. Jimmy Walker always found a way to take credit for anything that turned out well, just as he usually found someone else to take the blame for things that did not. He was brought back, hearing Mona repeat his name twice in succession.

"I'm sorry," he said. "I guess I drifted off for a minute."

She looked at him strangely. "I was just asking you if you would like to go to a club tonight, or just back to my apartment for a quiet evening. Do you think you're up to going anywhere?"

He took a deep breath, knowing the next few minutes would be difficult. "That's something I wanted to talk to you about," he began. I'm afraid I have some bad news. Not all that bad, just a temporary kink in the evening."

"What are you talking about, John." Her voice had grown apprehensive and he could see the look beginning to form on her face that always came when she found she was not going to get what she wanted.

"There's something I have to do tonight. It will only take an hour or so, unless complications come up, and then I can meet you back at the apartment later."

She was relieved, but only somewhat. At least he had not said he was spending another evening alone. The fact that he was leaving her, even tem-

267

porarily, was something she had not planned on and anything she did not plan on was an annoyance and any annoyance was something she considered intolerable.

"Oh, John, no. You said before you didn't even want to think about business anymore tonight and now you tell me you have to leave on business. I've been looking forward to seeing you all day. Can't you put it off, just for tonight, just so we can be together without any interruption? Just this once, John. I'll never interfere again."

There was a begging quality to her voice, like a child asking for something she knew she could not have. It made him uncomfortable trying to deal with it.

"This is something I *have* to do. I just *have* to see this person tonight. If I don't, I may not get a chance to again. Believe me, I don't want to, so please don't press me about it. I have a lot of things on my mind right now and I really don't need the extra pressure."

He could hear her foot stamp under the table. It was something he had never understood. How a grown woman could stamp her foot like a brat whenever things didn't go as she wanted them to.

"John, I'm sure it's not all that important." Her voice was haughty now and he did not like it.

"I said I have to," he said. "I'll pay the check and put you in a cab. The whole thing probably won't take more than an hour and a half and then I'll meet you back at your apartment."

"Well, perhaps I'll go see some friends." Her tone was bitchy and she had looked away from him, denying him the pleasure of her gaze.

"If that's what you want," he said. "If you're not there when I get there, I'll call you tomorrow."

Her head snapped around at him. He was saying exactly what she didn't want him to and it confused and upset her that she was losing control of the situation. "Oh, John, you know I'll wait for you." She reached across the table and took his hand. "It's just that I don't want you to *leave*."

She had emphasized the final word with another small stamp of her foot.

268

CHAPTER THIRTY-FOUR

He HAD PARKED HIS CAR ON FORTY-THIRD STREET between Eighth and Ninth avenues and he walked quickly toward it now, thinking only of what lay ahead. Mona had mellowed by the time he placed her in a cab and his mind was now clear of other problems. The drive to Harlem would take fifteen minutes, no more. And if Johnson was there he could take care of things and be back at her apartment by ten o'clock. He pulled the slip of paper from his pocket and checked the address again. Danny had come through for him again and it never ceased to amaze him the connections the little newsdealer had. He wondered for a moment if Danny would ever question it, if it came out that the old man was missing. It should never come up, he decided. But even if it did, Danny would simply assume that the old guy had skipped town because he found out the police were after him. He would have to take care of Danny somehow, he thought. Perhaps get him a job at Eatkins's factory if he wanted one, or maybe let him set up another newsstand outside the plant.

The car headed north in the traffic, past Columbus Circle, and on up into the ever-expanding west side. The pleasantness of the evening had brought people out on the sidewalks and he watched them walk along aimlessly, the way people in the city always seemed to walk when the tensions of the day had finally ended. He continued on, moving past Columbia University, which would soon be filled again with the children of the wealthy, walking about in their straw hats and later, when the weather grew colder, in raccoon coats. There was probably more bootleg booze sold in this neighborhood than in any other in the city, he thought, and he decided that one day there would be a great many wealthy young men walking around with white canes in their hands because of it.

When the car reached One Hundred and Twenty-fifth Street he turned right and headed toward Lexington Avenue. He had never worked in Harlem and was glad he did not work there now. The neighborhood was still good. There were strong ethnic ties, especially among the Italians and the Poles and Russians. It was still a place where many wealthy men kept their mistresses in pleasant apartments. But the darkies were slowly taking over, and he knew it would only be a matter of time before they overran the area and drove the whites away. The Italians would be the last to go, he thought. They always were. They were stubborn and they fought to hang on to what was theirs. They hated the niggers, he had heard them grumbling about the mulleys, the term used when they were being kind. Already Negroes owned jazz places along One Hundred and Twenty-fifth Street. They were living in the One Hundred and Thirties on the east side and only the west side of Harlem was still completely free of them.

Johnson lived on East One Hundred and Thirty-fifth Street and he hoped now that he lived there alone. If there were others living with him it would create problems he did not need and he realized he should have asked Danny to find out if he was married. But that would not have told him much, he decided. He had known Negroes who lived four and five people in a room and they weren't even related. He had never even liked to arrest one. Some woman would always show up at the stationhouse crying and begging for her man, claiming there was sickness in the family and that he was needed at home and finally evoking God, if necessary, as if she expected cops to give a fuck whether she belived in Jesus Christ or not. They were a worthless lot; he had decided that long ago and nothing he had seen had changed his mind. He had heard people try to make connections between the Negroes and the Irish and it had angered him to hear those connections made. The Irish had been poor and they had lived in filth and squalor and some still lived that way. But they had climbed out of it or were in the process of doing so. These people would never get out of it, of that he was sure. They liked it that way and it was something that anyone who dealt with them knew.

He passed Lexington Avenue and turned instead on Third Avenue. East One Hundred and Thirty-fifth Street would be one-way headed west and he wanted to park in front of the building, right in front of the door, if possible. At the intersection he stopped for a light and checked the street number again. Already the streets were dominated by the black men, sitting on the stoops of the tall five-story brownstones that filled every street. They looked at him sitting in his car waiting for the light to change, and some nudged each other. They knew he was a cop. They had a way of telling, these people, probably because they had something to hide, he thought.

He drove the car slowly along East One Hundred and Thirty-fifth Street, watching the numbers on the buildings slowly move toward the one he wanted. There was a small group of men standing in front of Johnson's building, most of them older men, and as he climbed out of the car they glanced at him furtively, looking away quickly when their eyes met his. He slammed the car door and locked it and walked heavily around to the sidewalk. The expression on his face was hard and rough. It was the look the police took on in neighborhoods where they were considered aliens, a look intended to keep the people they feared apprehensive. He walked straight at the group of men and they parted at the last moment, giving him access to the building. The hallway of the building was dark and dank and there were traces of mold on the chipped and peeling walls. There was a smell of urine in the hall and it sickened him and he tried not to breathe too deeply as he read the names on the mailboxes in the shabby foyer. Most of the mailboxes had been broken into more than once and some were twisted badly and no longer served a useful purpose. On most, the names were missing, but the old man's was clearly printed in pencil on the scratched and battered metal. Next to his name he had marked the number, 3-B.

Broderick climbed the dimly lit stairway slowly. On the way to the second floor he passed a young girl, nine or ten, he guessed, and she stared at him with suspicion, then hurried past, moving down and away from him as quickly as she could. On the third floor, under the stairwell, there were several trash cans and some sacks filled with garbage that had already begun to smell. The odor of cooking still lingered in the hall and mixed with the smell of garbage and the urine that seemed to be everywhere. He hated coming into these buildings. They reminded him of the one he too had been raised in. But the smell here was worse, he told himself. At the end of the dark hallway he found a doorway with the number 3-B scratched onto the brown, cracked paint. He hit the door solidly four times and waited. From behind the door he could hear movement, faint at first, then louder and directly behind the door. The door opened slowly, only a few inches at first and he placed his forearm against the wood and leaned his weight against it, forcing it open. The old man stood in the doorway, his features partially obscured by the light from a single uncovered light bulb that hung from the ceiling behind him. But it was the same man, the one whose face was so clearly etched into his mind. He looked at Broderick and his eyes widened and he took a step backward.

Broderick closed the door behind him. "Hello, Leroy. You and I have to talk."

He walked past him into the center of the small one-and-a-half-room apartment. It was shabby, furnished with battered old furniture, but it was clean and well ordered; it looked as though it was swept and dusted each day. There's a woman here, he thought. He walked over to a curtain draped across a doorway and pulled it aside, revealing a small but orderly kitchen. He looked around the room again.

"Where's the bathroom?" he asked.

"It's down the hall. I don't have one in de apartment."

The old man's face was still frightened. He could see that more clearly now with his face turned toward the light. He had a light brown complexion, almost the color of cocoa, and his hair was completely white. He was a thin man, no more that five foot seven, and some of the skin had begun to droop along his neck, seeming in conflict with his sharp, pleasant features. He held his chin up and his back straight but there was a slight trembling in his chin and there was no question about the look of fear that came from his eyes.

"You alone, Leroy?" Broderick asked.

"Yes, sir. I lives here alone," he answered.

Broderick took a few steps around the small apartment. "You expecting anybody."

"No, sir. I don't ever get no company. Not at night, leastways. What you want with me, Mr. Broderick?"

Broderick's eyes hardened on the old man. "You know who I am, Leroy?" he asked.

"Everybody knows who you is, Mr. Broderick. Your name was in all da papers." He had not moved, his feet seemed rooted to the floor. His hands hung loosely at his sides, the old fingers curling slightly in a nervous response. sponse.

Broderick stood about four feet away from him. His bulk seemed to fill half the room. He smiled at the old man. "But you know even better, don't you, Leroy?" he asked.

The trembling intensified in Leroy's chin. "I don't know what you means, Mr. Broderick. Why you here?"

Broderick ignored him. "How's your eyesight, Leroy?" he asked, his voice low and even.

"It's okay. It's good. What you mean?" His voice had taken on a small whine and his fingers were curling more quickly than before.

"You don't wear glasses?" Broderick asked.

"No, sir. I sees just fine."

Broderick shuffled his feet, looked down at the floor, then back up at the old man. "That's too bad, Leroy. I was kind of hoping your eyesight wasn't too good. You like your job at the Tombs, Leroy?"

The old man's nervousness was growing and he began fidgeting with his hands in front of him. "Yes, sir. I likes it just fine," he said.

"You see a lot of interesting things there, I guess?" Broderick said.

Leroy began to shake his head back and forth. "No, sir," he insisted. "I don't see nothin' 'cept what I'm supposed to see for my work. That's all. Honest, Mr. Broderick. That's all."

Broderick began to pace back and forth, his head down, as though he was thinking. He stopped and looked at the old man again. But this time he did not smile. "How'd you like to retire, Leroy? Go some place where it's warm and sunny and get away from this pigpen you live in?"

The old man's back straightened slightly. He was proud of his apartment, proud of what he had been able to make of his life and for a moment his fear left him. "I likes it fine here," he said.

Broderick reached into his breast pocket and withdrew an envelope he had prepared earlier in the day, watching the old man flinch with the movement of his hand. He opened the envelope and flashed the crisp, new bills inside, then returned it slowly to his pocket.

"Let's put it another way, Leroy," he began. "The way I see it you have two choices. You can take this." He patted the pocket that held the money-filled envelope. "And then you can retire. The other choice is that I'll have to use this money to buy flowers for your funeral. Now which is it, Leroy?" His voice had not changed. It was still low and even, the most threatening kind of voice one man could use against another, he knew.

Leroy's chin began moving furiously and the words came out in a constant stutter, an octave higher than his voice had been before. "Mr. Broderick, I ain't gonna say nothin' 'bout those three men. I didn't see nothin' and I ain't gonna say nothin'. What you done ain't none of my business. You jus' leave me alone and ain't nothin' gonna happen 'bout dat. I don't wanna go no place. I got family here and I ain't got too many days left. You let me spend them days with my family. Please, Mr. Broderick. You do that."

Broderick took a deep breath and looked up at the ceiling, shaking his head. "Leroy. You see? You're already talking about what happened that day. You're just going to have to retire one way or the other." He stared at him and continued speaking through his teeth. "Now which way is it going to be? A bus ticket to some place far away, tonight, with plenty of money in your pocket. Or is it going to be a ride in a fucking hearse?"

He took two steps toward the old man as he spoke the final words and watched Leroy move the same number of steps backward, trying to keep the same distance between them.

"Okay. I goes. I go any place you wants. You jus' let me get my stuff packed and we can go right now."

Broderick smiled and walked up to him, placing his hand on the old man's shoulder. Beneath the hand he could feel the old man trembling and he

273

squeezed the shoulder lightly. "You don't have to pack anything, Leroy. I don't *want* you to pack anything. You have plenty of money to buy yourself all you want when you get where you want to go. Where's that gonna be, Leroy?"

The old man looked up at him, the red veins in his eyes looking like a runaway road map, accented by the cocoa skin and the white hair. "I don't know," he said. "Where does you want me to go?"

"That's up to you, Leroy. Any place you want, as long as it's not here. How about the South? It's nice and warm down there."

Leroy shook his head. "No, sir," he said. "I comes from the South. I don't want to go back there, iffen you don't mind."

"You pick the place, Leroy. Chicago. Detroit. Maybe all the way to California. California is nice and warm."

"Could I jus' go to Jersey or maybe Philadelphia, so's my family could still come an' visit me?" There was a begging look in his eyes that faded as he watched Broderick shake his head.

"Too close, Leroy. I want you nice and far away. And if I find out you didn't go nice and far away I'm going to come see you again. You know that I can find you if I want, don't you, Leroy?"

The old man nodded his head. He had no doubts about what white people could do to coloreds. He had witnessed it his entire life and he also knew that no one would try to help him against this man. He had been expecting Broderick to come, but he had thought it would be at the Tombs. He had thought he might lose his job because of what he had seen and that had worried him. It was a good job and it had let him help his family. He could not understand why Broderick was afraid he would talk. Whites never believed his people. He knew that; he had seen it all his life. A man would have to be a fool to talk against one of them, to one of them. Coloreds talked only to each other and sometimes not even then when it concerned whites. He didn't hate them. He used to hate them, but he was too old now to hate anyone. All he wanted now was to be left alone. Jus' let this poor old nigger alone and let him die in peace, he thought. He looked at the big man in front of him. He was a powerful man and he could kill him with his hands. He was a frightened man, he knew that too. And he knew that frightened men were dangerous. Why are these white folks always so scared of poor niggers, he wondered. They afraid 'bout where we live and where we eats and everthin'. It had never made sense to him but he had accepted it because he had no choice.

"Well, where's it going to be, Leroy?" Broderick asked.

"Chicago," he said absentmindedly, not really caring.

Broderick smiled. "Good," he said. "Let's go. My car is outside."

They left the apartment, Leroy walking ahead of him, his shoulders slouching slightly for the first time. They went down the stairs slowly, the old man holding on to the rickety bannister to steady himself against the darkness. Outside, the men were still gathered in front of the building and they watched the two men move past.

"Where's you goin', Leroy?" a voice from behind them asked.

Broderick put his hand on Leroy's arm. "Just keep your mouth shut and get into the car." He opened the door and closed it behind him. The men in front of the building watched as it pulled away from the curb, but no one moved.

The car turned south on Lexington Avenue and then east on One Hundred and Twenty-fifth Street. The old man sat quietly, his back straight against the seat, his eyes staring straight ahead at the traffic. The converted gas lamps that lined the sidewalk cast a yellowing light halfway into the broad street, and along the sidewalks people were still walking, enjoying the newfound coolness of the evening. When they reached the East River the car turned south again, moving along the dark waterfront, and the streetlife disappeared, the buildings replaced by commercial businesses and warehouses. He slowed the car as he moved past them, glancing along the sidewalk to his right and at the flat open area to his left that ended abruptly at the edge of the river. He swung the steering wheel to the left and the car lurched into the flat open area and then came to a stop at the edge of the river. He turned to look at the old man. His eyes were wide and he was staring back at him. Even in the darkness he could see the fear that had again seized his face. It seemed to intensify with each second that passed.

"How come we stoppin' here?" the old man asked. His voice was trembling badly and for a moment Broderick was afraid he might try to run.

He looked at him for a long moment, trying to decide whether to speak. "You know, Leroy, it's like you said. You have family here. And I guess I could never be sure that you wouldn't come back to them, could I?"

The old man answered in total terror. His lips were shaking and the words seemed to run together all at once. "Mr. Broderick, I promises you. I ain't never comin' back. You ain't never gonna see me again. I promises you I won't. I promises you."

He continued to repeat the words, shrinking back each time he spoke them, his voice rising higher with each promise, his back pressing against the door. He raised his hands in front of him and they shook so badly they looked as though he was waving good-bye to someone.

Far down the river on Sutton Place, William Eatkins stood on his terrace watching the river slide past, enjoying the coolness that was intensified by the nearness of the water. He had just finished his evening meal and he was content now with his cigar and the river spread out before him. He expelled a breath of smoke and watched it waft out over the garden below.

275

CHAPTER THIRTY-FIVE

THE HEARING WAS HELD IN THE TWEED COURTHOUSE behind City Hall and the special Italian marble that Tweed himself had ordered installed lined every corridor of the cavernous, square building just as it had lined his bank account with equal beauty. Broderick entered the building at five minutes before ten o'clock with Mona beside him. He had suggested she not come but she had insisted, claiming it might be her one and only opportunity to see him testify as a police officer. It had not been a good week between them. He had been tense and he knew the tension would continue until the hearing was over. Only then could he put things behind him and he kept telling himself how a new life would begin then, the one they had now agreed upon.

In the corridor, outside the courtroom that had been set aside for the "informal" hearing, Chris Nolan stood with an aide and Broderick excused himself and walked up beside him.

"I see you brought your lady friend with you. You think that's wise?" Nolan paused. "You're still a married man, you know, and there are plenty of reporters around here."

Broderick shrugged his shoulders. He no longer cared what Nolan thought. "She wanted to come and there was no way I could keep her away. Besides, people know about her. How does it look for us in the hearing?" he asked.

"We have no problems," Nolan said. "Everything was all taken care of a couple of days ago, just like I promised." Nolan had the usual cigar clamped between his teeth. He looked at Broderick squarely. "You have any problems?" he asked.

"None at all," Broderick said.

Nolan smiled without removing the cigar. "In that case everything looks great for us. We have our man on the committee and he knows what to do. If things go as we plan there's going to be so much heat on this Lorch guy that nobody is going to have time to ask anybody else too many questions. But if they do, you just stick to your story, which is the truth, of course, and everything will be fine."

"What about that test you mentioned?" He glanced at the younger man with Nolan.

"Bill's all right," Nolan said, sensing Broderick's concern. "You can talk in front of him. As far as the test goes, there's no chance of that happening anymore. It shouldn't even come up."

Broderick glanced at the younger man again. He was tall and slender and his lips seemed permanently pursed; he had the look of an Ivy League lawyer about him and he was carrying a sheaf of papers under one arm. Broderick still did not like the fact that he was there.

"It sounds good then," he said to Nolan.

"The whole thing shouldn't take more than an hour," he answered. "I'll be surprised if it does. You and your young lady sit with us when you go inside. That way she won't be alone and I can explain things to her as they go along." He winked at Broderick and gave him a pat on the shoulder. "Don't worry," he said. "There won't be any surprises."

Broderick returned to Mona and took her by the arm and walked her a few steps down the corridor. "Chris said it shouldn't take more than an hour. So we'll be out early and I'll take the rest of the day off. And tomorrow we can kiss all this good-bye."

She smiled at him. "Marvelous, John. You have no idea how good that makes me feel."

They stood talking quietly for several minutes as people filed into the courtroom behind them. Nolan came up beside them and was introduced to Mona. He smiled at her through the cigar and then motioned toward the entrance of the courtroom with his head.

"It looks like they're ready to start. We better go inside." He said it as though giving an order and Mona noticed that it seemed to annoy Broderick. The fact that it did pleased her.

Mona entered the courtroom first with Broderick behind her, Nolan and the young lawyer taking up the rear. They entered one of the benches in the same manner, choosing one in the center of the courtroom. Before them, in the front of the courtroom, a table had been placed in front of the judge's bench to emphasize the informality of the hearing. There was an empty chair off to one side for the witnesses who would be called. Broderick studied the table. There were five men seated behind it, most of whom Broderick had seen before and one specifically who he recognized as a member of the city attorney's office. There were several men dressed in prison uniforms in the front rows to his left and he wondered for a moment which one of them was Lorch. Another uniform caught his eye and he turned and watched Inspector Garfoli walk down the center aisle and take a seat toward the front. He nudged Nolan.

"There's my friend, Garfoli," he whispered.

"Don't worry about him. Somebody's already had a long talk with him about some of his friends in Little Italy and he understands that he doesn't make trouble for anybody anymore."

"You mean he was . . ." Broderick didn't finish the sentence. He knew it wasn't necessary.

"Of course he was," Nolan whispered.

Broderick smiled to himself, wishing he could tell the other members of the squad what he had just learned. Maybe he would, he decided. After he resigned.

The man seated in the center of the long table rapped lightly with a gavel and called the hearing to order. Reading dryly from a prepared statement he detailed the events of the escape, the killing of the warden and the clerk, and the subsequent death of the three men in the prison coal yard.

Mona reached out and touched Broderick's arm when the coal yard was mentioned and he looked at her and nodded his head assuringly.

The man at the table continued reading, stating that it was the purpose of the committee to determine if anyone had been derelict in his duties and what steps, if any, should be taken to improve security precautions at the city prison. He then advised the clerk that the first witness could be called, and the name Louis Lorch was called out.

Lorch rose slowly from his seat in the second row. He had been sitting alone, away from the other uniformed guards, almost as though he had been ostracized. Broderick noted his size, large and raw-boned, as he walked to the witness chair and remained standing while it was explained that no oath would be required because the hearing was informal. He sat heavily in the chair and folded his large hands in his lap. He seemed placid, almost dull-witted, apparently unconcerned about what was taking place around him.

The man at the table who Broderick had recognized as a member of the city attorney's staff shuffled a pile of papers set out before him and began to speak without looking at the witness. He wore round, steel-rimmed glasses

278

perched on the top of his small nose, and it made him look like a skinny owl, Broderick thought. The nameplate in front of him said: Mr. Evans.

"Mr. Lorch. For the record please, what is your full name?" Evans began.

"Louis Lorch, Jr." The guard's voice was even and steady. The only show of emotion was a constant blinking of his eyes.

"What is your position with the city?" The attorney was still concentrating on his notes.

"Prison keeper."

"When were you appointed?"

"About May the first, 1915." His eyes blinked again in rapid succession as he answered.

The attorney looked up at Lorch for the first time. "Aren't you sure of the exact date?" he said.

"Yes, sir. May the first in 1915."

"On September the third, 1926, where were you assigned?"

"The Tombs Prison and Penitentiary."

"You were working that day?"

"Yes, sir. I worked the eight to four shift during the day." His eyes fluttered again.

Evans began tapping a closed pen against the papers, almost as though marking time for music. He picked up one, looked at Lorch briefly, and then began to read from it. "A communication addressed to you subsequent to that date reads as follows: 'You are hereby charged with neglect of duty and violation of institutional rules, regulations, and procedures of the department in failing to take reasonable and proper precautions in safeguarding prisoners and preventing their escape from City Prison, Manhattan, September 3, 1926. You are likewise charged with neglect of duty in failing to arm yourself on the date in question." He looked up at the guard. "Did you receive that correspondence?"

"I did," Lorch said, blinking again.

A murmur drifted through the room. No information had been given out about any charges being filed and Broderick smiled to himself, assuming it was part of the tactical game Nolan and the mayor were waging. The lawyer also looked satisfied, he thought. It was as though the charges alone were enough.

The city attorney was tapping his pen again, much like a cop might slap a blackjack against his hand during an interrogation. "You were also notified, were you not, that if you are a veteran of the Spanish-American War you are entitled to an attorney. Are you a veteran of that war?" he asked.

Lorch blinked as though he did not really understand the question. "I'm a veteran of both wars," he said.

"Which ones?" the attorney snapped.

"The Spanish-American War and the World War, sir."

"Then you are entitled to an attorney, aren't you?" Evans's sarcasm seemed calculated, intended to unnerve the guard. But he only blinked again, appearing not to notice.

"Yes, sir," he said after a short pause. "Yes, sir, I guess I am."

The lawyer drew a deep breath. "Are you so represented?" he asked.

A tall, gray-haired man stood in the front row. "Let the record show that Mr. Lorch is so represented," he said. "My name is William McIver."

Broderick noticed a small bespectacled man at the end of the table nod to the lawyer. He nudged Nolan.

"That's part of the opposition," Nolan said, adding the words, "a Republican," with a degree of disgust.

"Mr. McIver is well known to the city," the city attorney acknowledged, then ignoring him as though he did not exist, turned again to Lorch. "Now, Mr. Lorch will you tell this body in your own words just what occurred from your observation on the afternoon of September third of this year."

Lorch took a deep breath and then leaned forward in his chair as though he were about to tell his story to a friend. "Well, it was a little after one o'clock and I had gone to the gate to leave someone out. That's the main gate, I mean. And then I stood there for a while looking out the small window in the gate, as is my habit. Then I started back into the reception area and all of a sudden the door leading to the cellblocks swings open and these three men is standing there with guns. One of them, I since found out his name was Hy Amberg, he says to me, give us the key to the front gate and then he says a terrible name after that that I can't say because there are ladies in the room."

Muffled laughter sprinkled through the courtroom and the attorney rapped his pen against the table trying to quell it. "Go on, Mr. Lorch," he said.

"Well, then I says something terrible back to him." The laughter began again but Lorch continued, ignoring it. "And then I pushes him and dives behind the clerk's desk and rushes to the door that leads to the room we have our lockers in so's I can get my gun."

"Did these men try to stop you?" the attorney interrupted.

"Yes, they did, sir. They fired some shots at me, I'm not sure how many, but more than two." He paused for a moment. "But they missed," he added. The laughter began again.

"Obviously," the city attorney said, looking out into the crowd. "And what happened then?"

"Well, I heard some more shooting as I was gettin' my gun out of my locker. And then I went to go back out, when the clerk, Joseph Murphy, he came staggering in the room and he tells me he's been shot. So I try to help him and I tell him to stay there and I go to the door and kind of peek out, cautious like, and it's then that I see this Amberg fella shooting the warden. Then I tries to shoot him, but as I'm taking aim the others fires a lot of shots at me and drives me back into the room. Then they ran out when they hear the alarm going off."

The attorney stared at Lorch, placing both palms flat on the table. "Who set off the alarm?" he asked.

"I don't know, sir. It must of been one of the other guards who heard all the shooting."

"And why didn't you set off the alarm? There *was* an alarm in the locker room, wasn't there?" The trace of a smile had begun to form on the city attorney's face. He seemed to be enjoying his own talents.

Broderick was suddenly glad the man was on the mayor's side in the hearing. He not only looked like an owl, he had the predatory instincts as well.

Lorch had begun to blink again and shook his head slowly. "I just really don't know. I tried later, but it went off before I touched it. There was an alarm there all right. I just didn't think to set it off right away. I don't know why I didn't. All I thought of was getting my gun and stoppin' those men from gettin' out, I guess."

"And why didn't you have your gun with you while you were on duty?" The lawyer asked the question softly but he had moved up to the edge of his seat as though he were ready to spring out of it.

"Well, the warden, he didn't like us to wear it in the reception area. He thought it looked bad to the relatives who came through there to visit with the prisoners. He told us to keep it close by in case of trouble. I guess he never thought a prisoner could get as far as them three did without an alarm going off." Lorch sat stoically, awaiting the next question.

The city attorney let him wait, tapping his pen methodically on the desk. "And the warden is dead now, isn't he?" he said finally.

"Yes, sir. Prisoner Amberg shot and killed him."

"And the clerk, Mr. Murphy, is dead also, isn't he?"

"Yes, sir. They killed him too."

"So it's very convenient to use them as an excuse now, isn't it, Mr. Lorch?" The lawyer's voice had risen, but only slightly. He was staring directly at the guard, his face solemn.

"I don't know what you mean, sir," Lorch said.

The lawyer leaned forward until his chest touched the table. "Oh, I think you know very well what I mean." His voice grew steadily louder now, filling the room with his own conviction. "What I *mean* is that you are now trying to find a way to explain why you did not have your weapon with you as you should have. What I *mean* is that you are now trying to find a way to explain why you ran away. Why you didn't turn in an alarm. Why you abandoned your post in such an extraordinary act of cowardice."

281

The room had been overcome by the murmurings of the crowd and Broderick could barely hear McIver's voice as he rose to challenge the assault on his client.

Mona leaned toward him. "My God, they're really after that poor man, aren't they?" she said.

Broderick smiled to himself. You bet your sweet ass, he thought.

McIver's voice boomed out over the noise. "I object to this disgraceful line of questioning," he shouted.

"Not nearly as disgraceful as the actions of your client," the city attorney shouted back. "No further questions." He spoke the final words with a calculated degree of disgust.

The man seated at the center of the table rapped the gavel. He seemed confused by the outbursts of anger. Nolan leaned toward Broderick.

"I think all our problems are over," he whispered.

The man with the gavel asked McIver if he wished to question the witness. The gray-haired lawyer walked slowly forward. One of his arms hung loosely at his side as if paralyzed. "Indeed I do, sir," he said.

McIver waited for quiet, then waited still longer, drawing out the effect. He positioned himself away and slightly to the rear of where Lorch was sitting so his face was turned toward the roomful of people. He was playing to the crowd, not the committee.

"Mr. Lorch," he began, his voice quiet and even, forcing everyone in the room to listen, "I think you have explained very well your actions on September third of this year, actions which in no way could be considered cowardly. However, that is what the esteemed city attorney appears to want us to believe. Therefore, I have only a few questions for you." He paused, taking a sheet of paper from his breast pocket with his good hand and reading it over carefully. He looked at Lorch and smiled. "You told us you served in the Spanish-American War and the World War, is that correct?"

"Yes, sir. Both wars," Lorch said.

"And did you see any action in those wars? By action, of course, I mean battle."

"Yes, sir."

"In *both* wars?"

"Yes, sir, in both."

"I see." McIver looked at the sheet of paper again, drawing all eyes to it. He walked up next to Lorch and handed him the paper. "Can you read this and tell us what it is?" he asked.

"Yes, sir." Lorch looked at the paper and read it slowly.

"Do you know what it is, Mr. Lorch?"

"Yes, sir. It's a list of the decorations I received." He began blinking again.

"In both wars?" McIver's voice had taken on a note of surprise.

"Yes, sir. Both wars is listed here."

"Can you read some of them to us, please?"

"Yes, sir." Lorch looked down at the paper and hesitated.

"Go ahead, Mr. Lorch. Don't be modest."

Lorch drew in a deep breath as though reading was a chore for him and then began in a faltering voice. "The Spanish-American War. The Silver Star, for single-handedly destroying an enemy position, even though severely wounded and under heavy fire. The Purple Heart. For wounds sustained in attacking same enemy position. The World War. The Distinguished Service Cross, for rescuing three members of his patrol while under intense enemy fire and bringing each to safety in three separate rescues. The Purple Heart. For wounds received fighting an overwhelming enemy force." He hesitated and looked at McIver. "The rest of them's in French and I don't pronounce them too good," he said.

McIver smiled. "I think that will be enough, Mr. Lorch. We don't want to bore the gentlemen here with this rather extensive list. Suffice to say there are eight decorations in all." He turned to the committee. "These decorations, gentlemen, were provided to me over the telephone by the Department of the Army since there was not enough time to get them here by mail. You can, of course, confirm them for yourselves." He waited, allowing the information to settle. "I am also prepared to call other members of the staff at the Tombs to confirm Mr. Lorch's contention that the warden asked that weapons not be worn in the reception area." He turned, extending his good arm toward the other uniformed men in the front row. "If you wish I will do that now."

"I don't think that will be necessary." The city attorney's voice was quiet, barely above a whisper.

"In that case I have no further questions," McIver said.

"I move for a ten-minute recess," the city attorney said.

The shuffling of bodies leaving the courtroom began as soon as the gavel sounded its first note against the table. Broderick and Mona moved with the crowd, his mind still reeling with what had just taken place.

"My heavens, John. This is incredible," she said. "You simply don't know what to believe now."

He took her arm and led her into the hall. All the tensions that had begun to disappear had rushed back to him and he wanted to get to Nolan and find out what would happen now. He caught Mona looking at him, apparently noticing his concern.

"What's wrong, John?" she asked.

"Nothing." He smiled. "It just looks as though this thing is going to go on forever. I'm going to talk to Chris and see if he can't arrange it so I testify soon. Then we can get out of here." He lied convincingly, he hoped.

"But *I* think it's interesting," she said.

"Not after you've done it as long as I have." He squeezed her arm. "I won't be a minute," he said.

It took him several minutes to find Nolan. The crowd from the courtroom had clogged the hall and from the snatches of conversations he caught there was little question that no one would now accept Lorch as the mayor's scapegoat. It did not please him to hear it and when he finally saw Nolan off to the side talking with the city attorney he grew even more apprehensive. Broderick waited until Evans had left before approaching Nolan. The cigar was clamped angrily between his teeth and his annoyance seemed to be directed at the young aide who was still at his side.

"What happens now?" he asked Nolan as he stopped at his side.

Nolan looked at him, his face red. "Shit. That's what happens now. Shit."

"What does that mean, Chris?"

"It means we have some problems. It means there's no way we can blame this damned thing on a war hero," he snapped.

"What went wrong?" Broderick was groping for answers, almost afraid of what he might hear.

Nolan shot a glance at the young man standing next to him. "Someone," he snapped, "checked on Mr. Lorch and told us there was no problem."

The young man pursed his lips even tighter and looked down at his shoes. He looked like a fag, Broderick thought.

"So what happens now?" Broderick was watching Nolan's eyes, trying to grasp what could happen.

"So now we have to find somebody else to take the blame, if we can." Nolan said.

Broderick could feel his anger rise and he heard himself speaking before he even realized he had begun. "So who gets it now? *Me?*"

Nolan glared at him. He was not accustomed to anger directed at himself. Broderick did not care. He only wanted to survive the hearing. And then he wanted to get out.

Nolan's anger softened. "Of course not, John," he said. "You just did your duty. Unless the city attorney can cross up one of the other guards from where the escape started, then it's just one of those things. Nobody gets the blame."

When Broderick returned to Mona he was still not satisfied. He had learned long ago not to trust promises and he had trusted Nolan's and he had been wrong.

"Did you have any luck?" Mona asked.

"With what?" he said. He had forgotten his excuse for leaving her.

"With having your testimony moved up?" she said.

"No. It looks as though I'll have to sit it out." He was about to suggest that she go on and meet him later, but she interrupted him.

"Good," she said. "It really *is* interesting."

She had the silly look of a pleased child on her face and it annoyed him and he suddenly wanted to slap her and force her to leave. He would prefer to take his misery alone, he thought, and he was beginning to worry about his own testimony and the effect it would have on her; the word *scandal* kept returning to his thoughts.

"Don't be annoyed about it, darling," she said. "Just remember. This is the last time you have to do this sort of thing. Think about how much I'm enjoying it."

His body tightened at the thought. For a moment he wanted to take her aside and tell her what might lie in store for him. Tell her the entire story and then see how much she would look forward to the remainder of the hearing. But it wasn't her fault. He knew that. He also knew that everything was completely beyond his control. He had no choice. He had to trust Nolan because it was too late to do anything else. It did not make it easier realizing that Nolan had already failed. And still there was opposition somewhere on the committee panel, he had been told that much.

He sat with Nolan again when the hearing resumed, not because he wanted to, but because he felt safer being close to him. The city attorney questioned five other prison witnesses, together with another member of the panel, the frail, bespectacled man at the end of the table, the one who had nodded at McIver. Each seemed to be pursuing different objectives but neither achieved much success. The two guards who had been on the tier when the escape began handled themselves well, Broderick thought. Far better than he wished they had and it seemed clear that placing the blame on an individual would be difficult. When an administrator of the prison was called to testify the tenor of the questions changed, concentrating on existing security precautions and it began to appear that the ultimate blame might be laid to faulty procedures and the lack of enforcement of those that already existed. They're going to drag the warden out of his coffin and slap his wrists, Broderick thought. They even fuck you when you're dead.

It was noon when he was finally called to testify. He had been checking the clock on the courtroom wall and for a time he had feared that he would be forced to wait until after the luncheon recess. Mona squeezed his hand as he left his seat and he could feel the eyes of the spectators following him as he walked to the witness chair. He remembered how Lorch had been as he sat there. Unconcerned, almost childlike, and he could feel his stomach churning and he began to wonder if it was noticeable to everyone in the crowded room. He glanced at Nolan and received an assuring nod of his head.

The city attorney began the questioning, running through the identifying questions quickly. He seemed friendly, a sharp contrast to his handling of Lorch, but it still did not ease his concern. He had testified many times over the years and he knew how to answer questions. He knew he must not display any uncertainty or nervousness and above all he must not allow himself to become annoyed. Smooth and easy and precise. That was the way it was taught and it was the way he intended to do it. He kept his hands folded in his lap. He had been taught that too, a small trick, a way of keeping any sign of nervousness from surfacing. Cops were well schooled for the witness box. They could lie when they had to and sound like angels from heaven. And he *was* a hero in the entire affair and the more modestly he spoke about it the more heroic he would seem. He knew that too.

When the preliminary questions ended the city attorney asked him to explain, in his own words, what he had found when he arrived at the Tombs and what actions he and the other police officers present had taken.

Broderick began slowly, explaining how he had learned of the escape as he and Cordes were entering Police Headquarters and how they rushed to the scene on foot. He took special care to point out that neither he nor Cordes knew who had escaped until they arrived. He was fearful someone might take issue with the coincidence and he wanted to thwart any attempt before it began. The testimony was smooth, given in short, precise sentences just as he had been taught. He explained how he and Cordes worked their way up the alley behind the trash cans and he was careful to give Cordes equal credit. He almost smiled at one point, thinking how surprised Cordes would have been had he been there, listening to Johnny Broderick share the glory with a fellow cop. But he wanted Cordes to be very much a part of it now; he had seen his prepared statement and he knew it matched his own testimony in every detail.

He did not dwell on Cordes being shot; he said it matter-of-factly, knowing it would sound as though it was something every cop expected and that that alone would be impressive. Neither did he emphasize his own rush into the open to reach the coal mound. He simply explained that he ran there and that when he arrived he found all three prisoners dead.

The room was silent when he finished and he knew his testimony had produced the desired effect. If Lorch could get off the hook being a war hero, he could do the same by explaining how he had braved the gunfire of the alley. He had made the point that the gunfire had been heavy and everyone was aware who Amberg and the others were, what they had been arrested for, and that they had killed the warden and the clerk. If it was left at that, he would be as hard to blame as Lorch. The silence confirmed it for him and he began to feel easier about it. The approving nods from the city attorney that had persisted throughout his testimony made him more certain.

At the end of his account the city attorney attempted to reach out for a conclusion.

"And so, Detective Broderick," he began, "when you and Detective Cordes finally fought your way to the mound of coal that the three prisoners

286

had hidden behind, you discovered that they were all dead, apparently killed by their own hands, is that correct?"

"Yes, sir," Broderick answered. "All three appeared to have shot themselves."

"Thank you, Detective. I have no further questions."

Broderick felt a rush go through him and he started up from the chair. It was then that the small, bespectacled man's voice hit him. His nameplate identified him only as Mr. Williams.

"Just one moment, Detective. I would like to ask some questions." The man spoke with a slight lisp. He was smiling at him and Broderick could feel that his own face had flushed. He sat back in the chair clumsily. From the center of the room Nolan nodded to him, letting him know this lisping man was the opposition; it was something he had known instinctively. He looked straight into the man's face, removing any trace of emotion from his own.

The new interrogator continued to smile. "Detective Broderick, we are all familiar with your experience as a police officer. For the record, though, you are a member of what is termed the Industrial Squad, is that not so?"

"Yes, sir, it is."

"Am I correct in assuming that a major portion of your duties there involves dealing with labor difficulties?"

"In addition to normal police work, yes, sir."

"But, of course, your experience in normal police work is extensive, is it not?" He paused, then continued before Broderick could answer. "What I mean is you have been involved in numerous shooting and homicide investigations, have you not?"

"Yes, sir." Broderick was uncertain where the line of questioning was going and he listened carefully, certain the man was trying to entrap him.

"So like any experienced police officer your observations would be considered expert in those matters, is that not so?" The questioner removed his spectacles and began cleaning them with his handkerchief, as though the question really did not matter.

"I suppose to a certain degree it would," Broderick said.

The man replaced his spectacles and smiled again. "Have you seen the autopsy reports on the three prisoners?" Williams asked.

"No, sir, I have not."

"But you did see the bodies and checked to determine they were dead, is that right?"

"Yes, sir, I did." The question had sounded foolish and Broderick repressed a smile when he answered.

The man stood and walked toward him, carrying a large envelope. When he reached the witness chair he withdrew three photographs and handed them to him. "These are photographs taken in the coal yard, showing the

287

victims as they were found. Would you look at them please?"

Broderick looked at the eight-by-ten photographs. They were close-ups showing the head wounds of all three. Seeing them now brought a rush of uneasiness and for a moment he could see the faces of all three again as they flew back from the impact of the bullets.

"You'll note," the bespectacled man continued, "that Mr. Amberg was shot in the forehead, Mr. Dunniger in or around the mouth, and Mr. Berg in the left temple. Let's take Mr. Amberg first." He paused again, moving to the side of the chair so he could look at the photographs along with Broderick. "The wound to Mr. Amberg is almost in the center of the forehead. Don't you find that an odd place to shoot oneself?" he lisped.

Broderick stiffened slightly. "I suppose it is. Amberg was an odd man," he said.

"I see. Now Mr. Dunniger was shot in the mouth, not out of keeping with suicide, I'm told, but if you look closely you'll notice that the lower lip seems to be torn, but I suppose that could have been from the recoil of the weapon."

"I suppose so," Broderick said.

"Now Mr. Berg's wound, in the left temple. Do you know whether or not he was right- or left-handed?"

"I have no idea, sir." Broderick could feel his nervousness building and he knew that feigning ignorance would be his best defense. Christ, he hadn't even thought of that, he reminded himself. Another damned mistake.

"We haven't been able to determine that either," he said. He waited again, allowing Broderick to savor his own sense of relief. "But the medical examiner indicates that the wear on the fingertips of Mr. Berg's right hand would indicate he *was* right-handed. With that in mind, and also in the case of Mr. Amberg shooting himself in the forehead, would you not find these two facts to be *unusual?*"

"I wouldn't know, sir. I'm not an expert on suicide." There was some laughter in the room and Broderick glanced at Nolan and noted the concern on his face. He seemed to be trying to get the attention of the city attorney. He looked at Mona; she seemed confused, he thought, and her eyes were staring at him hopefully.

The bespectacled man ignored the laughter. "I understand that, Detective," he said, still smiling. "However, it would seem that in the case of Mr. Amberg, he would have to hold a gun like this." He formed a gun with his hand and placed the finger to his forehead.

"I don't see the point of this. I thought we were here to review the escape." The city attorney's voice was sarcastic again and Broderick assumed Nolan had finally caught his attention.

"I'm sure you don't." The small man's voice was calm and he was still smiling. "I'm well aware that City Hall does not want any problems in this matter. However, I believe I have the right to question witnesses and I intend to exercise that right."

Broderick looked at Mona again. Her confusion seemed to be growing. Nolan reached out and placed his hand on her shoulder and whispered to her.

"Now, Detective," the questioner said, turning back to Broderick, "if you'll look at the photographs again, please. I am told by reputable pathologists that when a person shoots himself there is normally heavy burning of the tissues around the circumference of the entry wound. Has that been your experience?"

"Yes, I guess so." Broderick's fingers had tightened on the photographs.

"If you'll look at the photographs again, I think you'll see that the burning appears to be absent."

Broderick studied the three photographs again. "I can't really tell from these pictures," he said. He shrugged his shoulders slightly.

"I see. Well, the pathologist's report indicates that there were powder burns but of such a nature that it would appear the shots were fired from two to four or five feet away. Does that strike you as odd?"

"No, sir. There was a lot of shooting going on. Maybe they were hit before."

"All three?"

"Look, I don't know." Broderick's voice rose a fraction and he fought to control it.

"Well I'm told that in that case there would be no powder burns at all—I mean, if they were shot from a distance during the gunfight. What does that suggest to you?"

"I don't know, sir. Look, there was a lot of shooting going on and I was trying not to get shot myself. It seemed to me that they shot themselves. If I was wrong, I was wrong. If police bullets got them"—he paused—"well, they were killers, weren't they?"

"Yes. I believe there were killers in that coal yard." He let the statement fall. "But let's go on. Detective, are you familiar with the scientific study of ballistics?"

"I've heard of it." Broderick shot another glance at Nolan. He seemed angry and his face had reddened again. Mona, in contrast, seemed unusually pale.

"You are aware then that this is a relatively new scientific technique of determining which weapon fired a particular bullet based on the lands and grooves made on said bullet by the rifling inside the barrel of the weapon?"

"I don't know how it works, just that some people claim it does. We don't use it in the department. At least I don't think we do." He was aware now that Nolan had been wrong again, that he was on his own and that ignorance was the only thing he could fall back on. Deep in his mind he wondered if this little man had the bullets in his pocket and his hands began to sweat.

"Detective, are you aware that I had requested that a ballistics test be made on the bullets that killed the three prisoners and on each of their weapons and on your weapon and that of Detective Cordes." He wasn't smiling now and behind his spectacles his magnified eyes were hard.

"No, sir." Broderick snapped out the words. He wanted to look at Nolan for some assurance. But he resisted it. He also wanted to avoid Mona's eyes at this moment.

"Well, the Police Department did not feel it was necessary. They were satisfied with their own investigation. I assumed they, too, felt that the fact these men were killers was enough in itself." He had started to walk away from the witness chair as he spoke. Now he turned and looked at Broderick again. "By the way, they told me I would need your permission to perform such a test. Would you object to such a test?"

The city attorney's voice boomed out again. "I object to this questioning and the innuendo that goes along with it. I don't think the detective should answer."

The small man was smiling again. "I'm sure you don't," he said. Then to Broderick: "Do you care to answer, Detective?"

"No, sir. I think I'll just go along with the department's position. They have the right to check my weapon if they want." He looked at Mona now. Her face was pale and although she was a full twenty feet away her face seemed closer, almost close enough to reach out and touch. He thought for a moment she might faint.

The small man's voice brought his eyes back. "Well, it's really a moot point, Detective. It seems the fatal bullets all disappeared from the coroner's office." A murmur rose from the spectators and he waited for it to subside. "Just one more question, Detective. Have you ever heard the name Leroy Johnson?"

Broderick's temples began to pound. He looked at Mona again, and her face seemed to have moved again, now within inches of his own, and her eyes were wide and frightened. "No, sir, I don't believe I have," he heard himself say.

"Well, let me see if I can refresh your memory. Mr. Johnson was a Negro about sixty-three years of age who was employed as a handyman at the Tombs. He resided, until recently, at 140 East One Hundred and Thirty-fifth Street. Do you recall ever hearing of or meeting him now?"

"No, sir." Broderick was fighting for control now and he felt trapped, helpless.

"Well, it seems that on the day of the escape Mr. Johnson was assigned to work in an area adjacent to the coal yard, so naturally he was sought for questioning. Were you aware of any of this?"

"No, sir."

290

"I object to this. What *is* the point?" The city attorney was clearly annoyed now and he slapped his hand against the table.

Mona sat in her seat, her hands gripped together, trying to control the trembling. For several minutes now the sounds of the questions and Broderick's answers had assaulted her like some terrifying verbal collage, mixing with her own memories that she wished now she did not have. She looked at Nolan and he placed his arm around her shoulder and patted it gently.

"What does all this mean?" she whispered.

"It's all politics," Nolan said. "Don't pay any attention to it."

"Will all this be in the newspapers?" Her voice sounded frightened and Nolan looked at her, confused by the question.

"Just the Republican papers," he said. "And nobody reads them." He smiled at her assuredly, then suddenly felt her body stiffen.

The argument with the city attorney had ended and Williams turned back to Broderick.

"I note your objection. *Now*, Detective. It seems that several days ago Mr. Johnson disappeared from his home. Several neighbors said he left with a large white man, who they thought was a police officer. Unfortunately, they seemed too frightened to try to identify him. Would you know who that man was, Detective."

The photographs crumpled slightly in Broderick's hands. "No, sir, I wouldn't. I don't know what you're trying to get at. I did my job as a police officer, and that's all I know about." He caught himself, realizing he was almost shouting.

The city attorney joined in, demanding to know the point.

"I feel the committee should recommend to the district attorney that the entire matter be more thoroughly investigated," the small man said.

"That's out of order," the city attorney shot back. "I want this entire line of questioning stricken from the record."

"I see," the bespectacled man said. He looked at Broderick and smiled. "No further questions, Detective."

Broderick sat stunned. He heard the city attorney ask for a luncheon recess and the sudden movement of the spectators. He looked up and saw Mona moving from her seat and turn abruptly for the door. He left the witness chair, dropping the photographs to the floor, and pushed into the crowd, going after her. He brushed aside questions from several reporters and caught up with her as she was turning into the small lobby that led to the main door. He took her arm and pulled her aside. She turned and drew back from him, her face pale with anguish.

"Where are you going?" he said.

"I just had to get out of here." Her voice was weak, distant.

"You shouldn't let that stuff bother you. It was political. I told you it was

291

going to be." He could feel himself trembling inside; everything seemed to be slipping from him. A reporter approached but he waved him off.

"John, how could it help but upset me. John, that man, Leroy Johnson. That's the name Danny gave you last week, the night you said you had to see someone. Now he's disappeared. What did you have to see him about?" There was a quivering in her voice. She seemed afraid of what the answer would be.

He pulled her aside, afraid others might hear her. "Listen, it was simple. I thought he might have been involved with the escape, that he might have smuggled the guns in. If you don't believe me, ask Danny. That's all there was to it. I waited for him but he was already gone."

"But they said he left with a man, a large man, a large white man." She wanted to believe him. He could tell from the sound in her voice. It was almost pleading for him to be right.

"It was probably some friend of Amberg's, that's all. He probably did smuggle the stuff in. Then he ran away. Listen, that guy was just trying to make something else out of it."

"Then why didn't you tell him that?"

"All right, I didn't. I never saw the old man so I didn't think it was important, Look, at least *you* have to believe me."

She stared at him for a long moment. "John, how did those men die in that coal yard? How did the bullets disappear? That man was acting like you killed them."

He reached for her arm but she drew away again, almost as though she felt he was covered with blood, he thought. "They killed themselves," he said. "It was just like I said."

She shook her head. "Oh, John, how could they? What that man said, it made it sound impossible. Why did the bullets disappear?"

He took her arm, forcibly this time. "Look, I don't know anything about that. I told you everything I know about it. I don't know what happened to the old man or the bullets. Let's just get out of here. We'll go someplace and we'll forget it."

She pulled herself free again. "But, John, it's not going to be forgotten. That man, he wants an investigation. There'll be newspaper reports about it. John, it's going to be horrible."

He looked into her face and the word *scandal* rushed into his mind again. "Look. What do you want from me? It was my job. Now that's over. We can forget everything. Things will be just the way you wanted. You'll see."

"Oh, John, how can they be? It's all so confusing, so embarrassing. What will people think of you? John, I have to think. I have to go somewhere and think."

"I'll go with you," he said, almost pleading himself.

She stepped back again as though she was afraid he would take her arm

292

and force her. "No," she said. "I have to be alone." She wasn't looking at him. Her eyes were staring into the lobby, not looking at anything.

"Should I call you later?"

She looked at him now. "Yes, call me," she said as she turned and started to go.

"Will you answer the phone?"

She turned and looked back at him. There were tears in her eyes and she seemed like a small, hurt animal. She didn't answer, and as he watched her go through the door he knew that the only voice he would hear would be Rita's.

Chris Nolan and his young aide came up behind him. "Trouble with the lady, John?" he asked.

"Yeah." He turned to face Nolan. He was angry. "It was pretty bad in there, Chris," he said. "Especially that ballistics shit that was supposed to be taken care of."

"They didn't lay a glove on you." Nolan had clamped down on his cigar, irritated by Broderick's obvious accusation. "Look, kid. There won't be any further investigation. We'll kill any motion to go to the D.A., and anyway he's a Democrat. He's not going to act on anything for one troublemaking son of a bitch of a Republican."

"Yeah, I know that."

"Then what is it, the woman? Forget her. She'll come around, and if not there are others. Don't forget, you're still Johnny Broderick, kid."

Broderick glared at him, wishing he could tell him exactly what he had just pissed away for him. "Yeah," he said. "There are a lot of them."

"Look, Johnny. The reporters want to talk to you. You go outside and see them and smooth things over. You understand?"

Broderick nodded and walked toward the door. Nolan watched him closely.

"Seems Mr. Broderick is annoyed with us," the young aide said when Broderick was far enough away.

"Yes, it does," Nolan said. "I think Johnny needs an object lesson. Maybe a few months back in uniform will get his head back down to size."

"His friend, Inspector Garfoli, should love that," the aide said.

"Well, we like to make everyone happy," Nolan said. "And who knows? Maybe we'll have the old Johnny back when it's over."

As he stepped through the door and into the sun-drenched heat of Chambers Street, he could see Mona standing at the curb, nervously waving for a taxi. She was running, he thought, not just walking away, but actually running, frightened by the few drops of ink she would have to live with in the morning papers. A cab pulled to the curb and she climbed inside. She did not look back and he felt his stomach sink. He wondered if there were still tears in her eyes and, if so, who they were for.

The reporters descended upon him and he spoke to them lightheartedly,

293

fighting for himself alone now, and he singled out those he knew, the ones who would be friendly and who, perhaps, might even influence those who were not.

Was he upset about the line of questioning? Of course not. Politics are politics, he insisted. When they asked about the old man, he let drop his suspicion that the old Negro might have run away because he was involved in the escape. The reporters seemed to like the idea and he knew they would speculate about it. On the question of the "suicides" Broderick left them laughing.

"Tell me, fellas, you think I wouldn't take credit for shooting them, if I had. I know I'm a modest guy and you all know it too, but—"

Their laughter stopped him. He knew City Hall would take care of the rest now. They would attack the small, bespectacled man, accuse him of political motives, and the department would see to it he got a citation to show its support. He hoped he could salvage things with Mona but he doubted it. Her uncle would jump on the scandalous aspect of it and intensify her fears, he had no doubt about that. But still he felt strangely relieved, perhaps just to be away from the hearing now, and it was difficult to concentrate on anything else.

He left the reporters and turned east on Chambers Street. He would walk toward Headquarters but he would not go there. His stomach was still churning from the morning and he, too, wanted time to think. He would try to reach Mona later. He would go there if necessary. There was still some hope and he would at least try. But he was still Johnny Broderick just as Nolan had said and Johnny Broderick had survived. He felt relief and the feeling overrode everything else. He flexed his shoulders, feeling the heavy muscles strain against his suit coat. His shoulders swayed again as he walked. It was warm now, but he would walk several blocks to work the remaining nervousness out of his system. He turned north on Centre Street and when he passed Leonard Street he did not look down toward the entrance to the Tombs and the alley. That was all behind him now and he would not think about it again. As he approached Canal Street the luncheon crowds thickened. He was hungry—he realized it for the first time and he decided he would go on to Lindy's and surround himself with people he knew.

Up ahead there was a small, slender man walking along the sidewalk. He dragged his right leg slightly, almost unnoticeably. Broderick almost staggered when he saw him and he felt his stomach tighten and his eyes were frozen on the man's leg. He fought for breath and then the man turned right into Canal Street and in profile he could see his Oriental features. He closed his eyes for a moment and then walked on. After a few blocks his shoulders began to sway again.

Epilogue

OHNNY BRODERICK WAS RETURNED TO UNIFORM AND
sent to a precinct in Queens but within months he was resurrected and
returned to the rank of detective, working his old Broadway beat for the next
twenty-one years. Throughout those years his reputation as New York's
toughest cop continued to grow, fed by some of the best known of the city's
newspaper writers. Throughout those years he also became the target of
numerous investigations involving police corruption and bribery, but in each
case he survived with the help of political friends and his supporters among
the press. His wife, forced into near poverty, finally obtained a legal separa-
tion, explaining to the courts that she and their daughter had been left abandoned and penniless. But Broderick never remarried and his private life,
friends later explained, became more solitary as the years passed.

In 1947, faced with another investigation of corruption, Johnny Broderick
retired. Two years later he decided to satisfy a longstanding ambition and
attempted to enter politics, running for ward leader in his old Broadway
district. But his opponents raised the scandals that had followed him throughout his career in the Police Department, and when the election returns were
counted, the voters, he found, had rejected him by an overwhelming margin.

After his election defeat in 1949, Johnny Broderick forever left the city he
loved and retired to a farm in the small upstate community of Middletown,
New York, a bitter and broken man. There, in 1966, living alone and forgotten, Johnny Broderick died in his bed on the morning of his seventieth
birthday.

The following is an article published in the New York *Herald Tribune* on

295

June 18, 1966, a few days after Johnny Broderick's death. The reader will note that certain historical facts were changed in the novel, some names altered, some fictional characters added, some dates changed and, of course, certain conclusions drawn, again that great presumptuousness that is what a novel is all about.

THE CITY'S TOUGHEST COP

Even the fat dictionary doesn't have such a word, but for a 20-year period until 1947, a common expression around town, especially in the Times Square area, was "to broderick."

It meant "rough up, clout, belt, clobber."

And the underworld coined it in grudging respect for a bulldog-faced cop who rarely used his service revolver, preferring to go in with his fists. While there have been scores of apocryphal stories about Johnny Broderick, who signed his name John J., it is a hard fact that his knuckles were so badly bent from banging the skulls of bad guys that Bellevue once used him as a live exhibit to show what the human fist can endure.

Johnny Broderick, who died Sunday, would be miserable on today's police force. He retired as a first-grade detective in 1947 after more than 24 years in the job.

In all probability, he'd be pelted with constant criticism today from groups accusing him of brutality—and in all likelihood he would have quit.

His view was "legalismo is a lot of bunk." For instance, he once walked into a cafeteria looking for a murder suspect. He saw him. The man identified himself, as requested. Johnny Broderick picked up a fully-loaded sugar bowl and knocked the suspect cold. As Johnny picked him off the marble floor, the detective pulled a loaded .38-caliber revolver out of the man's pocket.

"Case closed," said Johnny.

BRAVERY

Fellow officers regarded him as brave, all right, but also fierce and foolish. Along Duffy Square, "Broadway Rose" and bookies were laying 9-to-5 that their pal Johnny would be knocked off any day, in all probability by the likes of Jack (Legs) Diamond. For the notorious Legs Diamond was one of the many hoodlums whom Johnny Broderick whacked on the chin, picked up and dumped in an ash can, head first, legs flapping.

But Johnny fooled them all. He died of natural causes in the bucolic surroundings of his home near Middletown, on his 70th birthday.

Surviving are his wife; a daughter, Mrs. Marion Saranone; three sisters, and a brother.

To the end, he kept in touch with his New York, which he found distasteful in recent years. He felt that fists and nightsticks would clean up the town.

Young Broderick was born in the old East Side Gas House District, which now houses Stuyvesant Town. His father died when Johnny was 12 and the boy went to work driving a truck to support his mother. As a member of the Teamsters Union, he somehow met Samuel Gompers, president of the AFL, at a convention and Gompers took a fancy to the husky youth and made him a bodyguard.

He served in the Navy during World War I, where he excelled as a boxer. After nine months as a fireman beginning in 1922, he found that career tame and donned a police uniform in January, 1923. Possibly because he had a "rabbi" (a highly placed connection), he was a first-grade detective within five years. He soon became the best-known officer on the force.

He worked out of the so-called Main Office Squad, which meant he could go where he pleased. He liked Midtown, where he became as much a part of the scenery as Madison Square Garden, the Palace and Lindy's. Inevitably, he became the bosom buddy of the greats of the fight game, especially Jack Dempsey, who once reportedly remarked, "I'd take Johnny on in the ring if we fought under the Marquis of Queensberry rules—but not in an alley."

The cop with the thin lips and full, round face stood only 5-foot-9 and weighed about 175. But he had a mania for physical fitness, and worked out almost every day in Stillman's gym. He shunned tobacco and booze.

It was Johnny Broderick who, in 1931, went in and pulled James (Two Gun) Crowley out of a West Side building after hundreds of fellow cops laid down a siege and tried to smoke him out. By then, Johnny's knuckles were beginning to ache, so he developed the method of grabbing tie-wearing gangsters by the knot and twisting it till the felon fell back, almost choked to death.

In 1926, three inmates in The Tombs escaped, killing the warden and a keeper. Scores of police surrounded the prison. Johnny Broderick got there late. He picked up the top of an ash can, weaved his way into the Tombs courtyard, crawled on his belly to where the three convicts were hiding behind a coal bin. He had emptied his revolver by the time he got them, and he found them dead. The apocryphal story is that Johnny Broderick killed them. He did not—they had committed suicide, possibly because they saw him coming.

He knew all the big-time rumrunners—and they knew him. As long as they behaved themselves, they were not "brodericked." Old-timers along Times Square recall how Johnny picked up three punks who were misbehaving in a restaurant and threw them through the plate glass window—and then charged them with the breakage.

It was amazing, too, to see hoodlums slink out of eating places when he came sauntering in in his tight, custom-tailored light-weight suiting, wearing monogrammed shirts, handkerchiefs and underwear. . . .

Oh, there were times when he got his lumps. Before he was made a detec-

297

tive, a thug he had once beaten up telephoned and invited him to have it out. Johnny showed up—and walked into a room loaded with 16 gangsters. He broke a couple of noses before he emerged—bloody but in one piece. And he hung around until reinforcements came, when he got the thug who had invited him.

Besides the Main Office Squad, he was attached at times to other squads, known as Broadway, Strong-Arm and Industrial. Upon occasion he served as bodyguard for Dempsey and Queen Marie of Rumania. And he was really honored when in 1936 President Roosevelt specifically asked that Johnny Broderick be close to him on his New York visit.

He had detective partners who made names for themselves, too, such as Johnny Cordes, now living in retirement in Hollywood, Fla.

Johnny Broderick was busted from first-grade detective to patrolman in uniform in 1934, during the La Guardia regime, but in a few months he was a detective again, driving around in his Cadillac.

In 1949, two years after leaving the force, he took a fling at politics, seeking the Democratic leadership of the Times Square area. He got clobbered. But Hollywood paid him in excess of $100,000 to do his life story, the film being called "Bullets for Ballots," with, inevitably, Edward G. Robinson playing the part of the one-man anti-crime force.

DENIAL

He vehemently denied that he quit the police force under pressure to avoid a scandal. His political opponents so charged, saying he had been forced to retire because he had accompanied underworld figures to places such as Hot Springs "for the baths."

The detective, who won eight citations, always cringed when he heard this apocryphal story:

That Johnny Broderick walked into a funeral parlor where a Hudson Duster gangster was laid out and spit in the thug's eye.

"I brodericked him when he was alive," Johnny would say, "but it is against my religion to do anything like that to the dead."

He had a sense of humor and could tell stories on himself:

"One day I was in a detective squad room and I started to ride a rookie cop. He told me to cut it out. I refused. We went at it—right there in the squad room. He knocked me out. When he learned who he had done this to, this rookie fainted. He didn't know that I was THE 'tough' Johnny Broderick."

MILTON LEWIS